TURNING FOR HOME

Also by Sarah Challis

Killing Helen

TURNING FOR HOME

Sarah Challis

HEADLINE

First published in 2001
by HEADLINE BOOK PUBLISHING

10 9 8 7 6 5 4 3 2 1

British Library Cataloguing in Publication Data

Challis, Sarah
Turning for home
I.Title
823.9'14[F]

ISBN 0 7472 7237 9

Typeset by
Letterpart Limited, Reigate, Surrey

Printed and bound in Great Britain by
Mackays of Chatham PLC, Chatham, Kent

HEADLINE BOOK PUBLISHING
A division of Hodder Headline
338 Euston Road
London NW1 3BH

www.headline.co.uk
www.hodderheadline.com

For Alexander, with love

With grateful thanks for the advice of my friends, Charlotte Davis, farmer, Jane Galpin, trainer, and Nick Hoare, farrier.

Chapter One

Maeve Delaney found herself twenty-six years old and with exactly thirty-five pounds to her name. She had counted her money carefully and was oddly pleased to find that with the few stray coins retrieved out of pockets and from the bottom of bags, she arrived at a neat round sum. It seemed a good omen. She had, at various points in her adult life, had less in the way of funds, and at other times considerably more. Now, as she walked through Regents Park on a bright September day, she knew that something would have to turn up. It usually did. The positive things about her present position were that she had a roof over her head, even if you could not call a squat in Bethnal Green a home; that Mohammed had found a job as a waiter in an Algerian restaurant, so he was all right for the moment and he would not let her starve; and that she had put a thousand miles between her and the last disastrous man in her life, a man who had promised her the earth and had turned out to be a liar and a cheat. Despite her dangerously reduced circumstances, Maeve walked with an optimistic spring in her step and an eye for the beauty of the morning. When she happened upon a bench in the sun, she would stop and sit and empty her mind and wait for a solution to come to her.

She could, of course, telephone her father in Belfast and he would send an air ticket home. This was the ultimate last resort. Since she had slammed out of her home at seventeen in a storm of angry words and teenage defiance, she had only once asked for his help and that was when she was so ill with some amoebic infection that the nuns who were caring for her in Mexico thought that she was going to die. He had wired money for her flight and bombarded the convent hospital with panic-struck enquiries. However, when she was well enough to fly home, weak, pale and spindly, it took only

1

a few days for their relationship to whip up another storm like the one she had blown out on. The solid house shook, the windows rattled, and the newly hung, swagged and tasselled curtains stirred in the blast. Poor Bethany, the second and fairly recent Mrs Delaney and the architect of the new décor, cowered in fright. Not much older than Maeve, she was a lazy, gentle woman with doe-like, limpid eyes and a generous figure. Her very bulk seemed to smother her husband's rages like a blanket thrown on a fire. She stifled his vile temper with her passivity, absorbing his anger like blotting paper. Only when he had been particularly cruel did the fat tear slide down her cheeks and he would be overcome with remorse. How different was Maeve who rose up like a striking scorpion to sting, who matched her father in vicious temper and poisonous tongue. So it was and so it always had been. They even looked alike. Small, dark, pale-skinned, with a sort of vivid vitality in the turned-up nose and large, mobile mouth. Dangerous people. Clever, shifting, unpredictable. Maeve's father was a highly respected criminal lawyer. He might just as easily have been a brilliant crook.

Maeve's mother could never be called upon to bail her out. Juanita Delaney now lived in the south of France, her exotic, half-Spanish looks on the point of collapsing into dereliction. Over made-up, tottering about on high heels, smoking and drinking too much, her desiccated cleavage always on display, her once famous legs now thin as a chicken's, she terrified Maeve, who preferred to remember her as the dark beauty whom all the other girls at school had wondered at. Their own fat, powdered, pink and white mothers in their ugly stiff clothes had pushed forward like a herd of curious, nudging cows as Juanita swept into Speech Day in an outrageous hat, or drew up in an open car with a tanned, minor actor at the wheel. Maeve loved showing her off but secretly yearned for something more normal, more naturally maternal.

Her parents' unlikely marriage foundered when Maeve was twelve. Her mother dealt the final blow when she ran off with an excitable French film producer. Maeve had by this time already been despatched to boarding school, first in Ireland and then to a smart Catholic school near Windsor. Maeve had seen her mother only a few times since. Each time she had found her more alarming. The drink, the succession of ever less attractive and more hopeless men, the desperate attempts to hold on to youth and glamour, even as a child

2

Maeve saw her decline clearly and painfully. The fact that her mother was at heart a deeply selfish woman who had dedicated her life to preserving herself as a woman men desired, and that little else mattered to her, did not escape the knowing child.

Maeve walked briskly. Most of her actions were rapid. No dawdler, she. From the age of seventeen she had been on her own, making her own decisions. That way she knew if things fucked up it was her own fault. She liked that. Being free of people's influence. Her parents could do as they liked. It didn't matter to her. Let her father marry a single-brain-celled beauty therapist. Let her mother become a hideous old soak. They led their lives, she led hers.

Thirty-five pounds. She would have to get a job. She thought of the five hundred odd quid owed her by Carlos. She had pushed off and left him without collecting her back pay. The six months she had spent cooking on his charter yacht in the Med had begun like a dream in April and veered off into a nightmare in August. The partnership he had promised had ended in drunkenness and abuse. The gentle lover of the spring turned into a possessive demon. She had nothing to show for it except the remains of a tan and fading purple bruises.

Maeve, however, was not one to brood on past misfortune. Having voluntarily curtailed her own formal education, she was a great exponent of learning on the road, graduating from the university of hard knocks. Carlos could be written off as an experience. She wouldn't get caught like that again.

This morning she was on her way across the park to her friend Sophie's flat in St John's Wood, to cadge a bath. Good old Sophers was generous with her bath essence and had thick fluffy towels. Of course, they would be the best quality. They had been on her carefully chosen wedding list. Maeve thought of deep, steaming water with anticipation. She would baby-sit for Sophie's two-year-old twins, Freddy and Flora, in return. This was a good and fair arrangement appreciated by both parties. Maeve was not in the habit of feeling sorry for people as a rule. The fact that Sophie had been abandoned by her husband, Fergus, did not arouse much sympathy. If you marry a wanker and then have his babies, you get what you deserve, but all the same, poor old Sophers had had a tough time. She was too bloody nice, that was her trouble.

In the distance Maeve could see an empty bench, under the

trees but bathed in sunlight. That was where she would stop and have her think.

When she got there she sat down and drew up her knees like a little fishing gnome perched on a toadstool. Her problems were obvious. No money. No job. Nowhere to live. The job must come first and she would have to stay in the squat for as long as possible while she saved up to get somewhere else to live. She could easily get waitress work but it was so badly paid. The same applied to cleaning jobs. She spoke French, Spanish and Greek fairly fluently and she might try and get a job as a tour guide. She wasn't that keen on staying in London though. It was expensive and dirty and she felt out of touch with her own age group who seemed to spend hours in pubs and clubs and shopping for clothes. Ah, that was another problem. Her clothes consisted of little else than what she had been able to grab when she did a runner off the yacht. She had one pair of beaten-up trainers and two pairs of tatty trousers, T-shirts and a sweater. The black leather jacket she was wearing belonged to Mohammed. She couldn't buy much with thirty-five pounds. Not when she had to live on it as well. She didn't want to borrow from Mohammed who was so anxious to start sending money home to his enormous family in Egypt. Perhaps Sophie could lend her something to wear to go job-hunting? But Sophie was tall, nearly six foot. You could fit two of Maeve into most of her garments. Shit.

A well-dressed elderly man walked slowly past, with two Sainsbury's bags full of groceries. Maeve eyed them hungrily. She could see a packet of croissants on the top. Under his arm he carried a newspaper. He smiled kindly at the odd little elfin figure. Another drop-out, he thought. London seemed full of them, these strange young people with their closed, dead-looking faces and their grubby sleeping bags and dogs on strings. Even in the Blitz, which he remembered vividly, there had never been such abject misery. As he turned off the main path to walk towards his home in Primrose Hill, the news-paper slipped under his arm and the magazine folded inside it slid out and fell to the path. Rather deaf, he did not hear it drop and walked slowly on with his week's worth of reading material lying on the gravel. By the time Maeve came across it five minutes later, the old man was well away, disappeared across the busy main road towards his home. Maeve picked up the slim magazine which she had never read but had seen on newsstands. In fact, her father had once been asked to contribute a contentious article about the Northern Ireland peace process, and had been thrilled by the number of outraged letters he had got in response. Something interesting to read landing at her feet was a piece of luck for Maeve and a change from the tabloids people discarded on Tubes and buses.

She flicked through the magazine as she walked and the very first thing she read was: 'Carer/companion urgently sought for elderly, disabled lady living in own home in Somerset. Other help kept. Comfortable accommodation and excellent salary offered to the right person. Highest references essential. Some light cooking desirable. Car driver preferred.'

God, thought Maeve, I've found myself a job.

Sophie, however, didn't think so.

'Maeve, you're barmy. Nuts. It's a total waste of time. What kind of companion would you, of all people, be to a dribbling old crone? You're notoriously impatient. You'd hate it – you couldn't be stuck in the country in a creaky old mausoleum. Anyway, look at you – you look off the street. Completely dodgy. No one's going to let you near their granny.'

'Hey, Sophers!' Maeve protested. 'You know I've got a nicer side. I love your brats, don't I?' and she tugged Flora onto her knee. 'You don't mind leaving them with me, do you? You don't worry I'll lock them in a cupboard while you're out. I quite like old people.'

'You don't know any!' retorted Sophie.

Maeve considered. This was true, so she ignored it.

'I clean up OK – if I can get hold of some suitable clothes. References are no problem. You can write me one. Mohammed can write me another. God, I wonder if he *can* write? He can say he's a sheikh or something and I've looked after his Sultana mother. I'll write one myself.'

Sophie was horrified. 'My God! You'll go to prison!'

'Don't be silly. After all, I haven't really got anything to hide. I haven't got a criminal record. I don't steal. I'm not a pyromaniac. On those grounds alone I sound ideal. Come on, Sophers. Don't you see how it would be just right for me at the moment? I could save everything I earned, have board and lodging while I get revved up to do something else.'

Sophie looked doubtful. She loved Maeve who had shared a cubicle with her in the first miserable weeks at boarding school. She'd been a rock when Fergus had buggered off and left her when the twins were four months old. She had given practical help, taking the babies off her hands, cleaning the flat, which was worth much more than sympathy which just made her cry. But she had deep reservations about this current scheme. With a struggle Sophie tried to be more open-minded. She, who had only ever wanted a grand, white wedding and a big family of happy children, and a devoted husband, and an Aga and all that went with it, now found herself in a basement flat as a single parent. She had been forced to accept a life which she had never chosen and of which she basically disapproved. She believed in marriage and had meant every single one of the promises she had made at the altar. But it hadn't counted for anything. So why did it matter if Maeve was dishonest? The world seemed to reward shits. She had heard Fergus was seeing a blonde banker, while she was humping the bloody double pushchair up the steps of her basement flat, and collapsing exhausted in front of mindless television programmes every evening. No, she'd support Maeve.

'OK, pal. I'm with you. I'll be good at this type of thing. I mean, it could be my parents advertising for a keeper for my granny, couldn't it? I know what they'd expect. Let's write the reference first. Shall we say you were my kids' nanny? And listen. There's a charity shop round the corner stuffed with the sort of dreary clothes you'll need. I cannot wait to see you in a pleated, navy polyester skirt . . . but they're fashionable again, aren't they?'

Maeve half got up to hug her, still holding Flora on her knee.

'You're a star, mate,' she said. 'What a blast!'

While Maeve was in the bath they composed the reference Sophie was going to write. Maeve was inclined to get carried away and made herself sound like Mother Theresa, but Sophie toned it down and they were pleased with the final result. Sophie had some of her parents' grand, embossed notepaper in the bottom of a suitcase – 'I wrote my wedding present thank yous on it,' she said, wistfully – and they decided to use that.

Flora and Freddy toddled between them, fascinated by tiny Maeve in her bubble mountain. She scooped little mounds of foam and put them on their heads which made them roar with laughter until Flora biffed Freddy and he cracked his head on the side of the bath and the whole thing ended in screams. Maeve restored smiles in a second by submerging herself entirely under the surface of the water and then reappearing very slowly. The twins shrieked with delight, their fat little faces still shiny and wet with tears.

Maeve got out of the bath and skipped round the flat naked which made them roar all over again.

'Put some clothes on,' said Sophie. 'The whole street can see you.'

'They're welcome!' said Maeve. 'A penny a peep is considered quite cheap!'

When she did get dressed she had no option but to put her old clothes back on. Even Sophie's T-shirts looked like mini dresses on her tiny frame.

'When we've had a sandwich we'll go to Oxfam,' said Sophie. 'How much can you spend?'

'About a tenner,' said Maeve. 'I've only got thirty-five quid in the whole world. When we get back may I use your telephone to ring this number on the ad, and may I use this address? I can't tell the Snodgrasses that I live in a squat. I'll tell them that I live with a girlfriend and then should they ring for any reason, you can say I'm out and take a message.'

They ate a messy lunch, with the twins chucking Marmite sandwiches about and throwing carrot sticks on the floor.

'They're tired,' said Sophie. 'They'll sleep the moment they're in the buggy.' Then there was all the wiping down and changing nappies and pushing awkward little arms and legs into outdoor clothes.

'I don't know how you can stand this,' said Maeve. 'I'd just keep them naked and run a hose over them.'

'You wait. This old dear is probably incontinent. You'll be changing nappies soon.'

'Christ!' said Maeve. 'That's a thought. Wait a minute though. "Other help kept." That means there'll be a nurse or something, doesn't it? That will be her job.'

'Don't be too sure,' warned Sophie. 'I don't think they'd want a companion if there was a nurse.'

'Oh well,' said Maeve. 'I'll have to face that one when it comes. Get a move on, twinnies. We're going out. Sophie, how do you lug this great chariot up these steps ten times a day? It's like being a pit pony.'

'I just have to,' said Sophie as they hauled the double pushchair up to the pavement, each with a twin under an arm. 'There's no one to help me. I did complain about it to

Fergus and he said if I wanted the garden at the back, which of course I do, I'd have to put up with it.'

'What's he putting up with, I'd like to know. Except of course the huge disadvantage of being Fergus. But he must be used to that by now . . . like a birth defect.'

Sophie laughed. She plonked the twins in their seats and harnessed them in. Maeve took the handles and ran off down the road pushing the squealing babies. 'Come on, Soph! I'm going to try a wheelie!'

Should I be doing this? thought Sophie, watching the flying figure, all spindly legs and mass of dark hair. She followed behind at a walk. Aiding and abetting? She'll kill the poor old woman. Finish her off. Sophie had visions of an upturned invalid chair, wheels spinning after some madcap race, and Maeve cackling with laughter. She thought also of the other side of Maeve, the melancholy, dark side when she was in a gloom for days and no fit companion for anyone. No, she thought, I shouldn't be doing this, and she made up her mind to withdraw her assistance, put a stop to it while she still could.

The charity shop was ten minutes' walk away and by the time they got there Sophie still had not found the courage to tell Maeve what she had decided. She realised that she was childishly frightened to confront the inevitable flash of anger, the withering scorn. She felt like a schoolgirl again when Maeve, who bowled out opposition by her enthusiasm and force of personality, would get her involved in escapades she knew were a mistake. It was wonderful to bask in Maeve's approval and terrible to feel the cold of her displeasure.

'Listen, Maeve,' said Sophie at the door. 'I don't think I can do this. I honestly think it's a mistake. I do, really. You'll get into trouble, I'm sure. Something will go wrong – I mean seriously wrong. It's not that I don't want to help . . .'

Maeve turned on her, eyes blazing. 'OK,' she said. 'Fine. I very rarely ask anyone for help. I'll do it myself. Here,' and she pushed over the handles of the buggy. 'I'll see you around. You never did have any balls,' and she stalked in.

'Maeve!' wailed Sophie miserably, but she had already disappeared behind a clothes rail. All Sophie could see was an agitation amongst the garments as Maeve's hands worked furiously down the rack.

Oh bloody hell! Sophie wasn't going to be bullied. Not now she was a grown-up. She trailed back up the road. By the time she had reached the steps down to her front door the twins were asleep, little heads peacefully nodding. If she took them out of the buggy now they would wake and cry, but she couldn't get them into the flat without decanting them. She sat on the low wall that divided the strip of dirty ground at the top of her steps from the pavement. She didn't know what to do. Often these days she dithered about like this, feeling lost and directionless. Stupid things stumped her, like should she feed the children first when they were very tired and were likely to scream and throw the spoon away or put them down for a nap knowing that they would wake early, bellowing with hunger? Sophie closed her eyes and felt the sun warm on her face. She felt so tired. Sometimes she wished that she could just get up and walk off. Catch a bus going anywhere. Just walk away from this constant anxiety, this dragging weight of responsibility. She thought of Maeve utterly free of care for anyone other than herself and felt a stab of jealousy. Not for one single moment since she had presented the two scarlet, brawling scraps to the world had Sophie felt carefree. In those first nightmare months she had stood, breasts dripping milk, hair flat and greasy, stomach like a loose bag, trying to make sense of Fergus's accusations.

'Look at you!' he had shouted. 'Try to see what I see. You're a mess. I can't stand it.'

He had dragged her to the bathroom and had forced her to look in the glass. Her face stared back, eyes dead with exhaustion.

Flora gave a little snuffling sigh and opened and closed one small pink fist. Sophie stared down at her with love and horror. How could she even think such things? Always Sophie felt an irrational terror that she was going to be found wanting as a mother, that some government agency, some social worker would pronounce her inadequate. That Fergus would claim the twins. Each day she felt she faced this challenge. After all, she had been little use as a wife, how could she be so sure she was any good to the twins as a mother? This was the stick with which Sophie beat herself. She must not for one moment envy Maeve. No, it was Maeve who was destitute, deprived.

Sophie got to her feet and began to push the buggy slowly back up the road. Her legs ached and the sun in her face made her eyes feel heavy. She could almost close them and sleep as she walked. For something to do, she went into the bakers and bought some jam doughnuts. At the door of the charity shop she stopped and looked in. The three volunteer workers, usually rather brisk and unhelpful, anxious not to be mistaken for shop assistants, were gathered in an admiring group around Maeve who was prancing about in a beautiful little pink and gold checked suit. She saw Sophie and threw the door open.

'Hey! Look, Sophers! Come in. Chanel! What a find! What do you think? Isn't it brilliant?'

Sophie said nothing.

'And look! Children's jeans which fit a treat and a whole load of shirts and stuff. Oh, come on, Soph. Don't be a pain!'

'Yes.' Sophie shrugged. 'Well. You have to be pixie sized to wear that suit.'

'That's why it's only a tenner. There aren't many of us little teeny weeny Chanel pixies about.'

'Here,' said Sophie, her good nature surfacing as it usually did. 'I'll treat you. My father sent me a cheque this morning. Yes, you do look wonderful,' she admitted. 'Transformed. What about shoes? You can't wear trainers.'

'Can't wear dead men's shoes, me hearties,' said Maeve, in a Long John Silver voice, rolling her eyes at the rows of footwear. Sophie agreed that the worn shoes looked somehow sinister, still scuffed from previous outings and bulging in some cases where bunions or corns had pressed against the leather.

Maeve picked up her new jeans and a shirt and went behind a curtain to change. The assistants were arguing over how the till worked and rang up £2,500 and then £2.50 before they got it right. Sophie handed them a ten pound note.

'For the suit,' she said.

Maeve peered round the curtain, pulling up the jeans.

'You're a star, Soph!' she said. 'Oh that,' she went on, noticing Sophie staring in horror at the bruises now revealed on her ribs. 'Don't worry. The perpetrator is well out of my life. I gave him a black eye, what's more. A real shiner.'

They walked back arm in arm, the giant plastic bag of clothes hung from the buggy handles.

'Sorry,' said Maeve. 'Sorry to have asked you. I completely respect your decision not to perjure yourself. You've always been honest, haven't you? School didn't teach you to lie, did it? Not like it did me.'

'Look, Maeve. I won't *lie* exactly, but I will give you a

character reference and say about looking after the twins, and you can use my address. But you must promise me you'll be, you know, responsible.'

'Sure thing, babe. You know me!'

Sophie sighed. Unfortunately she did. With any luck, she thought, Maeve won't even get an interview.

Henry Bentham, who had placed the advertisement on the directions of his Australian wife, Bunty, stared gloomily out of the window of the bank. Mrs Tripp, his PA, had just brought him the news that Janet Cook had telephoned again. Mrs Cook was his mother's current carer and recently hardly a day went by when she wasn't complaining about something and threatening to walk out. He had had to deflect these calls away from Bunty, who would have exacerbated the situation by giving Mrs Cook short shrift. The truth was that they couldn't do without her until they had someone else to take her place. Henry closed his eyes and rubbed his white, domed brow. What was to be done?

Of course, his mother, now eighty-four, should go into a home. Bunty had done a lot of research and had found several perfectly acceptable establishments where she could take her own furniture, and one which would even admit Esau, her hideous old dog. The problem lay in her determination not to be moved from Charlton, her home in Somerset, and the fact that although she was more or less crippled with arthritis she still had full use of her faculties. She couldn't be bundled off against her considerable will. Charlton, of course, still belonged to her, although Henry intended to move there when he retired in five years' time. Bunty was eager to get on with restoration and improvements and was loud in her condemnation of her husband as weak and spineless in not dealing with his mother more firmly. Henry felt thoroughly battered in his position between two powerful women. Whatever Bunty said, he had in fact gained considerable control by taking over his mother's financial affairs and paying her an allowance, out of which came the wages of those who kept her at Charlton. Fortunately she was bored by accounts and housekeeping and left it entirely to him, her banker son, to tell her how much money she had at her disposal. He had been able to mislead her into thinking that she could hardly afford to go on living there. He couldn't exactly starve her out, but he

11

could make the comforts of a home look more attractive by contrast.

Then there was the problem of carers. Mrs Tripp had suggested placing the advertisement after Bunty railed endlessly at the expense of using agencies to provide the help his mother needed. Henry had pointed out that the sort of home he would have to put her in would cost more, especially when one considered that she might live to ninety or beyond. Janet Cook and her like always started well enough but it wasn't long before his mother was spitting out mashed potato on the carpet and making herself thoroughly disagreeable. The present complaint concerned her language. She had apparently called Mrs Cook a fat trollop. Mrs Tripp had laughed when she told him. 'Is she?' she had asked.

'Is she what?'

'A fat trollop?'

Henry had frowned and not answered. Sometimes Mrs Tripp surprised him. He turned from the window. The paintings Bunty had insisted he hung on the boardroom walls assaulted his senses. Great splurges and splashes of clashing colours daubed on by Aborigines, as far as he could remember. Anyway, the sight of them never failed to add to his irritation. Pressing a button on his desk, he said, 'Mrs Tripp, have we had any response to the advertisement yet?'

'Yes, Henry.' That was another thing. She had started to call him Henry since she had enrolled in Empowerment for Women in the Workplace classes. 'Three so far. Shall I bring them through?'

Henry sighed. 'No. Deal with them, will you? I can't waste any more time.'

In her office next door, Diana Tripp opened her drawer and took out a chocolate biscuit. She allowed herself a mid-morning treat as a stress buster. She reached for her pad. Three names were followed by a few notes she had taken. She put a line through one. A young male nurse was not suitable. The other two were possibilities. One was a retired housemistress from Yorkshire, a talkative spinster, obviously desperate for a roof over her head. The other was slightly odd. A young woman. Northern Irish. No proper training or career but a portfolio of rather off-beat jobs behind her. She had worked as a nanny and cook and had been on the staff of some Arab prince. Mrs Tripp's pencil hovered over her pad before she lightly pencilled a tick beside her name. She would ask for references, and would arrange for the two applicants to meet Henry.

Sophie took the telephone call. Thank God, she thought, that the twins were asleep and not bawling in the background.

'No, Miss Delaney is out at the moment. I am Mrs Manners, her landlady. Can I give her a message? Yes, I'm sure that will be all right. I'll tell her to ring you back if she can't make it. If you don't hear from her you can assume it's fine. She can bring her testimonials or references, whatever, with her. Do you want to give me directions to pass on to her?'

At the conclusion of the conversation Sophie put down the telephone with mixed feelings. She was right in it now. Up to the neck. The Chanel suit was hanging in her wardrobe and Maeve had arranged to telephone her at midday to see if there was any news. The appointment was for the following day. It seemed there was considerable urgency in filling the post. Sophie picked up the envelope containing the reference she had written. She took out the sheet of stiff, expensive paper and read what she had written. Yes, it was true that Maeve had looked after her children. It was true that she had always been reliable, honest and responsibly carried out her duties. It was true that she had known her for many years and that she was resourceful, competent and had a lively, outgoing personality. It was true that she was a talented cook. It was not true that she could thoroughly recommend her. Why not? she wondered. What was it about Maeve that was so unsettling, that seemed to attract trouble, that led her into uncharted territories where she herself would never venture? Maeve was a risk taker. That was it. She went further and faster than anyone else Sophie knew. She restlessly sought diversions and thought up escapades. Sophie could only comfort herself with the conviction that her friend would not actually harm the old lady, either accidentally or on purpose. She had too much basic good sense for that. But what else would she get up to? Sophie couldn't bear to think.

Maeve was ecstatic when she got the news.

'Hey! That's great, isn't it, Soph? Tomorrow, eh? I'll get Mohammed to write my reference when he gets back from work. He is brilliant, you know. Do you know what he's thought of? He has a friend who works at the Ritz and he's got him to snitch some headed notepaper. It was Mohammed's brainwave. It will be totally convincing. He'll write a whole load of Arabic stuff.'

Sophie groaned. She had serious doubts about this Mohammed character. Maeve had met him on a ferry somewhere off Greece. He had been on his way to England on a dodgy passport and with a dodgy visa. Typically, Maeve had befriended him. Sophie imagined that they were lovers but Maeve denied it, laughing. 'More's the pity. He's utterly beautiful but he's got a rich Swiss boyfriend.' Mohammed was in touch with a whole underclass of illegal immigrants in London and it was through them that he had heard about the squat and got the job in the restaurant. Maeve seemed wholly unconcerned by this flagrant law-breaking and this annoyed Sophie, who came from a long line of soldiers and civil servants and had an inbuilt sense of civic duty.

She was cross when the bell rang the next morning and she realised that Maeve had brought Mohammed to the flat with her. She could see dirty trainers and the lower portions of a chef's checked trouser legs displayed in her basement window when she went to open the door. She glared at Maeve, who bounced past her without noticing, saying over her shoulder as she went, 'Hi, Soph! I've brought Mohammed to meet you.' Mohammed beamed a smile of such warmth and beauty that Sophie was totally disarmed and within minutes was making him tea. He sat forward eagerly on her battered old sofa while Freddy and Flora stared at him, tongue-tied.

Sophie realised that she hadn't had a man inside the flat, at least not socially, for months and at the first opportunity went into her bedroom and sprayed on some scent and put on some lip gloss. Silly, really, she thought, considering his inclinations, but he was so very handsome. He smiled at her again when she re-emerged and she felt self-conscious smiling back. He was, of course, very dark, with short, cropped, black hair and glowing brown skin. His perfect aquiline features and large, slightly protruding eyes were coolly beautiful in repose; when disarranged by his broad smile and gleaming white teeth, he was even more strikingly attractive. Sophie was vague on classical art but thought she had many times seen his profile sculpted in marble and stone in the great museums of Europe. He was so very different to sandy, carroty Fergus, who went pink and peeled on honeymoon in the sun, and whose close-packed features and small

14

reddish-brown eyes gave him a foxy, weasely look. At least, Sophie could see that now. At the time she had been blinded by love, she supposed.

Mohammed drank his tea and smiled and Maeve went to fetch the suit out of Sophie's wardrobe to give them a dress rehearsal. Freddy and Flora continued to gaze, spellbound. Sophie sat down and smiled back. She was just about to embark on a series of polite questions about Mohammed's family and home and job when Maeve came charging back in. She had yanked her bunches of dark hair back into a knot and shoved all her hippy bangles up the sleeve of the suit so they were hidden. Her legs were quite brown and although she was barefoot and her feet were far from clean, she looked elegant and stylish and, Sophie had to admit, quite respectable and grown-up.

Mohammed was delighted. 'You look a different persons,' he said. 'These are wonderful clothesies.'

'You'll need a bag,' said Sophie. 'You can't take that ethnic thing.' She went off to find a smart leather bag her mother had given her.

Maeve hooked it over her elbow and swept about the room saying, 'How do you do? Have you come far?' in a queen voice to Mohammed and the twins.

Shoes remained a problem. 'I'll just have to wear me old trainers,' said Maeve, looking down at her footwear fondly.

'You can't,' said Sophie. 'They'll completely ruin the effect.'

'Ah,' said Maeve, 'no one will notice, and if they do I'll say I run everywhere – I'm in training. That'll seem energetic and impressive,' and she began to jog and shadow-box round the flat.

'No,' said Mohammed, who obviously had a lively imagination. 'Say you just come from caring for very old, sleeping lady and in theses shoes you are like little mousies, making no noises.'

'Brilliant, Mohammed,' said Maeve. 'They'll love it!'

'Don't you be counting your lucky chickens!' beamed Mohammed.

They're both mad, thought Sophie.

Sophie could be forgiven for thinking Maeve was not only without scruples but also free of any of the anxieties and responsibilities by which she herself felt besieged, and indeed as the little Chanel via Oxfam-suited figure pranced along the

City street that afternoon, Maeve looked the picture of buoyant confidence. Her skinny brown legs fairly twinkled along the pavement, trainers respectably white having been given a quick whirl in Sophie's washing machine, and the pink suit so cheerfully pretty and flattering that people smiled at her as she passed. Her dark hair bobbed along, knotted at the back of her head, and with a swipe of lipstick and some black eye pencil, Maeve looked both older and more attractive. In her hand she clutched Sophie's instructions about where to go when she got off the bus at Bishopsgate. In ten minutes she was due to meet Mr Henry Bentham at Bentham's Bank, the oldest and one of the few remaining privately owned banks in the country. But although she may have looked confident, Maeve was actually on edge and fearful. Sophie would never have guessed what it was costing her to face the forthcoming interview, how much she dreaded having her life held up to scrutiny, or how very deeply she felt she was a failure with little to offer anyone. Bravado and bullshit she was strong on, but lately she was finding it increasingly hard to get by on these empty, self-promoting qualities alone.

At twenty-six, Maeve realised that some of the hot-headed decisions she had taken earlier in her life had been mistakes. She knew she was intelligent, bright even, but grade As at GCSE meant nothing in today's marketplace, especially here in the City, where smart-suited girls in their twenties and early thirties, with PhDs and MBAs after their names, were two a penny. Of course they were not competing for the same jobs, but Maeve knew she could no longer boast 'I could have gone to university if I'd chosen to'. It sounded pathetic. Silly statements like that did not impress. She was no better qualified than the average shop assistant or waitress. She remembered her father shouting at her, 'You'll end up serving on the Pick'n'Mix counter in Woolworths!' He was right. Without qualifications she could have no aspirations.

The rest of her life did not bear much scrutiny either. To date she had not managed a single, truly successful relationship with a man. Unerringly, she chose the unreliable, the dangerous, the profligate, the cruel. Almost without exception she had found any affair she embarked on ended with a sense of failure and sadness. It seemed to her that she was not a woman who inspired true or lasting love. She did not know where she went wrong but from the earliest times the people

16

she had cared about and trusted had let her down. The two people she had loved most in the world, her father and mother, had not been able to stay together. At the time it had seemed to her that she was an inadequate child, that somehow she had not been able to forge the ties between the three of them which other children in secure families seemed to enjoy. She had not been strong enough, potent enough, important enough to make her mother happy and contented. Her father preferred the company of thick women and tarts. However hard she tried, Maeve could not transform herself and them into a family unit. They had remained three warring individuals.

This terrible sense of personal failure dogged Maeve. She covered it with a tough veneer, a careless attitude, and she tried very hard to be self-sufficient, to rely on no one. If she did not care, she could not be hurt. If she did not love, she could not be rejected. Yet she longed for the blast of being special, of being the reason someone got up in the morning. Maeve craved unconditional love. She did not believe she ever had been truly loved by anyone – not for herself, just as she was.

Her motives as she hurried up Bishopsgate were entirely selfish. She wanted a few months in which to earn a bit of cash and enjoy accommodation a little more salubrious than the squat. She needed a break to recoup, to gather her energies for her next onslaught on life. For the old woman she was about to profess such a caring interest in, she cared not a scrap. She was simply a means to an end. Maeve was sufficiently selfish not to exercise her imagination at all on her behalf. She remained a shadowy figure; her duties towards her to be despatched with the minimum possible effort. With any luck she wouldn't be too bothersome, and if she was, Maeve reckoned she could be more than a match.

It was with these convictions that Maeve swung open the heavy doors of Bentham's Bank and told the glossy receptionist that she had an appointment for 3.00 p.m. with Mr Henry Bentham.

With the advantage of hindsight, Henry realised that Maeve found him in a vulnerable state that afternoon. Mrs Tripp had just reported yet another complaint from Janet Cook regarding his mother, who it seemed had got it into her head that she wanted to give a party and had tried to order a great deal of drink to be delivered from a wine merchant in Castle Cary.

17

Fortunately the wine merchant had gone out of business many years earlier, but this was further evidence of her decline into senility and the difficulty to be faced in finding the appropriate person to look after her.

Maeve's appearance was not initially encouraging. She was far too young, her smile was too wide, her energy too palpable. Henry was used to dealing with rundown, apathetic creatures, still reeling from broken marriages or elderly parents dying off, leaving them redundant and in need of a residential post. In Henry's experience, these were the sort of women who found themselves filling the role of 'carer'. It had little to do with their capacity or inclination to care.

However, as he asked Maeve about her experience and her qualifications, Henry began to think that not only would she do, she might even prove capable of keeping his mother under control. She had, it seemed, filled several highly responsible posts in the past. One was even connected to royalty – Arab, admittedly, but impressive all the same. It seemed she had some understanding of the care of the elderly, had a basic first aid qualification (Maeve did not reveal it was obtained on an Australian beach as a lifeguard), could run a household efficiently, indeed she had cooked for several rather grand people, and worked two seasons as a chalet girl, and to cap it all she had been to the same school as his niece. He ran through working hours and time off schedule, explaining that the agency supplied relief cover. As he described the hours, Henry became concerned that he was not offering a high enough salary to ensure Maeve's acceptance and he mentally notched it up a couple of hundred pounds a month. He lied smoothly about his mother's health and the departure of her current carer, called his mother a 'dear', emphasised his affection for her and the degree of his concern over her welfare, adding that his wife, Bunty, was also devoted. Finally, he asked when Maeve could start. Hearing that she was immediately available clinched it in his mind.

Maeve sat patiently while he described Charlton. 'Not large but an inconvenient house, unsuitable for an elderly person but my mother is quite determined to stay there as long as she is able. It has been her home for nearly seventy years.' He explained its position on the outskirts of a small village and how a car was an essential and that he was happy to pay a portion of running costs. He outlined the financial arrangements he would make and how Maeve was to be responsible for keeping basic housekeeping accounts. He said that his mother only required the plainest of food and was a very small eater. She no longer entertained. She was sufficiently mobile to move about the house with help and in the summer she could go a little way into the garden. He explained that a cleaner came in three mornings a week and that there was also a gardener and odd-job man who did routine outside work. Maeve was to be responsible for his mother's washing and ironing although larger items could be sent to the laundry. She had her hair washed and set once a month by a travelling hairdresser. She had accounts with two large London shops from which she obtained various luxury goods and Henry himself monitored her spending. She enjoyed Scrabble and crosswords and it was hoped that Maeve would share this interest. He asked if Maeve had any questions.

Maeve looked him straight in the eye. 'Only one,' she said. 'Does your mother actually require nursing? I'm not qualified at all, you know. I can dole out pills and stuff, but that's all.'

'No, she doesn't,' said Henry, reasonably truthfully. 'What this post is about is making it possible for her to remain at home, providing the help she needs to live there. If her condition deteriorates, my wife and I are very conscious of the necessity of her going into a nursing home, but we have not reached that point yet. Now, if there's nothing else . . .'

He stood up and offered his hand. Maeve rose, took it, noting the wet fish handshake.

'I must discuss the matter, obviously, with my mother,' said Henry, 'but I would certainly hope to let you know very soon. We have your telephone number, don't we?'

Maeve said he had and with a jaunty wave of her hand, tripped out.

Henry sat back. He felt pleased. Rather a pretty girl, too, he thought, in that pulled through a hedge, Irish way. Good legs. Smart suit. Lively little face. His mother would like that. She hadn't cared for Mrs Cook's heavy, bovine appearance from the start. He rang through to Mrs Tripp.

'Do we have references?' he asked.

'Yes,' said Mrs Tripp, who had summed Maeve up fairly accurately and reckoned that she would provide entertainment at least. 'What did you make of her? Rather different from the usual.'

'I liked her,' said Henry. 'I think we could take her on a month's trial. She'd cheer Mother up a bit, I think.'

'Or finish her off,' added Mrs Tripp to herself.

'Did you get the impression she was keen to take it?' asked Henry. 'If offered?'

'Hard to say,' said Mrs Tripp. 'I'd have thought it was the last sort of job a young girl would want, but maybe for a few months . . .' She left the sentence unfinished.

'What about the other woman? The housemistress?'

'She telephoned this morning. Unfortunately she has had a fall and broken her ankle.'

'Offer the girl the job,' said Henry, who couldn't bear things hanging on and thought of Bunty's nagging. 'She'll do as a stopgap anyway.'

'Are you sure?' asked Mrs Tripp. 'We could always run the advertisement again.'

'No,' said Henry, 'We'll risk it.' He was looking forward to telling Mrs Cook she could go.

Chapter Two

In London, Sophie was disappointed but not surprised to hear nothing from Maeve. Her departure to the country had been typical. She arrived on Sophie's doorstep the day before she was due to leave for Somerset with two dustbin liners of stuff which she wanted Sophie to store.

'Look, Maeve. I have hardly any space at all. You can see that. Everything is bursting at the seams with the children's clobber. What is all this, anyway?' She reached into a bag and brought out an old exercise book. She flipped it open before Maeve could snatch it out of her hand. It was filled with Maeve's small and surprisingly neat writing, closely packed, page after page.

'It's private stuff,' said Maeve fiercely. 'Goes with me everywhere. Except this time I thought I could trust you to look after it for me. Since I'm not intending to be in this job for long. But if you can't, you can't.'

'Oh, all right,' said Sophie, relenting, as usual. 'If you promise me it's not junk but stuff that's really important. You can shove it in the bottom of my cupboard, where my shoes live. As long as it's not for long.'

Maeve kissed her head as she went past to the bedroom.

'Jesus, Sophie. How many pairs of identical shoes do you have? All polished and on trees. It's like a little army in here. On the march.'

Sophie closed her eyes wearily. Why did Maeve always make her feel boring and middle-aged with remarks like that? Didn't she appreciate you *had* to be tidy and organised when you lived in a tiny flat with two small children?

'When do you go?' she asked as Maeve reappeared. She went through to the kitchen and put the kettle on and spooned instant coffee into two mugs.

'Tomorrow morning. Twelve-thirty train from Paddington

21

to Castle Cary. Isn't it a lovely name? I'll have to get a taxi to the house. I told Mr Banker Bentham that I had a car, you see. He seemed to think I needed one for the job but, well, bugger that. Look, Soph, can I nick this squashy bag thing from your cupboard to take my stuff in? I need to look tidy on arrival, don't I? First impression and so on. The plastic shopping bag look is not appropriate. She's a lady. Did I tell you? Well, she is. Lady Pamela. Isn't it wonderful? Pure tea dances and tennis, isn't it? "Lady Pamela at the Opening Meet of the South Somerset Water Beagles at Little Gusset." '

'Or Great Chilpruff,' said Sophie, falling into the sort of silly game they used to play at school. 'With her friend Horatia Grebe Watling . . .'

'Oh, yes! Perfect,' said Maeve. 'Anyway, I'm off tomorrow. I'll give you a ring when I get there and have had time to look round.'

That was nearly two weeks ago and Sophie felt hurt that she'd heard nothing at all. As she packed up the twins' things – she was going home to her parents for the weekend – she reflected sadly on how she still felt envious of Maeve, at the same time as deploring her luck and her lifestyle. When they were at school she had listened to Maeve's tales of home and longed to swap her own conventional, safe, devoted parents for something more exciting. When Maeve went for holidays in the south of France, Sophie went to Cornwall. When she was kissed by a spotty boy from Radley, Maeve was dating a Corsican fisherman. When she had had her first under-age drinking experience, very brave, and got tight in the pub in Rock, Maeve was having sex in Nice. And so it went on. Even when she got married, which for Sophie had been a pinnacle of achievement, Maeve had been unimpressed, and indeed had sown a few doubts in her mind.

'What do you see in him, Sophs?' she had asked. 'Do you really want to spend the rest of your life with Fergus? Sorry, but it beats me.'

Sophie had been hurt and upset and had decided, after all, to have only young bridesmaids and pages. She had quite wanted to have Maeve walking up the aisle, behind her for once. She had hoped that Maeve might be envious. She should have known better.

And now here she was, living a half-life. She loved the twins, they were the best thing she'd ever done and more important to her than anything in the world, but the truth could not be escaped that while she was at home caring for them, on an allowance paid by Fergus, the rest of life was passing her by. She refused to call it a trap. Freddy and Flora could never be a trap, but she had to own that two children of under two and a half effectively imprisoned her. She had lost her freedom when they were born. She remembered how Fergus had not been keen on the idea of her pregnancy from the start. He'd said that it was too soon, that they weren't well enough established. Later, when she had found out she was going to have twins, she knew he'd be horrified. She hardly dared tell him.

He'd had a rage. Shouted and swore and kicked the furniture, his face red and furious, clashing horribly with his hair. He'd called her a stupid cow for getting pregnant. She hadn't told anybody that. Not even Maeve. It was too humiliating. He'd been coldly angry after that, which had lasted for weeks. Sophie had never been so miserable.

It was better now without him, she knew that, despite the relentless responsibility and the solitary drudgery. Going home to her parents was the one break she got and even this she felt she had to ration because her mother overdid it and always looked exhausted by the time they left. Her mother had wanted her to move back home after Fergus had left her. She had even found a little cottage to rent about a mile away. Sophie had been sorely tempted but made up her mind that going back would be a retreat. She would stick it out in London and make a valiant effort to be independent. She also wanted the twins to know their father; or perhaps not so much that, more that Fergus should not escape responsibility. If she moved back to her family it would allow him to behave as if she had never been. She wanted to be in London where she and the children were a reminder that their marriage had been real.

Careful, considerate Sophie, who always played by the rules, had made one bad error of judgement and was paying for it dearly. Maeve, on the other hand, who was rarely safe or sensible, seemed to emerge unscathed. Sophie envied her her freedom from responsibility, and this barmy job was a case in point. To take off and change one's life overnight, so utterly impossible for her, seemed hugely appealing. Sophie longed to know about Lady Pamela. She longed to hear the story Maeve would weave. She wanted to be touched by Maeve's vitality, to be reminded that the world was full of excitement and amusement and endless possibilities and not just a round of washing and feeding and shopping and worrying about GM foods and safety and driving carefully and child locks.

I always was a bit boring, thought Sophie, but now I'm utterly boring. Fergus was right. And then she thought, Bugger that. Of course I'm different to how I was, to how Maeve is. Being a mother is bound to make me different. I'm tired, that's one thing. I'm on my own, that's another. Flora and Freddy. It's them. They are more important than I am. I'm subdued by them. What I want doesn't count any more, and anyway I want what is best for them. I can never be like Maeve. To be truthful, I never could anyway. I'm the sort of girl who shops from a list and polishes her shoes. Maeve is a free spirit.

Sophie moved round the twins' room, carefully folding clothes and packing them neatly into a case. She caught sight of herself in the glass on the back of their cupboard door. She looked pale, tired and thin. Dressed in baggy trousers and a sweatshirt, with her straight fair hair caught back in a band, she looked, quite correctly, as if she made no effort with her appearance. She really couldn't be bothered. As long as she was clean, she couldn't see that it mattered. She made a wry face, remembering how she had put on scent and lipstick for Mohammed. She wondered how he was getting on. He had given her the name of the restaurant where he worked and told her to go there for a meal, to take the babies. He said they would be welcome. She smiled again thinking of what Fergus would think of his children associating with a homosexual illegal immigrant who lived in a squat. But Mohammed had been so nice, so warm and friendly and so genuinely interested in the children. She realised that she would like to see him again.

It was therefore with considerable pleasure mixed with disappointment that when Sophie went to answer her doorbell that afternoon, she found Mohammed standing on the step.

'Come in,' she said, 'but I'm just about to leave for my parents'. How are you? Have you heard from Maeve? I was only thinking about you this morning,' and she blushed.

Mohammed stepped inside. He looked swarthy and foreign in his leather jacket with his dark complexion. Sophie noticed that he wore two flashy gold rings and a gold chain of some sort. Really, he was not a possibility. Not even as a friend. OK, perhaps in his own country but too embarrassing here in London.

Flora and Freddy ran to him and he knelt down and opened his arms to them.

'How are they? These little angels. These little chickens.' Really, he was much keener on them than Fergus ever was. He scooped them up and began to throw them energetically into the air.

'Oh God!' cried Sophie. 'Do be careful!'

'Don't you worry,' said Mohammed. 'I have many, many nephewsies and nieces.' This did not reassure Sophie who thought that if that was the case one or two fatalities would be neither here nor there. 'I love childrens,' he added, beaming. He saw the piles of collected luggage and said, 'Now I can help you. So much cases is too much for you.'

'Well, actually . . .' Sophie had been worrying about how to load her car as well as watch the twins. She had decided to strap them into their buggy and leave them in the flat while she went backwards and forwards, but unless she could park right outside her door, she did not like to do this. These were the sort of logistical problems that dogged her. 'I'd be really grateful. But have a cup of tea or something first.' She glanced furtively at her watch. She could allow him half an hour.

Mohammed sat on her sofa with a twin on either knee. They both gazed at him in wonder. Flora patted his face and Freddy examined his rings with interest.

'I have come because I have had telephone message from Maeve. She is being very secret but she wants me to make visit to you to say she is all right and she wants come and see you next week on Monday's night. Tuesdays is hers days off. She asks you if this is all right. She telephones me at work. She does not telephone to you for some reasons I do not be understanding. But now,' and Mohammed produced something from his jacket, 'I have mobiles, so all is easy.'

Sophie was working hard to get the gist of this.

'Well, yes,' she said, 'it would be fine for Maeve to come on Monday, I'd love to see her. I'm longing to know all about it. Did she sound OK? Is she happy? I can't understand why she can't just telephone me. Have you got her number? Why can't I ring her?'

'This I am not understanding,' said Mohammed, shrugging,

'but she has my mobiles and she will telephone me and I give her your message. Also I tell you that I have now a room with a friend. Khaled, a friend from Cairo. I am writing you the address,' he took a scrap of paper from his pocket, 'with also my mobiles. Sometimes, I think, and you must forgive me, that you are needing a man to help. Maeve she say to look after her very good friend, and here I am, Mohammed.'

Sophie smiled. 'Thank you very much. Well, you couldn't have turned up at a better moment. It really would be a help if you could give me a hand with this lot. But on the whole,' she added, 'I manage very well.' She was relieved of a vague anxiety that Mohammed had come round to ask for help rather than offer it. She felt ashamed. She took the twins off to change them before the journey and handed Mohammed his tea and a chocolate biscuit, which was all she had to offer.

When she was packed and ready he carried everything, including the children, in several trips to her car. As she double-locked the door she had a treacherous thought about Mohammed's honesty. Was it wise that he should know her flat was to be empty all weekend? Oh well, it was too late to worry now. There he was further up the road, standing guard by her car. He courteously held the driver's door for her as she checked that he had strapped the twins correctly into their car seats. She did not want to offer him a lift but she could not drive off and leave him on the pavement so she took him to the Tube station, which wasn't really out of her way. His bulky jacket seemed to fill up the passenger seat and Sophie realised he was the first man she had driven in this car, which her father had given her six months ago. She pulled up on the double yellow line to let him out and then they shared a curious little moment in which he turned to look at her to say goodbye and their eyes met and held and something quite deep and unspoken passed between them. As Sophie drove away she felt quite shaken. What had it been? Was it pity she saw in his look? Concern? Sympathy? Affection?

Mohammed, left on the pavement, wondered at this strange English girl, alone in a way that could never happen in his country. He liked her plain pale face, her colourless hair, her clear, truthful eyes. She was brave and strong, but so very, very sad. He thought of her driving across London with her babies and how the little car seemed vulnerable in the traffic amongst the buses and lorries. His large, sentimental brown eyes filled with tears as he thought of the embracing warmth of his own family. He felt far from home and lonely. Sniffing, he went down the steps to catch his train.

Henry had had little difficulty in persuading Bunty that he had done well in securing the services of Maeve. Bunty did no more than half listen anyway because the only news she really wished to hear was that Lady Pamela was being packed off to a nursing home; anything else was of minor interest.

She and Henry lived in a large comfortable house in Putney, had a shooting lodge in Scotland and a flat in Switzerland. Adding Charlton to this list was not a pressing urgency except that Henry was due to retire in a few years and they had always planned to move out to Somerset when he left the bank. Charlton was not the house Bunty would have chosen but Henry was fond of the place where he had grown up and it was well-situated in rolling green country-side and yet not far from a mainline railway station. It was hideously old-fashioned and antiquated and it was for this reason that Bunty wanted to get her hands on it in plenty of time before they took up residence. In Bunty's view it had some major disadvantages. The first was that it was most definitely not a grand house but only a large farmhouse in the local style, with low ceilings and casement windows. There was not a room large enough for entertaining on the scale Bunty enjoyed. The drawing room was pretty, south-facing with a ham stone fireplace and windows to the garden but it was not sufficiently large to accommodate the numbers Bunty invited to her dos. The kitchen was positively primitive with a stone sink and old-fashioned cupboards and an ancient and temperamental Aga. There were numerous larders and game cupboards, an old dairy and cheese room, and back stairs leading to the attic rooms once occupied by female domestics and dairymaids. The main staircase was rather impressive with wide treads and a gracious sweep of banister. Upstairs there were six bedrooms and two hideous bathrooms which would have to be ripped out. There wasn't even central heating, only antiquated night storage heaters and open fires. There was a huge amount of work to be done and while Lady Pamela was still living there, it was impossible to make a start.

It annoyed Bunty to be thwarted in this way and she grumbled about it regularly. In the sort of unspoken understanding arrived at in most long-term marriages, it was accepted by Henry that he had married an energetic and forceful young woman with bouncy good looks in the blonde, brash, Australian style, whose physical attractiveness and personality far eclipsed his own. In return and to correct this imbalance, Henry had to pitch his position and spending power and on the whole to allow Bunty what she wanted in life.

Bunty was nobody's fool and knew very well on which side her bread was buttered. Now, at fifty-two, with her looks fading and growing a little stout, she still remembered the tin-roofed house she had grown up in Wollongong, outside Sydney. She had worked hard to free herself of the legacy of her family – her sluttish chain-smoking mother and unemployed father and the string of good-for-nothing sisters. When, thirty years ago, she secured a secretarial job in the Sydney offices of Bentham's, she could not have guessed, even in her wildest dreams, that she would catch the eye of awkward, tongue-tied Henry. Pale and tall and stooped, concave chested, spindly legged, he was the opposite of the bronzed, fit, muscular Australian male ideal, but Bunty had her eye on status and investment and she did not find it hard to engineer his falling in love and proposing. On the whole, she had never regretted it.

Henry was, as Bunty had suspected, disappointing as a man, and she sensibly subdued her physical urges and channelled her appetites into enjoying material pleasures. Spending money and entertaining her friends were her two pastimes and she did both expertly. Henry was a dull old stick and so Bunty took refuge in loud, noisy, party-loving friends and Henry picked up the tab. It was an arrangement which suited them both.

Their three children arrived with four years between the first two and six years separating the last, Charlie, who was in the sixth form at school. The eldest, Amanda, was married and expecting a baby, and Clemmie, the second, was engaged.

Bunty was an energetic and interfering mother for whom nothing was too much trouble as long as she could make the arrangements and implement the decisions. She induced a sort of semi-paralysis in her nearest and dearest, rendering them incapable of independent action. So used were they to her steamroller force that left on their own they came to a shuddering stop, unable to find their own momentum.

Henry's mother was one of the few people Bunty felt powerless to intimidate. Lady Pamela's age, her title and the memory of what her mother-in-law had been like when Bunty first arrived in England subdued her habitual bossiness. Thirty years ago Bunty had never met anyone like Lady P. and she found herself in the novel position of being rendered dumb in her presence. Ever since, she had never quite had the gumption to tackle the old girl herself or take the law into her own hands regarding her fate – you could hardly call it a future. Instead, she railed at Henry about his bloody mother, and he was forced to tread carefully between the two women.

Henry telephoned to tell his mother about Mrs Cook's replacement at seven thirty in the morning when he knew she would be awake and Mrs Cook was unlikely to answer.

Lady Pamela was still in bed. She had lain awake since five o'clock and had made her slow way to the bathroom, leaning on her walking frame. The damn thing caught on furniture and banged into door jambs. It took her a good twenty minutes to cross the landing and manoeuvre herself into position on the lavatory, which had a special raised seat and a handrail. Then there was the slow journey back. Through the landing window she could see the first flicker of dawn light the black squares of night. Another day. She could hear noisy snores from Mrs Cook's door. These few hours when she was awake and Mrs Cook still asleep were precious to her. She felt the house was her own again and free of the bustling interference of the dratted woman and her incessant talk.

She shuffled slowly back to her room. The electric kettle for her morning tea was left by the tray, set with cup and saucer and milk. She sniffed the cup and pulled a face. Bleach. The wretched woman rinsed the crockery in bleach-tainted water. Who cared if the old cup was stained brown? It was only tea. She lifted the kettle and could tell from its weight that Mrs Cook had not remembered to fill it the night before. A repeat of the journey to the bathroom was too much. No tea this morning. Another small pleasure denied. God, it was so maddening to be helpless.

Slowly, as she did everything these days, Lady Pamela sat on the edge of the bed and raised her old legs onto the mattress. Her nightdress caught up, revealing the blue mottled limbs, fleshless and scaly-skinned. Lady Pamela viewed them with distaste. She had once been known for her legs.

29

She remembered the feel of silk stockings, the exciting tug of suspenders, the warm soft flesh in between. Now this. And the smell of old age. She could smell it now, clinging to her. She refused to let that Cook woman bath her but had to accept help in and out of the adapted tub. It was a ritual which only took place once a week. No wonder she smelt. She pulled the quilt up and lay back on her pillows. Another day. Life was only worth living while she could remain here in her beloved Charlton. Once that went she would be ready to die. Her hands lying on the quilt were still beautiful; long fingers, knobbly with age, veined backs, but beautiful in shape and elegance. Her diamond engagement and eternity rings still sparkled. Bunty wanted to get her hands on those. Literally. They wouldn't fit her, of course, not with those plump, stumpy hands of hers. The rings would have gone to Lizzie had she lived. Beautiful, brilliant Lizzie. All that one could hope for in a daughter. She would have been fifty now, married many years, divorced perhaps, as so many of her generation seemed to be, with grown-up children.

As always, Lady Pamela felt the stab of loss. Henry's sister had died, struck with meningitis at nineteen, and nothing had been the same again. She had been a first year medical student, committed to doing good, to being of service, and how Lady Pamela had admired that. Her own life as the wife of a distinguished diplomat seemed idle and worthless by comparison. She had been so proud of her daughter's seriousness, her shining belief in herself. All gone. Wasted. And Henry left. Poor, dull Henry plodding up through the bank. She had loved him as a solemn, unimaginative little boy; loved him still, of course, but there was nothing between them, no point of contact. She remembered how Lizzie had sat on her bed in the mornings, how they had laughed and talked, shared wicked observations, exchanged books, telephoned, shopped together. Lizzie would have understood about Charlton.

Lady Pamela closed her eyes. She could still hear the snores. Soon Mrs Cook would be woken by her alarm and another day of irritation would begin. She was well aware that she needed Mrs Cook in order to remain at Charlton, but there were some things she could not tolerate. Better to be dead. But the body was strong, the heart robust, the doctor said so. Threatened her with years of life, which she had no use for. She switched on the radio beside her bed and the urgent voice of the early news presenter surged out into the room, relaying information about a world with which Lady Pamela felt hardly connected. Her own had shrunk to this bedroom, this tea tray, this old house, the old dog snoring in the kitchen and Janet Cook snoring across the landing.

When Henry telephoned with the news that he had found a replacement carer, Lady Pamela could not shake off her longing for a quick, merciful death. Sam, of course, she didn't want to leave. Or poor ugly old Esau. Apart from them, she had little truck with the living.

'What's the matter, Mother? You don't sound very pleased,' said Henry, annoyed.

'Oh, but I am, I am,' she said wearily. In her heart she thought, What does any of it matter? A selfish old woman, an old house, a lot of memories . . . none of it matters.

Later, she could not remember why Henry had telephoned.

Sophie drove back to London with mixed feelings about the weekend. It had been lovely to be at home, of course. Her mother had not altered her bedroom at all. The dressing table was still stuck with photographs of ponies and schoolfriends, the drawers of the chest still full of her old clothes, the bed still lined with an array of teddies and loved soft animals. It was so odd to lie in the familiar room in the morning and feel as if the clock had been turned back. Freddy and Flora were put into beds in the spare room next door, which had once belonged to Jack, Sophie's third brother. His cricket trophies and school photos were still there although Mrs Gladwell had removed her son's tits and bums posters and put them in the dustbin.

The most wonderful thing had been the opportunity to sleep. Her mother had got the twins up the minute she heard them stir in the morning and Sophie had been able to sleep on and on, managing for once to switch off the internal alarm which alerted her the minute she heard them move. Her mother had even brought her breakfast in bed at ten o'clock, with crisp brown toast and honey, treating her like an invalid. It was so marvellous to shut down completely and be free of any concerns about domestic details.

But in spite of this Sophie found herself disagreeable and impatient, unable to express her gratitude and irritated that her mother's loving concern seemed to stem from a belief that her daughter was a helpless victim of a gross injustice. It drove Sophie to defend Fergus and to feel she had to show that she could manage. The fuss over the twins irritated her too. It always led to them behaving badly, getting over-excited and difficult.

'Mum, just leave them. They're fine. Don't entertain them all the time. They don't get this attention at home. No, they don't need juice or a biscuit. Please, Mum.'

On Saturday afternoon her father had been cajoled into baby-sitting and Sophie and her mother had gone into Oxford to shop and Mrs Gladwell had insisted on buying Sophie clothes. She had an excellent eye and made Sophie try on some leather trousers and a red polo-necked sweater. 'You're so slim now, darling, they'll look fabulous.' They did. Her mother cheerfully passed over her credit card. She also treated Sophie to some glamorous new underwear.

'I can remember after you lot were babies, I longed for something sexy and pretty,' she said.

Sophie hadn't felt sexy or pretty for so long that she wasn't convinced that pink and brown lace would do the trick, but she was grateful to her mother for trying.

When she had arrived for the weekend, home had looked comfortingly the same as ever. The pretty, golden stone house in the village outside Oxford was where Sophie and her brothers had grown up. The road through the village was busier now with a constant stream of traffic, and no longer could a child ride a pony or a bicycle down the main street, but the lane where Sophie's parents lived was still a backwater. The house stood behind a high stone wall in which a wrought-iron gate was set, and the garden, since his retirement from a City bank, was her father's main hobby. The lawns were immaculately cut and rolled, the beds vigorously weeded. His spring planting consisted of bulbs in regimented lines in colour blocks. Keeping things under control was John Gladwell's motto. Keeping on top of it. Not letting the place go to pot.

The field beyond, where Sophie had kept her ponies, was let for grazing and was full of very white sheep. Her father had left the gate to the gravelled drive open and as she swept up to the back door she could see that he had already been out with his rake. Sometimes she suspected this regimentation, this emphasis on order, was what she had married Fergus to escape, but these were heretic thoughts when her parents had been so kind – her rock, her mainstay – when things had gone wrong.

She had opened the car door and unloaded the twins from the back. Even here, which she had always thought of as peaceful, she noticed there was the sound of traffic from the main road and the thrum of an overhead jet losing height before landing at Heathrow.

Her mother, hearing her car, had come to the back door and with cries of delight kissed them all and, arm in arm with her daughter, walked with them across the garden to Sophie's father, who was raking leaves on the lower lawn. The twins fell about in the red and gold piles and Jules, the old labrador, gave her an enthusiastic welcome. Sophie had kissed her father. He threw down the rake and put his arms round her, and she felt tears start into her eyes. Everything seemed a painful reminder of what she had lost.

On Sunday her mother had invited friends for lunchtime drinks. There was a youngish, single man whom she had just discovered. He was the nephew of friends and had recently started some kind of research post in Oxford. Sophie was appalled to overhear a kind of whispered explanation from her mother: '. . .had a really, really tough time . . . and she's such a darling . . .' Sophie had to scoop up Freddy and go into the kitchen to stop herself from screaming. It was as if she had some awful disability or condition which might at any moment flare up and embarrass everyone if they were not suitably warned beforehand.

When she calmed down enough to re-enter the room and eventually talk to the man, whose name was Mark, she found him depressingly introverted and dull. All the extra sleep and the drink made her feel overcome with torpor and she yawned twice while he was talking. The second time, he stopped in his tracks and looked offended and she had to work hard to explain that she suffered broken nights with the twins and that her yawns were nothing to do with his fascinating explanation of his work.

After a late lunch both she and the twins had a nap and her mother woke her with a cup of tea as it was getting dark. She sat on the end of her bed and said, 'Sophie, really, darling, both Daddy and I feel that you would be so much better off down here, near us. We can help you, you see, and that is what we want to do. Look how tired you are. You really can't go on like this on your own. Does Fergus *know* how hard it is for you? Why can't he pay for help for you, a nanny or an au pair? If you were down here we would lend a hand, give you a chance to get your life going again.'

'We've been through all this, Mum,' said Sophie. 'It's terribly kind of you, but I do really believe that I want to do it on my own. I can't come back here to where I was before, with everyone knowing me. I don't know why I feel like this, but I do. Fergus says he can't afford giving me extra for childcare. His solicitor says that I will have to meet the costs out of maintenance, but I can't. I might just manage an au pair but I've no room for one. A nanny is out of the question. I'd have to be working full time to even consider it.' She leant across and took her mother's hand. She tried to make her voice sound bright and confident.

'As I see it, I have about two more years of slog and then the twins can start at a nursery and I can look for a part-time job. I could move to a less expensive area, which is what Fergus always suggests, but where I am is so safe and quiet and I love the garden. Also it means that when Fergus has the children, it's only for a day at the most. It's easy for him to come to the flat and be with them there where all their stuff is and where they have a routine. I can go out for the day and it's not nearly as bad as when he used to take them to his mother in Suffolk for the weekend. It was worse than anything seeing them driving off. I could hardly bear it. And of course if I moved out of London that's what he would have to do, actually take them away for the weekend. Everything would have to be much more formal. As it is, if I want to go to the cinema or get my hair cut or something, Fergus just comes round. It means he's more involved.'

In actual fact, thought Sophie, this is a lie. He always said it wasn't convenient when she asked him. This was not a truth she wanted to share with her mother who patted her hand and stood up, looking out of the window.

'Oh Sophie,' she said. 'I find it so hard to see you in this situation. I'm sorry but I could murder that man . . .'

Sophie sighed. 'Don't, Mum. It doesn't make it any easier.'

Saying goodbye on Monday was awful. With the twins packed into the car, which her father had thoroughly checked over, tyres, oil, battery, anti-freeze, and her new clothes in their shiny carrier bag on the back seat, Sophie turned to hug her parents.

'Thank you so much,' she said, 'for everything.' Her eyes filled with tears. Her mother put her arms round her and her father held them both.

'I'm sorry,' she sniffed, 'to be so pathetic. It's you being so kind that finishes me off.'

'We're always here, darling,' said her father. 'You can always rely on us. We'll come at the drop of a hat if you need us.'

'Thanks. Thanks for everything and I'm sorry I've been so foul.'

It was her mother's turn to cry.

'Now come on,' said her father. 'This won't do. You'll upset the twins. Come on. Let's see a smile before you go. We'll be in London next week for the theatre, so we'll see you all soon. Now off you go and give us a ring when you get there.'

Sophie drove off, managing a smile and a cheery wave but out of sight she drew over into a field gateway and howled. She felt so damn sorry for herself. Freddy began to cry as well, so she had to pull herself together.

'Sorry, sweeties,' she said. 'Silly Mummy. She's better now. Do you know something? Maeve's coming to see us tonight. That will be fun, won't it?'

When Maeve finally banged on her door it was after ten o'clock and Sophie felt furious. She had stopped on the way home and bought steak and salad and supermarket plonk and now it was too late to cook. She felt too tired. The twins had cried and quarrelled most of the journey and had fallen asleep about five minutes from home. The flat felt cold and damp and unwelcoming as she dumped them both on the floor, their faces scarlet with crying and wet with tears.

'Be quiet!' she had cried. 'Be quiet! Both of you! I can't stand it. I'm doing all I can. I don't like it either.' It was stupid, she knew, to talk like this to babies. Her cross voice made them cry more determinedly and she snatched them up one at a time and dumped them unceremoniously onto their beds where they stood, shaking with outrage, their mouths large, red Os.

She unloaded the car and turned on the heating, closed the curtains and poured herself a drink. In a moment she would feel calm enough to hook them up, wash and change them into their night clothes and snuggle up with them on the sofa to read them a favourite book. It was her job to make their world safe and secure and certain even if her own seemed none of those things. She felt ashamed of her weakness and remembered the striking images recently flashed across the television screen of young refugee mothers carrying their crying, hungry babies across snowy landscapes or herded into tractor trailers, their homes bombed and burning behind them.

I have nothing to complain about, she told herself sadly. Nothing at all. She was glad that Maeve would soon be with her.

Maeve arrived by taxi, which was the first surprise. Sophie had fallen asleep on the sofa but was woken by her voice outside in the street, talking to the driver, before she rang the doorbell. There she stood, looking well, carrying Sophie's overnight bag and another small tartan suitcase and wearing a navy jacket and a soft red scarf. She kissed Sophie in a rush of outside air, and Sophie smelt expensive scent.

'Soph, darling, don't look so cross. I'm sorry I'm so late, but look,' she pointed across the room, 'your telephone is off the hook. I've been trying to get you.' Later Sophie thought about this and realised this could not have been true. Her cordless telephone did not even *have* a hook. It was typical of Maeve to brazen it out with a lie, and typical of her to accept it. 'I absolutely couldn't get away,' Maeve continued. 'You know, it's not like a nine to five job. You can't just leave when your time is up, and the agency woman had a puncture and was late arriving to take over. I had to get a later train.' Maeve's breath smelt of drink.

'But you've been drinking,' said Sophie, and then regretted it. It made her sound so whining and reproachful.

'So I have, matey,' said Maeve, burrowing in the bag and drawing out a bottle of expensive Scotch. 'Had a slug in the taxi. Here,' and she passed the bottle to Sophie. She dropped her coat on the sofa. 'Must have a pee,' she said and raced to the bathroom, leaving Sophie standing, bottle in hand.

Sophie felt very uneasy. She looked at the coat which seemed new and had a very expensive label. The coat, the taxi, the Scotch, the suitcase full of God knows what. The red scarf, which she picked up off the floor, was cashmere. What was Maeve up to? Sophie put the bottle on her kitchen counter. She did not want to touch it, let alone share its contents.

'Maeve,' she said when her friend reappeared. 'All this stuff. Where's it from?' Sophie was relieved to see that at least Maeve was wearing the clothes she had bought from round the corner.

Maeve glanced at her sharply. 'Hold on, matey. Don't sound so suspicious. Do you think I'm robbing her or something?'

This was exactly what had crossed Sophie's mind but she had to deny it. 'Of course not. But where? I mean, this coat must have cost a fortune . . .'

'Yeah. Thirty years ago. Come on, Sophs. Loosen up. Aren't you pleased to see me? I said I'm sorry I was late.' By now she was rummaging in the fridge and had found the steak. 'Heh, heh! What's this? Shall I cook it?' She splashed whisky into glasses and handed one to Sophie. 'Steak sarni? How about that? You've got a ciabatta in the freezer . . . lots of garlicky, mustardy butter. Not too late, is it?'

A moment ago, the thought of meaty cooking smells had made Sophie feel sick. Now Maeve had whetted her appetite.

'Sounds great. Sorry. I feel knackered. I drove back from home this afternoon. The twins were horrible. Or rather, I was. I got sick of waiting for you. Must have fallen asleep. Sorry.' She held out her arm. Maeve swiped at her hand. She was not one for physical demonstrations.

'Go back to the sofa,' ordered Maeve, 'with your drink. You can tell me how you are while I cook, and then I'll tell you all about me. It's quite a story.'

'Well, I'm fine,' said Sophie lamely. 'I mean, we're all fine. The weekend was nice, really. It was nice to get out of London . . .' she tailed off. She couldn't make anything of it. She found it impossible to talk about herself, to be entertaining. I'm so dull, she thought. 'Fine', 'nice', when in many ways we're not fine and it wasn't all nice. She didn't seem to have the vocabulary to describe how she really was, how she really felt. Always this brave face. To her parents and now, dammit, even to her best friend.

She felt an awful swelling in her throat and took a large gulp of whisky to quell the tears. I'm just tired, she thought. Tired and hormonal.

'But tell me,' she asked, 'why the mystery over the telephone? Why didn't you ring me? Why the messages via Mohammed?'

'Ah! Well, that's Lady P for you. A right old tartar. She likes to be in control of everything. There's only one handset, which she has had moved into her bedroom, and I'm not supposed to use it without permission. I could only ring when she was in the bathroom. I tried to get you a couple of times but you were always out. I knew I could catch Mohammed when he was at work. I'm getting all that changed, though. I'm not putting up with being treated like a servant. Where do you keep the mustard, Soph?'

'Cupboard to the right of the hob.'

Maeve was banging about in the cupboard, getting out the grill pan, then there was the wonderful smell of hot olive oil and garlic which always made Sophie think of holidays abroad.

'How are your parents?' Maeve shouted above the sound of spitting meat and the kitchen fan, which gave Sophie the opportunity to supply another 'fine' and 'very well'. She did start to cry then. Large, silent drops rolled down her cheeks as she sat, curled up on the sofa, nursing her glass. With a flourish, Maeve slid the sizzling steaks into the warm sections of bread spread thickly with aromatic butter.

'Yum,' she said and handed one on a plate to Sophie with a section of kitchen towel. It was robust, trencherman's food and required a lot of silent tearing and chewing. Talking was impossible for the time being. Maeve sat on a floor cushion at Sophie's feet with her back against the sofa. She hadn't noticed Sophie's tears.

'Now,' she said, wiping her mouth and taking another swig of whisky, 'I'll tell you all about it.'

Chapter Three

'Well,' said Maeve, 'I'll start right at the beginning. You know how it was when I left London? I wasn't exactly enthusiastic about the job per se, but at the same time really glad to get myself sorted out for the next few months. I got the train OK that morning – didn't wear The Suit but cleaned up pretty well and looked tidy and respectable, not at all alarming to an old lady. Got out at Castle Cary. Train whizzed on to deepest Devon or somewhere and left me and your bag at the station. Single-track line, all peace and quiet. Cows mooing, smell of something agricultural. That sort of thing. Car park full of estate cars and four-by-fours. No taxis. And me! Jesus, I thought. I'm not going to be able to cope with this. Not my scene. As soon as people know I'm Irish, they think I must have grown up in a bog astride a black and white pony. You know I didn't. I'm a pavement girl. Never had a pair of wellies in me life. Don't know the name of a bird. Can't tell an oak from an ash. A townie through and through. Where the concrete ends, so does life as far as I'm concerned. So there I was, looking at all this green and wet and thinking, Soph was right, this is a big mistake.

'Then a taxi arrived and I said, "Heh! Can you take me to this address?" and the taxi man said, "No problem, my dear," and piled my stuff in the boot. "Climb aboard," he said, and looked at me sideways. "So, what are you doing here?"

'Well, that's like the Irish – nosy. I'm used to that. "I'm come to take care of Lady Pamela at a place called Charlton. Do you know her?" I said.

'He looked at me again and said, "Bugger me! I don't believe it!"

'I looked at him and said, "Why not?"

' "You don't look the type," he said. "Not like the other ones."

39

' "Other ones? You mean there have been a lot?"

' "Oh, yes," he said. "There have been a few all right."

' "So, what's she like then?" I said.

'He thought for a bit and said, "Well, she's a real lady, that's for sure."

' "That could mean anything!" I said. "Tell me about the others."

' "Not like you!" was all he would say. All this time we were driving slowly through this dripping green countryside, stopping every now and then to let some sort of tank-like tractor get by, passing farms and cottages like you see on Christmas cards, but in crisp white snow with the sun shining, not in thick brown mud. Cows in gateways with mud up to their knees and dollops of muck on the muddy lanes. I felt as if I was going to be buried alive in a manure heap.

' "Aren't we there yet?" I asked. I'd been told it wasn't far from the station.

' "Nearly," he said. "Not far now. I do this run every two weeks with her boyfriend."

' "Her boyfriend?" I said. "Whose boyfriend?"

' "Hers," he said. "Lady Pamela's."

' "Lady Pamela's?" I said, thinking I'd misheard. "Lady Pamela's in her eighties. She can't have a boyfriend!"

' "Can't she! Every two weeks I'm booked to collect him off the London train. Spends the day at Charlton and catches the six twenty-five back again. A bit later in the summer. Regular as clockwork. Been coming for years, he has. Nice old gentleman. Mr Sam, I call him. An art historian is what he says he is. Writes books and that. Been her boyfriend for the last thirty years, so they say."

'Jesus, I thought. I felt a bit cheered up. Having a boyfriend seemed hopeful. As if it wasn't all bedpans and dribbling and dementia. Then we turned off this tiny lane at a little green triangle and through some gates and up to a really lovely house. I don't know what I was expecting exactly, something rather grand and Brideshead-like, I suppose, because Banker Bentham seemed so affluent. This wasn't enormous or grand but pretty and comfortable looking. The sort of house the BBC might use for a Jane Austen adaptation. A breeches and bonnets house with a big wide front door and windows set so that they sort of smile – you know what I mean? A house with a smiling face?

'There was a car parked in front. One of those little

fat-bottomed, polished ones in a horrible shade of limey
green. You know, the sort of colour you can't imagine anyone
actually choosing voluntarily. The sort of car which you
always find at the head of a queue of other vehicles all boiling
with road rage. It was packed with luggage – someone was
evidently all ready and waiting to move out. I paid the driver,
whose name was George and who gave me his card and told
me he'd come and rescue me if ever I felt desperate, and I was
just going to thump the knocker on the front door when the
door flew open and this woman came gushing out. Late
fifties, pink face, pink jumper, fat, trousers, little trotty high-
heeled boots, silly face. "I'm Mrs Cook," she said, "and you
must be Maeve" (she pronounced it Mauve). "All I can say,
dear, is that I wish you all the best. I'm very, very fond of
Lady Pamela, but I have to say that she has become very
trying. And rude. If there's one thing I cannot put up with it's
rudeness. And ingratitude."

'Good beginning, eh? Oh, Mrs Cook, personally I just adore
those two particular qualities. She took me into the house
and gave me a whistle-stop tour, ending up in a back
sitting-room place where she showed me piles of papers and
lists which she had pinned to a cork noticeboard. Names and
telephone numbers and the day's routine, that sort of thing.
She showed me Lady Pamela's pills and said she couldn't be
trusted to take them herself, and said she'd left supper
prepared in the larder. Then she was off and out of there as if
she couldn't wait to shake the dust off her feet. I stood at the
door and watched her leaving.

'When she'd gone I felt really weird. It was incredibly quiet.
The house was empty and still. Lady Pamela was supposed to
be having a nap upstairs. And there I was, plonked down in a
completely unknown place with this huge weight of responsibility on me. I could have called up George and got the hell
out of there and no one would have been any the wiser. But
I didn't. I went in, shut the door and, feeling like an intruder
– it's most peculiar snooping around other people's furniture
and possessions – had a better look round.

'It struck me that although there was loads of lovely
antique furniture and pictures and stuff that must be worth a
packet, the place hadn't had much spent on it recently. No
central heating, shabby old carpets, peeling paint, dingy
wallpapers. Incredibly antiquated kitchen and sculleries, an
old dairy sort of place and boot room filled with funny old

gardening hats and ancient shoes and a modern folded up wheelchair and a sort of commode affair which I didn't like the look of.

'Mrs Cook had set up shop in the little sitting room and had an armchair, electric fire and television. She'd left two dead pot plants, and a half bottle of Tia Maria, with no top on the bottle and dead flies floating in it. Supper, when I located the larder, was a few slices of that square, paper-thin wet pink stuff which passes as ham and a packet of instant mashed potato, two tomatoes and a tin of rice pudding. She'd employed a kind of scorched earth policy. George, I'm going to need you, I thought. A big stock-up at a supermarket is called for.

'At the front of the house there was a lovely sitting room with long windows which looked down a peaceful valley, and a quite grand dining room, but they had that shut-up, over-tidied feel about them as if they were sets for a play which had yet to start. The fireplaces were black and empty and swept clean. No fires had been lit for ages, I'd say.

'Then I went upstairs. I'd found a little creaky back stair which went up from next to the kitchen for the use of maids and underlings I supposed, but the front staircase was wide and carpeted in that old-fashioned way with a strip of deep red carpet up the middle of the treads. The walls were hung with hunting prints, mostly of elegant top-hatted men falling into ditches, and other pictures showing the slaughter of birds or deer or endangered species, I expect. Then I had a terrific fright because something stirred in the gloom on the landing, but it was only a small hairy dog which jigged about a bit in a friendly way. It was one of those shapeless little dogs which you have to look at quite hard to work out which way it's pointing. It looked fairly ancient and cob-webby. It scuttled off sideways, like a crab, into a room off the landing where the door stood open. I could hear a radio playing from inside, so I knocked on the door and a very wide-awake and young-sounding voice said, "Come in!" She wasn't asleep at all, just lying there in the half-light of the afternoon.

'I felt uncomfortable going into her bedroom with her in bed. She was lying, dressed as far as I could see, under the cover of a big old mahogany bed. She reached out and fumbled with a bedside light and I said, "I can do that!" and she said, "I am not completely incapable, you know," and then she knocked something over and swore – "Damn" or something innocuous like that – and then the light came on and we had a good look at one another.

' "Well!" she said. "You are far too young. What is Henry thinking of?"

' "No I'm not," I said. "I'm not anything like as young as I look. Like you." She liked that. I could tell at once she was a vain old woman.

' "Come closer," she said. "Why, you're tiny. Hardly bigger than a child."

' "About the same as you, I'd guess," I said, seeing how small she was. "But it's quality which counts, isn't it? I may be little but I'm a little good 'un, as they say about horses where I come from." I don't know where I got this from, it came into my head from nowhere. I mean no one where I come from talks about horses. Anyway, it struck a chord with her all right.

' "Of course, you're Irish. Where from? Do you know the Carews, the Castlemains, the Guinnesses? They were all friends of ours, of Bumper and me."

' "Know the names, of course. But my father is the first of my family to stay on at school after fourteen. To better himself. He's a lawyer. I've done my best to re-establish the family tradition of fecklessness, which is why I've ended up here – oh! That sounds rude . . ." but Lady Pamela laughed. She has a tiny little crinkly face and a wide mouth, like a little monkey, and white hair cut in a flat, straight bob.

' "Now what can I do?" I asked, trying to seem brisk and willing.

' "Go away while I get up," she said.

' "OK," I said. "I'll go and take my bags upstairs."

'I had a look at the other bedrooms and found where Mrs Cook slept, across the landing. She'd stripped the bed and folded the blankets but left a corn plaster and used tissues in the wastepaper basket. I decided I'd rather be right at the top of the house in a couple of attic rooms which had less overwhelming furniture and lovely views, even though the sight of all those fields might induce me to leap out of the window in despair.

'I chucked everything out of my bags and made up the bed with clean sheets from the airing cupboard and then went back down to ask if Lady P wanted a cup of tea. She was up and sketchily dressed in a tweed skirt which was rucked up at the back – caught in her knickers, I expect. "Don't you go downstairs?" I asked.

' "Not since my hip," she said. "That last one didn't want the responsibility of getting me up and down."

'I looked at the triangle formed by her armchair, the little table where she must eat her disgusting meals, and her bed. That was her life. I couldn't imagine where she put the boyfriend when he called. Not in the bed, surely?

' "I'll help you down, if you want," I said.

'She didn't acknowledge this generosity on my part, but said, "Where have you put your things?" I told her and she got really crabby and said I couldn't go upstairs, that I was to sleep where Mrs Cook had slept, that if I was upstairs I wouldn't hear her call if she needed help.

' "Oh yes I will," I said. "I've got hearing like a hawk," and the inappropriateness of this remark made us both laugh even though she was cross.

' "You're a ridiculous girl," she said. "I can't think what Henry thinks he's doing sending you down here. You'll have to go, you know."

'I ignored that remark and said, "Now, if you don't want a cup of tea, and don't need me, I'm going for a walk and then I'll see what I can do about this terrible supper we've been left."

' "You can't go for a walk," she said. "You're not free to go. It's not your time off."

' "I won't go far," I said, ignoring her. "Do you want to come, ugly little dogwog?" and I poked at him with my foot.

' "No, he doesn't," she said. "Esau won't go with you. He never leaves me." But he got up and wagged the end with a tail on it, and scuttled off down the stairs with me.

'You old bitch, I thought, and I had to smile. It takes one to know one, doesn't it, Soph?'

Maeve reached for the bottle which she had put on the floor beside her and splashed some more whisky into her glass. She offered some to Sophie who put her hand over hers. 'Can't,' she said. 'I've got to be up with the twins in the morning. I can't cope with a hangover as well.'

'Who'd be a mother?' said Maeve. 'What a price to have to pay for being fucked by Fergus.'

Sophie groaned. 'Don't remind me. Anyway, go on.'

'Well,' said Maeve, 'to cut a long story short, I explored outside and found amongst other things a hen run and a fair-sized vegetable garden. I had no idea where hens put their eggs when they lay them but I discovered a little sort of hinged door on the hen house and inside were four little nest boxes and four brown eggs. The hens didn't seem to object to me stealing them so I put them in my pocket. The veg garden had rows of sprouts and leeks and onions and also spinach and broccoli, so I went inside and got a plastic bag and collected spinach. I expected to get shouted at at any moment but there was no one around and it seemed quite reasonable to help myself if it was for Lady Pamela. I remembered Banker Bentham telling me there was a gardener and odd-job man and obviously this was his territory. I snooped around the sheds by the back door and found a coal shed which was empty and a log store which had a small pile of logs at the back. I also found a bicycle which seemed to be in reasonable order but had two flat tyres. By this time I'd long since lost the dog and it was getting dark, so I went back in and put on a lot of lights and found a radio for the kitchen, washed the spinach, set a tray with silver from the dining-room cabinet and nice wine glasses which I polished up on a cloth. Mrs Cook had told me supper had to be at seven o'clock sharp. I looked for something to drink but couldn't find anything in all the obvious places. I went upstairs and knocked on Lady Pamela's door and then went in and closed her curtains and tidied up the things she'd dropped on the floor and re-made her bed. She made me pass her her comb and mirror and lipstick and she painted on a mouth in roughly the right place.

' "Where is Esau?" she said.

' "No idea. He pushed off while I was looking around outside."

'She looked pleased at that. "I told you he wouldn't go with you," she said. It was a small triumph.

' "Would you like a drink of something? The sun's over the yardarm and all that stuff."

'She looked at me sharply. "Do you drink?" she said.

' "You bet," I said. "But I can't find anything downstairs. Where's it all kept?"

'She looked at me for a moment. I could see her wondering if I was a dipsomaniac. She must have decided that I wasn't because she said, "I've got some bottles up here. In the cupboard over there. Sam brought them." She indicated a door in the far wall which I opened to find a deep recessed cupboard – more like a dressing room – hung with rails of clothes and stacks of hat boxes and racks of shoes. There was also a cardboard box containing a large bottle of gin and some sherry and vermouth and some empty bottles as well. I pulled out the gin and the vermouth.

' "Gin and it?" I asked. "Is that what you have? Surely with ice and lemon, or a stuffed olive? Would I find something like that downstairs?"

' "As it is will do," she said, pointing out a heavy crystal glass on a tray. "I don't believe I said you could have one," she added. She could see that I was looking for another glass.

' "Oh, come on!" I said. "Share and share alike! I'm supposed to be a companion, aren't I? It's not very companionable to sit and drink on your own. Tell you what, when we've finished this bottle, I'll buy the next one. How about that?"

'She had to laugh. "Go on then."

'I shot off downstairs and came back with some ice in a bowl and a second glass. There was no lemon or olives. I don't know why I bothered to look.

'I mixed us a stiff one and then I found a paper and pencil and made a list of things I thought we needed and read them out to her.

' "My dear, do you think I'm made of money? What a ridiculous list. I hardly eat anything."

' "Well, I do. I'll get George to take me into the town tomorrow and I'll do a big shop. Here, let's have a refill and then I'll go and get your supper."

'When I brought her up a poached egg on a pile of steamed spinach she was genuinely surprised and pleased. She said she couldn't eat it all of course and that it would keep her awake and so on, but she gobbled it up all the same. I reckon she was half-starved. I ate mine off my knees in her room although she told me that Mrs Cook never ate with her. "Well, I hate eating alone," I said.

'Afterwards I asked if she wanted to do a crossword or play Scrabble and she looked at me as if I was barmy. All that stuff Banker B had told me was rubbish. She said, "Certainly not. I want to watch *The Bill*." So off I went to put my stuff away, which took about five minutes. I had a bit of a poke around the other rooms and got the hang of the layout of the house and found the bathroom I was supposed to use. It was freezing, with a one bar electric fire on the wall. It's a good thing we went to boarding school, isn't it Soph, and had all those years of deprivation of home comforts? Then at about nine o'clock I followed Mrs Cook's instructions and took up a hot drink and got the morning tea tray ready. Lady P makes herself a cup of tea in the morning because she wakes so early. I hovered around a bit and tried to work out how much help she needed to get ready for bed. I could see that the arthritis in her hands made buttons difficult, so I said, "Here, I'll do that," and unbuttoned her cardigan and blouse and tried not to notice the funny old vest underneath and the sort of chicken carcass look of her body. She couldn't manage her skirt, either, so I undid the button and the zip and then got the hell out of there, but not before she had time to say, "You may go," as if she was dismissing me. I heard her shuffling across to the bathroom to wash. I left it a bit and then knocked on her door and asked if she wanted anything, any help getting into bed, but she said, very sharply, "I'm not completely incapable, you know. You can turn that dreadful music down." She could hear the radio playing in the kitchen. "OK," I said, thinking, miserable old bat, "sleep well," but she didn't reply.

'The next day I met the daily, Mrs Day, ha, ha, who is a terrific talker, at full pitch, above the Hoover noise. I told her I wanted to light a fire in the sitting room in the afternoons and to get Lady P downstairs and she piled Mrs Cook's dried flower arrangements in the hearth and laid a fire on top of them. I opened the windows because it was a nice mild morning and we moved the furniture about to make it more comfortable. I didn't think much of her cleaning efforts. She just Hoovers central areas of carpet and moves dust around with a duster, but she was friendly and helpful. I thought I might find out all about everything from her but it seems she has only been "doing" Lady Pamela for the last few months. The original old daily was eventually retired – blind, deaf and one-legged as far as I can tell. In the afternoons Mrs Day goes and cleans at an air force base. She has a clapped-out old car and said she'd give me a lift if I ever needed one. She plays Bingo twice a week and goes to the pub with her husband on another evening so by my standards she leads a pretty racy life. Frank, her husband, is a cowman on a farm. She says he smells of slurry so she washes all his clothes with Dawnfresh fabric conditioner. We had a laugh about that.

'I asked her about the gardener and she said she saw him about but didn't speak to him much. He was a bit odd. Lived in a cottage on the lane. His name was Dick Jack, or Jack Dick, she wasn't sure. I went outside to look for him and found him digging up potatoes. He was about fifty, wearing a woollen cap and had one of those mad, straying eyes so that when I talked to him one eye was on me and the other was wandering over my shoulder – very disconcerting. He seemed grumpy that I'd picked the spinach and so I asked him what the arrangement was about vegetables and eggs and he said, "Well, she had no need for 'em. Never wanted any."

' "Who's she?"

' "That last one. The fat one. Only frozen stuff, she said. Allergic to eggs, and all."

' "Well, I'd like some every day, please. If you don't want me to pick stuff, then could you do it for me and leave it by the back door? And eggs, please." His eyes swerved about wildly.

' "You can bugger off," he said.

'I just smiled and said, "Thanks. I'll give Lady Pamela your message. I'd like some of those potatoes for lunch, please."

' "Bugger off," he said again, but he did bend over and pick up some potatoes and gave me three or four.

'So that was it. The local colour. I'd rung George and in the afternoon he came and collected me and took me into Castle Cary. I must admit that that was a pleasant surprise. It's a really pretty little old town with a winding high street and lots of dear little stone cottages, all beautifully kept with cats sitting in the windows among the geraniums. There's a wonderful ironmonger with bird tables and dustbins and plastic bowls set out on the pavement, and the butcher is called Lush! Isn't that wonderful? There is a grand town hall like something out of Thomas Hardy, with two white doves on the roof, a clock on the steeple and a wooden seat outside under a sign to Horsepond Lavatories and next to a holly tree covered in red berries. There are some interesting looking shops – one seems to sell nothing but tassels for grand curtains – and some olde worlde pubs. Banker Bentham has organised for me to draw money out of Lady P's housekeeping account, and the bank is beautiful with eighteen twenty-six carved in stone on the front. There is a really good supermarket in the High Street stocked with all sorts of expensive treats as well as tinned peas and white bread. I did a big shop and bought some wine. When George delivered me back he had a look at the bicycle and took it off in the back of his taxi to get it mended for me.

'I gave Lady Pamela lamb cutlets that night for supper. She said she couldn't eat them but she did, and we had a glass of wine.

'The wine and the food seemed to give her a sparkle. It didn't last for long though. She told me to take the dirty things away, that she was tired, that I was too noisy. I helped her get ready for the night and then left. When I closed her door and said, "Good night, Lady Pamela, sleep well," she didn't reply.'

Maeve yawned and stretched. 'That's it for tonight, babe. You look knackered and I'm pissed. Just let me have a duvet and I'll curl up on the sofa. God, it's nice to be here.'

'It's nice to have you,' said Sophie dutifully. She meant it, too.

'Maeve,' said Mohammed the following morning as their little party walked on Hampstead Heath in bright autumn sunshine. 'You are telling us so funny stories, but there is so much strange. How are you all alone in this old houses with the old lady? How do her families, her sons and daughters, let her be alone like this? They do not know you, you do not know them – yes, you are very kind girl, but they are not knowing this. You are strangers. In my country this is impossible. This old ladies would be living all the time with her sons and daughters. This is rich family but this is not good.'

Sophie was pushing the buggy along between Maeve and Mohammed. She felt happy. Mohammed on her left had his arm loosely over her shoulder, Maeve on her right had tucked her arm through hers. This easy physical contact was reassuring. It made her feel less isolated, less cut off from life, less like someone washed up and marooned by her circumstances. The sun was lovely and the trees, turning red and gold, glowed under the blue sky.

'It is weird, isn't it?' said Maeve. 'I mean, the family telephone quite often but frankly, anything could be going on. At least I'm reasonably caring. I mean she does complain all the time and I think old Henry and the daughter-in-law have given up really. They want an easy life and they want to keep Lady P's nuisance potential to a minimum. As long as she's not actually neglected and as long as her basic needs are met, they're just sitting it out. They take the view that she's had a good innings and can't last for ever. I'm just a sort of keeper really. But it is odd living so closely with someone and yet not having a normal, real relationship with them. I mean, I'm only there because I'm paid to be. Whether I like the old bat or not is immaterial. There was a daughter, I've discovered, who died young. She was the favourite, that's obvious. I suppose it would all be different if she were alive. But come to think of it, I certainly won't dance attendance on my appalling mother when she's in her dotage. Lady P's got a number of friends who telephone and call but they're all pretty ancient. The deaths column is the first thing she looks at in the newspaper every morning, to see which of them has dropped off the perch. Dying is the most interesting thing any of them do these days.'

Mohammed, who had been getting quite agitated, broke in, 'You English are so cold, so frozen, like your bloody country. At the end of her lifes, this old lady should feel love about her, not the caring of a stranger and this only for the money.'

'I'm providing a service,' said Maeve, 'and I daresay it's easier for me to be pleasant and kind than it would be for her family. I'm not required to be involved in any other way. She'd certainly hate it if I got gushy over her. She's actually quite a laugh. We were looking at some photographs the other day and I pointed to one and said, "Is that your husband?" and then something inane about him having an interesting face or something, to be polite, and she said, quick as a flash, "Bumper was a perfect bore. Certainly not interesting!" "But you were married to him for fifty years or more!" I said, and she replied, "There are worse things than boredom, you know."

'Fifty years!' said Sophie sadly. 'And mine lasted under two.'

'Count yourself lucky, babe!' said Maeve.

Mohammed said excitedly, 'All this I am not understanding. Here is beautiful sweet woman Sophie – no, it is the truth – with lovely childrens, and no man. Here is old ladies with rich families all alone in old ages with Maeve, who does not care for her at all, but only for herself, because she too is also alone. This is not possible for women in my countries. Always they have their families to care for them.'

'Wait a minute,' said Sophie, 'there is some element of choice here. My family begged me to go back and live at home but I didn't want to. That's why I'm alone. Apart from the Fergus defection, I mean. Maeve is certainly alone by choice and I gather that Lady Pamela is too. She actually wants to go on living where she does.' Sophie didn't like to say so but she thought she had read articles in *Marie Claire*, fierce, angry articles, about the dire state of female emancipation in Mohammed's homeland. She wasn't altogether sure that female circumcision didn't come into it somewhere.

Maeve had no compunction about voicing her thoughts. 'Yeah, and where you come from, mate, women don't get a choice,' she said bluntly. 'They're stuck with their families, who treat them as they like, like prisoners in some cases. Don't give me that crap. I grew up in a pretty dysfunctional family and I couldn't wait to get out.'

Mohammed looked offended and lapsed into sulky silence. Western women were a mystery. He had seen them baring their breasts on Greek beaches, wearing provocative clothes, doing whatever they liked. Behaving like men, in fact. It was all very puzzling. No wonder families in Britain could not function, with such women.

'Anyway,' said Maeve, 'however much you might disapprove, I've cheered the old bat up – fed her proper food, got her seriously on the bottle. Life's looked up for Lady P.'

'The whisky, Maeve? The clothes you were wearing? All that stuff in the suitcase?' Sophie hardly liked to broach the subject but felt she had to know.

'She said to take what I wanted. She'll never wear them. I had a fabulous go through her wardrobe, trying on all her old stuff. I'm almost exactly the same size as she was, although she's dead thrilled that my waist is a bit bigger. She loved it. It was like bringing back all her memories. I reckon she was a bit of a goer, you know. Bumper didn't go into the family bank. He was a diplomat, so they spent a lot of their life abroad in all sorts of exotic places. She was in Kenya not long after that Happy Valley scandal, and I gather it was all pretty racy. She's got Schiaparelli suits, Balenciaga, Chanel. Of course, most of it is impossible today. It should go to the V and A probably, but I took what I wanted. This coat's cashmere. Feel it.'

'The whisky, Maeve? The taxi? How come you can suddenly afford things like that?'

'Well, the whisky I did just slip through the housekeeping account. Don't look so shocked. If I work out how many

51

hours I put in, I'm getting about two pence an hour, so I feel entitled to some perks.'

Sophie groaned.

'And the taxi fare, dearie – well, I've got two weeks' pay and bugger all to spend it on down there, so why not? Made life a lot easier, and I was late, remember?'

'Now does the financial side of things work?' asked Sophie, wondering how soon Maeve would be rumbled.

'I get an agreed amount of housekeeping per week, which I can draw out of the bank in Castle Cary. Any extra bills I have to lob at son Henry. Stuff like the account I've opened at the offy.'

'What?' said Sophie, not believing her ears. Maeve would definitely go to prison.

'His seccy person said it was fine. I've got Sky TV being installed too, and I'm renting a video player. Henry can afford it. He's rolling. The old bat hasn't many years left, she might as well have as much fun as possible.'

'What about the boyfriend? Has he shown up yet?'

'Not yet. He comes next week. I'm going to pull out all the stops. Give them a really good lunch. Can you believe that Mrs Cook used to leave them a frozen supermarket quiche and bugger off for the day? Apparently she was really disapproving.'

It was the same old story, thought Sophie. Maeve was having an intriguing and interesting time and making her feel dull and plodding by comparison.

They stopped and sat on a bench and Freddy and Flora were released from the buggy. They played in the golden leaves and ran about laughing shrilly, their little faces pink and their eyes shining. They played a simple game of hide and seek, and as the children buried their faces in her lap, fat little hands clamped over their eyes while Mohammed hid behind a nearby tree, Sophie felt a great rush of love. She thought, I'm the luckiest person alive to have this moment.

Mohammed had stopped sulking. He loved playing with the children and knew instinctively how to entertain them. However, Sophie thought he looked tired and a bit outlandish in his leather jacket and a West Ham supporter's knitted hat. She smiled at him when he returned to sit beside her, and asked him how his work was going. It seemed that he was exploited, overworked and underpaid.

'Why do you do it? They can treat you like that because of

your status. Why don't you go home to your family who you miss so much?'

Maeve snorted. 'Soph, there's nothing there for him. No job, no future. He's sending everything he earns back home to keep them in bread and send his sisters to school. He has to stay here and work.'

Sophie looked at him sympathetically. Why can't everything be simple, she thought. People should have the right to work, have enough to eat, security. Love. Children should have fathers. Why does it go wrong the whole bloody time?

'But listen, you guys,' Maeve was saying, 'the weekend after next, I want you to come and stay!'

Chapter Four

'Henry,' said Bunty, a few mornings later, 'your mother's gone very quiet. How's that new girl getting on?'

They were having breakfast and Henry was annoying Bunty by concentrating on his newspaper, which he read methodically, folded into neat squares. Sometimes Bunty felt like being sociable and this morning was one of them. She had glanced at her own newspaper, a tabloid with large, arresting headlines, but had seen nothing of interest. She didn't care for foreign news which seemed to her to be nothing but starving black babies and unattractive, bearded Moslem men killing one another.

Dutifully, Henry put down his paper.

'It all seems to be going very well. Mother complained a good deal at first. Said she was too young, too noisy and so on, but I think she has got used to her. Mrs Tripp has dealt with a few queries from the girl asking about a new telephone – Mother exerted such iron control over the use of the one handset which, I have to admit, I didn't know. And renting a video player and so on seems entirely reasonable. No, on the whole, it all seems to be going very well.'

Bunty cocked her head. New telephones, videos. She did not like the sound of it at all.

'It's not a holiday camp, you know, Henry. Not the Savoy. I hope you made it clear that the girl pays for her own personal calls. What does she need a video for? She's supposed to be keeping your mother company in the evening, not watching videos. I hope you made that clear, Henry.'

'I didn't actually speak to her, Bunty. Mrs Tripp dealt with it and I gather found Miss Delaney quite aware of her duties.' Henry very much hoped that his wife was not going to get a bee in her bonnet and start interfering. It made such a welcome change to have peace on the Charlton front. Dealing

55

with Mrs Cook had thoroughly worn him out. However, he knew that it was more than his life was worth to mention Sky TV and the Racing Channel.

Bunty frowned. Whilst she was glad in a way that her mother-in-law was not causing upsets and taking up Henry's time, on the other hand she did not want things to go too well. The ultimate aim was to get Lady Pamela out of Charlton and into a home, and so the sooner the situation down there became untenable, the better. Bunty was suspicious of other people's initiatives and this girl sounded dangerously presumptuous. A video player indeed! Bunty was used to dealing with carers who meekly accepted things as they were, who did not feel they were in a position to suggest improvements or changes.

'She's got Mother downstairs, too,' said Henry. 'Every day, apparently. Even into the garden. It's cheered Mother up enormously.' Realising that this would not please Bunty, he added hastily, 'Of course, I fear it won't last. Mother will become impossible, as usual, and this girl, I'm quite sure, won't put up with it. Young people won't. I just hope she stays long enough to give us a breather.'

Of course, this was true, thought Bunty. It was sure to end in tears, and as she had said to Henry, this girl was to be the last. What with a number of key social events she was organising up to Christmas, Bunty realised that a lull in the ongoing saga of Lady Pamela was not unwelcome. In the New Year when they had returned from their annual trip to the West Indies and things had calmed down a bit, she would seriously set about finding a suitable home and aim to get her moved in by the spring. This irritating young woman, she supposed, should be encouraged to stay until then.

After Henry had gone to work, Bunty telephoned Radio Rentals and discovered that the cost of hiring a video player was in the region of eight pounds a month. Not too bad, she thought. Won't break the bank. But nevertheless the girl would need watching.

Not one to let things go, she telephoned Diana Tripp.

'No, Diana. Don't put me through to Henry. It's you I wanted to have a word with. Have you a moment?'

'Of course, Bunty. What can I do for you?'

Bunty's hackles rose. First of all, the uninvited use of her Christian name and second, the suggestion that Diana was graciously willing and in a position to extend a favour of some kind.

'This girl,' went on Bunty, 'this girl that you and Henry found to look after his mother. Henry says she's been asking permission to spend on various items. Now, Diana, I know that you are only trying to deal with these things so as not to bother Henry, but in future I would like you to refer them to me.'

There was a moment's pause. Even down the telephone line, Diana Tripp could feel the presence of Bunty's imposing bosom swelling with indignation and overwhelming opposition. She remembered her empowerment classes.

'Bunty,' she said, 'as Henry's secretary it is my job to screen and prioritise his telephone calls. He specifically requested me to deal with any matters relating to Miss Delaney, which I have done, with his approval.'

'Yes,' said Bunty, 'but in future you are to refer them to me.'

'In that case, Bunty, let me put you through to your husband. As his PA, I take instructions first and foremost from him. Having once been a secretary yourself, you will understand that.' Silently Diana Tripp yelled, 'Yes!' and raised a fist in the manner of a scoring footballer.

There was a pause while Bunty considered this.

'No, that won't be necessary,' she said coldly and added with as much implication as possible in her voice, 'I will speak to him this evening. Goodbye.'

'Goodbye, Bunty.'

Diana Tripp awarded herself a small chocolate bar from her desk drawer. Lesson Three, 'Saying No to Bullies', had proved effective. She looked forward to sharing this success with her trainer.

Sam Elwes, now in his eighties, no longer enjoyed travelling by train. The pilgrimage he made down to Somerset once a month was about the furthest he ever went these days, and the accompanying anxiety of departure and arrival times, purchasing his ticket through a thick glass screen, behind which the ticket seller's lips moved incomprehensibly, finding a seat, producing the same ticket later for the inspector – all these things conspired to produce in him 'a state', as he called it. There wasn't even a decent lunch to look forward to. But nothing would stand in the way of his seeing Pammy.

In the bag at his feet was a bottle of gin and some packets of crisps which he had grown rather partial to. Once he'd got up the stairs to Pammy's room, he'd pour them each a stiff one and they'd clink glasses and away they'd go. He couldn't count the number of places he'd drunk gin with Pammy. All over London certainly. And Paris. And years ago, when they'd met before the war, all over North Africa and Italy, and after the war, in Kenya and in Singapore. Their lives had crossed so many times, to begin with by pure circumstance – Sam was in the same regiment as Bumper – and later by design. Sam reckoned he'd loved Pammy for fifty-five years off and on, mostly on, and although she wouldn't say it, she'd loved him, too.

He'd had affairs, of course, few of which he regretted, but could never marry. Pammy's hold over him was too strong for that. It was Pammy who had shaped his life, who had made him the lonely old bachelor he was today. This was nonsense, of course. He'd never been lonely in his life. As a distinguished art historian he had had a fascinating and rewarding career. His sweet nature and generosity of spirit had made him friends wherever he went. He was a man much loved and still much sought after.

Sam's appearance had always predisposed people favourably towards him. As a young man he had been tall, blond and handsome; as an octogenarian, shrunk, stooped and certainly tubby, he was still impressive. His features had retained their pleasing alignment and his face, although creased and sagging with age, had lost little of its beauty. Always freshly shaved, his skin was pink and healthy-looking, his lips still full. The years had not dragged down the corners of his mouth, rather he looked permanently amused and benign. His striking blue eyes surveyed the world over half-moon glasses. He had had a full and happy life and it showed.

Now, as the train approached Castle Cary station, he stood up, fussing about his hat and gloves and stick and nearly forgetting the gin. Then, having made his way down the carriage, the electric doors of the train panicked him. He always feared that they would not open and he would be carried on down the line. There was a nerve-racking moment after the train had stopped when he pressed the door-release button and nothing happened. It was the same every time but it always unnerved him. He got down carefully onto the platform and felt, as usual, the twinge of excitement at the prospect of seeing Pammy. There was George waiting to help him, taking the bag out of his hand, asking him how he was, opening the taxi door for him, settling him comfortably into the back seat.

'So, George. How have you been keeping?'

Sam always asked this, and George always replied, 'Mustn't grumble, sir. And yourself?'

'Very well indeed, George. Very well indeed. Usual old aches and pains, but apart from that, very well indeed.'

'You'll be seeing some changes since your last visit,' announced George as they drove down the lanes to Charlton.

'Changes?' said Sam, alarmed. Change at his age generally meant for the worse.

'Oh, yes, there have been some changes,' said George, 'but for the better, mind. Or so I'd say.'

'In what way?' asked Sam, unable to envisage what could be better, apart from the lunch, that is.

'You'll see,' said George mysteriously.

They drew up in front of the house. It was a warm day and the front door stood open, which was unusual. As he struggled to get out of the taxi and collect his things he got a distinct whiff of something rather delicious in the air. George gave him a conspiratorial wink, and got back into his driver's seat. Sam banged on the open door with his stick, and called loudly up the stairs to where she would be waiting.

'Pammy! Pammy! It's me, Sam. May I come in?'

'I'm in here, Sam!' she called back from near at hand. The drawing-room door stood open and Sam went in. A bright fire was lit and the room looked comfortable and welcoming. Someone had reorganised the furniture and a small drop-leaf table had been moved in front of one of the long windows and set with cutlery and glasses for lunch. There was a tray of bottles on a cabinet. Sam could see ice and lemon. A large-screen television set had been positioned in another corner.

Pammy was seated in a comfortable chair by the fire. She looked just the same and extended a hand to him.

'Sam, darling. Lovely to see you, as always.'

'And you, my dear,' and he bent down to kiss her cheek and hold her hand between his.

'But what is all this? And you downstairs? My darling, how wonderful.'

'It's the girl,' said Lady Pamela. 'The Irish, as I call her. She's done it all. You'll meet her in a minute. Very full of herself, she is, and full of ideas. Exhausting, really, and doesn't know when to stop. A ridiculous girl.' From her tone, Sam knew that Pammy was delighted with her.

'So what has happened to that other one – the provider of disgusting meals?'

'Gone, thank the Lord. I have to hand it to Henry for finding the Irish. An unusual and imaginative choice for him. Oh! Gin! How lovely, darling. Look, she's set us up with a bar! You can put it over there and pour us both a drink straight-away. She'll be in in a moment if she can smell the gin. She's disgracefully forward. Really a most inappropriate companion for an old lady. Crisps – how delicious! Shall we have a packet each? My goodness, cream cheese and chives, smoky bacon, barbecued beef. Which sort, darling?'

Sam, busy pouring drinks, stopped for a moment to look out of the window. It was so long since this room had been used. It seemed such a great reversal to see it like this again with a fire lit and the furniture polished and Pammy ruling the roost. The retreat to her bedroom after her fall and operation several months ago had seemed somehow irrevers-ible, part of a slow decline which would lead, inexorably, to increased incapacity, senility, death. He had braced himself for it, as he had indeed for his own journey down the same road, scheduled, surely, for the not too distant future.

'Well. This is a great surprise!' he said, turning and handing her her glass, drawing up the chair opposite and then bending stiffly to throw another log on the fire. Esau snored gently on the hearth rug. 'Now tell me how it all came about.'

In the kitchen, Maeve had dished up the lamb and made the gravy. With the door open, she kept her ears cocked for what was going on in the drawing room. She wanted to be tactful and not go barging in on the old pair. Little, crisp roast potatoes rested in an entrée dish, as did creamed leeks from Jack Dick's garden. Despite his initial hostility he had left a fresh vegetable on the kitchen doorstep every morning, along with eggs once a week. When she had remarked on this to Lady Pamela, she had said, 'To be absolutely truthful, I'd forgotten about him. All those weeks upstairs and one loses touch with what is going on. He used to be a very good gardener, and good with the horses, too. I suppose it was Mrs Cook who told him to stop bringing vegetables to the house. She didn't like anything with dirt on it. I'd assumed the kitchen garden had gone in one of Henry's cost-cutting exercises.'

Right, thought Maeve, I've left them long enough, and she went across the hall and knocked on the door.

Sam looked up to see what he thought was a child of about fourteen standing there with a cloud of messy black hair, dressed in faded jeans and an orange and red striped sweater.

'This is the Irish,' announced Pammy.

Does she mind being called that? wondered Sam. Typically Pammy and not very sensitive to race relations.

'Hello, Mr Elwes,' said the girl, holding out her hand without a trace of an Irish accent and, 'How about my gin?' she asked Lady Pamela, laughing.

'What did I tell you?' said Pammy.

'Lunch is actually ready,' said Maeve. 'That is, if you are. Shall I bring it in in five minutes? I'll take my drink to the kitchen with me,' and without waiting to be asked she poured herself a sizeable glass of gin and tonic.

While she had her back turned, Sam gazed at her. A tiny but very feminine bottom, a narrow little back. Scruffily downtrodden trainers. She was so remarkably different from Mrs Cook that he was struck dumb. He found Pammy watching him with amusement. He raised his eyebrows at her and they exchanged looks.

'Five minutes, then?' said Maeve, turning and smiling at them dazzlingly, and went out with her glass. Sam went to wash his hands and then helped Lady Pamela out of her chair and over to her seat at the table, which was set for two. Maeve came back in with two plates, and then returned with a perfectly roasted little leg of lamb, burnished brown and scented with garlic and rosemary. Some thick slices had already been carved. She passed it to Sam to put on the table and went back for the vegetables and gravy.

'My dear, how delicious this looks. What a treat!' said Sam.

'It's a pleasure,' said Maeve. 'Now I'm going to leave you to it. Look, mint sauce here, and redcurrant jelly. No doubt you have masses to talk about. Shout when you're ready for pud,' and she left the room.

'Pammy, darling! What a find! How very clever of Henry!'

Lady Pamela agreed. 'It was, wasn't it? Although Henry can have had no idea how she'd turn out.' They helped themselves to vegetables and for a while there was no more conversation as they enjoyed their meal.

'She is a very good cook, of that there's no doubt. Spanish mother. Got it from her, I expect. Strange childhood. Parents separated early on. She went to St Theresa's.'

'But what is a girl like her doing here? Pammy, dearest, you must admit that looking after a difficult old woman in the depths of the country is hardly an attractive proposition for someone of her age.'

'I don't imagine she's intending to stay long,' said Lady Pamela. 'I think I'm a sort of stopgap. I rather hope she'll see me out.' The two old friends were able to talk about their impending deaths in this forthright manner, as if they had made appointments and were waiting for them to be confirmed.

They broke off as Maeve came in and removed their plates and then brought in an apple crumble and cream.

'I'm going to leave all this,' she announced, indicating the table, 'and go out on that bicycle while it's still nice. Just leave everything where it is. Lady P, don't forget the racing on the television. You said there was a big race this afternoon.' She was off before Lady Pamela could suggest that she and Sam always enjoyed coffee after lunch.

Reading her thoughts, Sam said, 'I can make the coffee. Or you can and I'll carry the tray through.' They did, however, leave the cluttered table as Maeve had directed. A lifetime of being waited on made doing such a thing for themselves unthinkable.

Later, as they sat with mugs of instant coffee by the fire, Lady Pamela put on her new television set and tuned in to the Racing Channel. As the horses galloped down to the start of the second race at Cheltenham, they both fell gently asleep.

Turning out of the gates of Charlton, Maeve cycled past the two picturesque cottages on the lane. Pretty as they were, they had tiny dark windows and a neglected, greyish-green thatch. The two front doors had not been painted for years. Maeve thought they must be damp and dismal to live in. Smoke curled out of a chimney and as Maeve wobbled slowly past she caught the flicker of a television set in a window and thought she saw Jack Dick sitting in front of it. Both gardens were immaculate and at the back where the ground rose to meet the fields behind Charlton, Maeve could see solid blocks of vegetables planted in chocolate-coloured earth.

The village began round the next bend. More cottages, one or two smartly restored with newly carved name boards, a cul-de-sac of uninspiring council houses, a garage which combined a rudimentary grocery shop and a post office, a few more cottages, Manor Farm, a handsome stone house with a yard full of black and white cows, a war memorial on a little triangle of grass, a village hall with a noticeboard in front, and that was it. The lane which crept through the village left it to wind up a wooded hillside – a hard push on a bicycle – and then there was a long twisting ride between high banks and hedges with fields on either side, past a couple of farms, both advertising bed and breakfast. Vehicles meeting one another head on had to squeeze into gateways to pass. An encounter with the milk tanker might mean reversing for quarter of a mile. Maeve knew from driving in the taxi with George that there was nothing else until South Charlton, two miles on, where there was a church and a pub and a primary school. She got off her bicycle to read the notices outside the hall. There was a flyer for a car boot sale, six weeks out of date, a bus timetable for the service, twice weekly, from South Charlton to Wincanton and a childishly coloured advertisement for a playgroup, also in South Charlton. The mobile library was now calling on Wednesday instead of Thursday. Someone had lost a black and white cat called Paddy. If he had any sense, thought Maeve, he'd be on that bus out of here. Looking for a Dick Whittington to go to London with.

It was very quiet. A young woman about her own age came out of one of the cottages with a baby in her arms, which she loaded into the back of a car, then drove off. Washing hung on lines in back gardens, a ginger cat sat on a gatepost but there was little other sign of life. Maeve wondered whether she could be bothered to cycle on into South Charlton. From what she could remember, it did not have much to offer either. She felt a huge wave of boredom. Really, she thought, I can't stand much more of this. How do people survive in such a place? It was beautiful, no doubt, but she preferred landscapes teeming with life – ski resorts, harbours filled with boats, Greek islands where the hills are dotted with white villages and there is a taverna round every corner. Everyone lives behind their doors here, there is no life on public display, she thought. She contemplated the state of her finances. She had saved about half of what she had earned so far and was a long way off real solvency.

63

She'd have to hang around for a bit yet. She'd really quite enjoyed sorting out the old girl, and took some pride in the success she'd had, but Maeve needed life to move on fast. She needed fresh challenges. She also, frankly, wanted a man. She did not believe she had ever been so long without some sort of love interest.

She got back on her bicycle and peddled slowly up the lane. She wasn't even in a state of preparedness – the clean knickers, clean sheets, shaved legs state of readiness, as Sophie called it, which was typical of her, thought Maeve who had had the best times without knickers or sheets. Beaches and boats, sand up your bum – they had been the best. She had heard people argue that the countryside was throbbing with sex but she could not see how or where. Maybe amongst the horsey set with those skin-tight breeches and emphasis on gripping with your legs. Maeve had never liked horses – well, they were all right in a field from a distance, as part of a view.

Maybe a farmer would do me, she thought. Perhaps if I hang around here on the bicycle, I'll meet one. The more rampant the better. She thought of Young Farmers Clubs and remembered reading in the local paper, left behind by Mrs Cook, of a branch in Castle Cary. She did not feel drawn to welly-throwing competitions or talks entitled 'Crimp or Dry Roll Your Own Feed'. Hedge-laying sounded more promising. Oh shit. Meeting men had always just happened. She would have to trust to luck as she had always done.

She glanced at her watch. It was two thirty. The pub would be closing so it wasn't worth the effort to ride further. She did a wobbly turn in the lane and peddled back. She noticed a drive going off to her left, which looked as if it went to the back of Charlton, between the railed paddocks behind the kitchen garden. She could see the roof of the house above the trees. She'd go home that way.

Lady Pamela woke with a start. Sam was up and out of his chair and saying something to Maeve who was loading a tray with lunch debris from the table. She wondered how long she had slept. The television was still broadcasting from Cheltenham.

Maeve looked over in her direction and said, 'Well, she's awake. I can ask her.'

'Ask her what?'

'About the horses in the field behind the courtyard. Who do they belong to?'

Lady Pamela thought for a moment. Horses? The world of horses seemed so very long ago. That was her world when Bumper was alive, when they had retired down here to Charlton.

'You mean the old mares? Two old mares? Are they still there? It's so long since . . .' and she tailed off.

'I wouldn't know if they were old or mares,' said Maeve.

'They are the two old mares. The last of the line. Bumper had success with his horses, you know. We had a very good mare called Ballerina, by the wonderful stallion Dancing Master. She started it all. Her progeny did terribly well. We had a lot of winners over the years. Those two are April Dancer and Sylphide Song. They must be at least twenty-two or -three. They'd retired when Bumper died. He wanted them kept on, it was in his will. That's why they're here. Jack looks after them. I told you he was good with horses.'

'I see,' said Maeve, disappointed. She had hoped that the horses would lead somewhere, not back to Jack Dick. Although not interested in horses herself, in her mind she connected them with racing and show jumping and a glamorous, fast-moving set of people.

'Are those two the last?' asked Sam. 'I thought there was still that horse which ran so well – won all his races. What was his name? Something else to do with Dancing?'

'That's right,' said Lady Pamela. 'Irish Dancer. He was the last runner we had. That was after Bumper died. But he broke down, didn't he, after Towcester? You were with me, Sam. It was the most horrible thing.'

'Broke down?' said Maeve. 'I didn't know horses had breakdowns. What, like he couldn't go on, life was too terrible?'

Lady Pamela snorted. 'I can't believe you're an Irish girl!' she said. 'Breaking down means the tendons go, the tendons in the legs. While racing, usually.'

'Is that the end then?' asked Maeve. 'Are they finished when that happens?'

'Not always. They can mend. There's a dreadful business called "firing", but it takes a long time. Racing again is always doubtful. We did have him fired in the end, but after a year he was scanned and it wasn't very encouraging so I decided to leave him be. As far as I know he's still at Mitchell's yard, where he was trained. Turned out with the young stock. Bumper left specific instructions about his horses. Left them provided for. Henry would have got rid of them otherwise. Bumper knew that.'

'Oh God,' said Maeve. 'It's like *Black Beauty*! Tell me about this horse. What did he win? I love his name – Irish Dancer. It's a lucky name. I have a really spooky feeling about it.'

Lady Pamela laughed. 'His sire was a good Irish horse, Leprechaun King. Our chap won or was placed in all his races. Qualified for Cheltenham. Looked to be the favourite, and then broke down in his last race. I'll never forget seeing him canter to the start, pulling like a train. Poor Jerry Murphy was on board and got thoroughly carted. A big ugly brute he was, like most of April Dancer's offspring. He had attitude, isn't that the term? Full of himself. So well, so fit. And then coming back, broken. Crippled. Hardly able to move. That was my last race, too.'

'So, how old is he now?' asked Maeve.

'Let me see. That was at least three years ago, so he must be eleven or twelve, I should think.' Lady Pamela paused, lost in thought, the years rolling back to other horses, other races and always the feeling that she was bereft because Lizzie, who had loved horses so much, wasn't there.

Maeve had filled her tray and stood now, hand on hip. 'By the way,' she said, 'and to change the subject, would you mind if I have some friends down to stay? You'd like them. Only for the weekend. Would you mind?'

Lady Pamela, brought back to the present, but still filled with aching loss, reacted sharply. 'What an extraordinary request! Who are these people?'

'Mates. My best mates. You see, there's bugger all to do here, you must admit, so I reckon, you know, if I'm going to stay, I'll have to import friends every now and then.'

Sam watched this exchange with interest. As in most arguments, he could clearly see the case for both sides. He could see also that Pammy had been drawn by some memory stirred by the horses into the painful country she visited from time to time. He had watched this happen so often over the years. Always he was excluded, unable to share her private grief, and he had learnt to sit it out, to wait for it to pass, like taking shelter during an air raid.

'This is my home,' began Lady Pamela, 'and I really think that you must understand—'

'Oh yeah,' interrupted Maeve, 'I know. You don't want to have everything disrupted, and I promise you it won't be. You'll hardly notice that they're here. They're very quiet – much quieter than me. I promise you, you'll like them. It will be like having a lovely house party. Like you used to have. Open the place up a bit.'

Sam cleared his throat. 'I think Lady Pamela needs to be reassured that if she allows this visit once, it lasts no more than the weekend and is never to be repeated without her consent.'

'Of course,' said Maeve. 'I mean, they're not squatters. They both need to get back to London to jobs and . . . so on.' She felt that now wasn't the moment to mention the twins. She was uncertain about Lady Pamela's fondness for small children. Or what she would make of Mohammed. 'Anyway. Think about it,' she said, and took the tray out to the kitchen. A moment later she put her head back round the door. 'Mr Elwes, how about taking Lady P for a little walk outside? By the time you get back I'll have the scones warmed and buttered for tea.'

'The girl's intolerable,' grumbled Lady Pamela. 'How dare she suggest such a thing? Charlton is my home and she is a paid employee. It is not a hotel, or should I say a hostel, for her friends. And how dare she tell you what to do with me. I will not be treated like an article.'

'Think of Mrs Cook,' advised Sam, who was himself thinking of scones.

Later, as they shuffled arm in arm down the path through the dying rose garden in the long shadows of the evening, Sam said, 'I should let her, you know.'

'Let her what?'

'Have her friends to stay. Only for a weekend. You might enjoy it. But I wouldn't tell Henry.'

Lady Pamela was silent. She would make up her own mind.

As it happened, Sophie could not, anyway, visit Charlton the following weekend. It was Fergus's Saturday with the twins. They had spoken on the telephone and he would come to the flat at ten o'clock to collect them and bring them back in the evening. Sophie wanted to know what his plans were for the rest of the day and Fergus resented this policing of his activities.

'Well, what time do you want them back?' he asked, pointedly ignoring her question.

'It isn't that . . . not what time I want them back, but what you can find to do with them all day. It's not easy when you haven't got a car.'

'I can bring them back here,' said Fergus.

Sophie dreaded this. The thought of Flora and Freddy in Fergus's flat, which he shared with a hard-drinking stock-broker, filled her with alarm. She imagined them playing amongst empty beer cans and overflowing ashtrays.

'Anyway, I can borrow a car.'

'But not with car seats. You'd better take my car.'

'For God's sake, Sophie. Stop fussing. Christ, you are a bore. Children have survived for most of the history of the human race without car seats and special spoons and safety locks.'

Sophie closed her eyes. It was the usual accusation – she was a bore. A bore about the children.

'OK,' she said. 'OK. See you at ten,' and she rang off.

Saturday now loomed ahead like a terrible ordeal to be got through. She tried to think of what she would do with the twins off her hands. The trouble was that the few friends she had kept up with were usually out of London at weekends or with partners sharing the only precious time they had together. She couldn't foist herself on them. After some thought she rang the smart hairdresser she used to go to when she was single and booked a cut and blow dry for Saturday morning. The salon was off Marylebone High Street and she liked the shops there and could spend a happy few hours mooching about. Later in the afternoon she would go home and sleep.

The trouble was, the salon had done her hair for her wedding. Simon had come down to Oxfordshire on Satur-day morning and washed and set it on giant rollers and turned it into tumbling curls and set the tiara amongst them just as she had wanted. She couldn't remember if he knew that her marriage had broken up. She would have to go through it all, she supposed. Shrug and say, 'Oh well. It didn't work out.' Use the ridiculous excuses people came up with for foundering marriages, to explain away their failures as human beings, their inability to choose the right person and to make them happy, to disguise the truth that they were unlovable. Going back there was a mistake. Sophie rang again and cancelled her appointment.

As she had expected, Maeve was angry when she told her on the telephone that, after all, she wouldn't be going to Charlton.

'Bugger Fergus!' she said. 'Change his weekend. Or leave the children with him and come yourself. Why not? He's perfectly capable of looking after them. Give him a chance. Why not? Sophie, don't be so pathetic. They'll survive without you for a day, you know.'

'I can't come all that way just for a day. I have to be back in the evening to put them to bed.'

'Why? For God's sake, Sophie, he is their father. He can put them into their fucking pyjamas, you know.' Sensing Sophie's resistance, she added crossly, 'Oh, I give up!'

'Just let me decide, Maeve. Stop bullying me. When they're a bit older—'

'They'll never be old enough for you to let them go,' said Maeve bitterly.

In her head, Sophie was persuading herself. Fergus could take them to his sister's. Claire would look after them. She'd trust them with her. Claire lived with her banker husband in Fulham and had three children herself, and a live-in nanny.

Later, after a drink, she rang Fergus. She could hear the television, or voices in the background.

'Are you having a party?' she asked.

'Only a few friends,' he said. 'Well? What is it?'

After she'd told him, he was angry, too.

'For God's sake, Sophie, why can't you ever make your mind up? It's extremely late to ask Claire. It's not fair on her. Why can't you think ahead and get organised?' This was so unfair, it made Sophie gasp. She had never changed arrangements before, whereas Fergus often did.

Later still he telephoned back to say that it was all right with Claire. She'd give Sophie a ring in the morning. He was warmer and kinder, a few drinks further into the evening.

'Where are you off to, then?' he asked. It had obviously struck him, or someone had pointed out, that a weekend invitation could only be a good thing. Sophie dating or remarried would be far preferable to Sophie the millstone round his neck.

Utterly exhausted, Sophie slumped on her sofa and picked at the bobbly cotton on the knee of her pyjamas. Maeve was probably right. She should be prepared to let Freddy and

Flora occasionally go to other people. She had become possessive and neurotic. She was so fearful for them when they
were away from her. Her head always filled with frozen
images of the ghastly freak accidents she read about in the
newspapers: choking on stray peanuts, falls from windows,
drowning in baths. Nobody but she could be trusted, nobody
was sufficiently aware of the dangers – not even her mother,
and certainly not Fergus.

Sophie was also fearful for herself. What was she without
them? She didn't want to find out. She wanted them to need
and love her unconditionally and she did not want to share
them with anyone else. Their reliance on her must not be
diluted. Did that mean she was jealously possessive? She
supposed it did. She remembered how the last time Fergus
had taken them for the day, Flora had cried when he was
leaving and had held on to his trouser leg with fat little
hands. Fergus had been delighted and touched, Sophie could
see, and she had felt stabbing jealousy and anger towards
Flora who had betrayed her.

Slow, hot tears rolled down Sophie's cheeks. Caring about
the children so much was evidently wrong, a symptom of a
sickness. Yet how could a mother love or care too much?

If I wasn't alone, it would be different, she thought. I would
have a balance in my life, a husband to look after and to look
after me, to share the children with. It's because I'm alone
that I'm unhinged. And I'm so tired. So tired.

Sophie woke on the sofa at three in the morning, cold, and
with a stiff neck. She shuffled about making a hot water
bottle and eating bread and butter. She should manage to get
a few more hours' sleep before the twins woke and, relent-
lessly cheerful, started another day.

Chapter Five

The day after Sam's visit, Maeve and Lady Pamela were sitting with whiskies beside the fire, the curtains drawn against a chill evening sky. The atmosphere between them was cordial. Lady Pamela had enjoyed seeing Sam and appreciated the difference Maeve's efforts had made. Although she hadn't said as much, she had been pleased that Maeve had been tactful and made herself scarce, leaving them alone to reminisce and gently revisit the past. She had been annoyed by Maeve's request to invite friends to Charlton, but Sam's advice she always listened to, and later the same evening she had told Maeve that she would allow it.

Now she looked across at her companion, noting how the light of the fire gave her pale face a glow of colour. The tangle of dark hair was bunched into a knot at a crazy angle on top of her head, her bony little hands held the cut glass of whisky up to her face, like a little squirrel with a nut. She was looking into the flames and, unsmiling, had a wistful expression. What a funny creature she is, thought Lady Pamela. Tough as nails, not really conventionally pretty, but there was something about her, energy, vitality, spirit, which she applauded.

Maeve was thinking how strange it was to be sitting there by a drawing-room fire with an old woman with whom she had no ties or connection. This could be her last night on earth, she thought, and she is spending it with me, who means nothing to her. All those years of a busy, privileged life, all those friends and acquaintances and travelling and parties – it has amounted to this. She did not feel exactly sorry for her. At least Lady Pamela could afford to be warm and comfortable. Maeve was aware from newspaper stories of elderly people dying alone in freezing flats, or suffering from malnutrition and neglect.

When she considered her own situation, Maeve also felt odd and misplaced, as if she had floated into a backwater, away from the mainstream where she had come to expect events to sweep her along and throw opportunities her way. Here, life had inevitably slowed to the pace of her elderly charge. Routine and order prevailed and each day slipped past with hardly a disturbance of the surface. Maeve had never had so much time to sleep and eat and read and she felt as if all her sharp, defining edges had blunted and as if the blood was moving sluggishly in her veins. The long periods of silence, the empty evenings, the solitary walks, the incredible sameness of the countryside spooked her. She had, up until now, instinctively sought life amongst the restless, rootless young people who collect around the edges of the world's playgrounds. She was used to rising late and sleeping with the dawn, blown away by dope or drink. She had learnt to steer away from introspection and rely on activity to keep her batteries charged. She wondered now what beast it was that she feared to confront. What it was that she would not allow to take shape in her mind.

Maeve found she did not welcome this rare opportunity to think and take stock of her life so far. Thinking too much could lead her to the black hole of depression which she knew loomed never far from her path. At Charlton, she had so far avoided slipping down into its depths, but it was there all the same. As she moved her glass to her lips, she caught Lady Pamela's look and for a moment was discomfited. She shied away from revealing anything about her feelings and she could sense a sort of intimacy in the air that made her uneasy. To move things along, she said hastily, 'Tell me about Charlton. About this house. Has it always been yours?'

'My father owned it. It used to be the dower house of where I grew up, Eastcott Hall. That was sold off after the war. It's a golf club and hotel now. The estate has gone. My only brother was killed in the war and Father lost heart. The title went to his brother after he died, and then when Uncle Tony died childless about twenty years later, the line became extinct. So, all gone. Only Charlton left. I came to live here when I married Bumper. It was Father's present to me.'

'So, what was Bumper like?'

'Bumper was rather fine in the war. He looked at his best in uniform and we met and fell in love very fast. One did in those days. It was the war, you see. It made everything urgent. One wanted to get on and live while one could. Many of my friends had married and I followed suit. A register office wedding we had, while he was on leave. Two friends as witnesses and then champagne at the Ritz. That was it. I telephoned my parents from honeymoon in Cornwall. They were shocked, of course, but it happened all the time in those days.'

Maeve was interested now. Lady Pamela was describing the sort of unpredictable behaviour which appealed to her. If she ever got married it would be like that.

'So what was it about Bumper?' she said. 'Why did you choose him?'

'Oh, he was a good-looking man then. Very tall and big. In those days he hadn't become pompous. Although you could never describe him as fun, he was attractive, definitely, and he was in love with me. As the war went on, his career took off and by the end, when he was very involved with drawing up peace treaties and reparations and so on, he became insufferably self-important. His work was engrossing. He had little time for anything else.

'Through quite a lot of the war and afterwards, I lived alone here at Charlton. This is where Henry was born, and later Elizabeth. Afterwards, when Bumper was a diplomat, we moved round the world a good deal, but Charlton was always home and I spent what time I could here. You see, a diplomat's wife had a role to play in those days. I was rather good at it. Entertaining, dressing up, knowing who was who. But one was always on parade and Bumper was a stickler for correctness. It was only when I came here that I could let all that drop and be myself. Bumper never had another side to him, you see. He was always rather stiff and proper, even off duty. He preferred to be in London, at the heart of things, where he could meet important men at his club, rather than down here with the children and me.'

Maeve thought he had a point there.

'After he retired, racing became his interest. He bought the mare I told you about, Ballerina, and she began it all. I made him put her with a trainer here in Somerset and although he still preferred to be in London, once he'd started a breeding programme, he spent more time here. But he always loathed the country. He considered our London house as home.'

'What sort of man was he, though?' asked Maeve, trying to

imagine him sitting here in the drawing room, trying to feel his presence in the house.

'Bumper was a cold man. I think that was why he was such a good diplomat. He never gave his feelings away. But he loved his horses. Once I watched him go out into the yard. Ballerina was in a box out there with her latest foal. He stroked her nose and then bent and kissed it. A very unlikely gesture if you knew him.'

Maeve tried to assess the marriage which Lady Pamela had hinted at. She thought of her own parents, the rows and screaming and banging, the heat of their arguments. How chilly Lady Pamela made her married life sound. All those years of duty and observing form. She wondered where Sam fitted in, but did not like to ask.

She could not imagine sticking with a man she found dull or pompous. Women of her generation wanted men as lovers and friends, not just providers. She knew she was a hopeless judge, falling for the worst and most unreliable men around, but at least they were entertaining. For a while anyway, until the charm wore off.

'What sort of father was he?' she asked.

'Oh, distant, I suppose. He did not particularly care for small children, and then they both went away to board and when they came back they had grown up and he was more interested in them.' Lady Pamela paused and Maeve could sense that there was difficult or painful territory ahead. She supposed it was connected to the daughter's death.

To retreat to safer ground, she said, 'Talking about men reminds me I haven't got one. Since coming down here I haven't even had a sighting. Mrs Day's told me about the air force base and how all the local girls go to dances there on the lookout for men. Her daughter's married an airman and her granddaughter, who's sixteen, has just had a baby which Mrs Day suspects was fathered by someone from the camp.'

Lady Pamela looked at Maeve. To talk so freely of the need for men, and presumably sex, was entirely novel. It was true that she had just revealed a little of her own personal landscape, which she would never have done to Mrs Cook, for instance, but this sort of gossipy confidence shared with a woman of such a different age and position was extraordinary. Maeve was treating her like a friend almost, or an equal. Lady Pamela could not decide whether she was flattered or disapproving.

Maeve read her look and grinned. 'Don't worry! The thought of going to cattle market discos does not appeal. I'm too old for that and I'm not that desperate. Yet. The pub's probably the best bet but I can't get there except by bicycle and so far I can't be bothered. When I get Sophie down with her car, then we can explore a bit further afield. Don't look so shocked. It's perfectly natural to seek a mate. I bet you went out on the pull when you were young.'

It was Lady Pamela's turn to smile. 'What a perfectly ghastly expression! I can guess what it means and no, indeed I did not. Meeting young men in my day was very formal. One was always introduced. Although, of course, the war changed things. Gave girls a great deal more freedom, especially if they were in the services. I drove an ambulance, you know, before Henry was born. In fact, my dear,' and her face took on an impish delight, 'I rather think we did go out on the pull, some evenings. My friend Joan and I used to go dancing and just see who would turn up. Sometimes a different young man took us home every night of the week!'

'There you are, then!' said Maeve. '*Plus ça change*, etc.'

She got up and refilled their glasses and threw another log on the fire.

'What was your childhood like?' she asked, settling back into the armchair and tucking one leg under her. 'I was just working it out. You must have been born during the First World War. It was all long skirts and hats and horses, wasn't it? And you were living up at the big house with armies of servants? Jesus, you've seen some changes in your life.'

'My childhood was completely unexceptional, but quite extraordinary by today's standards. I hardly remember my parents featuring in it at all. I had the most wonderful nanny, called Thomas.'

'Thomas?' said Maeve. 'A bloke?'

'Don't be ridiculous! She was known by her surname. All the servants were. Ellen Thomas, she was. I adored her and she was far more important to me than either of my parents. I spent virtually all my time with her. My brother was sent to prep school and then Eton, but I had a governess and never went to school. I was taught to love my parents and, of course, I did, but my real affection was for Ellen.

'When I was sixteen she left. I'd been to stay with cousins in France for the summer and when I got home my mother called me into the drawing room of our London house and said that Thomas had gone, left to take up a position with another family. I was absolutely shell-shocked, broken-hearted. I couldn't believe it could be true until I ran up to the top of the house where we had nursery rooms and found all her things had gone. She'd left me a little, stiff note wishing me well and a prayer book as a parting gift. After that I was treated as a grown-up and had my meals in the dining room with my parents. I was given a bedroom on the first floor and the services of one of the maids to help me to do my hair and dress.' She paused and looked into the fire. 'I don't think I ever really got over Thomas going like that.'

Maeve thought she detected a note of self-pity creeping into Lady Pamela's voice. She could not bear people expressing sorrow for themselves. She found herself quite unable to offer sympathy. She was incapable of the sort of murmured condolences that seemed to be asked for. Instead, her hackles rose.

She couldn't stop herself from saying, with an edge to her voice, 'About the same time, my family was emerging out of the bog and going to work in the mills in Belfast. My granny was a mill girl at fourteen. Going off to work in the dark in the morning, barefoot, and with her piece wrapped in a bit of newspaper. Bread and a strip of fat bacon to last her the day. I often think of her when I'm feeling pissed off for myself.' In truth this family history bordered on pure fiction. Maeve only vaguely remembered her father telling her something of the sort. The bread and bacon was a particularly imaginative touch.

Lady Pamela looked at her coldly. 'I will ask you not to preach to me, Maeve. I am too old for that. Those were different days. Hard days. Childhood was a luxury only the well-off could afford and even privileged children often lived under regimes which would be considered barbaric today. They had material security and were well-fed and clothed but they did not always feel loved or wanted. All sorts of cruelties were inflicted on them. Wealth does not necessarily buy a child happiness and security, you know.'

'Who are you telling?' retorted Maeve. 'OK, I agree. But being hungry and uneducated and living in crowded insanitary tenements wasn't fun either.'

'What sort of world do you think I've lived in? I've seen more poverty than you could dream of,' said Lady Pamela. 'All over the world. And many times I have found dignity and poverty go hand in hand.'

'It's OK for rich people to say that. You know, how the poor have something that money can't buy, but on the other hand how many rich people give everything away so that they can live like that too? Jesus said, didn't He, about it being easier for a camel to get through the eye of a needle than for a rich man to enter into the Kingdom of Heaven. That's because the rich are blind to other people. They live in their own world, protected by their money. They can't see all the suffering around them. Or they see it and learn to ignore it.'

'My dear, how good people are, how Christian, has nothing to do with whether they are rich or poor. It comes from within them. Or so I've found. Now let's stop this, because I think we agree in principle. Money is neither here nor there, but I can see that one can be rich and unhappy very much more comfortably than poor and wretched.'

Lady Pamela felt she was being restrained in not asking Maeve exactly what she was contributing to the lot of the poor about whom she felt so strongly. Or asking her whether an expensive education should not go hand in hand with the responsibility to use it wisely. As Lizzie had felt. She had been fired with determination to make things better, to train as a doctor and then to work against ignorance and disease and poverty.

As if she had read her thoughts, Maeve said, 'I didn't want to go to that school, you know. God, I had it rubbed in often enough how much it was costing. I'd have been happier at home, in a Belfast comprehensive. But they needed me out of the way and so boarding was the answer. I hated it. I felt like you did when you found Thomas had upped and gone. Fucking miserable. They didn't even want me back at half-terms.

'Do you know, once no one came for me. They'd got in a muddle about whose turn it was and I felt so fucking humiliated to be still sitting there hours after all the other girls had been collected that I rang for a taxi and got the driver to take me to a hotel in Windsor. I spent the weekend there, watching the television and calling up room service. By the time my parents realised they had mislaid me, I'd spent a fortune. My father had to pay it off with his credit card. Then I went to Sophie's for the rest of the week. She'd got the lot, of course – brothers, a pony, a mother who wore a hairband, a father who cut the grass and teased her. It was like the perfect family. They asked me questions all the time, especially her mother. Poor old Soph squirmed because she knew what she was at. "And where does your mother live now, Maeve? Oh, the south of France, how *lovely*. Has she remarried? Oh, so does she live alone? Oh, I see . . ." and so on. The more they learned about me, the more unsuitable I became as a best friend for Sophie.

'Just like you and the Thomas thing, I don't think I can ever forget that my parents did that to me, sent me to a posh Catholic girls' school in England. Me, an only child from a broken home, with an Irish accent, an alcoholic, nymphomaniac mother and a womanising, Republican father. I didn't fit in on any level at all.'

'They believed it was for the best,' said Lady Pamela stoutly, 'and for all you know, it was. It taught you self-sufficiency and independence.'

'Yeah,' said Maeve, 'it did that, matey.' She grinned. 'And another thing. It gave me Soph.'

Ah, Sophie. Sophie came as something of a surprise. When she arrived on Saturday morning, Lady Pamela did not hear her car draw up on the gravel, and only became aware of Maeve's visitors when the door of the drawing room opened and Maeve put her head round. 'They're here, Lady P. Shall I bring them in?'

Lady Pamela put down the racing pages of the *Telegraph*. She would have preferred to have had a moment to put on some lipstick and powder her nose. As it was, she had dressed more carefully than usual. Maeve had pointed out that her pale blue jumper was stained on the front – failing eyesight had let her down – and had helped her arrange a scarf and pin it over the offending area with a turquoise and diamond brooch.

'Isn't this pretty?' she had said, choosing it out of the jewel box. 'Sam gave it me, when Lizzie was born.'

Maeve had continued poking in the box, her head bent over the brooches and pins and earrings. 'You've got some lovely things. I'm surprised they're not in a bank vault or somewhere safe.'

'They would be if Henry had his way. He's always trying to run off with them. Bunty would like to get her hands on them, I know, but over my dead body, I say, which is exactly what will happen in the end. There isn't anything terribly valuable, mostly sentimental pieces which I don't want to be parted from, even now.'

'There,' Maeve said, as she pinned on the scarf. 'That looks cool.'

Lady Pamela held up a hand mirror. 'Thank you, my dear. Very cool!'

After Maeve had skipped off to finish the casserole she was cooking, Lady Pamela had turned over the pieces in her box, recollecting the locations and occasions they marked. The diamond pin had been a thirtieth birthday gift. The emerald earrings had been left under the soap in the Georges V in Paris, after one of the happiest weeks in her life. Bumper had given her the diamond fox to mark a winning horse. Lizzie would have had them all, of course.

Now, slightly confused, Lady Pamela looked up at the sound of Maeve's voice. A tall, thin girl with flat, colourless hair was standing with her back to the window, looking uncertain.

'This is Sophie, Lady Pamela,' Maeve said.

The girl moved forward and held out her hand. She had a soft, low voice. 'Thank you so much for allowing us to visit Maeve,' she said.

Lady Pamela looked at her face. With the light behind her it was hard to see, but she was struck by its smoothness, the soft, indefinite features, the large, gentle eyes.

'And this,' Maeve was saying, pushing someone forward, 'is Mohammed.'

Suddenly, and to her great surprise, a very dark and very beautiful young man bounded forward and was kneeling beside her chair and taking her hand in his.

'Ah! Lady Pamelas,' he said. 'My joys is over the moons.'

My goodness, thought Lady Pamela. It was a very long time since she had seen anything quite so handsome. Or quite so dark. Damn about the lipstick. She found herself in no hurry to withdraw her hand.

Sophie felt so ill with anxiety that she could hardly string two words together. Flora and Freddy had been collected as planned and, she had to admit, gone with Fergus quite cheerfully, strapped into the back of a borrowed car with their carefully packed suitcase in the boot with the cool box containing Freddy's goat's milk for his eczema and all the meals and snacks that Sophie had prepared for the weekend. Fergus had been brisk and businesslike, not bothering to look at the address and telephone number Sophie was giving him should there be an emergency of any sort while she was away.

'OK,' he said. 'Have a good time. Say goodbye to Mummy, kiddos.' Flora had beamed at her through the window of the car, opening and shutting a hand in imitation of a careless farewell. Freddy, she thought, had looked anguished for a moment as he realised that she was not coming. It was this image, of Freddy's little face creased with sudden grief, that haunted her. She had rung Claire's number after twenty minutes. There was no answer. Then Mohammed had turned up and she was forced to organise herself, and prepare to leave for Somerset. She rang again just before she locked up but there was still no answer. Could they have had an accident already? She checked her answerphone and her mobile telephone. No messages. There was nothing for it. She would have to leave. Mohammed was talking nonstop and kept getting under her feet in his effort to be mercilessly helpful. She dreaded the journey with him. He required so much attention.

'Look,' she said when they were sitting side by side in the car,' I have a really bad headache. Would you mind if I didn't talk?'

Then he was full of solicitous attention. He wanted to give her a head and neck massage.

'You can't. Not when I'm driving,' she objected, screaming silently, 'Leave me alone, leave me alone, *please*!' He nevertheless twisted in his seat and with strong fingers kneaded the back of her neck.

'This is so tight,' he remarked. 'It is no wonders yous have headaches.' Remarkably, after quite a short time, Sophie could feel that he was doing her some good. Her shoulders seemed to relax and drop from somewhere up round her ears to a more normal position.

'It is so strange, yes, for yous without the childrens? This, I think, is making so stressful. But father is good for childrens. I think so. You must be happy for them.' Sophie felt angry with him. How dare he volunteer his opinion, when he knew nothing about it?

'My fathers die when I am small boy. My fathers he had bicycle barrow in the streets of Cairo. He sell bread from big baskets. One day the polices come and say, "Where is yours licence?" He too poor for licence. They takes him to polices station and they takes from him his barrow. My fathers does not come home. Late at night my mothers tells me to go to polices station to say my fathers is missing. Policemens say to me, only a small boys, "Come with us". They takes me to morgue and show me my fathers, dead like meat on slab. He has had heart attacks. "Is this yours fathers?" they asks me. I have to run home for my mothers and my sisters, to tell them ours fathers is dead. This is very terrible thing.'

Sophie looked at him. 'Mohammed. I'm so sorry. What an awful story.'

Mohammed shrugged. 'Long times ago. But still I misses him. I want always to be good to his memories.'

'And your mother? How did she manage? How many of you were there? Children, I mean.'

'Seven childrens. My father's familys takes us in but my mothers is not happy. In two years' times she marries again.'

Oh dear, thought Sophie, dreading the wicked stepfather story she was sure she was going to hear next.

'He very good mans,' said Mohammed. 'He kind fathers to us all. He helps me with my schoolings to be engineer. He kind to my sisters. Then he, too, dies. Now my mothers lives in house he buys us.'

So, a reasonably happy ending, thought Sophie. Feeling sorry for Mohammed had, perversely, cheered her up and she felt a little calmer about her own children. She planned to stop when they were on the M3 and she would telephone again at a service station. She just needed to hear that Freddy was all right. Of course he will be, she thought as she drove along. Children survive terrible traumas. However, the picture of his unhappy face remained with her and haunted her the rest of the weekend, long after Claire had told her to stop worrying, that he was fine, playing with Ben, his cousin. She could even hear happy voices and laughter in the background and her heart ached even more.

This, then, was the Sophie who presented herself at Charlton. She was first struck by the prettiness of the countryside, so much more truly rural than Oxfordshire. Gentler, greener, wetter. As they left the A303 at Wincanton and threaded through the back roads and lanes, she felt as if they were entering a different country. Milking herds stood in muddy gateways, beef cattle grazed hillsides, fields were dotted with sheep. This was real stockman's country, with grass fields and high hedges and very little plough and wire. Mohammed, who had never been out of London, was speechless. So much grass. So much space. Where were all the people? Sophie imagined Maeve felt much the same. She wondered how she survived in such an alien environment. They got lost and then finally found the drive to Charlton.

What a pretty house, thought Sophie. The front door stood open in welcome and when they got out Maeve appeared, wrapped in an apron, and greeted them excitedly. She hung round Mohammed's neck like a limpet.

'A man, a man!' she squealed. 'God! I think I'll take you hostage.'

Mohammed looked pleased and swung her round like a child.

'Come on in,' she said when he put her down. They followed her through the hall and into a large untidy kitchen which showed all the signs of Maeve's occupation. The sink was full of washing up. Saucepans were piled on the floor. The Aga was stained and dirty. A small dog looked up from where he was nesting in a laundry basket of what looked like unironed clothes.

'Excuse the mess!' said Maeve. 'There's a heavenly cleaner but she hasn't been for three days and I'm buggered if I'm doing her job as well.'

Sophie's heart sank. She couldn't bear this sort of thing. The compulsion to clear and tidy was too strong in her.

'Lady P's next door,' Maeve was saying. 'I'll introduce you and then let's go to the pub for a drink. Lunch is all ready in the bottom oven.'

'Can you just leave her?' asked Sophie anxiously.

'For Christ's sake, Soph, don't start on that! I've just got you away from your children, which is a minor miracle. Don't start being all responsible here.'

'Well, can you?'

'Of course. She's not an invalid. Or ga-ga. She's perfectly all right on her own.'

She hurried them across the hall and into a pretty, bright drawing room. Sophie was relieved to see that it was fairly tidy and that Maeve had lit the fire. A tiny old woman sat in a large armchair opposite a large television set. She had white hair cut in a straight, smooth bob and despite her great age looked attractive in a pale blue sweater with a pretty scarf pinned at the neck. Her face was intelligent, the bone structure clearly defined under the powdery skin. For a moment she looked bewildered and then held out her hand to Sophie. Mohammed then leapt forward dramatically to crouch beside her and Sophie saw her eyes light up as they took in his youth and good looks. He uses his charm mercilessly, she thought. Even on this very ancient woman, it works. But, of course, she is the sort of woman who has always enjoyed men.

Later on, after the three of them had driven the short way to the Dog and Duck in South Charlton, they sat at a wonky oak table by the roaring open fire, half-pints of cider in front of them, a Coke for Mohammed, bags of crisps open on the table. The bar was quiet. A few locals slumped at the counter, slightly shaggy-looking men in jeans and work boots. A group of women sitting at a table with some children might or might not have belonged to them. Remarks were exchanged, and the children occasionally hung around the men, wheedling for more drinks and crisps. Both groups stared openly at Mohammed, who fresh from his conquest of Lady Pamela was more ebullient than ever. In the gloom of the pub his teeth flashed and the glamour of his exotic looks was heightened. One of the women whispered something to her friend and they both looked in his direction and smirked and giggled.

'Well,' said Maeve, looking about her. 'This isn't where it's at, that's for sure. Still, it's the first time I've been in a room with more than three people for a couple of weeks . . .' She tailed off as the door banged open and a man came in. He was about thirty, dressed in much the same way as the others but had more swagger and style. He was brown-faced, brown-haired and as he dug his hand into his back pocket to look for money he took in the room, turning to look at Maeve. 'Morning,' he said pleasantly in their direction.

The barman gave up his leisurely polishing of glasses. 'Usual, Rob?' he asked.

'Yes, please, Tom.' The men at the bar all looked up and there was an exchange of banter. Rob, it seemed, drove a lorry, a livestock lorry.

Sophie watched Maeve take him in. A few moments later she was on her feet, collecting their glasses, going over to the bar to lean beside him.

'Hi,' she said. He turned to look at her and smiled – not quite the megawattage of Mohammed, but not far off.

'Hi,' he replied. The men on the bar stools sniggered. In the next few minutes he had bought Maeve a drink and then made an arrangement to meet her in Castle Cary that evening. The seated women looked Maeve up and down – her neat little backside in the jeans with the artful split under the left buttock, the shrunken pullover, the expensive velvet scarf tied round her neck, the knot of thick dark hair. She had a sort of wanton appeal that they recognised. Forward, too. A goer. Rob was on to a good thing.

She brought Rob over to Sophie and Mohammed and introduced them. Mohammed looked cross. Sophie smiled.

'We're going to meet tonight, Soph. OK? Rob here says he and his mates go to a pub in Cary on a Saturday.'

As they drove back to Charlton, Sophie said, 'You are amazing, Maeve. He was only in the pub for two minutes before you'd nabbed him!'

'Ah! I'm a desperate woman, to be sure,' said Maeve cheerfully. 'He plays rugby, so there should be fourteen more – little, fast, scrummy ones and big forward ones. Something for everyone, eh, Mohammed?'

As it turned out only Sophie and Maeve went out that evening. Mohammed, whose religion forbade drink, said he was tired, and indeed he looked it. He worked extremely hard in the restaurant and also had a cleaning job in a primary school in the afternoons. He said he would like to stay behind and watch television. The space at Charlton was an obvious novelty. The room he now shared with his friend Khaled was tiny. 'If one of us is standing up, the others has to be in the beds,' he explained.

Sophie wondered at the propriety of leaving him alone with Lady Pamela. She sought a moment with Maeve in the kitchen as she washed up the mountain of dirty dishes and Maeve made scrambled eggs for supper.

'Listen, Maeve. Seriously. Is it really OK to leave Mohammed? I mean, what would Lady Pamela's family think?'

'What on earth do you mean? He's not likely to rape her or make off with the silver, is he?'

'Well. No. But it's not the arrangement they made, is it? I mean, they would expect you to be here . . .'

'What the fuck difference does it make? We'll ask her, if you like. She'll be thrilled to have him waiting on her every whim.'

Sophie could see she was wasting her breath but nevertheless felt uneasy, although when she and Maeve eventually left at about half past seven, the two of them were happily sitting by the fire watching *Blind Date*. Mohammed had agreed to help Lady Pamela upstairs and she had assured Maeve that she was quite happy to be left with him.

'We're going to talk about Cairo,' she said. 'Bumper and I were there for four years, living in a beautiful house on Zamalek Island in the Nile. I loved Cairo. I am going to show Mohammed my photographs.'

'See?' said Maeve to Sophie. 'Now stop being so pathetic.'

Sophie hadn't felt like going out at all but had to put on a bright face. She changed into her leather trousers and red sweater and put on some make-up and let her long hair loose.

'Wow!' said Maeve. 'You look fab.' She had changed into another pair of jeans which she wore with a pair of cowboy boots.

'These are my FMBs,' she explained, doing a sort of line dance routine. 'My Fuck Me Boots. Never failed yet.'

As Sophie drove to the town she felt terribly depressed. She didn't want to be going out, to sit in a crowd of strangers in a smoky, noisy pub, trying to look as if she was enjoying it. She was past all this. She hadn't enjoyed it the first time round and realised that she had hitched herself up to Fergus as a means to escape the awfulness of being single, unattached and looking for a man. She felt more secure as she was, withdrawn from the contest, out of the running, utterly taken up with her babies. She never even felt sexy these days. She didn't want to be forced back into the arena and it was typical of Maeve to get her out on some escapade like this. Still, she had the car, she could jack it in and drive back whenever she felt like it. Maeve could get a taxi home if necessary. Sophie would even pay for it.

Later, in the pub, it was exactly as she knew it would be. They fought their way through a crowd of young men and women and found a table with two spare places. Maeve went to the bar to get drinks and was gone for ages. Sophie couldn't even see her through the scrum. She fiddled with the beer mat on the table and tried not to listen to the conversation of the young couple who shared the table. It went on the lines of, 'Well, who was there then?'

'You know. The usual.'

'Was Di there?'

'No.'

'She said she wasn't going.'

'Well, she wasn't there.'

'What was it like then?'

'Same as usual.'

All this, punctuated by long pauses.

Glancing at the girl, Sophie noticed they were engaged. Christ, she thought.

Maeve came fighting back with two glasses of lager.

'Hurry and drink up,' she said. 'There's another room at the back. We're going to play darts. That bloody Rob's here with a woman!' Her eyes were sparkling and she radiated energy. 'Some slapper with peroxide hair and a pair of melons in a boob tube.'

Sophie did as she was told and they fought their way back the way she had come. Men lifted arms holding beer mugs to let them pass and one or two made suggestive remarks in the spirit of Saturday night in the local. The room at the back was just as crowded and, if anything, noisier. Rob came over and kissed Maeve on the lips to the fury of a blonde girl who glared at her ferociously. He kissed Sophie too and put his arms round them both.

'Hey! Guys! How about this then?' he shouted to his mates. Sophie took in a bunch of burly young men, some with shaved heads, who stood drinking and laughing round a darts board. Rob made some swift introductions and instantly Maeve was in there, laughing and flirting. There seemed to be some discussion about how much she weighed and she was lifted off her feet and passed round like a parcel before being put into the lap of a young man sitting at a table. Sophie knew herself to be hopeless at this sort of thing. She was too quiet, too tall, too restrained. She edged to the side of the room where the duller girls had gathered and found a bit of wall to lean against and a corner of a table to put down her drink. Someone asked her what she was having and another lager appeared. They were a welcoming bunch.

'Here. Do you want to sit down?' asked a dark girl who shuffled along a bench to make room for her. 'I'm Stella. This is Jane.'

'Hi,' said Sophie. 'I'm Sophie.'

The two young women were friendly. They both wore wedding rings. 'That's mine,' said Stella, indicating one of the shaven-headed men. 'Kevin. Jane's husband's Daniel, over there. They're all in the rugby club.'

'Oh, I see,' said Sophie.

'You're married then,' said Stella, indicating Sophie's ring.

'Was,' said Sophie. 'I'm divorced.'

'He's my second,' said Stella, nodding at Kevin. 'My first was a right bastard. Only lasted three months.'

Sophie smiled with relief. No judgement from this quarter.

'Dan's Jane's second too, come to that, isn't he, Jane? Although she wasn't married first time. Had the two kids though. He was a bastard too, wasn't he, Jane?'

Jane nodded cheerfully. 'Yeah.'

'So have you got children?' asked Sophie.

'Yeah. We've got three each. Only Jason's Kevin's like. Abby and Solitaire are Dean's, my first husband's. He was all right really until we got married. Allergic to marriage, he was, wasn't he, Jane?'

Jane nodded amiably.

'Oh, I see,' said Sophie. How remarkably they cope with all this, she thought. Sitting here in the pub on Saturday night with all this wreckage of family life in their wake and yet they seem quite unscathed. What survivors they are.

'What about you?' asked Jane.

'I've got twins,' said Sophie.

'Lovely! Do you hear that, Stell? Twins. I always wanted twins. Are they identical!'

'No, they're not, actually,' said Sophie, thinking, how extraordinary, I feel quite normal with these two. No explanations needed. No sympathy expected. All men are bastards seems to cover everything. Quite by accident she had fetched up in a haven of female solidarity.

'Your husband, was he . . .?'

'Yes,' said Sophie. 'A bastard.'

Maeve came to find her after the landlord had called 'Last orders' at least twice. She was pink-faced and slightly drunk and was dragging a man by the hand.

'Soph, you've got to meet Matt. He's a vet, but the great thing is, he lives at Charlton. Isn't it amazing? He lives at the farm in the village.'

Matt, also slightly pissed, held Sophie's hand for a long time and tried to find the words the occasion called for.

'Hi, Matt,' said Sophie. 'Well, that'll cheer things up for Maeve, having a drinking partner in the village.'

Matt, who had a lean, angular face and brown floppy hair, smiled and said, 'Cheer things up for me too, I can tell you. She changes the average age in the village by about twenty years or so!'

'Listen, though, Soph, another coincidence. Matt has just

been looking at that racehorse of Lady P's . . .'

'What racehorse?' asked Sophie.

'Didn't I tell you? I've discovered she's got this really good horse. It's wonderful – he's called Irish Dancer, named for me, but he bust up his leg and hasn't done anything for three years. Well, Matt has just had the leg scanned. He was asked to by the trainer. It's a coincidence, isn't it? And he thinks the horse is OK to race again. Tomorrow we'll load up Lady P and go over and see it, shall we? How about that, Matt? Will you come?'

'Can't. I'm farming tomorrow for my father. But I'll talk to Lady Pamela about it, if she wants. Mitchell was going to ring her anyway and ask her where she wants to go from here.'

'I see,' said Sophie, who felt far from interested and was anxious to change the subject to their leaving and going home. She glanced at her watch and wondered if it was too late to ring Claire and find out if everything was all right.

'Maeve, are you ready to leave?'

'OK, babe. I'll join you in a min,' and she pulled Matt off towards the door, no doubt to have a goodnight snog, thought Sophie. She said goodbye to Stella and Jane, thinking how the three of them had sat there the whole evening like doorstops, and went out to start the car. She saw Maeve and Matt groping in the car park and felt annoyed. It was so bloody undignified. Eventually Matt led Maeve over to her car and opened the passenger door and helped her in.

Maeve tried to get out again and Sophie yanked at her arm.

'For God's sake, Maeve, cool it. I'm not hanging around any longer. Either come now or make your own way.'

Matt, it seemed, had a lift with someone who was going on to a nightclub. Maeve had one of those maddening non-conclusive conversations, with the open car door between them, about when and where they would meet again. Finally she wrote her telephone number on Matt's wrist and allowed Sophie to drive away.

'Sorry, Sophs,' she said. 'But he's OK, isn't he? Couldn't let a good one like that get by me.'

'Didn't notice,' said Sophie, and then relented. 'No, he looked OK.'

'Did you have a good time?' asked Maeve. 'Sorry I never got back to you but it was so crowded and I got caught up with that rugby club lot.'

'It was fine,' said Sophie, thinking, how can she expect me to have enjoyed it?

'Of course, you couldn't drink, could you? Did you meet anyone?'

'Yes. Stella and Jane.'

Maeve sensed tension in the air. 'Don't be like that, Soph. You could have met just as many people as I did. If you won't make any effort—'

'Look, Maeve, we're different, OK? Just leave it at that. I can't behave like you do.'

'What do you mean, behave like I do? You make it sound as if I fucked the first fifteen before I'd finished my first pint.'

'Just leave it, Maeve. It isn't my scene, that's all.'

'No. Bloody miserable martyrdom's your scene . . .' And so it went on. They arrived back at Charlton in tight-lipped silence, Sophie feeling that she actually hated Maeve. As they slammed in they could hear laughter from the sitting room and opened the door to find Lady Pamela and Mohammed on the sofa together surrounded by boxes of photographs.

They looked up, beaming.

'I've had the most delightful evening with Mohammed,' said Lady Pamela. 'We've talking about so many places I remember so well . . .'

Mohammed's eyes were shining. Not since he had left home had he met anyone with such an interest in his country.

'He can't believe that Bumper and I were often guests of King Farouk. Quite a playboy, he was, I can tell you. We left in nineteen fifty and he was exiled the following year, after a military coup.' Lady Pamela noticed the glum faces and said, 'What's the matter? You both look rather cross. One thing I must mention, Maeve, is that Bunty telephoned while you were out. I answered the telephone of course, but Mohammed called from the study – he was looking for the boxes of photographs – and Bunty got very excited, thinking she heard a man's voice. I told her it was the radio, but I don't think she quite believed me. I think it would be just as well if she doesn't know that you have had friends to stay for the weekend. She rather likes to think that I am on my last legs, you know.'

'Shit,' said Maeve, glaring at Mohammed. 'Well, they won't be coming again.'

She went off to bed and left Sophie and Mohammed to tidy

up and help Lady Pamela upstairs. Sophie asked her if there was anything she could do, filled her a hot water bottle, made her a drink and filled the morning tea kettle. They had a long search for her glasses which they found under the sofa, and Esau had to be put out. He disappeared and Sophie had to wait by the open kitchen door and shout for him into the blackness. She tidied the kitchen and hung the tea towels on the rail in front of the Aga.

Mohammed appeared from upstairs and asked her if she was all right.

'Yes. Fine. A bit tired, that's all.' She smiled at him and he came to lean on the Aga beside her. With a finger he traced her chin. She hung her head, close to tears, and her hair fell in a curtain to hide her face. Gently, he tucked it behind her ear and raised her chin and kissed her. Utterly taken aback, she let his tongue find its way into her mouth and then kissed him back. Her body responded in a way she had forgotten and she felt a wonderful melting sensation in her gut. They kissed for a long time and Mohammed's hands moved over her breasts and then slid between her legs.

'No, Mohammed. I'm not ready for this,' she murmured. He withdrew his hand and eased it into the waist of her trousers at the back, and down over her buttocks inside her knickers. 'Oh God . . .'

Esau had been in a very long time and was snoring in his basket before Sophie and Mohammed turned off the lights and went upstairs.

Chapter Six

Maeve was up and banging around making breakfast the next morning when Sophie slunk downstairs. Sophie had hardly slept at all and was feeling elated, nervy and a bit shifty. She couldn't work out exactly why what had happened between her and Mohammed should affect her relationship with Maeve, but she felt awkward and unnatural. Maeve was whistling cheerfully and seemed to have forgotten the bad feeling of the evening before.

'Hi,' she said. 'Sleep OK? Sorry I left you to it last night. I was marginally pissed off, but all forgotten now. OK?' She slammed some bread to toast on the Aga hotplate and poured boiling water onto coffee in the cafetiere. 'Coffee will be ready in a sec.'

'Yes. Well, sorry if I was a pain. Here, I'll watch the toast.' Sophie wanted to ask if Mohammed was up yet but wasn't sure she could produce a sentence with his name in it without revealing everything. She turned the toast over, glad to have something to do, something she could concentrate on and avoid having to make eye contact with Maeve.

'Did you two stay up late?' asked Maeve innocently, loading Lady Pamela's breakfast tray.

This was Sophie's moment.

'Actually, Maeve,' she said, studying the toast and having to clear her throat between the two words, 'we did. You see, we . . . we sort of started . . . well, it just started with him kissing me and then . . .' She felt compelled to look up and caught sight of Maeve's face. She looked definitely hostile.

'What, you had sex?' she said bluntly.

'No! Well, not the whole way. But almost. I wasn't sure I wanted to, you know.'

Maeve laughed, although it was more of a short, derisive snort. She mimicked Sophie's words, ' "Not the whole way" . . . Christ, Soph, you sound just like a schoolgirl. Come to think of it, any schoolgirl worth her salt would have said yes to a bonk with something as gorgeous as Mohammed.'

Sophie felt unfairly under attack.

Maeve went on, 'Honestly, though, I'm glad. Do you good. Did he tell you about his boyfriends?'

Sophie wondered if Maeve was being deliberately cruel. She obviously minded.

'Yes, he did. You'd already told me, anyway.'

'Oh yeah. Well, as long as he told you.' Maeve shoved the two pieces of toast on the tray and went out. Sophie leaned against the Aga, feeling miserable. Maeve was reducing what had happened last night to something sordid and shameful. Sophie didn't want to lose how Mohammed had made her feel. She had regained a sense of herself. Her body, which had seemed for so long to be trapped beneath a thick, dense, impermeable skin like a kind of wax on a cheese, had stirred and responded to his caresses. She hadn't had to think about it or try. Sexual desire had just taken over, welling up as strongly as ever. For Sophie this was cause to celebrate. She had forgotten what it felt like and she had forgotten how good it was, how healthy and alive it made her feel.

Although Maeve had mocked, she had not taken Mohammed upstairs with her and invited him into her bed because she was not sure that she could cope with what this might do to her, and she was also restrained by a sense that such behaviour was unmannerly and inappropriate in a house where she was a sort of guest.

Maeve came back in and poured out coffee for them both. The silence felt cumbersome.

'Here,' she said, handing a mug to Sophie. She came to stand beside her, warming her bottom on the stove. Sophie moved over, staring into her mug.

'You can bet I tried it on with him. I mean, you don't meet many centrefold men like him, do you?' said Maeve. 'But he didn't fancy me. I'm not his sort. He likes softer, more mumsy women. He has boyfriends because that's what he got into in Greece when he was trying to find a way of getting over here. I don't think homosexuality is such a big deal anyway, in his culture. I mean, I think he intends to marry and so on.' She paused and then said, 'Look, Soph, I was jealous when you told me. He sort of feels like my territory, but I can see that's ridiculous. So it's OK.'

Sophie looked at her. 'But we're not going to have an affair. We're not going to go out together. We decided that last night. He doesn't want to any more than I do. It was just something that happened. To be honest, I didn't know I would feel like I did. I wasn't prepared for it at all. I didn't know that he even liked me much. He's so good-natured and kind that he's attentive to everyone, isn't he? And, Maeve, I didn't know that I would want it so much. It would have been really, really easy to have slept with him last night. I don't know how that would have made me feel this morning. I mean, AIDS is an issue, isn't it? And the twins make a huge difference to me, to how I feel I can behave. But Maeve,' Sophie turned to her friend with shining eyes, 'it was lovely. He was lovely. It was just so good.'

'Why's it so impossible then, you and him?' asked Maeve. 'Wouldn't you consider anyone who hadn't belonged to the Pony Club?' She couldn't resist sarcasm. Sophie was like a pathetic dog rolling over to be kicked.

'Maeve, you know why! It's just physical attraction on my part. I'd be using him, really. I don't want to be anything more than a friend. If you think about it, we don't have anything in common at all. Nothing to build a proper relationship on. He can see that too. He wants to go home and find a traditional Moslem girl to marry. We just got carried away, that's all.' She could see at once from Maeve's face that such considerations were something she would never have to grapple with.

'Well, good on yer, mate!' said Maeve, giving her a kiss. 'And never say never. I can't see what would be wrong in having a bit of a hot time with him, but there you are.' She went on, changing the subject, 'Now, I have a plan for today. I've just been speaking to Lady P about it. Will you drive us over to see this horse, Irish Dancer – Dancer for short? The place he's kept, it's only just the other side of South Charlton. Lady P has already rung the trainer and fixed up for us to go and have a look at him. Then back here, quick lunch and you and lover boy can head off to London before the Sunday evening rush. Hey, Soph! I've had a thought! You must introduce Mohammed to Fergus!' She giggled, and Sophie joined in.

'What would he say? Or his mother? She always looks as though she has discovered a bad smell. They are such appalling snobs. If it wasn't that it would cause the most dreadful hoohah, I would pretend he is my new boyfriend!' Sophie felt happy and light-hearted now, glad that she had got the situation out in the open with Maeve, and also glad, she recognised with a twinge of guilt, that Mohammed had chosen her above her friend. It was base of her, she knew, but the fact he liked her best was like a little kernel of pleasure that she wanted to tuck away and store.

Maeve banged up the stairs and tried to get Lady Pamela moving, but as usual the old woman would not be hurried and was at her most imperious.

'Fetch me the telephone,' she demanded. 'I want to ring Doug Mitchell, the trainer, again. Now what is his number?' and Maeve had to run downstairs to look it up. As far as Maeve could gather the telephone call was quite superfluous anyway. She seemed to have forgotten that the plans had already been made.

'This is Lady Pamela,' she announced in ringing tones. 'To whom am I speaking?'

Maeve winced. This morning Lady P seemed unreal, like someone on a silly television programme, parodying the old and grand.

Getting her ready took an age. She did not agree with Maeve's choice of skirt and several more had to be dragged out of the wardrobe before she would agree to a mustard-coloured herringbone tweed.

'It hardly fucking matters,' said Maeve under her breath. 'We're only going to see a horse, for God's sake.' Then the stockings were wrong and Maeve had to wrestle with a top drawer of rolled up woollen balls to find the exact pair she wanted. Then her gloves had to be searched for, and her tweed hat and field glasses which were eventually found in the washroom downstairs, hanging on a hook beneath an old mackintosh.

'Come on, come on,' groaned Maeve, who would have been out of the house in the twinkling of an eye and who found such delays an agony of frustration. It's deliberate. It's about power, she thought crossly. She's showing me who is boss.

Mohammed was despatched to polish up a pair of old brown field boots and Sophie told to get her brown bag out of her wardrobe and find her handkerchief. Sophie caught Maeve's eye and grinned. 'Ladies of the Bedchamber?' she murmured as they passed on their errands.

At last they got Lady Pamela into the car and Sophie had just turned the key in the ignition when Lady P announced she had left her spectacles beside her bed. Maeve had to unlock the house and run upstairs to look for them, only to find that they were in her bag all the time. Mohammed squashed himself into the back seat behind Sophie and massaged her neck while they waited. Lady Pamela shot him a glance.

Blimey, thought Sophie, she doesn't miss a trick!

Eventually they were off. It was a bright, windy morning with puffy white clouds racing across a blue sky. Sudden dazzling sunshine broke between them, almost blinding Sophie as she drove between the gold and red autumn trees. How pretty the country is on a morning like this, she thought as they left the valley and the village behind and climbed to the top of the hill. Far in front of them the landscape rolled like a puffy, green, quilted eiderdown, the small fields stitched with thick, black thorn hedges and threaded with trees. There was so much grass, and many of the fields were still full of grazing stock. Tucked into the wrinkled folds lay the farms and villages. It all looked so snug and secure, and as if man and nature had worked harmoniously hand in hand to produce such scenery. No wonder Lady Pamela loved it.

'It's just round this bend,' said Lady Pamela. 'Here. This turning on the right,' and they drove into a smart and orderly yard, with looseboxes on three sides and further ranges of barns and stabling behind. A good-looking man in his fifties came over and opened Lady Pamela's door. Maeve gave him the once-over. Quite fanciable, she thought, fit, healthy-looking and dressed in a tweed jacket, flat cap and cord trousers. However, he displayed no interest whatever in the girls in the car and concentrated on Lady Pamela, helping her out, enthusing about the pleasure of seeing her again and asking if she would like to come into the house for coffee.

Greasy bastard, thought Maeve. She was glad that Lady Pamela declined and then, trained in mannerliness, turned to introduce her, Sophie and Mohammed. Maeve saw Doug Mitchell look them over with a complete lack of curiosity, and said a brief good morning. He's only interested in money, thought Maeve. He knows who butters his bread, and that's his owners, not the likes of us lot. He can't be bothered with hangers-on.

He had turned back to Lady Pamela to explain the exact situation with the horse. He was at pains to confirm that he himself had been on the point of contacting her had Matt not passed on the news that the leg had been scanned and that the results looked promising. Maeve narrowed her eyes as she listened. She knew nothing about it, she admitted that, but there was something weasely about this man. He's bluffing. He's not really interested, she thought. Lady Pamela and her horse are not in his league any more. She's just an old lady and the horse had had a breakdown, or whatever it's called. All this pretending to care is just bullshit.

He was leading them across the yard to a tank-like four-wheel drive vehicle.

'Now,' he said, 'are all of you coming?' somehow implying that they were a sort of Sunday school outing, better left behind.

'Sure thing, mate,' said Maeve fiercely. Doug shot her a glance and then helped hoist Lady Pamela into the front seat. She was so light that with Mohammed taking one arm and Doug the other, she sailed up, like a child, showing a good deal of long pink knicker leg and stocking top, which made Maeve grin.

The others crammed into the back and Doug drove carefully out over two fields, beautifully fenced with wooden railings, to a further field where a herd of young stock were grazing. They looked up when they heard the engine.

'He's turned out with this lot. We'll go and catch him. You won't be able to pick him out from here, but we can drive on a bit further.' Mohammed was told to get out and open the gate, which he did, a bit sulkily. He looked out of place, thought Maeve, in his cheap London clothes, and she could see he was trying not to get his trainers dirty in the mud of the gateway. Doug tapped the wheel impatiently. 'They're probably his only pair,' she whispered to Sophie.

As they bumped across the field, the horses stopped grazing and bunched together, heads up, nostrils flared. They were obviously young. Even Maeve could see that. Leggy and light and nervous, they seemed ready to take flight. Doug stopped a few yards away from them and turned off the engine.

'There he is, Lady Pamela. At the back of the group. You'll pick him out in a moment. Of course he looks a bit rough. Not as you'll remember him.' Picking up a head collar from the floor of the jeep, he got out and moved towards the animals. He kept the head collar and rope behind his back and held out some horse nuts on the palm of the other hand.

The young animals parted and jostled about him. The big brown horse at the back watched suspiciously and then came forward to greet him. The rope was over his neck in a second and as he reached for the nuts, the head collar was slipped on his head.

'Christ,' said Maeve. 'Is that a horse or a potato?'

He was covered in mud, quite literally coated in a casing of greyish brown. It was plastered in his long matted mane and tail. His legs were filthy and hairy, his hooves overgrown and broken.

Lady Pamela said nothing. The horse had been roughed off and she would not have expected him to look any different. She could see that his ribs were well-covered and although he had lost a good deal of muscle over his neck and quarters, he still looked strongly made and was in fair condition. He had never been an oil painting. His rather large head looked coarser than ever with long whiskers and a lot of hair on the chin. The unmistakable broad white blaze down his nose was still an identifiable feature even though it, too, was muddy.

Maeve felt disappointed. In her mind she had imagined a beautiful, noble creature, like the racehorses she had seen parading in the paddock at racecourses. This character had little more glamour than a gyppo horse. Irish Dancer was a highly unsuitable name for him. She started to feel cold and bored. She didn't like Doug Mitchell and she didn't like this ugly horse. The whole outing began to seem like a waste of time.

Doug led the big, brown gelding to the jeep and Lady Pamela, helped from her seat by Mohammed, looked him over carefully. Stooping, she ran her hand down his legs and then looked up at the trainer thoughtfully.

'Look, Doug. You were always fair to Bumper. Now tell me the truth. What chance is there that he will come right and stay right? I know you can't guarantee anything with horses and I'm not asking you to make any promises, but what do you think his chances are?'

Doug was silent for a moment. Maeve looked at him. He was trying to phrase something in a way not to cause offence. She wondered whether he would be honest.

'Personally, Lady Pamela, and if he was mine, I'd have had him put down three years ago, and that's the truth. As he is now, the leg looks sound and Matt will have told you that the scan confirmed that the tendon seems healed. There's some scar tissue, of course, but it looks OK to do the job. But to be honest with you and to save what might be your next question, I don't want to take him on again. I don't think this yard would be the right place to train him. He is going to need a lot of individual and specialist care to get him fit very slowly after all this time he's been off, and frankly it's late in the season and I don't have the staff. I've got some quality horses here. My owners want results and I have a tight programme with them all. I just don't have the slack to take him on. You have to remember, too, that some horses don't come back well from injury. They are smart enough to remember what it felt like to gallop three miles and jump eighteen fences and then hurt themselves, and they say, quite definitely, "Sorry, mate. Forget it." '

There was a silence. Maeve was listening, interested again. This sounded like a challenge. Doug was making this ugly, muddy horse seem like a person.

Lady Pamela was thoughtful. 'Thank you, Doug. I appreciate your honesty. It is what I expected to hear. But with this horse I don't think we have to worry about any shortfall in the courage and guts department, although I agree that it's a possibility. I, too, have seen horses turned away because of injury who never have the nerve to run again.' She paused, and Maeve and Sophie caught each other's eye. Maeve raised her eyebrows quizzically and Sophie shrugged. She didn't know which way it was going to go either.

Lady Pamela went on, 'It seems to me, then, that we can allow him to retire peacefully and he can come home and end his days at Charlton, turned out with his mother, or we can consider giving him a second chance by sending him to someone else to train.'

Doug nodded. 'That's about it, Lady Pamela.'

The old woman held her chin for a moment in her gloved hand. She was enjoying this, the air, the bright morning, the sunshine, this man waiting to know what she had decided to do. She no longer felt old and helpless.

'I think the first thing is to bring him home. You can arrange transport, can't you? I will just have to warn Dick that I'm bringing him back and make sure we have everything in order, but I think the sooner the better. We still have the old horse walker in the yard. He can start on that immediately.' She patted Dancer's nose. He seemed to look at her gravely as if he was weighing her words.

Sophie and Maeve exchanged excited smiles. Good-oh! thought Maeve. She loved a bit of a stir. A bit of excitement. She turned round to include Mohammed but he was busy trying to wipe the mud from the sides of his trainers. All this was incomprehensible to him. So much talk about a horse, and not even a beautiful horse with a flowing mane and high lifted tail like he had seen ridden round the pyramids at Ghiza.

'Irish Dancer. It's a lovely name,' said Sophie. 'It makes me think of fiddle music and tapping feet. Look. He knows we're talking about him. He's listening.'

They had bread and cheese in the kitchen for lunch, the four of them, all talking excitedly about Dancer and his homecoming. Lady Pamela had to explain very basic concepts to Maeve and Mohammed. She told them that the horse would have to begin with perhaps six weeks of walking, building up from twenty minutes a day. This would strengthen and harden the legs. He could begin this programme at Charlton with Jack Dick in charge. Maeve was all for going to tell Jack immediately but Lady Pamela said that Monday morning would be soon enough. They would have to order concentrated feed and monitor carefully the change of diet as exercise put on muscle. When he was fit enough to start ridden work they would have to find someone else to take him on and get him ready to race. He would do weeks of trotting and then would have to do some faster work before he started to qualify.

'What do you mean, qualify?' asked Maeve. 'Qualify as what? He's been a racehorse already, hasn't he? You make it sound as if he wants to be a chartered accountant.'

'He has to do seven days' hunting,' said Lady Pamela, 'and then get a hunter's certificate in order to quality for point-to-points or hunter chases. Given that it's already early October, time is short and the sooner he gets started the better. Most horses will have been brought up from grass, getting fit since August.'

'Where does he go hunting?' asked Maeve. 'Round here?'

'With guns?' asked Mohammed. 'Bang! Bang? Why is this necessary?'

'Yes, round here,' laughed Lady Pamela, 'with the local pack. There will be a lot of racehorses qualifying. This is an area that produces good horses and there are some excellent yards. And no, Mohammed, never with guns. Hunting in

England is quite different from what is understood by the term in most other countries. This is hunting with hounds and mounted followers.'

'Wow!' said Maeve. 'I am so excited. I love this kind of thing – an odds against challenge. Hey!' A thought struck her. 'How much does all this cost? Can you afford it?'

'That is a consideration,' said Lady Pamela, 'but I think I have explained to you that Bumper left the horses provided for. It's the only trust that Henry hasn't taken over, and I know that there is quite enough to put the horse in training for a year. I rather feel that I owe it to Bumper to give this a shot. I know that had he been alive he would have made the same decision. He'd be so delighted to have his colours on the track again.'

'Colours? What do you mean?'

'Horses race wearing their owner's colours – or at least the jockeys do. You'll have noticed the spots and hoops, and stripes on their jerseys, and the colours on their caps? Bumper's colours were well-known in the steeplechasing world, thanks to Ballerina. White with orange crossbelts and armlets, orange cap.'

'Ooooh! Divine!' cried Maeve. 'I adore orange. It's absolutely the colour this year. It would look lovely on a nice brown horse.' She jumped up and skipped round the table. 'Oh, I love it!' she cried. 'Lady Pamela, we'll get you a fabulous hat to wear and you'll be presented with a cup by the Queen Mother, your combined ages about one hundred and ninety!'

'Enough of your cheek, Irish!' said Lady Pamela tartly.

Sophie and Mohammed, who in the warm kitchen both felt overcome by lack of sleep, smiled fondly at her and then at each other. With a start Sophie realised that she hadn't thought about the twins for at least an hour. I am definitely in a state of recovery, she thought.

It was hard to tell what Jack Dick thought of the prospect of having Dancer to look after. He stood in the kitchen at Charlton turning his woolly hat round and round in his hands, his heavy face working as he grappled with the implications of what Lady Pamela was telling him.

'Him's a difficult bugger,' he said at last.

'You may find him less so now he's older and completely unfit,' said Lady Pamela. 'But I understand if you think he may be too much for you. None of us is getting any younger.'

'He'll not be too much for me,' he retorted. 'When's he coming then?'

'Tomorrow morning,' said Lady Pamela. 'Could you check the horse walker is working, and get a box ready for him? We've still got suitable rugs and so on, I suppose?'

'Arr,' said Jack. 'I had 'em all put away, proper like, with mothballs and all. We've still got all the tack. I've kept it all oiled and that.'

Maeve slid a mug of tea to him along the table, and a plate of homemade oat biscuits followed. He eyed them cautiously.

'Go on,' she said, helping herself to a biscuit. He reached out to take the mug in his large red fist.

'I'll have 'em outside,' he said.

'He's thrilled,' announced Lady Pamela after he'd gone.

'Could have fooled me,' said Maeve. 'He looked about as thrilled as a turnip.'

The next afternoon when Maeve went down to the stables to see if Dancer had arrived, she found Jack in one of the boxes, grooming a big, sleek horse she didn't recognise. Watching him over the top half of the door, she saw Jack's face relaxed and happy, the granite features softened. He was whistling between his teeth as he worked the brush over the horse's quarters. The animal was restless and fidgety, lifting a hind leg as if he was about to kick, and snatching at the end of the rope with which he was tied to a ring in the wall. He turned to look at Maeve and with a start she recognised the long white nose.

'Jesus, Jack,' she said. 'Is that him? Is that Dancer?'

Jack looked up and a smile cracked his face.

'Looks better, does he?' he asked. 'Of course he does, the old bugger.' He had clearly been hard at work for some time. Dancer's previously filthy coat now gleamed and a pile of matted hair in the corner of the box indicated how much dead coat had come out. He had also thinned and shortened his mane and tail. Maeve was genuinely admiring. She gazed at the horse over the door. He now looked much more like a possibility. Even she could see his powerful rangy build was impressive.

'You've done wonders, Jack. When Lady Pamela wakes up from her nap I'll bring her down to see him. She'll be amazed at the difference. He looks more like a racehorse now.'

'He'll be needing clipping,' said Jack. 'He can't work with

all this bugger on him.' He indicated the horse's long autumn coat. 'And shoeing. Got to get his shoes on.'

Dancer turned and nudged him with his nose. Maeve saw an expression close to love pass over Jack's features. 'Bugger was born here,' he said. 'Right here in this box. He's come home, that's what. He's come home. All that,' and he indicated with a jerk of his head that he was talking about the racing yard, 'that bugger told her ladyship about not wanting to race again. He doesn't know the bugger. He's a right one, this is. A right tough one. He'll want to race all right.'

When Maeve telephoned Sophie later in the week she was full of horse talk. 'He's been shod now, Soph. Lady P loves to hear him clopping about in the yard. She says it's like the old days, and God, you should have seen the blacksmith. Farrier, I should call him, shouldn't I? He was all bulging biceps and a leather apron, and a big black beard. I've found out where he drinks. He said he'd come and take me one night. He was like a gladiator. And a girl came and clipped him, in what they call a blanket clip, and he looks like a racehorse now and old Jack Dick is besotted. His vegetables are right out of favour. He spends all his time down there in the yard exercising him on his horse walker thing or else what he calls "strapping" which is sort of banging him with a brush to build up muscle. Lady Pamela is thrilled. It's given her a whole new lease of life. We go down to the stables every day to see how things are going. Twice a day sometimes. She gets Jack to take off the horse's rugs and she stands and looks at him. She calls it letting the horse fill her eye. Do you know that expression? She says it means taking a little time to see where he needs building up, which bit needs work, whether he's good in his coat. That sort of thing.

'Matt has been to check him and thinks he looks well. Did I tell you that he has recommended somewhere to send him? A small yard run by a young woman trainer. She only has seven horses in training and she takes real trouble knowing them as individuals, so Matt said. Lady P was a bit off about a woman trainer but she's got used to the idea now. Jane Hedderwick's her name and she's close enough for me to cycle over to see him and she's a great girl. Always got the gin bottle on the table. She's had a real struggle getting started but now has some dedicated owners. Honestly, Soph, it's such fun. I never thought I'd get the hang of horses.' She broke off to giggle. 'Isn't that what people say, "hung like a horse"? But you know what I mean. I'm getting really quite interested.' She paused. 'Anyway, Sophers, how are you? And how are the Effs?'

'Fine. Fine. Really good, actually. The twins had a lovely time with Claire and I think Fergus actually enjoyed having them to himself.' Sophie did not go into what anguish this had caused her. It had made her realise that she preferred Fergus to be hopeless with the children. It gave her more control and it was easier somehow to deal with the view of him as an uncaring father rather than a loving parent whose concern for the children rivalled her own.

'And Mohammed? How was he on the way home? Did you stop in a layby for a bonk?'

'Maeve! No, we didn't, but we had a good talk and he was lovely. Is lovely. We're going to the cinema on Sunday afternoon. Fergus is having the children again.'

'Heh! This is a bit of a change, isn't it? Fatherhood for two weekends running?'

'Yes, it is. Fergus seems to want to. Flora and Freddy are excited about it too. They really enjoyed having him to themselves this last weekend. I think it's partly due to them growing up and being less sort of threatening.'

'Threatening? What do you mean?'

'I think they were threatening when they were real babies. Fergus was quite frightened of them. They were like little aliens. He thinks they're human now.'

'Good, Soph. It's good, isn't it?'

'It's a big step,' agreed Sophie, 'to acknowledge that your children are human. Now what about you and Matt Digby?' As usual Sophie found it easier to ask the questions. 'How is that going?'

'Like a bomb!' said Maeve. 'Unlike you, we have had sex in a layby. I'd recommend vets, you know. They have a real earthy, down-to-business approach. I suppose it's only natural if you spend most of your time with your arm up a cow's bum.'

Maeve was feeling as exuberant as she sounded. Having a boyfriend and the added interest of Dancer made all the difference to her outlook. Matt was fun. The stifling boredom of the village was transformed by him. He worked long hours but was usually ready to go for a drink and take her out somewhere on a Saturday night. He was clever and brainy and she respected his expertise. She loved his powerful, mud-spattered car with all the drugs and syringes in the back, and hearing about his surgeries and his farm visits. She had never before had such a respectable, steady sort of man in her life. She loved seeing Digby names in the churchyard and hearing Matt talk about the farm when he was a boy and his grandfather farmed the land. She liked the continuity of it, the strength of family ties, the rooted feeling, the sense of belonging. It went totally against her nature, and the life she had always led, but suddenly she found it strangely attractive.

Sex, too, was part of it. She and Matt both had a basic animal need and she had made it clear early on that she was as eager as he was. He was an urgent lover, pressing his mouth down hard on hers, making her lip bleed, forcing her hands out of the way as he struggled with her clothes. They made love everywhere but in a bed. The back of his car, in the barn, in the churchyard, in the pub car park. It seemed in the beginning that their appetite was insatiable. Matt wondered at his luck. At thirty he had missed the boat in terms of the first flush of local girls, most of whom were now married with children, and recently he had not had the time or inclination to start a new relationship. Maeve had dropped into his life like a blessing, and he was delighted by her uncomplicated attitude to sex. They never talked about love, which he would have shied off anyway. Love didn't come into it. Not for the moment anyway.

Whenever Maeve felt bored she had taken to sloping off down to Manor Farm. The first time she had turned up to find that Matt was out, she had stood and shouted by the back door until his father, Commander Digby, had come out of the feed barn to see what all the noise was about.

'Hi,' said Maeve. 'I thought there must be someone in.'

Commander Digby removed his cap and looked at her, saying nothing. He was tall and lanky, like Matt, and dressed in green overalls with the sleeves rolled up to reveal sinewy brown forearms. His bushy grey eyebrows hung over deep-set and startlingly blue eyes. He was still a good-looking man.

'I'm Maeve,' she said.

'Ah,' said the Commander. There was a pause while he considered this information. 'Should I know you?' he asked, reasonably politely.

'Well now,' said Maeve, cheekily, 'how do I answer that? I'd say you'd be missing something if you didn't. I know your son, Matt.'

'Ah,' said Commander Digby again. Something stirred in his memory. Had Matt mentioned a girl? He seemed to think he had.

'Now, aren't you going to ask me in for a cup of tea?' said Maeve, affecting a very Irish accent, which she could turn on and off like a tap. 'It's half past four and I'm sure you could do with one yourself, and in here,' she indicated the supermarket bag she had dangling over the handlebars of her bicycle, 'I have some biscuits and a cake for you.' She smiled coquettishly.

Commander Digby had not been talked to like this in living memory. Feeling quite disconcerted, he mumbled something and pushed open the back door to allow Maeve to enter. Not bothering to remove his mud-splattered boots, he followed her into a back scullery where he washed his hands at a stone sink and dried them on a filthy roller towel. He couldn't remember what sort of state he had left the kitchen in, but at a guess it would be the usual muddle of dirty plates and papers. Since his wife had died fifteen years earlier, things had gone downhill. He supposed he could push this extraordinary girl into the drawing room but he wasn't sure what sort of condition that was in either.

Once inside, Maeve seemed not to notice. She put the kettle on to boil and looked for some mugs. The draining board was piled with them, dirty and left to soak with an inch or two of brownish water in the bottom. 'This is just what me father does,' she said chattily. 'I can never see why he just doesn't wash the thing up and be done with it. Now where's the milk?' David Digby had anticipated this request and had already got a bottle out of the fridge and was sniffing it anxiously. Definitely cheesy.

Maeve poured the water into a brown teapot and sat at the table, pushing away the litter of breakfast and post and other detritus. She cut the Commander a hefty slice of sponge cake and put it on a plate. 'Now there you are,' she said. 'I'll bet you two don't look after yourselves properly.'

Commander Digby gave up the search for a milk jug and sat down opposite. Maeve smiled at him. 'And I'll bet another thing. I bet I'm not the first woman who's been round here trying to seduce you with her baking. Flaunting her iced fancies, I'll be bound.'

The Commander looked startled and then broke into a laugh. 'Well, since you mention it, yes, there have been one or two . . . some rather determined,' he said.

'Well, you don't need to worry,' said Maeve cheerfully. 'I'm not after your body, or your money or your farm. I'm just dying for lack of company. Lady Pamela is watching the racing – or asleep, more like. Jack Dick is grumpy and has just driven me out of the yard, and I'm at such a loose end, I don't know what to do with myself. You don't mind, do you? I won't stay long. Her ladyship will want her own tea soon.'

Commander Digby finished his cake and said, 'May I?' before scoffing another large slice. He watched Maeve from under his brows. Her bright little face and upturned nose and laughing wide mouth appealed to him. She was dressed in a most alarming fashion in a series of V-necked oversized sweaters which seemed to be falling off her shoulders. Underneath, and quite visible, was a tiny, black lace bra. Her mass of wildly curly dark hair was bunched into a knot at the back of her head. The milk was definitely off, he noticed.

'I'm not very sociable,' he said awkwardly, 'but always delighted to see you.'

She seemed to take this as an invitation to prattle on about how she had come to Charlton. A quite extraordinary tale. It was a relief she didn't make any attempt to be interested in the farm. It was so trying, answering inane questions about the herd. Most women seemed to think they should show an interest.

'That's great, then,' said Maeve taking her mug to the cluttered sink and pouring it away. 'I'm not much of a one for clearing up myself, so I'm not offering to do this for you, but I'll leave the cake and the biscuits. Fair exchange? And I'll come again!'

After she'd gone, wobbling away on her bicycle, trying to wave at the same time, David Digby worried that he smelt of cows or worse. He'd spent the morning pulling a heifer out of a ditch. After a bit, he knew, one failed to notice oneself.

Thus encouraged, Maeve took to visiting Manor Farm frequently, letting herself in and out of the back door and putting on the kettle to make tea or coffee. She usually brought a fruitcake or shortbread and Commander Digby looked forward to seeing her and always made her welcome. Maeve, for her part, enjoyed being in a house of men without another woman. It reminded her of the days when she was at home alone with her father, between various of his live-in women. Those had been the best times, when she could rule the roost and be the centre of attention. He spoiled her then, allowed her her own way and treated her like a grown-up companion. No wonder she hated the subsequent interlopers who stole his attention and wanted to impose rules and bedtime and treat her like a child.

Maeve wondered whether she would like to live at Manor Farm. She tried to imagine being satisfied with village life, with the routine of the farm, with the utter predictability of it, with the plodding nature of the local people. She thought of Lady Pamela with her Dior dress and embassy balls and handsome, sophisticated men in white ties and tails. The old lady loved Charlton, it was true, but she had had that other glamorous, fast-moving, thrilling life as well. She had really lived. Maeve knew in her heart that backwater life was not for her and that Charlton could only be a peaceful interlude. Sometimes as she walked back over the fields, stumbling over the ruts and sliding in the mud, she wondered whether she could get Matt to leave, to travel, to find work in a more exciting environment. She had seen television programmes about glamorous vets dealing with exotic animals in Africa. Maybe when she was ready to move on, Matt would come with her. For a while at least.

For the time being she was happy with the change that Charlton represented and although Lady Pamela could be maddening, she got on with her surprisingly well. The worst aspects of the job were the solitude and the long periods of inactivity. She found that the caring, the helping in and out of the bath, the fetching and carrying, the providing of meals and comfort, the companionship, she actually enjoyed and was good at. She was much more patient than she had believed possible and she took pleasure in her role. She had never had to care physically for anyone before. True, she had cooked in chalets and on yachts, but this was different. Lady Pamela relied on her for more or less everything and Maeve enjoyed this relationship. As a child she had been shifted between a variety of slipshod au pairs and nannies and she remembered what it felt like to be ignored or treated with indifference, to have ill-prepared food slapped down on a table and be left to eat alone. She could remember being treated as a boring nuisance, being grumbled about on the telephone, having no interest taken in her little achievements at school, like when she swam her first length of the swimming pool, or got a red star for spelling. She took pleasure now in being a better sort of companion.

Together she and Lady Pamela walked round the autumn garden, Maeve asking questions about the shrubs and plantings. She admired the late roses and asked their names, she was promised the beauty of the spring garden, first white with snowdrops and then thick with tiny yellow daffodils. Lady Pamela struggled to remember Latin names and raked in the past to recall when she had planted the azaleas on the bank or dug out the little pools of the water garden.

Some evenings Maeve dragged out the boxes and albums of photographs. She was less interested in places than she was in people. She sat cross-legged on the floor in her ripped jeans, spreading the photographs around her. 'Who is this? God, a duchess – she certainly looks grand. Is this Sam? Cor, he was good-looking. And this is you in that heavenly dress. You've still got it, haven't you? Dior. Blimey, what a life you've had! What glamour! God, I would have loved it!'

'It wouldn't have suited you for five minutes,' retorted Lady Pamela. 'One had to be frightfully well-behaved in the diplomatic service. Everyone else had all the fun.'

'Hmmm,' said Maeve in an unconvinced tone. Lady Pamela kicked at her with her tiny foot.

After a while, especially after a whisky, Lady Pamela would doze off, waking every now and then with a start. Maeve prowled restlessly around the house, opening cupboard doors, rifling through drawers. In Lady Pamela's room she found what she was looking for, a whole drawer of photographs of a girl, as a baby through toddlerhood, childhood and then as a young adult. This had to be Lizzie, whose image was so conspicuously missing from the masses of photographs downstairs. Maeve held up a studio portrait under the light. She was fair, fine-boned, very pretty. She had been photographed in that odd way with naked shoulders and a string of pearls. She looked, despite this staging, young and fresh and innocent.

What a waste, thought Maeve.

Underneath the photographs were bundles of letters and other packets. Maeve picked up one and read in clear, neat handwriting, 'Darling Mums, It was wonderful to see you yesterday, and a million thanks for the food. We shared the chocolate cake after lights out. It was absolutely scrummy . . .' Maeve put it gently back with the others and replaced the photographs and shut the drawer. She tried to imagine having that sort of relationship with a parent. She had never bothered writing to her own mother after she had come home from prep school and found her dutiful weekly letters, full of information about school food and the weather, opened but clearly unread at the bottom of a pile of bills and circulars. Maeve tried to imagine loving someone and having one's love returned unequivocally. She couldn't. She slid the drawer open again and found a small passport-sized photograph of Lizzie aged about sixteen. She pushed it up her sleeve and closed the drawer.

Lady Pamela knew that she would have to deal with Henry. When she woke at her usual early hour, she lay in bed and listened to the silence of the house. She was so much more mobile these days that going to visit the bathroom took much less time and effort, and she could rely on Maeve to have remembered her morning tea tray. There was now a tin of homemade ginger biscuits as well, and she and Esau enjoyed one each as the first treat of the day. Looking around her room, it was certainly a good deal more untidy than when Mrs Cook had held sway. Maeve left clothes lying over her chair and never bothered to hang things properly or put shoes on trees. Drawers were not neatly shut and often shoved home with edges of clothing caught. She was a ramshackle sort of girl, of that there was no doubt. Mrs Day dusted round the muddle, but Henry would not be impressed by the air of neglect. On the other hand, mused Lady Pamela, she could point out how she had put on weight since Maeve had arrived, and how much more active she had become.

Then there was the money. Although vague about the cost of living, Lady Pamela knew that Maeve's style was not pinchpenny and that expenditure must have rocketed since she had arrived. How long would Henry allow it to go on? And the horse? She felt nervous about the decision she had made on the spur of the moment. She should have consulted Henry. Even Sam said as much. When she had telephoned to tell him, there had been a silence and then he had said, 'Isn't the Irish getting in a bit deep with this? Is it really wise to start something like this at your age? Aren't you getting a bit carried away?' And of course he was right. The rush of adrenaline, the feeling that life was surging around her again had been a heady mix. It made her feel powerful enough to see off the spectre of Bunty and a nursing home. But how could she be sure that Henry would not interpret her decision to put a horse back in training as an act of crackpot irresponsibility and a manifestation of senile dementia? What she must do was to get him down to Charlton and work on him. Without Bunty. Definitely without Bunty.

In the event, Henry had anyway been planning a visit to see his mother. Bunty had flicked through her diary and announced that she did not have a single spare day, but that when they returned from the West Indies after Christmas and the New Year she was intending to go down to Charlton and stay for a few days, arranging various meetings with architects and planners and garden designers. They really could not delay any longer and Henry was to tell his mother so. That very morning she had received a brochure for a new sheltered housing development in Sherborne which looked extremely attractive and might be the answer to the problem of what to do with Lady Pamela. Really, she was too busy to deal with it now, but in the lull of the new year she would give it her full attention.

So Henry drove down to Somerset on his own. His large, expensive car purred along and he listened to Classic FM with the heater keeping the temperature comfortably warm. He felt cocooned from the raw, cold November day outside and all the stresses of his busy life. The bank was the least of his problems. Charlie, their son, was causing him concern. His housemaster had been on the telephone yesterday to say that he had been caught smoking for the second time that term and that a third offence would mean suspension. Bunty was angry with the school for taking this line, saying that all seventeen-year-olds smoked and that the housemaster should get real. She did not seem to take on board that rules had to be obeyed. There had been other incidents, too. Drinking. Being caught out of bounds. He was clearly being as much of a pain at school as he was at home. Henry wished that the school could just deal with it. Punish him, gate him, whatever, but just deal with it and not expect him to come up with any answers. He didn't know why Charlie behaved like this and he didn't know how he could stop him. He had rather supposed that all teenage boys went through this stage. He couldn't say that he had himself. He had been too frightened of his father, and there hadn't been much opportunity for misbehaviour when he had been growing up. The school he

had been sent to was miles from anywhere and the more
ambitious boys had to cycle seven miles to a pub to get drunk
and then wobble home without lights, stopping to be sick in
the ditch. He had never been invited to join them.

He turned off the M3 and on to the A303. The wider
landscape of the chalk downlands opened up, promising clean
air and long views. He flashed past Stonehenge, even today,
in the gloom of winter, encircled by strings of tourists. He
passed a Little Chef and felt hungry. He was supposed to be
having lunch with his mother, but God knows what this girl
would produce. He had a couple of bottles of wine in the back
which would make the food more palatable. Nearly there
now.

It was with no feeling of fondness or nostalgia for a happy
childhood that Henry turned into the village and then into
the drive. He had always known that Elizabeth was the most
loved and when she had died Henry had seen just how little
he could make up for his mother's loss. The serious, shy little
boy who had grown up at Charlton in the shadow of his
younger sister developed into a young man with a keen sense
of his own inadequacy. If in any way he blamed his mother,
he never showed it. Playing the dutiful son was a well-
rehearsed role. Warmth or real feeling did not come into it.

Drawing up outside the house, Henry turned off the ignition and sat for a moment, lost in thought. He was startled to
see his mother appearing round the side of the house,
walking unaided, except for a stick, carrying a basket of
winter flowers and a pair of secateurs in her hand. She raised
the stick in greeting.

'Hello, darling. Good journey? Come on in out of the cold.
The Irish has a fine lunch for us!'

She had, too, thought Henry as he drove away in the dark.
That beef casserole had been delicious, followed by a crisp
sweet apple charlotte with real creamy custard. Henry loved
comforting school food. Bunty was into Pacific Rim at the
moment, which he hoped would pass. His mother certainly
looked far better than the last time he had seen her, and in far
better spirits. The girl had rearranged things quite sensibly,
making the drawing room more comfortable and more cheerful and moving the little dining table into the window. His
mother had made a great fuss about the joy of the new
television and the Racing Channel and he had to admit that it

would be mean to deny her that pleasure if it meant so much to her.

The truth was that she was being looked after much better than he had thought possible and he felt a sense of relief that this was so, and that nothing was required of him personally, other than writing the cheques. There, too, it was his mother's money he was spending. His father had left her well-provided for and her current expenditure, although increased of late, was still hardly denting the income she received. She was unlikely to be able to live at Charlton for very much longer and Henry was generous enough to want her to enjoy it while she could. She was much less trouble than she had been and while things were running smoothly he was inclined to leave well alone.

It was after lunch, when the girl had brought in the coffee, that the subject of the horse had been raised. Henry had not forgotten the horses. He knew exactly the cost of keeping them and had been aware of the monthly trainer's bill for something that he considered to be of as little use as a seaside donkey. It didn't therefore surprise him greatly that his mother had to make a decision about the horse's future. As long as there was sufficient evidence that it might run again he was in favour of bringing it back into training. If it was no use, he thought he could exert enough influence to have it put down. If it came good, it could be sold at the end of the season. Either way, it would be less expensive than allowing it to continue in luxury retirement. If he presented it like this to Bunty, even she might agree. According to the terms of his father's will, the horses were taken care of and any moneys left after their demise was to be donated to the Injured Jockey's Fund, so it would be no skin off Bunty's nose anyway. Henry had tried to alter the terms years ago, but they proved watertight.

Henry might have guessed the little Irish girl was behind all this. She was a pretty little thing with all that wild dark hair. He remembered her neat bum as she bent over to throw a log on the fire and a small breast brushing his arm as she leaned forward to lift a dish from the table. He would like to have sex with a girl like that. Small and quick and dark. He did not find it difficult to imagine her without her clothes. He hoped she would have large brown nipples and a mass of dark hair between her legs. Small and dark and dirty.

Henry decided to drive straight back into London. In his

desk drawer he had one or two telephone numbers which he felt he must urgently call. As he was bypassing Basingstoke, he suddenly remembered the wine. He had only drunk half a bottle and the rest, now he thought about it, seemed to have been spirited away. It was expensive wine too. She was up to every trick, that girl. Henry found this thought rather exciting.

Chapter Seven

Christmas was going to be a major event. Maeve had resolved that if she was going to spend it at Charlton she was also going to enjoy it. She could not remember the last time she had had a traditional Christmas and she was determined to make it a success. In the absence of a proper family, she wanted to be surrounded by her friends.

Henry and Bunty had made their usual arrangements, it seemed, to spend Christmas with their children and another family of old friends in the West Indies. They took the same villa every year. The weather and the food could be relied upon and London in the run-up to Christmas would, as usual, be exhausting. A totally relaxing, switch-off time was what was called for. Bunty would pack a Marks and Spencer Christmas pudding and that was all she would have to think about.

Last year Lady Pamela had been a problem. She had had flu in November and was frail and crotchety. Mrs Cook, anxious not to be stuck with her, had had many telephone calls with Henry trying to find somewhere the old lady could be posted off to for the holiday period. Lady Pamela had, of course, become even more determined not to be moved, saying she could manage perfectly well on her own. Sam, too, had been ill and could not come down to Charlton, and finally Mrs Cook had been bribed to stay for Christmas Day and an agency carer, at great expense, had taken over on Boxing Day until Trish Holmes, a retired nurse who had helped with Bumper, came for her customary two weeks in January. Mrs Cook had heated up two foil trays of turkey dinner from the supermarket and the ungrateful old woman had not touched it. Esau ate it in the end, and then was sick.

It was therefore with much relief that Henry heard from Diana Tripp that Maeve had telephoned to say that she would

115

be happy to stay with Lady Pamela over Christmas on the understanding that she could have two friends to stay and that Henry would meet the extra housekeeping expenses. Henry thought this sounded perfectly reasonable, and when he rang his mother to check that it was something to which she had no objection, in the back of his mind was the thought that he didn't much care if she didn't agree. She would have to put up with it. He thought briefly about the extra cost of lighting and heating and wondered if he could deduct something from Maeve's salary. On second thoughts, he realised it worked out far cheaper than sending his mother into a residential home or organising outside help. No, he would be generous on this occasion. However, he decided it would be wise not to tell Bunty.

In a state of great excitement, Maeve went to sit on the end of Lady Pamela's bed one morning. She was wearing a T-shirt which barely covered her bottom and, Lady Pamela couldn't help noticing, a tiny pair of knickers. For a moment it reminded Lady Pamela of Lizzie. She is so unselfconscious, she thought. At her age I had to be grown-up. I was a mother of two and the wife of a rising diplomat and running a household of twenty.

'Look, Lady P, this is our guest list. What do you think? You and Sam, me and Matt, and his father, Soph and her two, Mohammed and maybe Khaled, and Mr and Mrs Day, who are going to be on their own otherwise. That's ten or eleven. What do you think? We can open up the big dining table and I'll get a whopping turkey and do the whole works. I'll get Soph down here on Friday and she'll help. Christmas is Monday, isn't it? She could bring Sam. Or, perhaps he's more comfortable on the train? The twins would probably be his idea of a nightmare. I'm going to make Christmas puds and mince pies and a Christmas cake. I've found an ancient *Good Housekeeping* in the kitchen which has got all of that old-fashioned stuff in it. And we'll have a tree. Where can we get a tree from? Would Jack Dick know? Jesus, I've forgotten him. We can't have him on his own, so that's another one.'

Lady Pamela watched her excited face and thought, What a child she is. Christmas had long since ceased to be of any interest at all to her. It was more of a nuisance than anything else. In an increasingly shaky hand she wrote out cheques for her grandchildren and sent Henry and Bunty a hamper from Fortnums. Henry dealt with everything else. She wondered whether she could face what Maeve was describing. She supposed that she and Sam could take refuge together. It would be lovely to have Sam.

She wondered where she had put the Christmas catalogues she had been sent from various London stores. She would enjoy choosing gifts for everyone if she was going to have a party. What an extraordinary gathering they would be. What would Bumper have thought! Dining with the cleaner and handyman! He would turn in his grave. This thought rather cheered Lady Pamela. She had always enjoyed shocking Bumper. Certainly, it couldn't be worse than last year with Mrs Cook and her plastic turkey. She would telephone Sam when Maeve had gone and see what he thought.

Sam was faintly worried. 'My dear girl! Can you cope? So many people! Well, yes, I'd love to come. I was hoping I would be asked. You know, the Irish really can cook and that is a great attraction. One has so few pleasures left. Now, as to all these other people, I think it would be wise to make it absolutely clear when you expect them to depart. Do not, on any account, allow it to be open-ended, or you will still have them at New Year. People have no manners nowadays. They have no sense of when they should leave. One practically has to have them evicted.'

Lady Pamela had become rather deaf and her telephone conversations were held at full concert pitch, so that Maeve, passing on the landing, heard most of this exchange. She put her head round the door. 'Don't worry, Lady P, only four days at the most. I promise. I'll get rid of them all on Boxing Day. I want to go racing with Matt. He's course vet at Wincanton, so we get in free.' She twinkled mischievously. 'Now, how do you think I knew what you were talking about?'

The following days were filled with preparations. Maeve made invitations decorated with the corniest of robins and holly and sent them to the guests. She ordered turkey and ham, chipolata sausages and streaky bacon from the butcher. She made puddings and a cake and mince pies and the house filled with the delicious scent of spices and baking. She made ice cream with real vanilla pods and thick yellow cream from the dairy farm in South Charlton. She made a huge pheasant casserole for Christmas Eve and a shepherd's pie for the deep freeze. The kitchen was littered with crossed out shopping lists and Mrs Day arrived to a mound of washing up every morning. She did not mind because she was looking forward to Christmas Day. She had enjoyed telling her friends that she and Frank had been invited to spend the day at Lady Pamela's, and not to do the washing up either. Better than the British Legion Christmas Social, which was the alternative. Frank was a bit worried that he wouldn't get his stout to drink, but Maeve had already enquired what was his tipple and had added it to her list for the off-licence.

Maeve then telephoned Diana Tripp, who had just rolled back from an office Christmas lunch for which employees were being billed £25 a head. 'Don't worry about the accounts,' Mrs Tripp told her. 'Send them to me and I'll deal with them. Do you know how much their holiday costs? Well, I do, because I've just paid the cheque for it. You give the old girl a good time. They can afford it.'

Maeve was struck with a sudden thought. 'Hey, what are you doing for Christmas, matey? How about you coming down to join us? It would be such a blast!'

Mrs Tripp felt choked. She had drunk too much and had a splitting headache, and the thought of Christmas, as usual, alone with her widowed mother and the television and a pale roll of reformed turkey breast, made her want to cry.

'We couldn't do that,' she said. 'We don't know anyone, and Mother's eighty-two and deaf as a post.'

'Doesn't matter. Half of us are eighty. We go from eighty-four down to two. Go on. More the merrier. Really, I mean it.'

And she really did, Mrs Tripp could tell. She put down the telephone and had a little sniff and a chocolate biscuit from her drawer. They wouldn't go, of course. Mother wouldn't hear of it, but it was a lovely thought.

In all the years she had worked for Henry he had never once asked her how she spent Christmas.

The weather conspired against Maeve. While she wanted it to snow – all deep and crisp and even – it remained warm and wet and grey. Some days it hardly seemed to get light at all. She struggled indoors with branches of berry-bedecked holly which Jack had cut for her and stuck sprigs wherever she could. The dark, glistening green and the drops of scarlet lent the rooms immediate festive cheerfulness. She bought a bunch of mistletoe in the town and nailed it up in the hall. Jack had promised to bring her a tree nearer the time and she thought that she and Sophie could decorate it on Christmas

Eve. Lady Pamela thought there were some old decorations somewhere and they could look for them later.

When Maeve took the short cut to the village to see Matt, she foundered through mud so thick that it sucked Lady Pamela's old rubber boots off her feet. I couldn't stand this, she thought. If this was my life and this was all I'd got, this mud and wet, I'd go raving mad. How can people put up with it? She longed to feel pavement beneath her feet and see the winter sky aglow with lights. She longed for the sound of traffic and canned music and to feel the jostle of shoppers on crowded pavements. She missed the warm smell of beer and cigarettes when a pub door was pushed open and the beckoning room full of loud voices and music and raucous laughter. She missed the raking, lascivious looks of men on the loose and the sort of evenings that could lead anywhere. And here she was, galumphing along a country track with half a cold shepherd's pie in a plastic bag and one of Jack Dick's cabbages. I'm like something out of Thomas Hardy, she thought, only without the ravishing on Willoughby Chase to look forward to. Unfortunately.

Recently Matt had been very busy and was hardly ever in. Two of his partners had flu and he was working twice as hard to cover call-outs in his part of the practice. When he came to see Maeve in the evening he often went straight to sleep in the kitchen armchair, the sleeves of his shirt and sweater still rolled up to reveal reddened forearms, the glass of whisky she had poured him clutched in his hand. It was unhealthy weather, he said. Mud fever and foot rot were rampant. Calves born in the reeking indoor yards were coming down with infections; pneumonia was rife. To Maeve, it seemed the country was awash with mud and disease. If it hadn't been for Christmas she would have sunk into gloom. As it was, she kept everybody's spirits up.

This winter evening as she walked up the path to Manor Farm she saw, lit up like a tableau in the living-room window, Commander Digby perched on his shooting stick in front of the television, watching the News. Matt had told her that if he sat on the sofa or anything more comfortable, he went to sleep and missed what he wanted to watch. The carpet was full of little tufted holes.

Maeve went round to the back door and crept in. Matt was asleep in the kitchen on the battered old leather sofa. A plate with two dried-up sausages was plonked atop a pile of

Farmers Weekly magazines on the floor beside him. Maeve felt a rush of impatience. It seemed to her that Matt was succumbing to the slowness of this place, that his blood moved through his veins as sluggishly as her feet through the mud. He was too young to doze his way through life. She stood above him and shook his arm. He grunted and then opened his eyes. She smiled at him, ferociously, and watched his coming awake reactions, the moment of wondering where he was, of putting two and two together. He sat up scratching his head. His shirt was undone, revealing his smooth belly and the fine hairs running in a slender dark line down from his navel. Maeve sat beside him and ran her finger down his chest.

'Heh!' she said. 'Wake up!'

'I didn't realise I'd fallen asleep,' said Matt, looking confused. 'What time is it? Had I promised to see you, or something?'

'No. I just came round. On the off chance.' Maeve was deliberately provoking. 'You're not doing anything, so let's go out. Let's go to a night club somewhere. Come on! Have a night out.'

'Are you joking?' said Matt. 'I've been up since six. I got home at seven this evening. I'm not going anywhere.'

'Too right!' said Maeve, crossly. 'You've said it. Look at you! The living dead.'

'Maeve!' Matt protested. 'That's not fair. I'm absolutely rushed off my feet at work. I've had a bloody awful day. No time for lunch. One call out after another. You, on the other hand, don't have enough to do. That's what the trouble is.'

'What do you mean? It's exhausting looking after a cross old lady. And depressing for someone my age. That's why I need a bit of life.' She sat down next to him on the sofa and draped her legs across his lap. 'And I need sex,' she added wickedly.

Matt pushed her legs off and stood up to put the kettle on the Aga. 'It's always about what you need,' he said. 'What about me? Are you at all interested in what I need?'

'You don't have needs,' said Maeve hotly. 'Just "don't wants". You don't want this, you don't want that. Everything negative.'

'I'm sorry if that's how it seems,' said Matt grimly with his back to her, staring at the kettle, noticing how dirty it was, how its sides were smeared with a sort of black grease. When his mother had been alive, he thought he remembered that it had shone. 'Today I had to shoot two heifers which I couldn't calve. I then saw a herd where all the new calves have rotavirus-induced diarrhoea because the farmer could not afford to vaccinate the mothers. It's touch and go whether any of them will survive. I suppose that's why I don't seem very cheerful. I'm bloody tired too.'

Maeve felt a pang of remorse. She picked up the plate with the sausages on it. 'Good supper, though?' she asked.

Matt turned and couldn't help smiling. He caught her wrist. She put down the plate and they kissed. She moved his hair out of his eyes. I love his lean, bony face, she thought. She liked his wide mouth and his straight white teeth and the rather deepset dark eyes, ringed now with shadows.

Her mood softened. 'Sorry,' she said. 'For making you cross. You're right. I'm bored. Not enough to think about stuck there at Charlton. Lady P's grumpy at the moment. She gets these moods. I'll catch it when I get back – she tries to stop me going out when she's feeling sorry for herself. "Sod it," I say. "You don't own me." Here, I've brought you and your dad a shepherd's pie. Half a one, anyway. And a cabbage. Could you eat it now?'

Matt looked interested and took a fork out of a drawer and a bottle of Worcester sauce from the larder. He sat down at the kitchen table and ate the pie as it was, cold out of the dish. Maeve looked round for something to drink.

'Dad's got the whisky in the drawing room,' said Matt. 'I don't think we've got anything else.'

'Well, I won't disturb him,' said Maeve. 'Does he go to sleep on that shooting stick?' She laughed. 'You two are a right pair of eccentric old bachelors, aren't you? Do you realise how dotty you both are?'

'We're ordinary country people, that's all,' said Matt, wiping his mouth. 'God! That was good. Here, come and sit on the sofa with me. The kitchen's the only warm place in this house.'

Maeve made a pot of tea and they sat companionably, her head on his shoulder, her feet tucked up beneath her. Matt stroked her hair – her 'bindweed hair', he called it – twisting the strands round his fingers and watching them spring back into curls like little coils when he released them.

'This is peaceful,' he said. 'Maeve, it's so nice when you're quiet and relaxed and not bitching about something.'

121

Hmm, thought Maeve. Nice for you, maybe, but not for me, matey. I'd suffocate if it was like this every night. It would kill me.

Later Matt drove her back to Charlton and she found Lady Pamela asleep in her chair, snoring gently, mouth open. The news she was sleeping through was about Northern Ireland and the latest shooting in defiance of the precarious peace. The next item concerned the widespread abuse of children in local authority homes.

If it had not been for Christmas, Maeve would have been up and off, to a warm and sunny country where children were loved and cherished and old people sat outside their houses in the evenings shouting greetings to those who passed by, and life bubbled like a spring. Christmas kept her going.

Sophie was also buoyed up at the prospect. Initially, her parents had been concerned when she told them she was not joining them as they had expected. As they got used to the idea they wondered if, for once, it might not be a pleasant change to have a grown-up Christmas, on their own and without any of the usual fuss and extra work. They realised that Sophie was excited and happy and were glad that she was spending the holiday with friends of her own age, where the twins were also welcome.

Fergus, Sophie discovered, was going away skiing with friends, and she surprised herself by not caring much or wondering how he could afford it. He, too, was surprised and pleased that, when he brought round presents for the children, Sophie was calm and rational and he got away without the tearful scene he had anticipated. As a rule he dreaded going to her flat and always came away ridden with guilt and angry that she made him feel like that. She had had her hair cut into a modern shorter shape, all spiky and odd lengths. It suited her, he thought, made her look less flat and sort of dragged down. She was looking rather pretty. He wondered if she had got a man and also wondered, as he walked to the Tube station, whether he did not detect in himself the smallest pang of possessive jealousy? Would she be in bed how she had been with him? Not in the what-went-where sense, but the way she used to whimper with desire and shout when she came? The way she always felt hungry afterwards and got up to bring toast or biscuits back to eat in bed? Fergus was growing rather tired of his blonde banker, who was becoming too demanding and bossy, and as a consequence his feelings for Sophie were a little fonder and he was able to remember how he had once felt about her. After their separation and then their divorce he had denied the integrity of their early relationship. It had been a necessary part of the liberating process he had had to go through. It was safe now to acknowledge that he once had, indeed, loved her.

Sophie's parents had wisely given her money for the twins, rather than toys, and she pushed them down to Baby Gap and bought them fleecy clothes for the country, and bright knitted hats and gloves. Flora would not wear her hat and kept throwing it off onto the pavement, but Freddy loved his and pulled it down over his face to make Sophie and Flora laugh. She also bought them shiny yellow rubber boots. She couldn't think what to get everybody else. She spent ages choosing Maeve a lovely soft leather bag with a beaded trim, like a fashionable Navaho Indian might have knocked up. She bought Lady Pamela a large photograph album for all her future pictures of Irish Dancer. The men were so difficult. She got Commander Digby a box of Turkish Delight, Matt some thermal gloves, Jack a scarf, Frank a torch, Mrs Day some delicious orange-smelling bath oil. Mohammed's gift was a complete blank. What could she give someone who meant to her what he did?

Sophie had been surprised to find what a difference her encounter with Mohammed had made to her. He had restored her sense of who she was, as distinct from being the mother of the twins. Her brain seemed to have stirred into life beneath the grey sludge of permanent tiredness and depression. He had made her feel alive again. Sometimes she wondered what it said about her that she had been so altered at discovering a young man was sexually attracted to her. Was it reprehensible that the reawakening of sexual desire, to feel desirable again, had jolted her back to life? Did it mean that she was wholly vain, shallow, incomplete without the approval of a man? Oh blow it, she thought, for whatever reason, it worked, and God! She was grateful. Her body seemed replenished. She felt healthy and strong again. She enjoyed looking at herself, catching glimpses in shop windows of her tall figure, her new hair. One evening as she sat on the sofa drying her hair, after the twins were in bed, she held up her hand mirror and studied her face, the new network of fine lines, the loss of youthful bloom, girlish looks all gone. Suddenly it was like looking at a stranger. Then she tried smiling and laughing at her reflection, noticing the dramatic effect on her face, the widening and lifting, the softening of mouth and eyes. I must do it more often, she thought. When I look animated, I am an attractive woman. From then on, she deliberately held the eyes of men who looked at her, and smiled, and, with pleasure, noted the effect this had. For the first time for ages she liked herself.

In the end, she bought Mohammed a sweater.

There was a query from Maeve about whether Sophie could collect Sam and bring him down to Charlton with her, and then a second call to say that he had changed his mind and was going by train after all, and then Mohammed telephoned her to say that he now knew he had to work until the Saturday before Christmas and had to be back at work on the Wednesday after. He planned to travel down to Charlton by train on Sunday morning. He still did not know what Khaled was planning to do. His voice was warm and kind as he expressed concern about her travelling alone, and Sophie felt cared for and secure in his affection.

She rose early on Friday and was ready to leave London as soon as she judged the morning rush hour would have thinned. It was raining and the street outside glistened with a greasy film; the opposite houses were purple against the ugly orange-lit sky. The twins were over-excited, Freddy rather fractious and tearful and Flora bossily interfering with the packing – wanting a different coloured mug, different cereal, a different choice of toys. She was much further advanced with her talking than Freddy and was now putting three-or four-word sentences together. The main thrust of her energy and her newly acquired vocabulary seemed to be directed towards ordering the world to her satisfaction.

After Christmas the twins were starting at a playgroup for two mornings a week. Sophie found it hard to believe that they were about to climb aboard the system which would sweep them along until they were young adults. It seemed to underline their growing up and their growing away from her. The cosy life in which the three of them had been cocooned was now only temporary. Very soon they would all be pitched out to face the world.

She realised now how much she had dreaded this change.

Other mothers seemed to welcome this first step towards independence but to her it had loomed like an approaching rain cloud. She had found herself pretending to her mother that the highly prized places at the playgroup marked a jumping-off point, a chance to get her life moving forward again, while all the time she feared it. All it would do, she had reflected sadly, would be to highlight that she had no life. There was also the attention the twins received, just because they were twins, and then the inevitable questions and the revelation that she was a single mother. She felt she wore that status as if it were branded on her forehead, or like a thief with the stump of a severed hand. She could imagine the sympathetic faces of the other mothers gathered round the school gate, singling her out, whispering explanations, when what she wanted more than anything else was to be part of a proper family, not a lopsided, limping, fatherless affair.

But lately – since Mohammed, in fact – she had felt different, more confident, more buoyant, less apologetic. It wasn't her fault, she reminded herself, that Fergus had left. She cared less what other people might think and was more hopeful for her future.

Now, as she drove out of London with the children singing to each other in the back of her car, she was glad that things were as they were, that she was going to spend Christmas with Maeve, that she felt whole again and not a broken half of a failed marriage. She smiled at herself in the driver's mirror. It's going to be all right, she thought. I can look the future in the face. I will survive.

Sam, too, was looking forward to Christmas. The last few years he had been alone in London. He had attended midnight Mass at his local church and then had lunch on Christmas Day with some old friends who lived in comfortable splendour in Kensington. For three old people it seemed pointless and rather obscene to exchange expensive, unwanted presents and eat and drink too much. The prospect of a proper country Christmas with his dearest living friend was an altogether more attractive proposition, and he liked the idea of Maeve's oddball friends joining them. And there would be children. For Sam, who loved children and had been denied fatherhood, this was a special bonus.

He took his velvet smoking jacket down to the dry-cleaner

and went by bus to Knightsbridge to buy some pretty Christmas tree ornaments and a box of crackers. The shops were crowded and hot and outside the light was already fading, although it was still a drizzly early afternoon. The shop windows threw stained-glass colours onto the wet pavements and the sound of carols blared from within. Sam supposed he would have to think about presents for everyone. He had already chosen a beautiful shawl affair for Lady Pamela in a fine cobwebby design and knitted in the colours of a Scottish hillside. It was so fragile that it folded into a tiny silk envelope. He hoped she wouldn't think it too old-ladyish and intended to tell her he had imagined her young and beautiful, wearing it over her naked shoulders and across her lovely breasts, with a rosy nipple poking through the soft wool tracery. A naughty thought for an old man, but he had loved her completely and could remember exactly the sexual arousal she had evoked. In a way it was a relief to be old and past all that agony and yearning – but the memories of love-making were as fresh as if it had all been yesterday.

It was amusing that young people felt they had a monopoly on sex, that it was invented by and for them alone. He could imagine the Irish in bed. In fact he had had a girlfriend not at all unlike her – tiny, with little upturned breasts, a handspan waist and a feminine little bottom. She had been a vigorous and demanding lover, with sharp little teeth and a temper to match. No wonder the young vet, whatever his name was, was so smitten by Maeve. It was pure sex, he would have thought, driven entirely by lust – and nothing wrong with that. But it did not match up to what he and Pammy had shared, that rare and potent mix of deep love and friendship and mutual physical desire. Their love had sustained them for nearly all their adult lives and would see them out. Lust, on the other hand, was rarely enduring and could be easily transferred from one object of desire to another. He remembered how, for him, Pammy lit up a room by her presence, how the sound of her voice could send shivers down his spine, how a glimpse of her at a distance could send a jolt through him like an electrical charge. She wasn't everybody's cup of tea. Of course, he knew that. One did not love with one's eyes shut. Yet her faults were as dear to him, in a way, as her virtues.

Caught up in the throngs of London Christmas shoppers, Sam was jostled off the pavement. His mind was far away. He had so many enduring memories and sometimes they seemed more real and to have more substance than what was going on around him. A van driver swerved and hooted. 'Watch where you're going, yer stupid old git!' shouted the young man, leaning across the wheel and gesticulating wildly. Sam hurriedly tried to remount the kerb and, tripping backwards, fell heavily amongst the carrier bags and the feet of the Christmas shoppers.

If Maeve had more understanding she would have seen that the run-up to Christmas was a tough time for Matt. Not only was the practice under strain because of illness, but his father was going through another period of depression. Farming, and particularly beef farming, had been hard hit by a variety of factors and every evening Commander Digby would sit with his accounts spread on the dining-room table, sunk in gloom. His suckler herd was worth less every day, while costs remained the same, or were rising. There was no further room for economies to be made. Already he and Matt did virtually all the work. Bert, the cowman, now well over seventy, was more of a hindrance than a help, but he had to remain in his cottage. It would be unthinkable to evict him – he had lived there all his life. Anyway they could not afford to pay the wages of a younger man. It seemed to David Digby that Bert had lost his nerve with the stock. Twice recently he had been knocked over by a cow with calf, and was now understandably reluctant to go in among the beasts. He could be used as a sort of bollard, to fill a gap and stop animals turning the wrong way, and he could drive the tractor and help with strawing down the yards, but that was about all.

In addition, the buildings needed some investment. There was no electricity in the bottom yard, which made calving down there very difficult, and the roof needed attention. The fact that the byre was a listed building did not help. More paperwork and applications for grants might elicit some funding, but the bulk of the expensive pantiling would have to be met by the farm. At the moment there was no income to cover such expenses. They were losing money every month. Matt worked for nothing and only charged for the drugs he used, and even so the situation was dire. Last week the prices at Frome market were the lowest recorded for years, and yet the calves they were producing were as good as ever. He could stare at his paperwork as long as he liked, but it did not alter the fact that he was going broke. The bank would not increase the farm's overdraft; a few more months and a decision would have to be made. Things could not go on as they were.

Matt did what he could. He had some ideas about the direction the farm could go – a smaller herd, diversification into holiday cottages, subletting to a livery business – but found that his father turned an unresponsive countenance and a deaf ear to anything he suggested. Matt was willing to work on the farm whenever he had a free moment, but in no way was he allowed to feel like a partner or as if he could have an input into decision making. When things were bad his father simply shut him out, retreating into silence and bad temper. It was as if an admission of the true state of the business would be to reveal a personal failure, which at all costs must be denied. Matt felt trapped in an impossible situation.

Watching his father limp about the yards, he saw an old man who could no longer manage the heaviest of the work. An unspoken decision had been reached where the most difficult jobs, particularly the stock handling, were left to Matt. When he asked about market prices, he knew they were losing money and he felt that he was aiding and abetting in a mutual deception – that this way of life was sustainable and they could continue as they always had. Sooner or later, he knew that he would have to blow the whistle. Quite what that would mean he did not know. What would his father be without the farm?

Maeve had also become a worry. Matt had simply not had time to spend with her and she was often irritated by what she interpreted as his lack of effort and interest.

'Are you telling me that you just can't tell them, your partners, and that practice receptionist person who's always bleeping you, that you're not available this weekend?' she would say. 'For God's sake, you've got to have some life of your own. You didn't spend all those years qualifying to be pushed around, did you? Christ! You're so bloody meek and accepting.'

'For God's sake, Maeve, meekness has nothing to do with it. I am a junior partner and we work on a rota. It's true I probably get more of the unsociable call-outs than the others, but that's how it is in any practice. The one at the bottom always gets shat on.'

Sometimes, when they did meet, he was too tired to take

her somewhere noisy and bright, to the lights and clamour she longed for. Sometimes he was too tired even for sex, and Maeve, as Sam had guessed, was not a patient lover. Matt felt torn. He was fond of Maeve and loved her company and having a girlfriend had filled a need that he only now realised was like an aching void in his life. But they were not really compatible. They both knew that. Her lack of interest in the country, her longing for excitement, for clubs and dancing, set them worlds apart. That was it, exactly, worlds apart. She would never fit easily or happily into life in Somerset and he could not imagine living anywhere else. Well, of course, that wasn't strictly true, there were lots of places he could live, but all, of necessity, in the country, which she hated.

However, he had got a week off between Christmas and New Year and was really looking forward to going to Charlton on Christmas Day. It would save him from another tortured Christmas at his aunt's, with weak, warm gins before lunch, the Queen's Speech afterwards and a lot of constipated conversation in between. He was glad that Maeve had asked him and glad that her friend, Sophie, was going to be there too. Female company was what he and his father craved, he realised.

His father seemed quite agreeable as well, although he had expressed surprise at being included. Maeve had kissed him on the cheek and said he was the man she most wanted to sit beside her, that she always loved a sailor, and he was utterly charmed. He had even been into Sherborne and bought her a Christmas present, standing awkwardly just inside the door of the shop while they wrapped it up, like a large, nervous horse about to bolt. He had chosen her a wicker basket filled with God knows what lotions and bath oils. It came from a shop which smelled like a tart's boudoir manned by two terrifying women with gleaming lips and nails, but he hoped she'd like it. He had thought about getting something for Lady Pamela, or Matt, but the shops and the people overwhelmed him and he thought he would call it a day. It had been years since he had been called upon to do any shopping. He was happier on the telephone, ordering the cow nuts.

Despite Maeve's efforts there were some things she could not control. The news about Sam's broken wrist was the first calamity. Lady Pamela seethed with fury when she heard that he had had it X-rayed and set in A&E and was discharged the

129

same night to go back to an empty flat.

'What has happened to this country? How old people and children are treated is a measure of how civilised a country is. Sam's treatment is brutish, barbarian, totally uncaring. It is a disgrace. What can I do? Who can I telephone? Damn it that Henry has gone away already. He could have got on to Lord Melton . . .'

'I don't think anything like that helps any more, you know,' said Maeve. 'The world's changed. Doesn't Sam have anyone who could look after him? No relations anywhere?'

'They all live in South Africa, or France. He is all alone, which is why he needs me. How can I get to London?'

'Well, you can't, matey, that's for sure,' said Maeve. She refrained from asking what help Lady Pamela thought she would be, anyway. 'I know,' she said, jumping up. 'Let's telephone Mohammed. I bet he would go round and look after him. School has broken up so he isn't doing his cleaning job this week.'

Lady Pamela tried to think of objections but was too distressed. Maeve had a hurried telephone conversation which she could not grasp and then said, 'That's fixed. He's delighted to help. What he's going to do is telephone Sam when I ring back with his number and then he'll go round and see to him this morning, sort him out, and then go off to work this evening. He can do that every day, and then – listen to this, this is brilliant – his friend, Khaled, is a taxi driver and he'll bring them all down here on Saturday in his car. Sam would pay the petrol, wouldn't he?'

It was all moving too fast for Lady Pamela who was still very distressed by the sound of Sam's weak voice on the telephone. She was filled with a terrible fear that she might lose him, that he was going to slip away from her. She did not want to be left. Death itself held no fear for her, but loneliness did.

'You'll have to do it,' she said, rather crossly. 'I don't know what you mean. I can't cope with all this . . . Mohammed and whatshisname. You'll have to do it. Why are they coming here, anyway?'

'Christmas, matey. It's Christmas!' said Maeve, dialling Sam's number.

When Sophie drew up at Charlton on Friday afternoon, she was clearly in a state of agitation. She got out of the car and said to Maeve, who had run out from the kitchen to greet her, 'Freddy's not well. I first noticed in the car. I didn't know what to do. I nearly went back, but I'd got so far. Now I think I should have done. What about Lady Pamela and Sam? They don't want to catch something from him at their age. Look, poor little chap. He cried most of the way and I've dosed him up with Calpol and he's fast asleep now.'

Maeve peered into the back of the car. Freddy's chin was slumped on his chest. His face was scarlet and wet with tears. His breathing was shallow and noisy.

'OK, babe. Keep calm. Let's get Flora in and everything out of the car. Leave him there if he's asleep. We can call the doctor if he's really ill.'

However, the moment they unpacked Flora, Freddy woke and started to scream again. Sophie lifted him out of his seat and he buried his face into her shoulder, crying miserably. They carried him into the kitchen and tried to make him have a drink. He seized the cup with both hands and drank a noisy mouthful, and was then sick. Flora started to cry in sympathy.

'Look. You shut it, matey!' Maeve told her. 'You're in charge now, you know. This is a crisis. We need a big girl, not a crying baby.'

'Me not baby,' said Flora crossly.

'Well, I don't know about that. Now you pick up your teddy and take Freddy's squirrel. What's he called? Oh, Squirrel. That's original. We'll go and show them where they are going to sleep, OK?'

Sophie wiped poor Freddy's mouth and face and pulled his arms out of his jacket. She could feel his little body burning through his clothes. He was obviously running a very high temperature. She thought of meningitis, and then remembered Lizzie. Oh God! She wished she had turned round and driven back to London. Better to have a sick child at home, even if it meant a lonely Christmas. She pulled off Freddy's T-shirt and was astonished to find his little body covered in red spots.

'My God! Maeve! Quick! Come and look at this!'

It was Lady Pamela who came into the kitchen, walking quite briskly on her stick.

'Sophie, my dear. Whatever is the matter? Oh! Chicken-pox, poor lamb. Calamine lotion when it starts to itch. Plenty to drink. He'll be all right. Little ones like Freddy don't get it too badly. It's me and Sam who could get shingles, of course.'

'I'm going home,' said Sophie. 'I can't bear to think we might infect you all, and shingles is ghastly.'

'Don't be absurd. Put the little chap to bed and when he's asleep come down and have a stiff drink. My dear, it's lovely to see you all.' She pecked Sophie's cheek. 'You've heard about poor Sam? His Christmas shopping injury? Do you know that Maeve has organised a car for him with dear Mohammed in attendance? They're arriving tomorrow. I can't tell you the relief that Sam is all right and that it wasn't a hip. Hips are very often the end at our age, you know, and he was so looking forward to Christmas. Maeve's cooking, more than anything. Now take poor Freddy up to bed. He's not itching yet, is he? That will come later, when he feels better, as far as I can remember. Yes, I know it's a bore, Sophie darling, but it's not the end of the world.'

There was a bang on the kitchen door and Matt stuck his head round.

'Matthew, you've had chickenpox, haven't you?' asked Lady Pamela. 'Poor Freddy here has got it for Christmas.'

'Jesus. I think I've had the lot. Cow pox and everything,' said Matt, coming in. 'Hi Sophs!' and he kissed her warmly. 'Where's Maeve?'

'She's upstairs being organised by Flora,' said Sophie. She turned to Lady Pamela. 'Thank you so much for being so welcoming. I mean, we turn up here with the plague, and you take it all completely in your stride. Thank you so much.'

Matt looked at her. She's a nice girl, he thought. A really nice girl. She looked rather prettier than usual, and there was something affecting about the sight of a young mother with her little boy's face buried in her shoulder while she gently stroked his head. He smiled at her across the kitchen, and she smiled back, her face lit up, her eyes warm. Matt felt a real surge of what the season was supposed to be about – goodwill to men, wasn't it? And women.

'Don't be silly,' said Lady Pamela tartly. 'Bumper and I lived abroad for so long that one got used to having one's arrangements turned upside down by typhoons and military coups and so on. Chickenpox hardly registers on the scale of inconveniences. Now do take him up and put him to bed, poor sweet.'

Sophie stood up and went to the door. Matt followed her.

'Is there anything I can bring upstairs?'

'Our stuff is dumped in the hall. Thank you.' And off they trooped.

Lady Pamela sat down on a kitchen chair. Goodness, she thought. Either she was watching too much sex on television or there was something very potent in the air between those two. How she had smiled at him. How he had responded.

She looked round the kitchen, which was a complete shambles as usual. However, she knew Maeve would have some delicious meal under way. There was no point in making a fuss about the filthy floor or the table upon which one could not have found the space to put down a tea-cup. What did it matter as long as Sam was all right and that little boy was going to have a restless night or two but was going to live to enjoy his third Christmas? She heard the sound of feet upstairs – Flora made an astonishing amount of noise for a little scrap – and voices. How different it made the house feel to have young life coursing through it again. She peered at the kitchen clock. It was five twenty. She wondered if it was permissible to pour herself a whisky.

Sophie finally got Freddy settled and asleep, and Flora had her supper and agreed to go to bed as long as various lights were left on and Esau was on the end of her bed and there was the correct arrangement of soft toys around her and Sophie and Matt and Maeve all kissed her according to a strict protocol she imposed, and Matt tickled her until she screamed.

'She's an appalling flirt,' Sophie said to Matt in the kitchen as they nursed gin and tonics. 'Have you noticed? I wonder if it's because Fergus left us. I mean, do you think Flora subconsciously tries to ingratiate herself with men?'

'Shut up, Sophie!' said Maeve. 'None of us want to wonder about Fergus, OK? Or the effect he has had on you, his children, the stockmarket, the pound, the weather, the environment or anything else.'

'Oops! Sorry,' said Sophie, pulling a face at Matt.

Matt looked over his shoulder at Maeve, who was yanking something out of the oven. 'Come on, Maeve. It was quite an interesting question. Flora *is* a flirt. But I think all little girls are, actually. Certainly my sister's two are. They're always asking me to marry them. I live in fear of the social services overhearing them.' He got up to get them all another drink and Sophie offered to set the table.

133

'It's only us four,' said Maeve. 'Let's have our supper on our knees. It's *The Bill* on the telly. Lady P won't want to miss that. It's a double Christmas programme. Twice the vice to mark the occasion of the birth of Our Lord.' She was mashing potatoes in a saucepan on the Aga. Sophie got up anyway and began to clear the table and stack the washing machine. 'Can't stop, can you, Soph?'

'Well. This is one thing I can do – be a scullery maid. You've done so much. Thank you for getting our rooms all ready.' She put her arms round Maeve from behind. 'Thanks for everything. You really are a friend.'

'Look at us two lezzies, Matt!' called Maeve, making a joke of it, and turning in Sophie's arms to hug her back, still holding the potato masher in her hand.

'Oh God,' said Matt coming back with the gin. 'I think that's one of my fantasies!'

'What? Three in a bed? Sex with two lesbians?'

'No. Sex with mashed potato.'

They had a happy evening. Matt lit the fire and Maeve produced a delicious supper of pork and beans and French bread to mop up the juices, followed by a sharp chicory salad. Sophie went up and down stairs countless times to either a crying Freddy or a naughty Flora. Lady Pamela dozed until *The Bill*, and then turfed them all out so that she could watch it in peace and at full volume. They regrouped in the kitchen where Maeve tried to make Matt take them out for a drink.

'There's no way I can go, Maeve,' said Sophie. 'I can't possibly leave Freddy. You two go.'

'Come on, Matt. Just a quick one. I'm fucking sick of this kitchen.'

'OK,' said Matt unwillingly. 'I'd rather stay here, but if you really want to. Are you sure you don't mind, Soph?'

'Not a bit. I'll help Lady P to bed. I know her routine, and then I'll have an early night too.' She was glad to allow Maeve a bit of freedom.

As it turned out Matt did not want to drive far and so he and Maeve went to the nearest public house in South Charlton. For once the bar was full and lively and the fire was burning brightly in the grate. As Matt ducked under the mistletoe pinned over the door there was a cheer from the regular drinkers, and when he turned and caught Maeve by the arms and lifted her off her feet to kiss her on the mouth, the noise grew. He had only just put her down and turned to the crowded bar to catch the barmaid's eye when Rob, who had been drinking steadily all the evening, emerged out of the crowd and, seeing the opportunity, caught Maeve himself. Wondering what the increased roar and the interest in something happening behind him was, Matt turned and saw Maeve with her legs wrapped round Rob, snogging him enthusiastically. He made a good-natured gesture and found a bar stool to rest his bottom on, his back turned. A moment later, Maeve was snuggling against his arm, her face flushed and excited.

'You didn't mind, matey?'

'It's Christmas, isn't it?' Matt smiled affectionately, but it felt as if a wedge of ice had been driven into his heart.

The next morning Sophie found Maeve up bright and early and whistling cheerfully in the kitchen.

'God! Is that the time? I was up with Freddy at five this morning and I must have gone back to sleep.'

'How is he? I'm just doing Lady P's breakfast. Do you want me to make some toast for the children?'

'Flora will have some. I don't know about Freddy. I'm just going to grab a cup of tea and then I'll go and get Flora up. Freddy's still asleep. He had a rotten night.'

'And so did you. God! Who'd have children?' Maeve slammed some more toast in the toaster and as the kettle boiled she filled a cafetière with water.

A thrown-together breakfast tray lay on the table. Sophie tidied it up and put a spoon on for the marmalade. She made herself a cup of tea with a tea bag and as she was looking in the fridge for the milk, she said to Maeve, 'Did you have a nice time with Matt? I must say he is unbelievably nice. I'm really happy for you.'

'Yeah, it was fine,' said Maeve, 'but actually I've got some quite exciting plans. You know I've got a holiday due after Christmas? Lady Pamela always had this arrangement with a carer who she gets on well with – a retired nurse who is keen on the garden, I gather. She always takes over at the beginning of January for two weeks. I thought I'd go to France to where I used to be a chalet girl. You remember me telling you about Pierre? He managed one of the ski resorts out there. I telephoned him a few days ago and he sounded really pleased. He's got somewhere I can stay and then I found a really cheap flight, and so I'm off on the day after Boxing Day. Can't wait.'

'Is Matt going?'

'Are you joking? I couldn't get Matt away from his bloody cows. No. I'm going on me own, matey.'

Sophie stirred her tea, considering. 'Will Matt mind?' she asked. She should have known better.

Maeve flared up. 'Why the fuck should he? What's it to do with him?'

'Sorry. I just thought you were . . . well, you know, sort of going out.'

'That doesn't mean he owns me.' Maeve picked up the tray and flounced out.

Sophie trailed back upstairs with her tea. She wondered if Maeve had decided to go as a sort of challenge to Matt. A throwing down of the gauntlet. Was she waiting for a reaction? As she got dressed she considered the intricacies and subtleties of the mating game and was very glad that she was in a state of retirement.

On Saturday afternoon Mrs Day came to keep an eye on the children for a couple of hours. Frank was working and she was quite happy to be out of the house which they were now sharing with her granddaughter and baby Cheyenne. Frank hadn't wanted this arrangement but she had told him they had to take Tracey in. There was nowhere else for her to go. Her own mother, Diane, was living on an air force base up in Scotland and Tracey refused to join her. She was vague about who the father was and seemed to treat the baby as a minor inconvenience, lugging her about like a toy. This afternoon she had taken her into Yeovil. Mrs Day didn't like to think what she got up to, hanging round the shopping precinct, showing off the new pram. According to Diane, Tracey had disclosed that she'd had her slip up amongst the flowerbeds in the middle of a roundabout in the centre of Yeovil. After a disco. Mrs Day worked backwards and thought it was probably tulips then. The Council did lovely tulips in May. Not that it made any difference.

She enjoyed looking after Freddy and Flora. Their mother wasn't much better off than Tracey when you thought about it, but at least they had a proper routine, not like poor little Cheyenne who was here, there and everywhere, eating hamburgers and all sorts and out till all hours. Her social worker said they should set a curfew, but Mrs Day would like to see her try. Freddy was still a bit hot, poor little chap, and scratching away at his spots, but he didn't have too many of them. Flora was a right little madam, but she did make her laugh.

Sophie drove Maeve, Lady Pamela and Jack Dick over to see Irish Dancer. Jane Hedderwick had telephoned and said that she was going to gallop him on Saturday afternoon – would they like to come and watch?

'Well, certainly, if we can get there,' said Lady Pamela.

'Of course we can,' said Maeve. 'Soph can take us. And we must take Jack. He'll want to see how Dancer's doing.'

So Sophie's little car was stripped of its baby seats and Maeve and Jack squashed in the back together, which made Sophie want to laugh so badly that she daren't look in the driver mirror in case she caught a glimpse of his face. Lady Pamela sat in state in the front passenger seat, and off they went.

Jane, a tough fit-looking young woman in her late twenties, was in the yard saddling up three horses when they drew up.

'Hello!' she said. 'I'm really, really pleased with him and thought you would like to see how he is working. These two have been up since August and are both qualified already, so they have a definite edge on him. They should be racing fit in three weeks or so, but I don't think he'll be far behind. I've had him out twice now with the hounds and he'll do his next five days after Christmas. I can't say it was a fun experience. It's like sitting on a coiled spring, and he was in a lather in about ten minutes. It took me all my strength just keeping him steadyish at the back. With a leg like he's had I'm not taking any chances.'

As she was talking she was whipping off rugs until Dancer was revealed in his full glory. He really did look well, even Maeve could see that. His coat shone and he was lean with muscle. Jack ran his hands over his flanks and down his legs. The suspect leg was bandaged.

'I keep it bandaged for work and put on ice packs afterwards. So far it's OK. It swells a bit when he's standing in but goes down with exercise. The tendons seem hard, but it's the elasticity we're worried about – has he still got the "ping" left after being fired? You see,' she explained to Maeve and Sophie, 'the tendons are like strong, thick elastic bands. After they've gone once it's always hard to know whether they will ever come back, heal up, as tight as before.'

Sally, the yard groom, appeared with a tiny saddle and a bridle and she quickly tacked him up. 'I love this horse,' she told them. 'He's such a character. He loves people. He's dead nosy – always got his head over his door watching what's going on. He's always trying you out in the box, but he'd never hurt you.' She tightened the girth. 'I'm riding him this afternoon. He's strong, as you know, but he doesn't take such a hold with me. Seems better with ladies. More considerate.'

The other two horses were now ready to go and two teenage boys sprung up on to them with the agility of monkeys. Sally checked her helmet strap and Jane gave her a leg-up. The instant she was in the saddle, Dancer came alive, arching his strong neck, rounding his back like a cat. He moved with a real swagger, a 'look at me' show-off prance. Making no attempt to hold him back and still on a loose rein, Sally patted his neck and let him move forward in front of the others. After a moment he visibly relaxed; the strong muscles loosened and his stride lengthened.

'She's a sympathetic rider,' said Jane. 'She goes with him. Doesn't fight. Encourages rather than dominates. He hasn't been used to that. Right, Lady Pamela, do you think you could climb up into the Land Rover? It's too far to walk and the mud in the gateways is awful. It's not very far. Look, I work them up the hill you can see. We've just finished putting down an all-weather track. I'll park at the bottom there and you will be able to see nearly all the way round. You've got your field glasses? Good.'

A few minutes later they had bumped over a couple of fields and were watching the three riders trotting around the edge of some set-aside land. Sally had kept Dancer in front and his long stride ate up the ground.

'When they turn that last corner they canter on the flat and then pull up the hill,' Jane told them. 'It's hard work but very strengthening for heart and lungs. Second time around they'll press on a bit. Sally will take it easy and the other two will go ahead.'

Jane lapsed into silence as they watched the horses working. Dancer's canter looked uncomfortable and irregular to Sophie, as if he was pulling hard and throwing his head about. Sally was crouched up in her stirrups now, trying to hold him back, and the other two passed him as they hit the upward slope of the hill. When the gradient started to tell he dropped his head and concentrated, but the fitter horses had the advantage and kept their lead. At the top they disappeared from view for a moment and then reappeared the other side going gently downhill, and fast. As they swung round, again on the flat, all three riders moved up a gear. The leading horses were galloping now, flowing along effortlessly, their young riders perfectly balanced. Dancer was fighting again, and then Sally let him have his head. He seemed to drop his shoulders and his mighty quarters powered him along, and for the first time Maeve and Sophie saw what he was all about.

'Jesus Christ!' said Maeve, clutching Sophie's hand. 'Will you look at that!' The big bay horse had moved past the other two, each stride covering that little bit more ground, his ears pricked, his neck extended.

'The old bugger!' said Jack – the first words he had spoken. 'The old bugger loves it.'

Jane was looking at Lady Pamela. Her hands, holding up her field glasses, were shaking. When she lowered them her eyes were wet and she scrambled in her pocket for a handkerchief. 'The wind,' she said briskly, 'the wind has made my eyes water.'

The party was complete on Christmas Eve afternoon. It was getting dark and foggy and Sophie had brought in the logs and lit the fire when Khaled's battered taxi drew up. Sam emerged from the back seat, helped with loving tenderness by Mohammed. On his arm, he tottered into the house and to the drawing room where Lady Pamela got up to greet him. Sophie quietly shut the door behind him while there was a noisy reunion amongst the rest of them. Maeve was shrieking and Mohammed and Khaled were full of laughter and jokes. The hall filled with luggage and presents and coats and they spilled over into the kitchen, where Sophie put the kettle on for tea. Maeve had made scones especially for Sam and they loaded up a tray and took it in to the old couple, who were sitting side by side by the fire, Sam still in his overcoat and looking pale and shaky. Sophie noticed that they were holding hands. Sam kissed her and Maeve and asked to be forgiven for not rising. He said his old ribs had had a battering. Maeve poured out their tea and spread jam on the scones for Sam, and they left them alone again.

In the kitchen Maeve and Khaled argued about a tape of

music which Maeve said he had borrowed, and it was noisy and fun. Mohammed caught Sophie's hand and kissed it. He already had Flora on his knee. He had heard all about poor Freddy and had been up to see him dozing fretfully in his bed. In a moment Sophie was going back up to him, where she had spent most of the day. She would bath him and read him a story. Mohammed said he wanted to come and help.

Matt arrived and there were introductions to be made and more noise. Maeve got the men tree decorating with Flora, while she cleared up in the kitchen. Lady Pamela and Sam were going to dine alone in the drawing room. Sophie had made a little Christmas table arrangement with holly and winter jasmine and the last of roses which had escaped the frost, and Maeve had put candles on the white cloth.

Mohammed took Sam's case upstairs to Lady Pamela's dressing room where Maeve had made up a bed for the old man. He hung his coat on a hanger and unpacked the suitcase, hanging the smoking jacket still in the plastic cover from the cleaners. He drew the curtains and turned down the bed, checking that the bedside light was working and that there was everything that the old man might need. Mohammed enjoyed caring for people. He was glad that Maeve had put him and Khaled in the empty bedroom next door. He would hear if the old man called or needed anything in the night.

Sophie finished reading a Christmas story to Freddy and helped him open the last of his advent calendar windows. Flora, excited by being the centre of attention downstairs, grabbed at hers, which was propped on the table by Freddy's bed, spilling water from his mug over it. She screamed and tried to grab Freddy's, which made him cry, and Sophie nearly smacked her. It was what she needed, she knew, but it was Christmas Eve and she wanted to put them to bed peacefully and happily. Mohammed came in and showed Freddy a little toy mouse he had in his pocket, and in a moment Freddy was entranced, while Sophie took Flora off for her bath.

Washed, powdered, smelling sweetly of vanilla, her hair curling damply on her neck, and in a clean white nightie, Flora was at her best. Sophie hugged her. Together they put a stocking across the foot of each of their beds and left a glass of milk and a mince pie on the window sill for Father Christmas. It was much later before Sophie was allowed to tiptoe out of

140

the room, her heart full of tenderness at the sweet innocence of her children, now sleeping peacefully.

She went to retousle her hair and put on some lipstick and scent before going back down. The house felt strangely stuffy with all the fires lit, and on an impulse she opened the front door and went outside for a breath of cold, night air. The fog had lifted and there was a beautiful, clear sky, pierced by shining stars. She walked to the side of the house and banged on the kitchen window.

'Maeve! Come out for a minute. It's so lovely.'

A moment later a dark figure came out of the back door. Sophie caught her hand. Maeve's hair smelled of mince pies.

'Look, Maeve,' she said, pulling her into the glistening garden. 'Look at the house. Isn't it wonderful to see all the lights on, all lived-in and warm and cosy and full of happy people. And look at the sky. The fog has cleared. Look at the stars.'

'Doesn't that mean there's going to be a frost?' said Maeve.

Chapter Eight

In some ways Christmas was all that Maeve had hoped it would be. She and Sophie had tossed a coin to see who would get up at six o'clock to put the monster turkey in the oven. Sophie lost, but was awake anyway. Both the twins had been in bed with her since five o'clock, stockings unpacked, tangerines eaten, and had now fallen back to sleep. It would have been nice, thought Sophie, to share this first Christmas they could understand with their father. She felt lonely and as if she had to work extra hard at exclaiming in excitement and pleasure. She wanted to say 'Look at Freddy's face!' as he delved joyfully into his stocking, and 'Do look at Flora!' as she ripped off wrapping paper with concentrated determination. It was sad there was no one to share it with.

She crept out of bed and on the landing could hear Lady Pamela's radio playing softly and Sam's door showed a strip of light beneath it. Their age set them apart, thought Sophie, with the altered rhythm of old minds and bodies, waking early, sleeping less, nodding off during the day. These dead-end hours of early morning were theirs alone.

She was surprised to find the light on in the kitchen and Sam in his dressing gown, boiling the kettle for early tea. She thought with regret that they hadn't remembered to put an extra cup on Lady Pamela's tray. Sam kissed her and wished her a happy Christmas. He is such a lovely old man, she thought. Even at this grim hour he looks fresh and pink and clean, with no trace of stubble or bad breath and his hair already combed. She, on the other hand, must look quite alarming in an old stretch cotton nightie and bare feet. I have no standards, she thought sadly. Here's this ancient chap with a broken wrist and yet he still makes the effort to look spruce in the morning as a matter of self-respect.

They shuffled around, getting in each other's way as Sophie

wrestled the turkey, already stuffed and prepared, onto a roasting tray and into the oven. There was something repellent about its flabby, damp skin. It reminded Sophie of her own cold, mottled legs playing hockey at school, and the agony of embarrassment when brothers came to watch matches and enjoy the opportunity provided by the tiny games skirts to size up their sisters' friends. She washed her hands and accepted Sam's offer of a cup of tea. She took it back upstairs to bed with her, carrying Sam's as well.

He parted company with her outside Lady Pamela's door, thinking how extraordinary it was for him, an old bachelor, to share an early morning ritual with a scantily dressed young woman whom he had only met the night before. Ghastly grey dishcloth nightdress, but a nice figure, he could see. Quite a Christmas treat, and here was dear Pammy sitting up in bed wearing her lovely shawl. Not quite as he'd imagined, but lovely all the same. She moved over and he propped himself up on the pillows beside her. What more could he ask for?

Maeve was right about the frost. Overnight the weather had changed and when it got light they were enchanted to find a world as white as if it had snowed. The sun rose low in a blue sky and the garden sparkled with tiny coloured points of ice. A cock pheasant strutted on the lawn and behind him the hills rolled away under a silver blanket into the hazy distance.

After breakfast Sophie set the table in the dining room, using the best silver, cleaned by Mrs Day, and putting out crackers and little bowls of sweets and nuts. She trailed holly and ivy down the middle of the white tablecloth and placed red candles in the candlesticks. Maeve had organised a seating plan and although Sophie was slightly worried about how the children would behave at a grown-up meal, she thought that there were enough kind helpers in the party to take the strain off her. Freddy, if he was well enough, was going to sit between her and Mrs Day and Flora between Mohammed and Maeve.

She and Maeve had prepared all the vegetables the day before and they had a pact not to allow Mohammed into the kitchen so that he could enjoy something of a holiday. Instead he offered to bring in the logs, keep the fires burning and amuse Freddy. Khaled was more than willing to help Maeve. He clearly fancied her and couldn't take his eyes off her pert bottom in her tight jeans. He was the very opposite of

Mohammed, being short, stout, heavy featured and jowly with a large, hooked nose and bulbous eyes. He looked fierce, Sophie thought, and would make a very scary taxi driver, but in fact he was good-natured and cheerful. He was already a great friend of Sam's and had promised to play chess with him after lunch.

Mohammed raced about after Lady Pamela, fetching and carrying and generally acting like a lady-in-waiting. He thought of her as being the nearest thing to royalty he was ever likely to meet and treated her accordingly.

Sophie decided to take Flora to the ten o'clock service at the parish church in South Charlton. It wouldn't seem like Christmas without church. Flora was happy to go as long as she was allowed to choose what to wear and which of her toys and books to take with her. Where does she get this militancy from? thought Sophie. Such determination to get her own way. Because it was Christmas, Sophie slapped on some lipstick and blusher and wore the cashmere sweater her parents had given her in a gentle duck-egg blue and her leather trousers. She was glad she had brought her old winter coat, which was long and sweeping and would keep her warm if the church was freezing.

It seemed odd to join the gaggle of families crowding up the church path and in at the old grey stone porch. Just the two of them amongst all these strangers at a time of year when Sophie had always been surrounded by family. However, just inside the door she recognised Matt's father, Commander Digby, who was handing out carol sheets and then she saw Matt disappearing into a pew towards the back. At the same moment he turned and saw her. He beamed and mouthed 'Happy Christmas' and indicated that they should join him. Gratefully Sophie slipped in beside him and hauled Flora onto her knee. Matt kissed them both. Sophie noticed that he smelt of something sharp and medicinal and that his hands had a red, raw look about them.

'Been calving,' he whispered. 'Up since six.'

'Me too,' said Sophie. 'Not calving. Obviously. I had an appointment with the turkey.'

'How's Maeve?'

'Oh a high.' They both smiled.

'She loves it, doesn't she? A party. She needs people more than anyone I know.'

Somehow, although this was said with no hint of criticism,

Sophie felt that one was implied. Then the procession of choir, mostly late-middle-aged women, a few children and one or two men, trooped in, followed by the bearded vicar. He wished them all a happy Christmas, commented on the beauty of this special day, and announced the first carol. Flora stood up on the pew and clutched the carol sheet, pretending she could read, and when the singing started joined in tunelessly but with gusto. Sophie had difficulty stopping her at the end. She would willingly have added a verse or two as a solo. During the reading of the Christmas lesson she climbed onto Matt's knee and gazed up at him solemnly. He poked her in the tummy and she wriggled and giggled and Sophie had to make a face at them both.

Later they kneeled side by side at the Communion rail, little Flora disappearing between them. The vicar had to dive down to find her little blonde head and lay his hand on it in blessing. Sophie felt moved and sad. She realised that they had the appearance of being a proper family, like those on either side of her, where fathers carried babies in their arms, and mothers, on whom the burden of Christmas fell most heavily, looked exhausted, holding the hands of over-excited children.

These days, no longer feeling quite so deeply aggrieved, Sophie just wished that things were different, that her children were not being denied what she felt was so important – a proper family with a father and a mother. She still couldn't really believe that living with her could have been so intolerable that Fergus would leave his children rather than stay. He had never given her the chance to try and put things right, she felt. She had trained herself to deny she still loved him but she knew that she would have done, if they had stayed together. It would not have occurred to her not to love the man she had married, in an entirely dutiful way. She now wondered at the nature of the love she had felt. Was it real if it grew out of this sense she had of what was right, appropriate, dutiful, rather than the sort of fiery passion Maeve went in for? I don't think I have a passionate nature, thought Sophie. I'm too mild. Too dull. Which was why the sexual attraction she felt for Mohammed had been such a pleasant surprise. No duty there. Just a terrific urge to have a bonk. It was good. It was great. It made her smile even here in church, on Christmas Day.

After the service, Matt was stopped and greeted on all sides on the way out. It seemed he was a popular local figure and many of the people who had crowded into the beautiful little church were farmers who knew him well. Sophie noticed that the women – wives, daughters – eyed her up and down, clearly wondering how she fitted into his life. He introduced her properly to his father who was collecting the carol sheets and then walked with her in the dazzling sunshine to her car, holding Flora's hand.

Flora, rather over-awed by Matt's presence, had behaved very well in church and had demanded that he take her up to look at the crib when the vicar invited the children to come to the front to see the little wooden baby Jesus surrounded by the carved animals. During the children's carol 'Away in a Manger', Sophie and Matt had tears in their eyes trying not to laugh when Flora had taken her own line with tune and words and delivered her version to great effect, to the open-mouthed admiration of a little girl of similar age in the pew in front.

As they stood in the sunshine at the door of Sophie's car, Matt said, 'Has Maeve told you about this skiing jaunt of hers?'

'Yes, she has,' said Sophie noncommittally.

'I've got some days off between Christmas and New Year. We could have spent some time together, the lack of which she's always complaining about. I don't know why she went off and booked this holiday then. Do you?'

Sophie pulled a face. 'I suppose she felt like a change. You know it's hardly Maeve's scene down here. I'm amazed she's lasted so long. And seems to love it . . .' she added hastily.

'Oh well,' Matt sighed. 'She's a law unto herself, anyway.'

'Yes, she is,' agreed Sophie. 'And she'll be back. Don't worry.'

As she drove back to Charlton she wondered why Maeve did not take more care of Matt. He was the nearest she had ever got to a decent, honourable sort of man, unlike the rogues who littered her past history. No doubt this Pierre person would be just like all the others.

She's mad, thought Sophie. I can't understand her.

Christmas lunch was splendid. The guests started to arrive at twelve thirty and the house was warm and bright and welcoming with blazing fires and stiff drinks. Mr and Mrs Day were the first. Mrs Day had a gin and tonic, which went straight to her head, and Mr Day his stout. Sam, enjoying a dry martini, engaged him in conversation about his cows. Commander Digby and Matt were next and the noise level rose and happy laughter increased. Maeve, who was on her third martini, lost interest in the turkey and the roast potatoes and Sophie went backwards and forwards to the kitchen, checking that all was still half under control. By the time it came to making the gravy, she too was long past caring. She tripped over things in the kitchen, giggling happily with Khaled who, like Mohammed, touched no alcohol. It was useful having someone who was sober to lift the great golden bird out of the roasting dish and later to carve it into delicate creamy slices. Khaled sharpened the carving knife at length and wielded it like a warrior.

The roast potatoes were crisp and burnished, the sprouts turned in butter and nutmeg, the bread sauce creamy and fragrant. Maeve came reeling in and had to lean against the wall.

'Christ,' she said. 'I am totally pissed. Here, everyone!' She raised her glass. 'Happy Christmas!'

Sophie made the gravy in the turkey pan and checked that the Christmas pudding had not boiled dry. She started to put together two dishes of lunch for the twins. Freddy was much better since a sleep in the morning and was now hanging round her knees saying he was hungry. She passed him little slivers of turkey as it fell beneath the blade of Khaled's knife.

In the drawing room Mohammed filled glasses and passed round smoked salmon on little triangles of brown bread. Mrs Day had another gin and went very pink in the face. Lady Pamela looked round the noisy room and felt distinctly tight herself. She remembered the last few dreary Christmases she had spent here alone and marvelled at the change. She caught Sam's eye and gave him a private smile and held the softness of his beautiful shawl to her cheek. He smiled back. It was so wonderful being with him. Maeve had promised that after lunch the very elderly should be allowed an hour or two of peace and she knew that they would doze beside the fire together. She glanced at Maeve who was noisy and excited with two hectic spots of colour on her pale cheeks. She looked very pretty in a tiny leather mini-skirt and a red polo-necked sweater. She was teasing Matt about something and he was laughing too.

Commander Digby was talking to Frank Day. They had discovered identical political views and were having a fine time lambasting the government. Mrs Day was chatting with Mohammed, who was looking more handsome than ever in a beautiful cream polo-necked sweater Sophie had given him for Christmas. Lady Pamela realised that Sophie and Khaled must be on kitchen duty. There was a delicious smell of cooking wafting in, and then Khaled was at the door, calling them to take their places at the table and Mohammed was helping her out of her chair and offering his arm so that she could lead her guests into the dining room.

How beautifully Maeve and Sophie had decorated the table, how pretty and bright it looked with the candles lit and the shining colours of the crackers, and the dark green of the holly and the ivy. Here was Sophie, carrying Freddy, and Mohammed rushed forward to help her get the children seated on cushions at the places specially set for them with their plastic place mats to protect the white damask table cloth. Sophie looked pretty too, thought Lady Pamela. Less strained and tired and with more animation and sparkle in her eyes. She smiled gratefully at Mohammed and he pressed her hand. There was something tender between those two.

At last everyone was seated and Maeve remembered that Jack Dick had not appeared.

'He was outside the back door a moment ago,' said Sophie. 'He won't come in. He wants to eat in the kitchen. He's a bit overwhelmed.'

Maeve jumped up and took Jack's place setting out to the kitchen and put his cracker and napkin by his place. Sophie piled his plate high with food. Maeve put a tumbler of whisky by his plate. He came in then, sidling through the back door. Relieved of his woollen hat, his remaining silver hair was very flat and close to his head. He could almost have been a trendy character actor with his knobbly artichoke nose and bushy eyebrows. He had smartened up for the occasion in a check shirt with straining buttons and a bright blue hand-knitted cardigan. On his feet were a pair of very white trainers. He sat down happily, much comforted to be on his own, with Esau for company.

Then they were all eating and raising their glasses to the cook, and Maeve was laughing and happy, wearing a paper crown with a gold star pulled from her cracker. Sophie helped Freddy with his food and when he started to get restless she let him get down and he trotted off into the kitchen to find Jack and to give Esau a sausage as a Christmas present. Flora was totally taken up with flirting with Mohammed. Sophie looked round the table. Everyone was happy and talking and laughing. It was all thanks to Maeve.

Later, when Sophie looked back on this moment, especially in the light of what was to come, she was glad that she had caught Maeve's eye and, raising her glass to her friend, had said, 'To the best mate a girl could have!'

The afternoon slumped. Over-fed, with alcohol-induced headaches, the party disbanded. Lady Pamela and Sam withdrew to the drawing room to nod off in their armchairs with a tray of coffee and brandies. Sam had indigestion from his enthusiastic participation in Maeve's cooking and his broken wrist ached. Commander Digby, very flushed and stimulated by Maeve's attention, said he must go to do his evening round of the stock, and Jack Dick went to feed the horses. His sprouts had had a profound effect and he went out of the back door propelled by little bursts of farting, like the puttering of an outboard motor. He had been deeply moved by the gifts that Maeve and Sophie produced for him. 'I'll be buggered,' he kept repeating, flushed with whisky and pleasure.

Maeve and Matt had disappeared and Sophie would not allow Mr and Mrs Day into the kitchen to help clear up. 'You are our guests,' she said.

Frank had enjoyed himself far more than he would have believed, but now wanted to go home and watch the television in peace. The gin had made Mrs Day emotional by now, and she was kissing everyone and repeating herself. Frank bundled her into the car and, still shouting goodbyes and thanks, they drove off with six of Maeve's mince pies in a tin for later, when they had room for them.

Sophie took the children up to their beds for a nap and they snuggled down quite willingly with their new toys to play with. She went back down to the empty kitchen and made a start on clearing up. She started the dishwasher and put the silver into hot soapy water and then went back and forth to the dining room, clearing the table, deciding what to do with leftover food. There was still enough to feed an army. She wondered what her parents were doing, and her brothers. They had telephoned in the morning and she had spoken to them all except for Archie, who was in Australia. Fergus had telephoned from France to wish the children a happy Christmas and they had shrieked with excitement to hear his voice.

Sophie was daydreaming as she washed the silver and did not hear Matt coming into the kitchen. He had put on his coat and his new gloves – Sophie's present to him, although she said it was from the twins – and said that he must go. Sophie had made up a dish of cold turkey and bacon rolls for him to take back to the farm for supper and she started to hunt for cling film.

'Are you walking?' she asked.

'Yes. Father took the Land Rover.'

'Do you mind if I come with you? I need some fresh air. Where's Maeve?'

'She's asleep. Zonked. Yes, do come.'

'I'll just walk to the village and back. I shouldn't really leave the children.'

Sophie collected her coat and they set off together. The sun was setting in a violent orange-streaked sky. The air was clear and cold. Pheasants called across the valley and the village in the distance looked frozen, pretty as a picture with threads of smoke rising from the cottage chimneys. They walked in silence, boots crunching on the ruts of the track. Sophie's nose started to run in the cold. She was just about to say that she had better turn back when she felt Matt take her hand in his. He had taken off the gloves and his hand was very warm. They walked on. Sophie did not withdraw her hand. She felt confused, wondering if this was just a friendly gesture. Somehow it seemed very intimate, even more so when Matt started to caress the back of her hand with his fingers, back and forth, soothingly. She turned to look into his face in bewilderment.

'God, Sophie,' he said, looking anguished. 'Do you feel like I do?'

It was dark when Sophie returned to the kitchen at Charlton. Khaled was unloading the dishwasher and restacking it with the next load. Sophie joined in, blaming the cold for her pink cheeks. She began to wash saucepans and then the moment she dreaded arrived. Maeve came in, rumpled and stretching.

'Hi,' she said. 'I've had a lovely sleep. Where is everybody?'

'Around. Mostly sleeping,' said Sophie.

'Have you been out?' asked Maeve. 'You've got a very healthy glow.'

'Just for a walk,' said Sophie. 'I needed some air. All that food!' She scrubbed hard at the bread sauce pan.

'What, with Matt?' asked Maeve, picking at the turkey. 'God, do you know, I feel hungry again.'

'Yes. Just a little way,' said Sophie with her back to her. She felt her knees trembling.

There was a silence and then Maeve said, with her mouth full, 'Did he say anything about tomorrow? We're going to the races – he's the course vet or something – but he thought they might be off with this frost.'

'No. I don't think so,' said Sophie, finishing with the saucepan and putting it on the Aga to dry. She wiped her hands. 'I'd better go and see if the Effs are awake. I don't want them to sleep too long or they'll be up all night.'

Once outside the door she found her heart was pounding. What had she started? What had she got herself into? Matt had taken her by surprise. She hadn't for one moment considered him as anything other than Maeve's boyfriend, but now, after what had happened, she couldn't turn the clock back. It was like the situation with Mohammed, but much worse. Already they were guilty of treachery and already a sneaky self-interest was creeping into Sophie's heart. She could sense it and she didn't like it one bit.

The next morning was all activity with both sets of visitors busy packing cars and preparing to leave, Khaled and Mohammed back to London, Sophie to her parents for New Year. Sam was staying on for a few days. Mrs Day was going to come in every day until Trish Holmes, the carer who was taking over from Maeve, arrived.

Sophie was glad to be busy. The weather had changed again and overnight the frost had gone and it was dull and grey with a raw, aching cold. Every time someone went out of the front door with a bit of luggage to the waiting cars, the cold invaded the house, and 'Shut the door!' was Lady Pamela's frequent cry. Freddy seemed much better and his spots were already fading. It was Flora's turn to be crotchety and Sophie wondered if she was about to go down with chickenpox. It would be more than likely. Mohammed caught her alone on the upstairs landing and tried to kiss her. He took her into the bedroom he had shared with Khaled and kissed her again. She drew back, feeling confused. After Matt everything was different.

'I have been wanting to do this all the days,' he said. 'Sophie, you are so beautiful womans.'

'Thank you, Mohammed. Thank you for everything. You've been so wonderful. So good to everybody. Most of all, good for me!'

A moment later they were interrupted by Lady Pamela's door opening. Sophie jumped back, startled, and Lady Pamela, who had emerged and glanced through the open door, instantly read her expression. Sophie blushed. She began a loud conversation about New Year plans, in what she hoped was a normal voice. Lady Pamela said nothing but started slowly down the stairs. Sophie groaned. Again she felt underhand, caught in the act. Mohammed started to tell her that he had arranged to help Sam when he returned to London. He was going to go round every day to help him with various chores and the shopping. He planned to reduce the hours that he worked at the restaurant and give up his cleaning job. He was very happy about this arrangement.

'But what about visas and work permits? You could both get into trouble,' said Sophie anxiously.

'Mr Elwes has many friends who will help me. No worries,' said Mohammed.

Yes, I'm sure he has, thought Sophie, and they will all be over eighty and totally without any influence.

'Don't always be worrying for people,' said Mohammed. 'You frown and spoil your pretty faces.'

'Yes, I do too much worrying,' said Sophie. 'But I'm working on it.'

With the car packed and the children scooped up, changed and dressed for the journey, they were ready to go. It was eleven thirty. Sophie's mind worked furiously. When was Matt likely to come and collect Maeve for the races? She longed to see him again. But it was stupid to hang around. What could he say, in front of everybody? No, it was better to go now, before he arrived. She trooped from room to room saying her goodbyes and thank yous. Lady Pamela leaned to kiss her cheek.

'Take care, my dear,' she said. 'And be careful.'

What does she mean? thought Sophie. Be careful driving? Looking after the children? Or does she think I'm having an affair? With Mohammed? Sam kissed her too and said that he hoped he would see her in London. Quite genuinely, she said she would love that.

In the kitchen she hugged Maeve. She could smell the scent that she nicked from Lady Pamela in her hair. They rocked with their arms about each other.

'Have a wonderful holiday, Maeve, and thanks a million for the fab time you've given us. It's been so great, I can't tell you.'

Maeve kissed her and said, 'Get on with it, you silly bag. You did most of the work, anyway. I was too drunk.'

'Only at the end,' laughed Sophie. 'You did everything else.'

'You'll be coming again soon, won't you?' said Maeve. 'To watch? To see Dancer's first race? I'll need to hold your hand.'

'I'd love to. I'll speak to you when you get back from Val d'Isère.'

Khaled and Mohammed escorted them to the car and helped pack in the children. Sophie kissed them both. Khaled felt like a stout barrel as she put her arms round him. He was a nice man. She had discovered that he had a wife and children in Egypt, and he was going back to visit them after the New Year. He was a safe family man. Mohammed embraced her, self-conscious in front of his friend, mindful now of propriety. He kissed her on both cheeks and promised that he would be in touch. Then there was nothing for it but to go.

As she steered carefully down the tiny lanes, foot poised above the brake on every corner, she met a dark car driven fast from the opposite direction. Obediently she reversed into a gateway she had just passed, to let it by. As it drew level, the driver lowered the window and her heart missed a beat as she realised it was Matt.

'You're not going?' He sounded desperate.

'Got to.' She shrugged, trying to seem casual.

'When can I see you? When can we talk?'

'Well, not now,' she said, indicating the twins. 'Here,' and she tore a page out of her diary. 'This is my parents' telephone number. I'll be there for a week. Ring me there.'

'Darling!' he whispered.

'Don't,' said Sophie. 'Wave goodbye to Matt, Effs.' The children obediently waved and Flora set up a howl because she wasn't allowed to climb out to see him properly.

'Look what you've started,' said Sophie, smiling ruefully. 'Making all the girls cry.'

Chapter Nine

'You can't go like that,' said Matt, winding down the window as Maeve came out of the house, ready to hop into his car. 'I know it's only Wincanton Races, but you'll give the locals a fit, dressed like that.'

'What's wrong with me?' asked Maeve crossly but taking no notice and getting in and slamming the door.

'You look, well, extraordinary,' said Matt.

Maeve looked down at herself. She had on a sweatshirt which she wore inside out so the number sewn on the back appeared as a faint reversed shadow and she had customised the neck by slashing it into a V. Underneath she wore a series of strappy vests which all managed to be visible, as did her customary black bra. A purple and orange scarf was draped round her neck. Below this was her tiny leather mini-skirt, then fishnet tights on her little birdlike legs and her battered old cowboy boots. Her hair was loose and stuck out from her head in a wild wedge of curls.

'Well, I'm all for extraordinary,' said Maeve. 'It's like this, or not at all, matey. What's wrong anyway? I'm perfectly decent and I've got this,' she showed him Lady Pamela's cashmere jacket, 'if I feel cold.'

'Well, for God's sake put it on when we get there,' said Matt. 'This is Somerset not Notting Hill or wherever you wear that kind of get-up.'

'Oh, piss off!' said Maeve. 'What's the matter with you? You tight-arsed prick.'

Matt started the car and they drove the short distance in brooding silence.

That was how the day started and more or less continued. Later Matt wondered whether he had deliberately orchestrated the quarrel, but he could not see that it was all his fault. When they arrived at the course he had to go and report to the clerk, and on his advice Maeve disappeared to the bar to wait for him out of the cold. She had her member's ticket pinned provocatively to her bra. When he caught up with her later she was already tight. She had found one of the men who worked in Jane Hedderwick's yard and they were buying each other whiskies. She ignored Matt and he told her he was grabbing a burger and had to get back down to the stables to do a blood test. He gave her a twenty pound note and told her to get some lunch. She pushed it back at him.

'Keep it!' she said. 'I'm going to have a sandwich in the lorry with Steve. Jane's here with two of her horses. So you can sod off back to the stables.' This insult made her giggle and she swayed on the bar stool. Steve looked embarrassed and asked Matt if he would like a drink.

'Sorry. I'm on duty,' he said. 'Thanks all the same.' He felt awkward and annoyed. Maeve was putting him in an impossible position. He did not care if she wanted to spend the whole day getting pissed, but it would look to others as if he did. He touched Steve's arm in a matey gesture and then went quietly away.

He had a busy afternoon. The cold was miserable and although the racegoers had a good day with some exciting racing, he had a lot of routine work to do and the unpleasant task of destroying a horse which had fallen and broken a leg. He was stiff with cold and tired as the last race drew to a close. There had been no sign of Maeve all the afternoon. He had thought she might sober up and come to look for him, feeling remorseful perhaps. Now he supposed he'd have to look for her. Pushing through the departing crowds he worked his way into the lorry park. He had seen Jane when she had brought her horses down to the paddock before their races. They'd exchanged pleasantries and general chat about Christmas and she had said, 'Maeve's with us in the lorry. Keeping us all amused. Come and have a drink when you're through – that is, if we haven't gone by then.'

'OK. Thanks,' said Matt.

He imagined she would be packing up and ready to go by now but he could see her dark blue horsebox, still with the ramp down and a girl swilling out the contents of a bucket. He stomped over and knocked on the door of the living accommodation. The windows were steamed up with condensation and when Jane opened the door he could see a lot of people inside, all looking flushed and happy. There was a hubbub of noise which quietened down as she said, 'Hi, Matt. Come on in and have a drink. We've had quite a good day. Second and third was better than we expected.' She stood back to let him climb up into the lorry. Maeve was perched on someone's knee, drinking out of a mug. She looked pink-faced and excited. The living space was full of people and gear. A tin trunk was stacked with neatly rolled bandages and folded rugs and the tack was hung on hooks along the partition. The two horses munched at their hay nets, rugged up now and warm, their manes crinkly from where their plaits had been unpicked.

Matt stood feeling awkward until Jane passed him a large polythene box with a few rolls left in the bottom. 'Ham and cheese,' she said. He took one and realised that the knee Maeve was sitting on belonged to Rob who often drove for Jane if she was short-handed. Rob caught Matt's eye and grinned sheepishly and pushed Maeve off.

'My leg's gone to sleep,' he said.

Wearily, Matt realised that he did not care. He was too cold and too tired. All he wanted was to get home, help his father with the cattle and then lie in a long, hot bath. Jane offered him a whisky.

'Thanks, Jane, but I'm driving. In fact I've only come to collect Maeve. Are you coming?' he addressed her.

She did, but sulkily, stomping across the car park without saying a word and then when they were in the car she ranted at him about how he had been in a foul mood from the start, how he had spoiled the day, how he was a miserable sod, how she had better fun without him.

'Evidently,' he said, looking down at his knees.

'Too right, I do, and whose bloody fault is that?' said Maeve.

It seemed to Matt that she could only blame him, that reasonable discussion or analysis of their relationship was beyond her.

'Well, there's no point in going on like this. I think we should end it. Call it a day,' he said, turning the ignition. It was easier not to look at her. He swung the car out onto the road. This was not the time to bring up Sophie but nevertheless he felt a nasty taste of double-dealing in his mouth, colouring his words.

'Yeah. Well, that's fine by me,' said Maeve, and continued to rail against him all the way home. He let it flow over him.

It was the usual stuff – he only cared about himself and his bloody work, and the farm, of course. He was selfish. She came at the bottom of his list of priorities. All he wanted was a fuck. The same old story. What girls always said.

The New Year brought with it a bitterly cold east wind and a lowering of spirits. Sam went regretfully back to London. He had a hospital appointment in the first week of January and a couple of luncheon appointments which he did not feel greatly interested in. He had passed a quiet and happy New Year's Eve with Lady Pamela and they had toasted each other in champagne which he had bought in Castle Cary. A few days after Christmas, George had come in his taxi to collect them and they had shuffled round the supermarket together, buying a few basic groceries. Lady Pamela bought some smoked salmon and a lemon for a little celebration on New Year's Eve and they got some tins of soup. There was still plenty of cold ham and turkey to eat after Christmas and Jack had brought in leeks and potatoes from the garden, but they had neither the appetite nor inclination to bother with cooking. They had spent the quiet days after Maeve's departure sitting together in the drawing room beside the fire which Sam laboriously made up, lifting the logs with one hand. Jack came in and filled the log basket each morning so they were well looked after. In the afternoons they wrapped up warm and walked round the garden or a little way towards the village, just fast enough to get their old blood circulating so that when they returned indoors they felt warm and their cheeks were pink. They watched racing on the television, dozed, shared *The Times* crossword and talked. It was a precious, companionable time and Sam had loved it.

Now as his train drew into Paddington, he felt despondent. His wrist ached and he disliked the thought of his cold, empty flat. He knew that country life would not suit him in the long term while all his interests, apart from Pammy, lay in the city, but he had so enjoyed Christmas and being surrounded by lively young people. He thought about Mohammed coming in to help him and wondered whether the arrangement would be satisfactory. There wouldn't be a great deal for him to do, but it would be a help to have someone who could take books back to the library, for instance, run his errands and do his shopping. The truth of the matter was that he needed someone to share his life with. Mohammed was starting tomorrow and Sam was glad.

He didn't like leaving Pammy. When they had said goodbye she had felt so tiny in his arms. He couldn't help but wonder whether it would be the last time that they held each other. When they had parted in the war, when the danger was great, they had solid, vibrant youth on their side. They felt invincible. Now they were just frail husks. The flicker of life could so easily be snuffed out.

These were morbid thoughts which must be expelled. It was unlike him to feel gloomy. Perhaps it was the fault of the painkillers or whatever the pills were he was swallowing three times a day.

The train drew into Paddington and Sam hauled his case out of the luggage compartment. Carefully he got down off the train onto the platform. A kind young man passed him down his case. There were no trolleys or porters, of course. The young man, bundled up in a padded jacket and with an enormous backpack to wrestle with, offered to carry the case. It was really too kind. Sam gave him his most charming smile. While the rest of the world seemed awash with rudeness and barbarity, Sam moved in his own monoclimate where good manners and civility prevailed.

As he followed the padded jacket down the platform, he saw a young woman struggling with a pushchair and thought of Sophie and her twins and wondered how they had enjoyed New Year's Eve. He would telephone when he got settled back into a routine and invite her to luncheon at his club. She was a nice girl, rather old-fashioned, he thought. A bit wet, perhaps, as gentle girls often seem. Unlike his Pammy. Or Maeve, for that matter.

He thought of Maeve who had blasted out of Charlton like a whirlwind. She had had some sort of row with Matt. The Boxing Day Races had not been a success, apparently. He gathered Matt had been busy on duty and Maeve had spent the whole afternoon in the bar and was drunk by the time the last race had been run, and was ready for a fight. Sam had heard them at it in the car outside, when they got back – Maeve screaming and swearing, Matt trying to reason with her. Then she had got out and slammed the door of the car, still shouting, and Sam had heard her knocking things over in the kitchen. Matt had sat in the car for a bit and then when it was clear she wasn't going back out to him, had driven off. He had his work cut out with that one, thought Sam.

He and Pammy hadn't seen Maeve for the rest of the evening. She must have been packing after a fashion because there was a lot of going up and down stairs and moving about. She made no attempt to get supper or tidy up. She clearly thought she was on holiday already. The following morning she put her head round the kitchen door where Sam was making toast and coffee and announced that she was off. She was a most extraordinary employee. Sam thought she might have been more solicitous and concerned about them both, but no, she reminded him that George was booked to take them shopping and that Mrs Day was coming in every day until Trish, the replacement carer, arrived, and then she had gone, blowing him a kiss and calling, 'Look after yourself!' He assumed she and Matt must have made it up, because his car was waiting outside to drive her to Gatwick to catch her flight.

Pammy had been unsurprised and unconcerned. 'That's the Irish for you,' she said. 'Wild as a hawk. She always makes one feel she looks after one as a favour. Left no address or telephone number, did she, but I don't doubt she'll be back. She needs the money and in her way she's fond of us. The change will do her good. I believe they party all night at these sorts of resorts. Quite a change from us dull old things.' Sam had smiled at her fondly. She had been quite a party girl herself.

Outside the station the wind whipped past Sam as he hurried to keep up with his case, whisking the sheets of an evening newspaper into the air and scuttling litter along the pavement. The kind young man guided him into the queue for taxis. Sam asked where he was going and then suggested they share a cab. He would pay of course and it wasn't far out of his way to drop the lad off at King's College halls of residence.

Wherever Sam went he was a life enhancer.

After Sam had gone Lady Pamela felt more tired than usual. Without him she didn't feel like getting up or eating a solitary breakfast and she couldn't face the performance of lighting the fire so she sat by two electric bars and felt cold. The wind was punishing and she gave up going for a daily walk. The steely grey sky was glowering and unfriendly and the garden had the bleached look of a daguerreotype. There was nothing to go out for.

Mrs Day was understandably subdued as she went about her work. After Christmas, Frank had been given three months' notice. His boss was giving up the cows. For the first time in two hundred years there would be no dairy herd at Clayhills Farm. Mrs Day didn't like to think about the future. At over fifty, the prospects were not good for Frank. He had sunk into a deep depression and was hardly talking. Anything she said to try and cheer him up was met with either silence or a monosyllabic answer. One thing was certain and that was that he wouldn't get a job with cows again. Dairy farms were going out of business. Clayhills was one of many. The local paper was full of notices of dispersal sales. Fine herds were going under the hammer every week, old stock to the slaughterhouses, cottages sold to weekenders, milking parlours lying idle while planning permission was sought to turn barns and farm buildings into expensive second homes. The countryside would never be the same again.

At least, thought Mrs Day, as she banged the Hoover into the furniture, they were in a council house and not a tied cottage. She would have to try and get more work. There were more poorly paid part-time jobs aimed at women than anything for men. She'd applied for a job at the cheese factory in Frome where the milk came from France now, so they said. If she got it she'd have to give up Lady Pamela. She'd miss coming to Charlton, miss Maeve and all her carryings-on, but she'd have to go where the work was. She hadn't said anything to the old lady yet. No point in getting her upset when there was nothing settled. She'd told her about Frank, of course, and she'd been very kind, very concerned for them.

Mrs Day left the Hoovering and went outside the back door to have a cigarette. She supposed she'd have to give that up next. Bloody shame it was, when you'd worked all your life and couldn't afford a packet of fags. After a moment she stubbed it out. A waste, really, but it was too cold to stand out here. The wind was wicked.

If anybody was marginally more cheerful it was Jack Dick. The week after New Year, Lady Pamela had tottered out to where he was feeding his fowl and had asked him if he would like to go with her to watch Irish Dancer school over practice fences. He had been pleased to be asked. He stumped off to get his coat and went round to the front door to wait.

Trish, a comfortable, retired nursing sister of the old school, had arrived to replace Maeve, and was more than willing to drive them over to the yard. She liked an outing and the weather had improved a little but it was too cold to want to spend long in the garden, which was her real passion. She took her *Express* to read in the car and hoped they might stop in Castle Cary for coffee on the way home.

When they arrived at the yard, Jane Hedderwick came out to greet them, her long fair hair pushed under a woolly hat, and bundled up in warm clothes.

'Morning, Lady Pamela,' she said cheerfully. 'I'm glad you could get over, despite the cold, because I want you to see your horse. I've put him over our practice fences a couple of times now and I had him out hunting on Christmas Eve. We had a bit of fun, quite a good run and popped over five or six small fences, and what pleases me is that he loves it so. It just lit him up and I reckon we did three weeks' work in three hours. There's no problem about him coming back sour. He loves his jumping.'

'I told you that,' said Lady Pamela. 'All Ballerina's offspring loved jumping. They're not the fastest, but they jump and stay.'

Jane led the way across the yard. 'Did Maeve get off on holiday all right?' she asked. 'She was on great form on Boxing Day.'

Lady Pamela shrugged and sighed. 'After a fashion. She blew out like a whirlwind.'

Jane laughed. 'And with a hangover, I bet.'

She explained that she was going to take three horses down to the field and school them together. She introduced them as Bounty Bay, an experienced steeplechaser who had won three races and been placed several times last year. 'And he's better than ever this season,' said Jane. Then Jackpot Lad who was a novice, but well bred and promising. Dancer was the third.

'It will be interesting for you to see him working alongside these two,' said Jane. 'Bounty has been jumping well and Jackpot isn't bad. Neither of them have Dancer's experience but he's had a long time off and he's having to polish up his jumping. Now if you don't mind I'm going to have to love you and leave you. I'm short-staffed and so I'm riding Jackpot. If you take your car down the lane and stop at the second gateway on the right, you can see from there.'

Trish, obligingly, drove and parked as directed and Jack

helped Lady Pamela out of her seat. They leaned their arms on the gate and watched the three horses having a warm-up canter round the field. It was a bitter January morning. Even so, the country looked beautiful. The pearly sky and the grey hills seem to swim together in a watery mist in the distance, while the closer shoulders of land stayed resolutely green. There were some ewes with new lambs down in the bottom of the valley and the sound of the flock drifted across the frozen landscape. Lady Pamela pulled her knitted hat down further round her ears and concentrated on the horses. Irish Dancer looked well. His hind quarters had built up with muscle and he was lean and fit. Jack couldn't take his eyes off him and breathed noisily through his nose as he concentrated on the horse's movement.

'Look at the bugger. Look at that stride,' he said admiringly.

Sally was riding him, as usual, and in her quiet way she dealt with his bursting energy and settled him into a strong working canter, concentrating his power behind the saddle, preventing him from throwing his head about and becoming unbalanced. He was clearly very keen and pulling hard. He had a competitive attitude, always wanting to be in front. All three horses worked round the field a few times and then took the wider circuit where four brush fences had been built in a line. They came into them fast and grouped together. From where she stood Lady Pamela could hear the drumming hooves and the sharp snorting breaths. She watched Dancer's ears come forward. This was what he loved. He took off a stride too soon but floated over the fence. Sally had to sit well back not to get jumped off. The second he got absolutely right and out-jumped the other two, which gave him a lead as they galloped into the third. Again he got the stride wrong. Up in front, he stood right off the fence and once more his athletic jump got him out of trouble. He landed ahead, galloping on, looking for the next fence.

Jane shouted at the other riders to pull up and the three horses circled, falling back to a canter and then a trot. They walked over to the gate, snorting and excited. They all wanted to go on. Sally, her cheeks pink, her eyes watering from the rush of cold wind, patted Dancer.

'He feels fantastic,' she said. 'He's got one hell of an engine.'

'What did you think?' Jane asked Lady Pammy. 'From where I am, he looked to jump really well. He's a bit erratic but never makes a bad mistake and the great thing about him is that he lands galloping. He makes up ground on his fences every time. I have to admit, I'm really excited about him.'

'I told you he could jump. Because of his size he takes a lot of work to get fit and I would say he has a way to go yet.'

'Yes, and he needs some more schooling,' said Jane. 'He hasn't forgotten much, just the finer points. He's over-enthusiastic at the moment. Too full of himself. He needs to settle and concentrate.' Her excited horse spun round and she continued the conversation over her shoulder. 'I wondered about running him in blinkers. And later I'd like to ask you about who you'd like to ride him. I'm going on now, if you don't mind. I don't want them to get cold.' It was the horses she was referring to, not the frozen jockeys. 'Come into the house for a coffee.'

Jack helped Lady Pamela back into the car.

'Well?' said Trish, folding up her newspaper and wiping the steamed-up windscreen with her glove. 'How was the gee-gee?'

Lady Pamela smiled. 'Encouraging, I'd say. Wouldn't you, Jack?'

Trish had to abandon her idea of a cup of milky coffee and a selection of homemade cakes and biscuits in the Castle Coffee House and instead followed Lady Pamela into Jane's cluttered kitchen. Inside the back door there was a washroom full of clean girths and numnahs hung on racks to dry, all neat and orderly. The kitchen table was littered with forms and bills and racecards. Jane pushed them aside and invited the ladies to sit down. A ginger cat and a Jack Russell terrier were scooted off chairs onto the floor. Jane put the kettle on and got out mugs and opened a packet of shortbread. Talking as she went, she made up a tray to take outside. Jack had said he'd stay and help with Dancer and Jane made a cup of tea for him and coffee for Sally and her stable girls to have in the tack room.

When she eventually took a seat opposite Lady Pamela, she had a racing calendar in front of her.

'Now,' she said. 'I think we should run him first in mid-February. He'll be racing fit by then and the ground should suit him. February tends to be a wet month and Doug Mitchell says he ran best on the soft. Hard ground is out anyway, with the leg to consider. However, I don't want to run him if it is really deep. Not with that leg to worry about. I mean, it may be absolutely fine but I don't want to take that sort of risk so early on in the season.'

'That all sounds very sensible,' said Lady Pamela. 'Where do you think he should run?'

'I would say a nice little track – nothing flashy first time out. Newton Abbot, perhaps, in a middle-of-the-road Open Hunter Chase. We want to pick the right race where he doesn't have to carry a weight penalty for his past achievements. We don't want more than twelve stone on top.'

Trish helped herself to another biscuit since she clearly wasn't going to be offered one. This horse talk went right over her head but she could see Lady Pamela loved it. She could understand how it would be rather exciting being involved with a racehorse. She always had a flutter on the National and the Derby, but that was as close as she'd ever been. She had assumed all trainers were men – those horse-faced or weasely-looking men interviewed after races on the television, in their camel coats and trilby hats. Jane was not what she expected and she approved of her; liked her forthright manner, her well-run house. There was a place for everything, nothing left to chance or muddle. The papers on the table had already been stowed into two baskets as she talked, marked 'bills' and 'other'. The pin board by the telephone was covered in lists, some neatly ticked off. This was a busy, workmanlike place, she could tell that at a glance.

'So,' said Jane, 'if you agree to the general plan, my next question is who should ride the horse, and here I have a suggestion to make. Sally, the girl you've met, who was riding him this morning, she rode point-to-points for me last season and did really well. She likes the horse and gets on with him. I would have every confidence with her on board. What do you think?'

Lady Pamela paused. Women jockeys were not part of her experience. Bumper had always disapproved of them. She hesitated, remembering the sheer enjoyment on Sally's face as she pulled Dancer up after the practice session. She was a good rider. Lady Pamela's reservations were more to do with the risks involved, the accidents, the falls that could put the girl into hospital with broken bones; the crashes which could smash her pretty face. You did not gallop and jump several tons of horse without running considerable risks. She could not help but feel it an inappropriate sport for a girl.

But why shouldn't Sally race if she wanted to do it and had the ability? Hadn't Lizzie been told that being a doctor was a difficult job for a woman? That surgery was a man's world? That she should consider nursing as a more suitable career? How furiously Lizzie had dismissed these views. How excited she would have been to see a girl like Sally compete with the men. She made up her mind.

'I would be very glad if she would ride Dancer,' said Lady Pamela.

'Great,' said Jane, beaming. 'I hoped you'd say that. She'll be thrilled.' She drained her cup. 'Have you finished? Shall we go and tell her?'

Two days after Christmas, Flora's spots appeared and, as with most things, she set about having chickenpox with style. She was literally covered in scabs, even inside her nose and ears and down her throat. The kind doctor who was called out to her said it was unusual for a child so young to have it so badly. She was feverish for four days and by New Year's Eve she had exhausted both Sophie and her mother. Sophie was terribly glad that she was at her parents' home where there was enough space for her and her mother to take it in turns to be with Flora while the other could disappear to catch up on some sleep out of earshot, and where Freddy, who was by now much better, was not disturbed every time Flora woke in the night.

Sophie's parents were very kind and patient and Sophie felt hugely grateful to them for seeing her through. Her father took Freddy out in the car and when the weather wasn't too miserable they went for happy, pottery walks with the dog. Freddy enjoyed the special attention and started to talk in a spurt of new words. Sophie felt relieved to have him taken off her hands while she dealt with poor Flora. New Year's Eve was not going to be an event. In fact when it came to it, Flora slept peacefully for the first time since they had left London and Sophie went to bed herself at nine o'clock.

The whole time Sophie thought about Matt. He hadn't telephoned and she couldn't understand it. He had seemed so desperate when she had last seen him in the car and she had expected him to ring that night. Or the next day. Nothing. She re-ran their conversation over and over again, racking her brains for something she had missed. He had definitely said that he would telephone her. Could she ring him? A hundred times not. What had happened between them had seemed so special, so wonderful that she couldn't believe that he had dropped her, but nothing would make her telephone him first. Why not? What was wrong with ringing for a chat? Perhaps he had lost her parents' number. After all, she had only written it on a slip of paper. If he had, no one else could help him. He didn't know her parents' name or where they lived. *Had* he lost it? Almost certainly, she decided, in which case the only sensible way to end this torment was to ring him. With her hand on the telephone she stopped herself. No, she wasn't going to lay herself open to being hurt and disappointed.

Sophie's mind raged and the days went by. Every time the telephone rang she thought it was him and it never was. She couldn't believe that he could do this to her. Why had he said that he thought he was falling in love with her if she now meant so little that he couldn't even ring?

The chickenpox made it worse. Trapped in the house, nursing a fretful child, she had little else to think about. She was tired, exhausted from disturbed nights, but her brain was not engaged and she filled it with thoughts of Matt. She thought she had grown out of this. With Mohammed she was completely in control, able to enjoy their friendship without a moment's anxiety. Now Matt had taken her straight back into the victim zone, where she felt struggling, helpless, defence-less. What was the matter with her? Why did she misunder-stand relationships, misread the signals, get it all so wrong? Did it mean that she was always going to be hopeless with men? Always be let down? Always arrive at a set of expecta-tions that were hideously off balance? Always misjudge the emotional climate?

She had been sure that Matt was sincere when he told her his feelings. She had responded because she was so flattered. Thrilled, really. She hadn't dared think of him as potential man material because he was Maeve's. This was a whole area of difficulty. Was Maeve now the reason he did not telephone? They had talked round and round this already. She had told him that she would never come between him and Maeve and he had assured her that she wouldn't, that Maeve was tired of him anyway, that they weren't really suited to each other, that Maeve had more or less told him to get lost.

Now, Sophie was not sure. She quite definitely would not start a relationship with him if he was still going out with Maeve. Never. He had convinced her that it was near enough

167

over but would not promise that Maeve knew and did not mind. He was, she thought now, deliberately vague about this and said that they still had to sort it out and make the final break but repeated that Maeve understood, and that she felt just the same as he did. Sophie did not know what to believe.

At the end of her week with her parents, Flora was distinctly better, well enough to trot about and quarrel with Freddy. The spots were less itchy and she was less fretful. Sophie had her first undisturbed night's sleep and woke feeling calmer and more philosophical.

Just let it be, she told herself. What will happen will happen. Give things time and they will sort themselves out.

She drove back to London trying to retain this frame of mind but she couldn't and before long she was back to the agonising. Why, if he didn't mean it, had Matt said all those things? She thought about how he had held her hand. It seemed so gentle and, well, sweet somehow. How could a man who did that just cast you off a moment later? Perhaps, she thought in panic, by not telephoning him she was giving him the impression that she didn't care either. Perhaps he was waiting to be reassured by her. Perhaps he was as full of anxiety as she was. Perhaps not.

As she unlocked the flat and pushed aside the post which had accumulated on the mat, her hopes soared. Had he written? She quickly leafed through the envelopes. Bills, late Christmas cards, a couple of postcards, one from Fergus. Nothing from Matt.

The twins were excited to be back and started to race through the rooms, jumping on their beds and bumping into one another. The answer machine was winking. Sophie pushed the button to hear that she had twelve messages. She saw down to listen to them, her heart thumping.

The first was from Matt. 'Soph. Hi. You must have given me the wrong number. This is a London number you've written and I'm sure you said you were going to Oxford. I'll keep trying anyway. I love you, Sophie.' The second was also from Matt and the third and the fourth and the fifth and the sixth . . .

Stupid, stupid. Sophie sat down on her sofa and cried and laughed in equal measure. Freddy and Flora jumped on her in excitement and Freddy put his little arms tight round her neck.

'Mummy not sad,' he said quite distinctly and emphatically.

'No, darling,' said Sophie, kissing him. 'Mummy not sad at all.'

Later, when she had put the children to bed and tidied up the remains of the unpacking and put a load of washing in the machine, Sophie went through to her bedroom and combed her hair and put on some lipstick. She looked at herself in the glass. Here I am, she thought, and Matt loves me. He says he has fallen in love with me. Looking back she saw a long pale face with a pink mouth, so she put on some blusher and stroked some grey crayon round her eyes. She looked better now. A woman who just might be loved by a good-looking, nice man.

She went through to her tiny, tidy kitchen and took a bottle of wine out of the fridge. She opened it and poured herself a glass. She checked the clock. Eight o'clock was a good time to telephone. In the sitting room she switched on the table lamps and found a tape of favourite music to put on the stereo, to play very softly in the background. Curling up on the sofa she took up the telephone and carefully dialled Matt's number. He answered almost at once.

When Sophie spoke, her voice sounded high and tight as if she had had to press it out of her chest. And ridiculously eager.

'Matt,' she said. 'Hi. It's me. Sophie.'

'Oh Sophie! God, Sophie. What happened? I've been nearly out of my mind.'

'I'm terribly, terribly sorry. I must have written down my own number instead of my parents'. You had me in such a state. I didn't realise I'd done it. I'm so sorry. I've been out of my mind too.'

'You have? Why, because I hadn't rung you?'

'Yes, of course.'

'Oh Sophie, I'm so glad!'

'What, glad that I've been miserable?'

'Yes. I can't tell you how glad I am of that!'

They both laughed. Sophie took a sip of wine and found that she was smiling. A ridiculous great ear-to-ear beam.

'When can I see you?'

'I don't know. How can we see one another? Can you come up to London? Fergus has the twins this weekend but not overnight . . .'

'I'll come to you. I'm playing rugby on Saturday. I could come after the game.'

'You can't stay here,' said Sophie immediately. 'I'm sorry, but I'm not ready for that and not when the Effs are here.'

'OK. No, of course not. I completely understand. What about Sunday? Can I come for breakfast?'

'What would you like, sir? Bacon, eggs, sausage, fried bread?'

'Yes, all that, and you. Especially you.'

When she eventually put the telephone down, half an hour later, Sophie felt utterly happy. She stretched on the sofa and lay back looking at the bumpy plaster on the ceiling. Four more days and she would see him. Four days and five nights and he would be here in this room with her, changing it for ever. Nothing, in fact, would ever be the same again.

When Matt arrived on Sunday, he was later than Sophie had anticipated. She had dithered about, not knowing whether to start cooking him a fry-up, and then worrying that it would make her whole flat smell, including her. She didn't want his first scent of her to be of bacon fat.

She had tidied everything after the twins had left with Fergus, vacuumed the carpets, cleaned the bathroom, put out fresh soap and towels. She had spent more money than she could afford on flowers and the flat was full of them. Wine was cooling in the fridge. She had changed the sheets on her bed and sprayed them with scent and then while she gave her home a final check she panicked, thinking it looked too tidy, too impersonal, a reflection of a dull character. She ran out and bought a Sunday newspaper and spread it about on the sofa and dented the cushions to look as if she had been relaxing waiting for him.

She put on the radio and made herself a cup of coffee she didn't want and went to check her appearance. Inevitably she was in the loo when the doorbell rang and she had to hurry, pulling up her pants and trousers, worrying that he would hear her flushing the lavatory, and then there he was, on the doorstep saying something about getting lost and driving past the top of her road at least twice before finding it. He was wearing a waxed jacket, crumpled and battered, and a yellow scarf. His brown hair was long and flopped to one side and his face, Sophie thought, looked nicer than ever, with deep creases in his cheeks when he smiled and even, white teeth.

She felt oddly formal and heard herself saying, in her mother's voice, 'Do come in,' and hastily added, 'God, I sound like my mother. I'm so nervous.'

He kissed her then, a long kiss, and she kissed him back and it was as good as she remembered, not wet and sucky, just urgent and exciting as his tongue found hers and his hands went up the inside of her sweater. She had put on a pretty lacy vest, anticipating removing at least some of her clothes, and in a moment he was pulling her sweater over her head.

He stopped then and said, 'Sophie, Sophie. God, I've wanted this so much.'

'Take off your smelly old coat,' she suggested.

He did, dropping it onto the floor. The flat already looked more lived-in with a few clothes scattered about. She led him to the sofa and lay back on it as she had done a few evenings before. He sat beside her and looked down at her face and then her breasts and the rest of her. He slipped the vest down off her shoulders and groaned when he found she was wearing no bra. He bent his head over her breasts, sucking at one nipple while stroking the other in an upward movement which made Sophie squirm with desire. She could feel herself getting to a point where she would not want to stop. She sat up and pulled his sweater off and undid his shirt. He slid on top of her then and she felt the silkiness of his skin against hers. One of his hands was reaching down to undo her trousers. Sophie stopped him.

'No?' he asked. She covered his mouth with hers.

When they broke off, she whispered, 'I'm not ready, Matt. I'm sorry. I want to take it slowly.'

'That's OK, baby, that's OK.' He stroked her hair and ran a finger along the line of her chin. 'I'm sorry if I've rushed things.'

'You haven't, you haven't, but it doesn't feel right to me yet. Sex has always been a bit of a thing for me. It makes me feel terribly vulnerable. I can't just do it. Maeve says I'm like a schoolgirl – a sort of professional virgin.'

'I'm glad. I'd rather it was like that – that you don't feel pressurised.'

'Shall we go to bed, though?' asked Sophie. 'I'd like to lie with you and feel close.'

'Oh darling!' said Matt.

He thought he had never seen anyone as beautiful as he followed her narrow naked back into the bedroom. She was so slim and yet her hips were rounded and her breasts were full and rather low. She looked so vulnerable, soft, white. He was glad that she didn't work out and hadn't attained one of those muscle-bound bodies he found unattractive.

In bed she was sweet, gentle and shy. Her eyes seemed to widen and blur into a soft focus as they kissed and stroked one another. Matt took it very gently and most of the time they lay in each other's arms and talked.

Sophie said, 'This is the first time for over two years that I've had a man in my bed, and that was Fergus. Sad, really, but worth the wait.'

Matt kissed her shoulder. 'Don't make me wait for ever, darling.'

'Heh! We've only just met. This is pretty advanced stuff for me!'

'You're lovely. Wonderful. I've been dreaming about you. I can't believe you're here in my arms.'

'I can't believe it really either. I made poor Fergus wait until we were engaged before I'd sleep with him. What's happened to me? Have I turned into a slag?'

'Definitely,' said Matt, 'and I'm so glad.'

'All the things which restrained me then seem to have gone. You know, I married expecting it to be for life and I wanted to save myself for my husband. To be really his. That was my life plan. I couldn't just have affairs or live with someone. That wasn't what I wanted. It seems sort of self-important to think that now. As if I overvalued myself and my virginity. Fergus knocked on the head any self-esteem I had.'

'It sounds old-fashioned but I expect there are a lot of people, especially girls, who feel like that. It's true that men tend to go out and shag randomly, but in our hearts I think we like that idea as well. We're genetically conditioned to want faithful partners.'

'Hmm. An ideal. The reality is different. Here I am, half naked in bed with you and we hardly know one another.'

'We know enough. The important things. And this is the best way to learn.'

Sophie turned to look into Matt's brown eyes which were flecked, she saw, with yellow. There was nothing in his expression to alarm her or make her regret her impulsiveness.

'Tell me,' she said, taking his hand and lacing her fingers through his as she stretched luxuriously, 'when you first noticed me . . . first wanted me.'

'I noticed you straightaway, but you were playing at being a prefect, if you remember, while Maeve was being the naughtiest girl in the school and I was aiding and abetting. You were very disapproving.'

'Matt,' wailed Sophie, 'that's not fair, I was only—'

Matt just laughed and tickled her.

'Then I thought you looked really pretty on Christmas Eve. I certainly noticed you then, but it was Christmas Day in church that made me see you properly. You were so sweet with Flora and I just suddenly felt I loved you. Sitting next to you, it felt as if we belonged. Right, somehow. You are so lovely and calm and kind and . . .'

'Sexy,' prompted Sophie. 'Sexy, remember. It's sexy I want to be.'

'And sexy,' agreed Matt, raising himself on an elbow to lean over her and kiss her. 'Very, very sexy.'

It was four o'clock before they had breakfast although earlier Sophie had padded into the kitchen to get a bottle of wine, corkscrew and glasses to carry back to bed. After that they kissed and dozed and talked and Sophie became more relaxed and uninhibited. Now they sat on opposite sides of her little kitchen table eating bacon and eggs and drinking mugs of tea. Matt had put on a towelling robe that he had found behind the bathroom door and Sophie was wearing her prettiest knickers and Matt's checked shirt with sleeves rolled up. She wore it like a trophy. Under the table Matt slid his toes up her leg until they were gently probing between her thighs and she felt herself moved with desire again.

What a lovely upside-down day, she thought and then remembered that it would soon have to end.

'Maeve is back on Tuesday,' she said. 'What happens then, Matt?'

'What do you mean?'

'Don't be evasive. You know we've got to straighten this out. We'll have to tell her.'

'I know. I will.'

'How will you? Are you going to collect her from the airport?'

'No. I can't. I can't take the time off. She knows I can't be there. We'd talked about it. She's going to get the train. I'll try and see her as soon as possible.'

'I'm dreading this,' admitted Sophie. 'Whatever you say, I think she'll be furious. I've seen her angry and it's fearsome to behold.'

'She's got nothing to be angry about,' said Matt stolidly. 'We'd more or less agreed to break up.'

'It's this "more or less" that worries me,' wailed Sophie. 'How do I know that Maeve feels the same way as you? I thought you two were very palsy-walsy at Christmas. I wouldn't have suspected that you were on the point of splitting up.'

'Well, we still get on well,' said Matt, 'but not as lovers. It's that that doesn't work. Maeve knows it. She's always complaining. For instance she suggested that I give my job up and go on some world trip with her. She's got no idea of what the real working world is like. I can't possibly go off like that. I can't leave the practice when I've only been there for two years and I can't leave my father and the farm.'

'Of course you can't, but it's typical of Maeve to come up with some crackpot scheme like that. She's never made herself responsible for anything.'

'Yes, typical,' agreed Matt.

Together they were constructing their defence.

On Tuesday evening Sophie was dreading a telephone call from Maeve, fresh from her holiday and full of chat. However, the telephone remained silent, until ten o'clock, when Matt rang.

'Have you seen her?' asked Sophie, almost at once.

'No. No chance. I'm not even sure she's back yet. I can't remember the time of her flight, can you? But I'll see her tomorrow. I'll take her out for a drink at lunchtime and tell her then. Darling? What's the matter? You sound so on edge.'

'I can't help it. I am. I just don't know how she's going to take it. She has a really fierce pride, you know. She'll think I stole you.'

Matt sounded less concerned. 'She'll be OK. She made it clear to me that she didn't want anything serious. She's always accusing me of being dull. She virtually dumped me by going off on this skiing jaunt just when she knew I had time off I wanted to spend with her.'

'But she sort of tests people like that. She has to test their feelings. She's always been like that. She can never really accept that people aren't going to let her down and so she's always on the defensive. Challenging. Pushing friendships to the brink. Oh Matt, I'm so happy and at the same time sick to my stomach with guilt. But you have to admit that I didn't

174

throw myself at you, or anything like that, did I?'

'Definitely not. Sadly.'

'Will you promise to telephone me the moment you've told her?'

'Of course. Now don't worry so much.'

But Sophie did. She could think of little else. Whichever way she tried to frame it, what she had done was treacherous and she knew it. There were two other certainties in her mind. The first was that her disloyalty could not be undone. It was like a permanent stain on her friendship with Maeve. It would always be there between them. The second was that, however shame-faced it made her feel, her heart sang with happiness that she and Matt had found one another.

As it turned out it wasn't Matt who telephoned to tell Sophie what had happened when Maeve got back to Charlton. When the telephone rang on Wednesday afternoon, it was Jane Hedderwick on the line. Her voice sounded cold and businesslike.

'Sophie? Sophie, this is Jane, Jane Hedderwick. Sophie, I've had the devil of a job tracking you down. Look, I can't talk on the telephone but you need to get down here as soon as possible. You can't leave Matt to cope with this on his own. After all, Maeve is supposed to be your friend.'

Chapter Ten

Sophie drove down to Charlton with a suitcase of hastily collected clothes for herself and the twins thrown into the back of the car. All the way she thought of things she should have done before leaving London. She realised that she had forgotten Freddy's goat's milk and the twins' new rubber boots. She had never left anywhere in such a disorganised state, but after Jane's telephone call it seemed imperative to get on the road. She felt agitated and distracted and her thoughts keep returning to Charlton and what awaited her there. The traffic trailing west out of London was heavy, with new roadworks and temporary traffic lights. Twice she nearly drove into the rear of the car in front as she failed to concentrate on the stop start procession.

She had tried to telephone Matt but he had his mobile switched off. Lady Pamela eventually answered the telephone at Charlton, but was confused about Maeve.

'She's away, skiing,' she announced, and then, 'But how stupid of me. Of course she's back. She was here this morning. No. I'm afraid I don't know where she is at the moment. Who is that? Sophie, did you say? I'll tell her you telephoned, my dear.'

Sophie's little car crawled on and just where she had hoped to make up time, a section of the motorway was under repair and reduced to a single lane, causing considerable delays. The whole journey took nearly an hour longer than usual and it was dark by the time Sophie turned off the main road to negotiate the lanes to Charlton. Miraculously the Effs had been terribly good. She had played them their story tapes over and over again and Flora for once hadn't screamed and struggled in her seat. What was more, they had both fallen asleep and although it would play havoc with bedtime, it had made driving much easier and gave Sophie the chance to examine her feelings. She could not stop her mind racing, going over what Jane had said and then preparing the statement she knew she would have to make. Jane would not elaborate on the telephone but she gathered Maeve was with her. She had no one else to turn to, thought Sophie. At least, not down in Somerset.

Feeling in the wrong and guilty was a new experience for Sophie, whose whole life, as she saw it, up until now had been lived on the straight. Well-mannered, respectful, polite, she had been a model and much-praised pupil at school. She had never lied, deceived, cheated, and her rebellious teenage years passed harmoniously. She considered herself a good person and had always had this view reinforced. In fact it had never been hard for her to be kind and considerate. These things came naturally to her with her mild, peaceable nature. 'Sophie is a joy to have in the House,' read her school reports. 'Sophie can always be relied upon.' Honest, upright, law-abiding like her forebears. That was how she saw herself. It was Maeve who was unreliable, bitchy, selfish. Maeve who had made other girls cry with her vicious tongue and who made life hell for the weaker teachers. It was Maeve who lied more easily than she told the truth. Now she was getting a dose of her own medicine.

However, Sophie did not like feeling she had done wrong and her guilt sat uneasily on her. She comforted herself by thinking that Matt was, anyway, far more suitable for her than for Maeve. She felt privately that her background and family and interests and everything else drew them together. Good, solid, middle England. If he had had the sense to realise this, it was hardly her fault.

Not only that, Maeve's careless treatment of him had its own reward. She couldn't just ride roughshod over people, thought Sophie. She always had and usually got away with it. Now she had met her comeuppance. This time she had gone too far. Again, Sophie felt she couldn't be blamed for the outcome. Maeve had effectively driven Matt into her arms.

Sophie just hoped that she could hang on to these justifications when it came to it. She couldn't trust herself not to fold completely, to be rendered speechless, defenceless, especially if she didn't have Matt with her. They needed to stand shoulder to shoulder and gain strength from each other. They were partners in crime.

For the last couple of miles Sophie was held up behind a

milk tanker. She drove with uncharacteristic aggression, right on its tail, willing it to let her by, but the driver was oblivious, cruising along at his own speed, slowing right down at all the bends.

At last she turned into Jane's yard. Her headlights picked out Jane's horsebox and Land Rover, but Matt's car was not there. Sophie felt dismayed. She wanted him. She needed him if she was going to have to face the music. As she sat in her car a moment, trying to rally herself, she saw what she thought was the Charlton bicycle Maeve used, chucked down by the back door, not even leaned against the wall, as if the rider had been in great haste. Sophie had a terrible sense of foreboding. She got out and unpacked the twins who ran about the yard with no warm outdoor clothes on, splashing through the winter puddles in their shoes. She didn't shout at them to stop, but went straight to knock on the back door of the house. It was opened nearly at once by Jane, who was dressed as usual in her yard clothes, worn jeans, a sweater covered in hay seeds and a fleece gilet, her hair tied back in a knot.

'Come in,' she said shortly, unsmiling and not attempting any conversation, not asking how the journey had been or saying that she was glad to see Sophie.

'Come on, Flora. Here, Freddy,' called Sophie, gathering them up before stepping into the yellow square of light which marked the threshold. Her heart was thumping. Jane's coolness had made her cheeks burn and she felt flustered and uncomfortable.

The first thing she saw was Maeve slumped at the kitchen table. Her face looked extraordinary. Her holiday had left her tanned but with panda rings where her sunglasses had protected the skin around her eyes which were glazed and puffy.

She looked up when Sophie came in and said, 'Here's the other fucking Judas.'

All Sophie's resolution fled and she instinctively went to her and put her arms round her. She smelt a great gasp of whisky-loaded breath as Maeve pushed her off.

'Get off me, you fucking bitch.'

'Maeve. Don't. I'm so sorry. Maeve, we didn't think it would hurt you. Honestly. Maeve, please.'

'Oh, fuck off,' repeated Maeve. Her words were slurred and Sophie realised that she was very drunk.

Jane, leaning on the door, said off-handedly, 'She's put Matt in hospital. Hit him with the bottle of duty free she'd bought him. Can't say I blame her, frankly.'

'In hospital? My God. Is he all right?'

'Few stitches and a headache. A lot less than he deserves. It's just as well it was only a bottle that came to hand and not a pair of garden shears or I think his masculinity would have been in danger.'

Maeve stood swaying.

'Why have you got those with you?' she asked, pointing at Flora and Freddy who were standing, open-mouthed, behind Sophie. Flora thought Maeve was being funny and began to laugh and jump up and down, hanging on to her mother's hand.

'Stop it, Flora,' said Sophie angrily. She turned on Jane. 'I can't deal with this with the children here. Can't you take them somewhere? Give me a few minutes with her?'

Jane, unwilling to be helpful but seeing the sense of this, said, 'Hey. You two. Want to see some puppies? They're out here in the washroom. But you've got to be very quiet so as not to frighten them. Come on. On tiptoe. Here, hold my hand, Freddy,' and she led them out, shutting the door behind her.

Sophie went back to Maeve and put her arm round her again. Maeve threw her off and turned to deliver a smacking blow across the face. It took Sophie completely by surprise. Her nose cracked under the blow and her eyes watered. She stepped involuntarily back, tripped over the leg of the chair Maeve had been sitting on, and sat down heavily on the floor. Maeve, who saw her suddenly disappear from sight under the table, collapsed with laughter. Loud, shrieking noises came out of her wet open mouth and Sophie looked at her in shocked astonishment. She had never been struck in her entire life. Maeve roared and bellowed. Tears streamed down her cheeks. Sophie wanted to cry. She held up her hand to try and staunch the flow of blood and mucus from her nose. Down under the table, she looked up at Maeve who, in her moment of triumph, placed a foot on her chest, and with hand on hip raised an arm in a mock victory salute.

'Take that, matey!' she said, between gasps of hilarity. 'Two down. Two nil to me,' and promptly passed out.

Jane cautiously opened the door and poked her head into the kitchen.

'What the hell is going on?' she asked, alarmed by the screams and seeing two bodies on the floor, one bleeding.

Sophie wiped at her face with a bloodied hand and sat up. 'She hit me,' she said. 'But I think she's drunk herself unconscious.'

Jane came in, shutting the door behind her. 'We'd better get her into bed. Jesus, this is all I need.'

She handed Sophie a roll of kitchen paper and she mopped at her nose and then went to the sink to wash her face. The water ran violently red and Sophie wondered whether her nose was broken. It was throbbing and felt peculiar. After a minute or two she managed to stop the bleeding.

Giving the twins instructions to stay and look after the puppies, the two women, each grabbing an arm, hauled Maeve through to the sitting room. Jane ran upstairs to get a sheet and blankets and they made up the sofa and rolled Maeve onto it and then onto her side. They propped her up with cushions. She looked small and childlike like that, noisily asleep with her mouth open.

'If she's sick she won't choke,' said Jane, 'but my God, she'll suffer in the morning.'

Sophie stood looking down at her. Matt and her feelings for him seemed very far away. Her thoughts now were entirely with Maeve.

'Do you want me to stay and sit up with her?' she asked Jane. 'I can't just leave her like this with you.'

'She'll be OK. I had to get you here because I couldn't cope with her and the yard. I didn't dare leave her on her own in the state she was in. She was fighting drunk. Remember, she'd had three hours to sober up before you arrived. She'll be all right now that she's passed out. She'll sleep it off. You'll have to go to Lady Pamela's. That other carer person left this morning, when Maeve got back. It's nothing to do with me but I think you'll have to hold the fort.'

'Is Matt at home?' asked Sophie.

'No idea and frankly I don't care.' She paused and lit a cigarette. She looked at Sophie through narrowed eyes. 'I would have thought better of you two. According to Maeve, she and Matt were almost engaged and you are her oldest friend.'

It was Sophie's turn to look amazed.

'Engaged? That's completely untrue. That's a typical Maevism. She'll say anything to dramatise the situation,' she cried. 'The truth is that they had agreed to break up. Or sort of,' she added lamely.

Jane shrugged. 'Well, I don't want to get involved. It's absolutely nothing to do with me. You'll have to sort it out between the three of you. Maeve can stay here tonight and then I'll send her back over to Charlton in the morning. God knows how she got here as drunk as she was. She came on that bike, you know.'

'I guessed as much. I saw it outside.'

Sophie went to the mirror above the fireplace. Her nose was red and her nostrils were crusted with dark dried blood. With her pale tired face she looked plain and unattractive. She was glad that Matt wasn't there to see her. Now she'd faced Maeve she felt relieved, but limp and exhausted like a deflated balloon, all soft and shapeless. It was a more comfortable state than the taut tension of the drive, when the unknown had strung her up as if on a wire, but she now felt too weary to cope with anything more.

Flora started to cry for her from outside the door. She and Freddy had quarrelled over the puppies. There were just three little pinky white, black-spotted piglet-like creatures and although she had been told not to, Flora had picked one up and then dropped it. Bramble, the mother, had growled and Freddy had cried and so Flora had hit him.

All this Sophie gathered through the crescendo of screams. She caught Jane wincing and said, 'Look, we're going. I'm sorry.'

'That's OK,' said Jane, a trifle guiltily. 'I'm not used to children. Give me dogs or horses any day. Are you going to Charlton?'

Sophie supposed they were. She hadn't had time to sort it out in her mind but she had a sense of responsibility to Lady Pamela. She imagined that she would be worried now, anxious that it had got dark and that there was no sign of Maeve.

When she turned into the drive at Charlton the lights were on and she could see Lady Pamela moving about in the kitchen. She told the twins to stay in the car and she knocked on the front door. When it remained unanswered she ran round to the back and rang the bell and called, 'Lady Pamela! It's me! Sophie!' Lady Pamela opened the door and stood peering into the dark. She had a lemon in her hand and Sophie imagined that she had been pouring herself a drink.

'Lady Pamela, it's me, Sophie,' she repeated.

'Sophie? My dear. What are you doing?'

'Well. It's Maeve, really. She's not . . . um . . . not well enough to come back tonight. She's at your trainer, at Jane's. She's asleep, in fact, and so I've come just to keep you company. If that's all right. Only I've got the twins in the car. May I bring them in?'

'Maeve's not well? What is the matter? She's just been on holiday. I really don't know about you and your children. I wasn't expecting you. I'm not sure I can have people to stay now.'

'I know. I'm sorry. But I don't mean that I'll be here like a guest. I'll do Maeve's work . . . whatever she does for you and then I'll go the minute she gets back in the morning. I didn't like to leave you alone.'

'Don't be ridiculous. I'm not disabled. I can manage perfectly well.'

'Lady Pamela, please. Let me stay here tonight. It would make me feel slightly better. I owe it to Maeve, in a way. I can't explain all that's happened here on the doorstep.'

'Very well,' said Lady Pamela, still annoyed, Sophie could tell. 'You'd better come in. And bring your children, I suppose.'

God, thought Sophie, I've never had such chilly receptions. I'm in everybody's bad books.

It took her half an hour to get the children in and sorted out. In between she tried to telephone Matt but there was no answer at Manor Farm. Upstairs their rooms had been left from their stay at Christmas and the beds were still made up. The kitchen was tidy and clean – a far cry from how it looked under Maeve's occupancy and although there wasn't much food, Sophie made everybody scrambled eggs for supper. She put a match to the drawing-room fire and Lady Pamela had her supper on a tray. After she had cleared away and washed up, Sophie bathed the twins and then let them run around upstairs long after their bedtime as a reward for having been so good on the journey.

Later she went in to Lady Pamela to ask her if she would like a whisky. A pot of hyacinths stood on the table in the window and the room was filled with their heady scent.

'Those are lovely,' said Sophie.

'Trish brought them with her,' said Lady Pamela, and added, full of meaning, 'She, at least, knows her job.

183

Understands what is expected. She wouldn't allow these sort of situations to arise . . . to unsettle me. I always knew that Maeve was entirely unsuitable. I told Henry so.'

Sophie looked at her pinched, irritable face; it reminded her of Flora when things displeased her. Sophie was embarrassed that it was her presence which was causing the aggravation. She had never been in a position like this in her life.

'Lady Pamela, I'm sorry. I'm only doing what I thought was best. I completely understand that you don't want me here but I felt I couldn't abandon you tonight.'

'Abandon me! How dare you! You make me sound like a bastard baby on a doorstep. I can hardly be abandoned in my own home. I don't know what you've got to do with it anyhow,' said Lady Pamela tartly. 'It's nothing to do with you, is it?'

'Only that I'm Maeve's friend. Or was,' said Sophie, sadly, bending over the fire.

'What on earth do you mean?' said Lady Pamela. 'You must tell me. I am tired of this mystery. Of not knowing what is going on.'

Sophie straightened up and sighed. 'All right,' she said. 'I'll tell you.'

When she had finished there was a silence and she looked across at Lady Pamela, wondering whether she had fallen asleep. However she was wide awake and her shrewd old eyes were watching her closely.

'What a muddle!' she exclaimed. 'And very naughty of you and that Matthew. No wonder Maeve is upset. More with you than with him, I daresay. Couldn't you have waited until she'd got back, until you had a chance to speak to her?'

'Of course I could have. But I didn't think like that. I took Matt's word for it, I suppose, that it was over between them.'

'Hmm. It looks more as though you took advantage of her being away.'

'No. Really. It wasn't like that at all.' Sophie felt her face colouring up as she realised she was under attack again. There was a moment's silence in which Lady Pamela observed her stonily. Sophie found she could not meet her eye. She stuck out her long legs and studied her feet, side by side in their well-polished loafers.

Then Lady Pamela said, 'Let me speak to you frankly, Sophie. I am an old woman and I believe I can say what I want at my time of life. It appears to me that you are a young

184

woman who has had everything in life handed to her on a plate. I was very much the same. You have always been provided with everything you want. You have a loving home, loving parents, you are financially secure and you have every confidence that this is as it should be for a girl like you. It is what you were brought up to expect from life, if you played by the rules. You strike me as a girl who respects rules, who likes the reassurance of knowing that you are in the right. The opposite of little Maeve, in fact, who makes up her own rules as she goes along and couldn't give a monkey's for anybody else's. Most of her life, I daresay, she has been in the wrong in other people's eyes.'

Sophie felt acutely uncomfortable. Her nose throbbed and was swollen and red on one side and her head ached. She was aware that what Lady Pamela had said was not intended as praise for her or a criticism of Maeve. She had the uneasy feeling that there was worse to come.

'It puzzles me, this business about your marriage and the twins,' went on Lady Pamela. 'It puzzles me that a modern, intelligent girl could become pregnant accidentally, especially when she knew that her husband was so opposed to having children. Now, of course I only know what Maeve has told me, Sophie, but I believe that your pregnancy was intended. I think that you had decided that that was what you wanted next, that that was what was right – you married and then had babies. The fact that Fergus didn't want to start a family wasn't going to stand in your way. Underneath that gentle exterior is an iron will. No doubt you felt that he was confused, that he did not know what was right and that when the babies came along, he would be as thrilled as you. Anyway, you were going to have what you wanted and you would deal with the consequences. The fact that Fergus wasn't prepared to forgive you was something that you hadn't bargained for. His behaviour was against your rules and you don't possess sufficient imagination to see how it was going to be. I think he did behave badly, but I can perfectly understand why.'

Sophie gasped. 'How can you say that?' she said. 'You know nothing about it. Nothing.'

'Yes, I do, and if you will allow me to continue I will tell you why. When I married Bumper I had every expectation of a good marriage. He was handsome and clever and he adored me. Only later I discovered that it wasn't all as straightforward as that and that Bumper could never love me in the way I wanted or needed. By then I had had a child, Henry, and I had also met and fallen in love with Sam. Sophie, my dear, the rest of my married life was a compromise. I remained with Bumper because I believed that marriage was for life and I felt a strong sense of duty towards him, but not enough to stop me having an ongoing affair with Sam. Bumper and I lived together perfectly amicably and I did everything I could to be the sort of wife he wanted and needed. In a way I think he was relieved that the more passionate side of my nature was being looked after elsewhere. We never spoke of it and Sam and Bumper remained friends until Bumper died.'

'This has nothing to do with me,' said Sophie. 'Frankly, I don't agree with that sort of thing. I believe in fidelity. It's nothing like my life, which for some reason you feel in a position to criticise.'

'Wait. I'm coming to that,' said Lady Pamela. 'What I am telling you is that I never had the courage to follow my heart. I didn't want to hurt Bumper or spoil things for Henry, and selfishly I didn't want to throw away the wonderful security Bumper gave me. Sam was then only an academic. He had a little private income and later made money from his books, but he could not have offered me anything like the lifestyle which I enjoyed with Bumper. I also disliked the sort of scandal and publicity which a divorce would bring in those days and in our circle. Like you, I did not approve of that sort of fast behaviour. Sam knew that too and did not pressurise me to end my marriage. In a sense we both used Bumper. It was a dishonest and cowardly way to live one's life and, Sophie, I regret it. I regret that for all those years I congratulated myself on my sense of duty, on my high ideals, on being really rather wonderful. If anyone was guilty, I felt it was Bumper for being dull and unimaginative.

'Sophie, like me, you are more than capable of self-delusion. You need to examine what you do and why, and try to see things as they really are. Maeve, I believe, is truly honest. She's selfish and naughty and lots of other things but she is entirely true to herself. If the boot had been on the other foot and she had stolen your boyfriend, she would have said, "Sorry, we fancied each other and had a bonk." Are those the right terms? She's honest. Do you see what I mean? She wouldn't blame Matt for not making the situation clear to her, or the fact that you were away on holiday. She would recognise her own nature. Her own motivation. Do you see what I'm saying?'

'But we didn't "have a bonk",' said Sophie primly. 'I wouldn't. I didn't feel it was right.'

'There you go again,' said Lady Pamela. 'Seeing yourself through rose-tinted spectacles. If I know you, you wouldn't sleep with him because you wanted to keep that trump card up your sleeve. Much more to do with your strategy for entrapment than anything else.'

Sophie was dumbfounded.

'There's nothing wrong with that. It's an age-old trick, but be honest with yourself. Now a word of friendly advice. If you and Matthew do fall in love – and I can see that you are very well-suited, I thought as much at Christmas – come clean about everything else. Admit to Maeve that you stole him, that you thought he was too good for her, that you valued acquiring him above her friendship, because you did think that, didn't you? It's a salutary experience to realise what a little shit you really are. Admit to Matthew that Fergus wasn't such a bad man and that you behaved abominably in deliberately becoming pregnant, especially when you knew that there were twins on your side of the family and that there was a strong likelihood that you would have them too. Show him that you've grown up.'

In her entire life Sophie had never been called a little shit. This is unreal, she thought, sitting here in this house, nursing what may well be a broken nose, with an eighty-year-old, rather grand old lady, who is calling me a four-letter word. She almost laughed. Yet somehow everything that was being said to her was gathering momentum, like a fireball rolling through her brain. I've never seen it all like this, she thought. Is she right? It sort of adds up. But I'm a good person. A careful person. She's got me wrong. I've never been in trouble and I don't feel in the wrong now. I'm only here because I'm dutiful, responsible. Unlike Maeve who is drunk on someone's sofa.

'And you've always been spoilt,' continued Lady Pamela, 'like me. Encouraged to be easy on yourself, to see others as at fault and feel yourself somehow superior.'

'Stop,' said Sophie. 'This isn't fair. Why are you attacking me like this? I've done nothing but try and help you, be kind, make up for Maeve's irresponsibility.'

'Maeve isn't here because you and Matthew have kicked her in the teeth. You wouldn't have to stand in for her otherwise.'

Sophie was silent. That at least was true.

'You don't like to think of yourself as selfish and ruthless, do you?' observed Lady Pamela. 'But we all can be, to a degree, given the chance. Maeve knows it and is quite open and blatant about it. You know where you are with Maeve. It's those that don't recognise it in themselves who are the most dangerous, and that is you, Sophie dear, and me. For years and years I made poor Bumper suffer, and Sam. Oh yes, poor Sam.'

Sophie thought, She's lost it, the stupid old woman. She's drunk too much and she's senile and confused. She doesn't know what she's saying.

'And Henry, of course. A long list of victims. Now I am very old I can see it quite clearly but I certainly couldn't at your age, Sophie. So my plea to you is to be honest. To yourself, to Maeve, to your ex-husband, and to Matthew.'

'Right!' said Sophie, full of hostility. 'Thank you very much. And I am so sorry. Since I seem to be cast as the villain of this piece—'

Lady Pamela patted her hand and laughed. 'Don't take yourself so seriously, my dear. I'm not accusing you of being wicked, just blinkered and misguided. Now, allow me to overcome my earlier bad temper by thanking you very much for coming here tonight and for caring about me. I do appreciate it.'

'That's OK,' said Sophie, gruffly. She felt overwhelmed. Bulldozed.

'I'm ready for bed, if you would be so kind as to see to Esau.'

As she helped the old woman up the stairs, Sophie said, 'What do you mean about making Sam suffer? He doesn't look as if he has suffered much to me.' Still hurt and offended, she meanly wanted to belittle the emotion, reduce the drama of Lady Pamela's story.

'He has suffered because he never knew he had a child,' said Lady Pamela, pausing on the stairs. 'Elizabeth, you see. Elizabeth was his.'

Later that night both women lay restlessly awake under the curving tiled roof of Charlton. Sophie felt cold and tired but sleepless. At two o'clock she went downstairs to fill her hot-water bottle to thaw out her feet and made herself a cup of hot milk. What Lady Pamela had said to her littered her mind with pieces she could no longer make any sense of. It seemed that she was being blamed for being from a happy and secure home and for having quite ordinary middle-class expectations. Well, yes, she had had a clear idea of what she had wanted when she had married Fergus and she would admit to anyone that with the advantage of hindsight, she probably hadn't married for all the right reasons. As for her pregnancy, it had been an accident in the sense that she had forgotten to take the pill for a few days. Or not so much forgotten as allowed her supply to run out and been a bit careless. Took a risk.

Now, as she fetched a mug from the neatly ordered cupboard and filled it with foaming milk, she had to admit that risk-taking was not part of her usual behaviour. A calculated risk, then. Calculated? Did that mean a risk that she had calculated was worth it because the almost inevitable outcome was what she wanted? If she hadn't become pregnant that month, would she have repeated the risk-taking the next and the next? Yes, she would have. Until the desired result was achieved. A pregnancy which she could claim was an accident, an act of God, a perfectly forgivable mistake. Lady Pamela was right about that.

Subsequently, when Fergus had been so horrible about it all, Sophie had no difficulty in lining up her family and friends behind her. It was all 'poor Sophie', and her father, his eyes brimming with love and concern, had told her that as a man he could not understand how Fergus could behave as he did. Sophie felt vindicated, the innocent and injured party. But Lady Pamela was right. She had deceived Fergus who had trusted her to look after contraception. She knew that he wanted to wait to have children – of course they had talked about it in the early days and she had been alarmed how unenthusiastic he seemed, and so she had set about getting her own way. She remembered her elation when her next period was late. The thrill of feeling that her body had responded to her desire and that the tiny egg she remembered from cross-section diagrams in boring school lessons on reproduction was there, inside her, ripening and growing and unfurling into a baby.

The next few weeks were magical and mysterious. Sophie had said nothing but had waited, serene and untroubled, as

189

her womb, that dark and velvety chamber, began its secret processes. When finally she went to the doctor she had hardly needed him to confirm that she was three months' pregnant, and it was then, when she felt safe and triumphant, that she had broken the news to Fergus. Horrible, angry, unkind Fergus. She had hated his shouting and moods and sulking that polluted the atmosphere her baby was growing in. When it was confirmed at seven months that she was expecting twins she dreaded telling him. She was a victim then of his anger but she was able to turn in on herself, exclude him, as she concentrated on the drum of her womb and the miraculous life it contained. She had been happy those last months, like a ship in full sail, supported and praised and remarked on by everyone. How well she looked, no sickness, no high blood pressure and the excitement of twins! Had they chosen names? Two of everything! Fergus had skulked and scowled but publicly, at least, had put on a brave face. He had even been to ante-natal classes with her. She was confident then that when he saw the babies and held them in his arms his heart would be moved with joy and pride. Sophie thought that she had got away with it.

Afterwards when it had all gone wrong, after the excitement was over and exhaustion had set in and she wept and could not cope, when she really needed Fergus's love and support, then she learned at what price she'd got what she wanted.

Sophie sat with her mug at the table in the Charlton kitchen and thought, She was right about me, the old girl! I've never thought about it honestly before. Nobody has forced me to. Not even Maeve who was too much on my side because she loathed Fergus from the start.

But what about Matt? If she had stolen him, whatever she did now could not put right her treachery to Maeve. Lady Pamela was perceptive in saying that she had dismissed Maeve's claims to him and felt that her own were more legitimate. She was right in saying that she had allowed what had happened to happen because she wanted him and wanted him more than she feared hurting Maeve. Oh God! What a mess she had got into.

But what she couldn't get clear was what Lady P had meant by all that stuff about being true to yourself, acting honestly. Did she mean that she ought to say, 'Yes, I stole him off my best friend and although I'm sorry, I think it was worth it'?

What difference would that make? And all that about Sam and Bumper and Elizabeth. Lady Pamela's own incredible tale hardly threw light on her present circumstances.

She finished her milk and went to the sink to rinse the mug. Esau was making a lot of snuffling noises in his basket and she stooped over him. His breathing was shallow and fast and she could see his sides heaving. She stroked his coarse hyena-coloured hair but he paid her no attention. His little beady eyes were open and fixed on some far horizon. She hoped he was all right.

Lady Pamela heard Sophie moving about and guessed that their night-time conversation had disturbed her. She could not remember now exactly what she had said, but she regretted the fact that she had offered advice. It was foolish of her to think that mere age bestowed wisdom or that the lessons of her own life were in any way applicable. The world was so different now. In her day people behaved differently and had different expectations. 'It simply isn't done' was a good enough reason not to break the rules. Elizabeth had been the best thing, the most precious gift, and at the time she had thought the only possible course was to pretend that she was Bumper's child. For everybody's sake. The burden of this deception had been terrible to bear but it was necessary to save everybody's feelings, to avoid a terrible upset. Sam could not have married her. In fact they were attempting one of their separations at the time and he was living in Italy. Henry needed her. Certainly Bumper did. She was essential to his career. The poor baby needed a proper start in life, not the stigma of being a love-child, a bastard. She had no choice.

Maeve, of course, would have behaved differently. She would have run off, left Bumper after a year or two, gone her own way. Been true to herself, as she called it. If Lady Pamela had done that she would have followed Sam to Italy, left Henry, divorced Bumper, brought Elizabeth up in an atmosphere of love and warmth, lived a careless, reckless, Bohemian life. Where would it all have ended? She couldn't tell. She didn't know. She had done what had seemed best for everyone. It was loving Sam that had caused the trouble, where she had first gone wrong; but loving Sam and having Elizabeth were the best things in her life.

The night seemed endless. Her legs ached in bed and she had indigestion. What had seemed clear to her when she spoke to Sophie was lost in a mist in her mind. There were no answers and the questions were too difficult. One did what one felt one had to do.

She was dozing off at last when there was a knock on her door and Sophie's voice saying urgently, 'Lady Pamela! Lady Pamela! I'm sorry to wake you, but it's Esau. He's not well.'

It was Matt who came out to see the little dog. Lady Pamela telephoned as soon as the surgery opened and Matt appeared at the door a couple of hours later, looking battered and sheepish. He had some stitches along the line of his brow, covered by a plaster. He hardly glanced at Sophie, who bundled the twins out of the kitchen and took them into the cold garden to get them out of the way. By now she had a black eye and looked ghastly, she thought, what with the effect of a sleepless night as well. The garden was dour and damp and a cold east wind blew from the hills. She felt chilled and miserable and went to sit in the decaying summerhouse while she waited.

Lady Pamela sat in the kitchen armchair with Esau wrapped in her old dressing gown on her lap. His tight little body was a heavy lump and she fondled an ear and talked in a low voice to him. His breathing was difficult and his sharp little eyes had lost their brightness. She held one of his little brown paws in her old hand and said to Matt, 'Now, you must be honest. He's fifteen, you know, so he has had a very good innings, and he couldn't bear to be ill. This last week I have noticed that his hind legs have given way a couple of times and he hasn't eaten. If his time has come I must know.'

She was remarkably calm and in control, thought Matt as he bent over the little body. His presence was registered at least because Esau's bottom lip drew back in a weak snarl. He had always hated vets. Matt listened to his heart and checked his pulse before squatting on his heels and saying, 'Lady Pamela. You want me to be honest and I will be. His heart as you know has been irregular for a couple of years and the heart pills he has been on have done the trick up until now. However I think there is kidney failure as well and signs of general distress. We can try a course of antibiotics but my feeling is that his number is probably up.'

'Very well,' said Lady Pamela staunchly. She stroked the paw she held. The pad was rough as sandpaper and the old nails scuffed and blunt.

'I can take him away with me now,' suggested Matt.

'Certainly not. I want you to put him to sleep here on my lap in the kitchen.'

Matt left them while he went to the car to get his case. In the silence of the kitchen Lady Pamela wrapped Esau up a little more snugly in her dressing gown and shifted him so that she could see his face. His eyes had closed and his bushy eyebrows gave him the appearance of an old man sleeping.

'Good old boy,' she said softly, 'my dear, funny, ugly boy.' Esau's ear twitched. She thought he could still hear her.

Matthew was back then, filling a syringe, asking her if she was really all right. She dropped a kiss on the rough head on her lap and nodded. It was all over quickly and painlessly. The little dog drifted off in Lady Pamela's arms and she could not be sure when his spirit actually left him.

'It's over now,' said Matt. 'I can take him away with me or if you prefer I'll bury him in the garden.'

'Thank you. That would be very kind,' said Lady Pamela stiffly. She was still holding his little front paw in her hand. He left them then and went out to find Sophie. He knew Lady Pamela needed a few minutes alone and that pride and dignity prevented her from showing her grief. As the door shut, Lady Pamela allowed the tears to slide down her cheeks.

'Oh Esau, Esau,' she wept. 'My little friend. What will I do without you?' She felt a terrible wave of grief and loss and sadness for things gone as she covered him up. She would never have another dog. With his passing she was saying goodbye to the life she had shared with him, the evening walks when the trees cast long shadows across the summer fields, the river where he used to jump in and swim energetically up and down with his head held high like a lady anxious to keep her hair dry. She thought of the harvest fields when he had hunted amongst the bales while she and Sam dawdled along hand in hand. He had been a companionable, faithful, wilful little creature. His sturdy little body was still warm in her lap. She couldn't believe that he wouldn't sit up, shake himself and jump down to go and inspect his bowl in the hope that a miracle might have occurred and unexpected food arrived. She thought of his lopsided scuttle, his eager little face, his enthusiasm for life. She thought of him in his younger days cannoning about the fields, barking at the horses. She would ask Matt to bury him in the spring garden, amongst the irises, where he had spent many an hour intent

193

on searching for hedgehogs. She needed to tell Sam. Sam should know. Sam had loved him too.

In the summerhouse Sophie cried when Matt told her that Esau was no more. He sat beside her on a wobbly, rotten seat and held her hand and for a while they said nothing and then Sophie, sniffling, said, 'Why is everything suddenly so horrible? Especially when I've got you and it should all be wonderful.' She smiled at him through her tears and put out a hand to touch the plaster on his forehead. 'I told you she's something else when she's angry. She used to break windows at school.'

'Jane told me she bopped you one as well,' said Matt, kissing Sophie on her black eye. 'I called in there this morning to see what had happened. I wanted to telephone you here last night but I didn't like to ring when I got back from hospital. It was late and I thought it would disturb Lady P.'

'You could have rung my mobile,' complained Sophie. 'I had an awful evening. Lady Pamela got stuck into me about doing the dirty on Maeve. She basically said that I wasn't honest and that I deceived myself and others by pretending to be nice. Something like that anyway. She quite approves of us though – I think she said we were well-suited. Then she told me some extraordinary story about her and Sam and Bumper. That Elizabeth wasn't Bumper's child, but Sam's.'

'That's been local knowledge for years,' said Matt. 'It was obvious, I believe. No one could understand how Bumper put up with it. My father remembers that he was really good to Elizabeth. Adored her, in fact.'

Sophie stared at him. 'How extraordinary. It's sort of ennobling in a way, isn't it? To have the generosity to love another man's child? Anyway, how was Maeve this morning? Did you see her?'

'She was still hogging it on the sofa. Jane said just to leave her to sleep it off. No doubt she'll be round soon. Darling, I'm so sorry for all this.'

'It's more my fault. She's my friend.'

'Yes, I know, but I had no idea that she would go berserk like that. It was true what I told you – that I felt she wasn't interested in me. She was just using me really, to stave off what she called Concrete Deprivation.'

'But friendships go deep with Maeve. She doesn't bother with social sort of friends – if she likes you, you're a mate.

She'd do anything for you. We really have behaved badly. God, I wish we'd waited until she came home and talked to her before we embarked on falling in love, or whatever you call it.' Sophie felt uncertain whether she could assume that Matt really did feel he loved her.

He kissed her and said, 'I hope that's what we can call it. It's certainly what I feel. I can't stop thinking about you, Sophie. You're in my head all day long.' He pulled her towards him and she laid her head on his shoulder. She felt secure and protected.

'Me too. I mean, you are in mine. But have you felt like this before?'

'Never. Not like this. Never bowled over like this.'

Sophie had to get up then to sort out the Effs who had both fallen over in the mud. Flora had found a long stick which she was waving about like a sword. She screamed when it was removed and lay on the path on her back, drumming her feet on the ground.

Matt looked on with admiration. 'God! She can put on quite a display, can't she?'

'Yes. She's unspeakably horrible sometimes. Flora! Stop that at once. OK. We'll leave you there. Goodbye,' and they walked away, Matt to find a spade and Sophie to show Freddy the stone rabbits on the edge of the lawn.

Flora lay where she was and after a bit stopped bellowing and watched the seagulls up high in the sky. She was still lying there when Maeve peddled up the path, whistling.

'Wotcha, Flora. What are you doing there?'

Flora opened her eyes very wide so that she could take in Maeve and the bicycle, but did not move. 'Being howwible,' she said.

'Yeah. Thought so. Come on, you can sit on the saddle if you like.'

Later, in the kitchen, Sophie made them all coffee and the children sat on cushions and had juice and biscuits.

'So,' said Maeve, looking at Matt and Sophie, 'I'm going away again. I'm going to Ireland for a week to see me old mates. You can stay here, Sophie, can't you? It'll be nice for you to be near old dearly beloved over there.' She indicated Matt who was leaning against the Aga.

'Maeve, I can't. The twins are due to start at a playgroup. I can't just move in here. Anyway, what about Lady Pamela? She won't agree.'

'Tough titties,' said Maeve, stretching and yawning. 'You can sort it out between you. You're good at making plans behind my back.'

'Don't be like that, Maeve. It's not fair. We've both said we're really, really sorry.'

'Yeah. Well, I'm not ready to forgive you yet. I want a lift to the station, Matt. Give me ten minutes to pack.'

Chapter Eleven

'I am very sorry,' declared Bunty, whose tone made it clear she was not in the least sorry,' 'but I can only see that dog's departure as a blessing. He was always going to be a problem when we move your mother, Henry.'

'Yes, dear,' said Henry mildly from behind his newspaper. He could see the truth in what Bunty was saying but he also had a pang of sympathy for his mother who had telephoned that morning to tell him of Esau's demise.

'She did love him, though,' he added. 'God knows why. She could hardly speak to me this morning.'

'Well, I'm not saying that she wasn't very attached to it, but that is a sign of old age and loneliness. She'll feel better when we've got her moved and she can make friends with the other old people. Now, Henry, are you listening? I'm going to Charlton next week, remember, for three days. I'll be back in time for the Australia House reception on Saturday evening.'

'Yes. You've been through all that.' Henry folded his newspaper and brushed crumbs from his trousers. He sensed an early escape would be advisable. Standing up, he made for the door.

'Now before you go I just want you to look at these garden designs,' said Bunty, clearing a space on the table and spreading out sheets of grid worked paper. 'I think the tennis court here, don't you? I want all these trees down and a Japanese stone garden, here. It's so old-fashioned with all these itsy bitsy beds and arches. We want to think vistas, Henry.'

Henry murmured something noncommittal. Actually, he thought, Charlton had rather nice vistas already, of rolling fields and cows and distant villages.

'And look, Henry,' said Bunty, spreading out a fan of colour photographs. 'A Mexican theme, all terracotta and hot oranges, and this steamed willow and coppiced ash "hedge"

197

which doubles as a garden seat. Fabulous. All Peregrine's work, Henry. Fabulous.'

Henry could see all too clearly the direction this was going in and looked at his watch.

The holiday in the West Indies had revved Bunty up and she was unstoppable. This morning her tanned face and beady blue eyes were shining with the prospect of a challenge. She had come home ready to take on all comers and that included his mother. In fact, Lady Pamela was at the top of the list.

'Are you staying at Charlton?' he asked as he collected his briefcase and looked out to see if his car and driver had arrived.

'Of course. What did you expect? I'm not spending out on a hotel while that place is half empty. Peregrine too. He's staying.'

'Have you warned the girl?' asked Henry anxiously.

'I telephoned yesterday and spoke to her. She seems half witted, Henry, but I got the message across in the end. She said she'd get the rooms ready. We can always eat at the pub in West Chitton in the evening but it won't hurt her to earn her keep for a change and do us breakfast and lunch. Strange thing, I thought I heard children, little children crying in the background.'

Henry shrugged. 'Television probably. Last time you thought you heard a man, remember? And Mother? Does she know why you are going down there? Does she know about her visit to the Old Malthouse?'

'She knows we're coming to look around and do the preliminary survey. She pretends she doesn't understand, the wily old crow. She doesn't know that I'm taking her over to look at the sheltered housing. I thought it was best just to jump that one on her.'

'Here's the car,' said Henry with relief, leaning to peck Bunty's cheek. She was not paying him attention. She had turned back to the garden plans.

'Peregrine wants the pared-down purity of the Zen garden to meet the informality of the English country garden,' she explained. 'John Galliano has this mix in his garden in Paris . . .' but Henry had gone. He did not know who John Galliano was anyway.

Sophie sat at the kitchen table at Charlton in despair. Bunty had terrified her on the telephone and she felt like a rabbit caught in the headlights of a car.

What was she to do? She couldn't go on pretending to be Maeve and she dreaded the repercussions of admitting to Bunty that Maeve had gone off and left her to cope with Lady Pamela without any consultation.

It had not been easy, to be stranded at Charlton like this. She had had to telephone Fergus and tell him where she was and ask him to contact the nursery school and ask them to hold the children's places for a couple of weeks. She had to lie and say that they were still ill with chickenpox and she was keeping them in the country until they were completely better. Fergus was annoyed. He disliked plans being changed and he was aware that the school would charge him for the weeks missed. He was suspicious of the sudden relapse after Sophie herself had told him that they were much better. Something was up and he did not like being messed about.

Lady Pamela was not easy either. Since the demise of Esau she had been crotchety and uncommunicative. Sophie was less confident than Maeve and too anxious to please; Lady Pamela, like most strong-willed people who sense insecurity, became domineering and tetchy. Maeve would have ignored her complaints and given her the like it or lump it treatment which worked so well, but Sophie did not have it in her to speak to an aristocratic old woman as Maeve did. With Sophie Lady Pamela got the upper hand. She complained about the children and the noise and the food and Sophie became more and more nervous and distracted.

Matt tried to be supportive and helpful and the best moments were when he turned up in the evening after the twins were in bed and Sophie was getting Lady Pamela's supper. They had the kitchen to themselves and opened a bottle of wine and enjoyed being together. Matt loved watching Sophie move between the sink and the stove wrapped in an apron, chatting and unselfconscious as she prepared the food. He loved the angles of her plain, well-bred face and the way she ran her hand through her short hair and the long line of her neck. He came up behind her and put his arms round her and buried his face in her warm shoulder. She smelt of lemons and grass. He loved kissing her slowly from the little soft ivory-coloured spot behind her ear down the length of her cheek to find her mouth. He kissed the satiny skin of her underarm and learned the arrangement of bones and sinews of her long hand so that he would know them anywhere. He stroked her hair back from her face and ran his lips over the soft transparent down at her temples. He loved being with her. He felt at peace in her company and when she was anxious and tense he loved reassuring her and feeling that she needed him. He went back and forth to the twins who had become naughty and attention-seeking since being ill, read to them and took them drinks and rearranged Flora's toys as she demanded, opened the door on the landing, left this light on and closed that curtain, until they went to sleep.

But Matt could not help Sophie out of this corner. If Bunty was intending to come to Charlton after the weekend, Sophie would have to deal with her. Making up the beds and doing the meals was nothing, coming up with an explanation for Maeve's behaviour was much harder. Sophie supposed she could say that Maeve had been called urgently back to Ireland for family reasons and that she was holding the fort until she returned. But she was such a bad liar. Bunty was sure to want to know details, when exactly Maeve was returning, maybe even speak to her on the telephone.

Sophie telephoned Mohammed. He was thrilled to hear from her and anxious to help when she told him of her problem. She had to gloss over the true nature of why Maeve had bunked off. She felt embarrassed to tell Mohammed that she and Matt were in love, as if in some way she was being unfaithful to him. Mohammed, however, made it easier by telling her that he was going out with a Swedish girl he had met on the bus on the way to Sam's.

'Ah, these blondies,' he said enthusiastically.

'Have you any idea where Maeve might be staying in Ireland?' said Sophie. 'I mean, I can't stay here for ever.'

'I think she goes to her homes. She is not in London or she ring Mohammed.'

'Maybe you are right,' said Sophie. 'I could always telephone her father and say I am trying to trace her. I needn't tell him any more than that. I'd better go, Mohammed. Lady Pamela wants her lunch promptly at one o'clock and I haven't begun it yet. Give my love to Sam and Khaled.'

Later, as she took Lady Pamela her coffee after lunch, she broached the subject of Bunty's proposed visit.

'She's coming on Wednesday. She said she was bringing her designer with her, so Mrs Day and I had better make up beds. Do you mind which rooms I put them in? I hope to God Maeve will be back by then. I'll telephone Ireland this evening. I've got to know when she's coming back.'

Lady Pamela sniffed. 'I don't care to think of my telephone bill.'

'I'll use my mobile,' Sophie replied patiently.

Thwarted of a grievance, Lady Pamela sniffed again. She was tired of being disagreeable but hadn't the strength or the inclination to behave better. She knew she should be grateful to this girl for her kindness. She had no obligation to take Maeve's place or to look after her so conscientiously. Of this Lady Pamela was well aware, but it was still in an irritable tone that she said, 'It's an extraordinary state of affairs. You here, with those babies. I don't know what Bunty will think, or Henry. How can I possibly explain to them?'

Sophie felt close to tears. 'Well, what do you suggest I do?' she replied. 'I don't want to be here either, but I can't just walk out on you.'

Lady Pamela softened. She looked at Sophie's trembling mouth and filling eyes and said, 'I know, my dear, and I am grateful. I realise that I have been ungracious and I am sorry. The truth is that since Esau went, I haven't felt quite right. I am sorry to have been so disagreeable. I also know very well that Bunty intends to put me into a home at the first opportunity. This visit is no doubt paving the way and I don't know how long I shall be able to resist her. My only hope is that I die first. Don't look so shocked. It would be much the best all round.'

'Would she really do that?' asked Sophie. 'Shove you out against your will?'

'I suppose she'll have to prove I am incapable of living here, of managing in my own home. Maeve was a sort of bulwark, you see. I think it annoyed Bunty that Maeve and I rubbed along together quite successfully. As long as I had Maeve willing to stay and look after things, I was safe. When Bunty finds that Maeve has gone and that I have only a very temporary arrangement with you, I think she'll consider that the time is ripe to strike.'

Sophie considered this. She could see the sense in what the old woman was saying. In a way, she could also understand Bunty's argument. It was mad for Lady Pamela to rattle about alone in this big house. A comfortable, warden-assisted flat with central heating would be much more sensible. Her own grandmother had been moved into this sort of sheltered housing not long before she died. Then Sophie remembered, with regret, how her grandmother had hated giving up her home and how the life had seemed to drain out of her once she had been moved. There was more to this than what seemed sensible, she thought. It was altogether more complicated and had something to do with the human spirit.

'What I think we'll have to say,' she said, 'is that Maeve has had to go home, urgently, for some reason or other, and that I have come for a few days to take her place.'

'Hmm,' Lady Pamela considered. 'I rather think that Bunty will regard this as a natural break. She'll tell Henry to instruct Maeve not to return.'

'Then we must find Maeve,' said Sophie. 'We must find Maeve and get her back to Charlton.'

It wasn't until Tuesday evening that Sophie eventually tracked Maeve down. She dialled her father's Belfast number with a thumping heart and a dry throat. She realised that she was frightened of speaking to her. She could not bear more confrontation. She had already spoken to Mr Delaney who confirmed that Maeve was in Ireland, he wasn't sure where, but that she was staying the following night with him. 'It's all she'll spare me,' he complained in his high, nasal Northern Irish voice, 'and here I am, her father.'

He had a soft spot for Sophie who from school days he thought was a good influence on his daughter. She was the sort of well-behaved and polite young woman he would have liked Maeve to become.

'I'll tell her you called,' he said. 'No doubt she'll want to telephone you back for a gossip.'

Some chance, thought Sophie.

'I think it would be better if I rang her,' she said. 'It's really very important and she might forget.'

'Nothing wrong, I hope? She's not been getting into a scrape, has she?'

'No, not at all. Nothing like that. It's, um, about a friend. Maeve needs to know what's happened . . .' Sophie trailed off. She didn't want to be more specific.

On Tuesday the telephone was answered on about the third ring. It was Maeve.

'Maeve, it's me, Sophie.'

Maeve's voice was strange and cold when she realised who it was. 'What do you want?' she asked abruptly.

Sophie waded in. 'Look, I can't talk for long, but you've got to come back. Maeve? Are you still there? It's Bunty. She's here at Charlton with some designer person. He's quite sweet actually and wearing a pair of really hip trousers with ragged seams on the outside. They look as if they've been made in an occupational therapy workshop.' Sophie hoped she might make Maeve laugh, but there was no response.

'Anyway, Maeve,' Sophie ploughed on, 'she wants to put Lady P into a home. She told me so yesterday when she arrived. She's taking her to look round one on Friday. You must come back, Maeve. I can't deal with this. Bunty just makes me agree with her all the time. I seem to cave in at once. We need you, Maeve. Lady Pamela says Bunty will stop you coming back. She'll say you aren't needed. Lady P says she'd rather die than leave Charlton. Maeve?' There was silence on the end of the line. 'And Maeve, poor Esau has died and Bunty sees that as another obstacle out of the way. He can't be used as an excuse. His going is like the end of a chapter.'

Again there was silence, then, 'OK, matey,' said Maeve, in her normal voice. 'I'm on me way. If I fly to Bristol tomorrow morning, I'll have to borrow the fare off me father; and tell that bastard Matt to come and meet me at the airport. Heh! Listen, I haven't forgiven you, right? And how's that black eye?' With relief Sophie realised that there was a trace of amusement in her voice.

'Maeve, I am so sorry,' she said, 'but I do love him.'

'Pass the sick bag,' said Maeve, and rang off.

Bunty and Peregrine were hard at work pegging out the garden when George delivered Maeve to the back door of Charlton the following midday. Sophie had had to pay for the taxi from the airport because Matt said he could not possibly take time off in the middle of the day, but she felt it was worth it when she looked up from stirring a white sauce to see Maeve banging through the door. She was wearing an oversized ethnic-looking sweater made up of huge loopy stitches in various shades of pink and cyclamen and a pair of tight orange jeans. She looked fabulous, Sophie thought. The twins shrieked and left the house they were making out of cardboard boxes and rushed to grab her round the legs.

'Hi there, Effs!' she said, picking up each round the middle and holding them under her arms like two fat, squealing piglets.

Sophie hurried across and put her arms round her. Maeve's wiry little body stiffened but she didn't push her away.

Instead she plonked the twins back down and said, 'Where are the bastards?'

'Outside. I am so glad it's cold. They must be freezing. They're pegging out the new garden. Lady Pamela's in the drawing room watching them through the window. I can't bear it.'

Without a word, Maeve went through into the hall and Sophie heard her talking to Lady Pamela. Sophie followed to where she could see them standing side by side at the long windows. In her bright colours Maeve positively glowed against the grey gloom of the January landscape.

'Don't worry, matey,' Maeve was saying. 'If you don't want to go, you're not going.'

'There's nothing you can do to stop it,' said Lady Pamela. 'I'm afraid Bunty has made up her mind.'

'Then she'll have to unfucking make it,' said Maeve. She gave Lady Pamela a rabbit punch on the arm. 'Come on, Lady P. Where's your fighting spirit? Sorry about old Esau, by the way. I quite loved him too. Is he buried out there?' She indicated the garden. Lady Pamela nodded. Maeve scowled through the window at the two figures who were measuring and banging in pegs in the distance. 'I wish he'd rise from his grave and bite Bunty, don't you?'

Lady Pamela had to smile. Maeve was so childlike in her passions and this ridiculous notion that they could somehow hold out against Henry and Bunty. But having her back was somehow strengthening.

'Here,' said Maeve, 'I bought you a present,' and she dived into a plastic bag she'd left at her feet and pulled out a bottle of Bushmills Irish whiskey. 'Come on, let's have one now and then I'll go and give old Sophers a hand with the lunch. This is for you from my father, by the way. He bought it at the airport. Like most Republicans, he's always keen to toady up to titles.'

'How uncharitable you are! It's most kind of him,' said Lady Pamela, 'and yes, let's have a stiff one right away. However, before we do, I must first say, Maeve, that your going off like that and simply leaving me here with Sophie was outrageous. Utterly disgraceful. Sophie has done her best, but it has been a most inconvenient and unsuitable arrangement for us both. You are never, do you understand, to behave like that again?'

Maeve had turned her back and was sloshing whiskey into tumblers. She started to whistle softly under her breath and then began a nonchalant humming. 'Oh, sorry,' she said when Lady Pamela stopped to draw breath. 'Were you talking to me? I don't believe you could have been, because you must surely be very glad and relieved to see me again. Without me, your number's up, Lady P, as well you know. I'll have you understand I was quite tempted to stay on in Ireland, but no, duty called and here I am, and you, to be sure, must be grateful and pleased.' She handed Lady Pamela a glass and twirled the golden liquid round in her own. A soft, peaty smell rose from the spirit and she gulped a fiery mouthful. Lady Pamela observed her silently, a wry expression on her face.

'Very well, Maeve,' she said. 'We'll say no more about it. However, good manners should have dictated that you spoke to me first.'

'OK. I'll grant you that,' said Maeve cheerfully. She grinned. She realised that she was glad to be back. It felt like coming home. 'This wee flit to Ireland was more for effect than anything else, you know,' she said. 'I didn't really want to go away again but I needed to give Matt and Sophie a kick up the pants. You know about them, don't you? I can see you do. Well, I couldn't think where else to go and me father is always complaining that I never keep in touch, especially at Christmas and so on. All that family crap. But as usual, one evening was quite enough, and he wasn't too disappointed when I announced that I had to fly back to Bristol on the first available flight in the morning. Having me in the house unsettled Bethany, grown more bovine than ever now that she's pregnant. She sat on the edge of her seat as if she was preparing for a nasty shock whenever we were in the same room together.'

Maeve prattled on but she did not tell Lady Pamela that her father had not only bought her air ticket but had handed her a cheque as well. 'It's yours. You've had an insurance policy mature,' he said.

'A what?' said Maeve, to whom insurance, policy and mature were foreign words.

'A policy I took out when you were a baby. It's your money. In your name.'

'Jesus,' said Maeve, holding the cheque. It was far more money than she could dream of. 'I need never work again.'

'Hardly,' said her father, smiling. 'You'd get through that in about two years. Put it in a savings account. A building society.'

'Jesus,' said Maeve again. There was no need at all to return to Charlton. She could tell Henry to stuff his job, leave Sophie to sort it out, let Lady Pamela be put in a home. Never see any of them again. As soon as this thought had occurred to Maeve, she knew she had to go back. She knew she wanted to.

Sophie had made lunch of boiled bacon, baked potatoes and leeks in white sauce. Maeve set the table for Bunty, Peregrine and Lady Pamela in the drawing room, and the kitchen table for herself, Sophie and the twins. She heard Bunty come in the front door, clattering about and exclaiming loudly about the filthy weather. She couldn't catch Peregrine's replies.

Bunty went through to the drawing-room fire, rubbing her cold hands together. She had mud on the back of her trouser legs, Lady Pamela was satisfied to see. She had had her hair cut very short which seemed to emphasise her determined chin, and her tan looked exotic in the cold northern light. Around her neck she wore a string of shells and driftwood and possibly feathers. No doubt the work of one of her aspiring designers, thought Lady Pamela. To her it looked like the contents of a wastepaper basket at the end of a child's seaside holiday.

'I don't know what your gardener does, but it certainly isn't keeping those beds under control,' Bunty remarked.

'He does have everything to do outside, you know,' said Lady Pamela, 'and the horses.'

'Ah! The horses,' said Bunty significantly. 'I'm amazed to hear from Henry that you've put a horse back into training. Amazed that you can afford it, I mean. We certainly couldn't.'

This was such arrant nonsense that Lady Pamela ignored it. 'Yes. It's very exciting. He's looking quite promising at the moment, although of course he hasn't run yet. His first race is in two weeks at Newton Abbot. He's got quite a following, you know. The Days are going, our young vet and his father, Jack Dick, George the taxi driver, Maeve, certainly. Sam, of course.'

Bunty sniffed. It was not a list to impress, in her view.

'What are you drinking?' she asked, spotting the glass on the table by Lady Pamela's chair. 'Whisky? At lunchtime? Is that really a good idea?'

'Yes. It really is,' replied Lady Pamela. 'At my age I can do what I like.'

'Well, Peregrine and I will only have spring water. Has that girl got some in the kitchen?'

Hearing this, Maeve darted across the room and sat down casually at the kitchen table.

Bunty stopped short when she saw her. She looked from one to the other girl for an explanation.

'Well,' she said, 'who are you?'

'Hi!' said Maeve sweetly. 'I'm "that girl".'

'Who? The Irish one, whatever her name is?'

'Yup. That's me,' said Maeve, not getting up. 'I'm back! If it's water you want, it's in the tap. Bottled water is far too extravagant, don't you think?'

Later, as they sat down to lunch and Maeve was helping Sophie cut up the twins' meat and Flora was demanding to have only pink on this side of her plate and only white on the other, the atmosphere was strained, until Maeve looked across at her friend and said, 'OK, Soph. I'm over it now. But I have to say I think you two were bastards. Matt and I might not have been getting on so well but you didn't have to move in there quite so fast. You could at least have waited till the sheets got cold.'

'I know, Maeve. I feel really bad about it.' Sophie made a contrite face and held out her hand and Maeve took it across the table and gave it a squeeze.

'Actually,' she said, 'you're right in a way. Matt suits you much better than me. After a bit he'd make me want to murder him. He's too sensible and reasonable. Give me unpredictability, a bit of danger. I need to be kept guessing.'

Sophie didn't know whether she should try and defend Matt against this slur, apparently of dullness, but thought it better to let it pass.

'I was thinking, you know,' said Maeve, 'about you, Soph. First of all Mohammed and then Matt . . . I realised that since Fergus and all that trauma, you've become much more attractive. Pre-Fergus you were a bit smug, you know. Little Miss Perfect. Now you've been knocked around a bit, you're much more human, more vulnerable, and I guess that's what men like. And you've got better looking. Being thin suits you. No wonder they're all falling in love with you.'

Sophie smiled. 'Hardly all,' she said.

'Anyway,' Maeve went on, 'I think you and Matt are good news. I really do.'

'Thanks,' said Sophie, overwhelmed and sniffing.

'Only don't do it again,' said Maeve. 'No more stealing my men. I saw Jack Dick first, remember.'

'Has Jack Dick got a willy?' asked Flora, looking up from arranging her plate.

'Oh God,' said Sophie, 'how do I answer that?'

'Of course he has,' said Maeve. 'All boys and men have willies.'

'Oh,' said Flora, considering. 'And my daddy?'

'Yes,' said Maeve, 'and what's more, he is one.'

It did not take Maeve long to win over Peregrine. He was a tall, fair, etiolated young man with a pretty face and silky yellow hair. He was clearly finding Bunty's adoration and attention a little suffocating and kept trying to slope off to the kitchen to see what Maeve and Sophie were doing.

'Here comes Golden Delicious,' said Maeve, as he appeared that evening when she and Sophie were drinking wine and eating cheese and apples in the kitchen. He and Bunty had had steak and chips in the pub, but since Bunty was temporarily off alcohol she had not suggested he had a drink. Rob and various of his rugby mates who had been in the bar had sniggered at the roughly hewn, arts and crafts trousers and the pashmina carelessly knotted at the neck, and snorted into their beer when they heard Bunty address him by name. Of course they assumed he was homosexual, which he wasn't.

'Well, you shouldn't go around dressed like that,' said Maeve, when he complained to them. 'This is red meat country. If you waft about like Tinkerbell, of course they'll think that. Have you got a girlfriend?' She handed him a glass of wine.

'Yes,' said Peregrine. 'Big and black and gorgeous. She's a dancer.'

'Good for you,' said Maeve. 'Come on, sit down and tell us about her.'

At that moment Matt appeared at the back door. He looked abashed at seeing Maeve, and Sophie flew across to him and took his arm. He was still wearing a plaster across his eyebrow.

'Maeve's come to save the day,' she said. 'I couldn't cope with Bunty and her horrible schemes. Maeve's come back to see her off.'

'Great,' said Matt nervously, and then sensing an amiable atmosphere, went across and put his arms round her. She allowed him to give her a hug. 'Are you going to knock her out?' he asked.

'Possibly,' said Maeve. 'This is Peregrine, her gardener.'

'Designer,' Peregrine corrected.

'Great,' said Matt again, floundering.

'Now, Matt, tell me about Dancer,' said Maeve, sitting back at the table and pouring him a glass of wine. 'What's the crack?'

'I was down at Jane's yard yesterday,' he replied. 'She's pleased with him. He seems in good order. He's been working well, apparently. Sharpening up his jumping. That's the thing about Jane, she really knows how to improve a horse.'

'I can't wait to see him again. I missed you, you know, while I was away. I missed the whole yard buzz. I told me father I'd got into racehorses. "Ah, well, it's in the blood," he said. "Your grandfather was a bookie and most of the family were drunks or gamblers." As if I'd reverted to form!'

They were chatting and laughing when Bunty reappeared, wanting coffee. She looked surprised at the party going on in the kitchen. Every time she went in there someone new had arrived. Really, she thought, Charlton was being used like a hotel. However, on being introduced, she liked what she saw of Matt. She approved of professions and someone had once told her it was harder to qualify as a vet than as a doctor. She was also favourably disposed towards him as Esau's executioner and she had a few minutes' talk with him about the necessity of recognising when the moment had come to put a beloved pet to sleep. She made it sound as if she personally had to struggle to come to terms with this decision and, like Sophie, Matt found himself agreeing with her while at the same time disliking what she was saying.

'Now,' she said pointedly to Maeve, 'since I imagine that you have resumed responsibility for Lady Pamela, I am taking her over to the Old Malthouse in Sherborne tomorrow morning. She is not yet aware that we have put her name down for sheltered accommodation, and I anticipate some resistance, but she will love it, I know, when she has looked round and met the manager and some of the other old people. I want her up and ready by ten.'

Sophie looked at Maeve. This was her moment, but Maeve simply nodded, smiling agreeably.

'Sure,' she said, 'I can do that for you, Bunty. The old girl needn't know where she's going.'

Sophie felt dismayed. Where was the resistance? The heroic stand?

Annoyed by Maeve's cheeky use of her Christian name, Bunty turned and directed her next remark at Sophie. 'Now that Miss Delaney has reappeared, you presumably will be leaving tomorrow? I realise you have kindly stepped into the breach for your friend here, but this is hardly a suitable household for young children. So many valuable things about . . .' Her implication was clear and Sophie blushed.

'Actually,' said Matt, 'Soph's coming to stay the weekend with me, my father and me, at Manor Farm. You must be terribly grateful to her for helping out like this. You could have had a real crisis if she hadn't dropped everything and come.' Sophie looked at him gratefully and Bunty had the grace to look slightly uncomfortable.

'Of course,' she said, 'although it was extraordinary to arrive here and find this arrangement had been made with no reference to us, Lady Pamela's family.'

'Crisis management,' said Maeve. 'No time for niceties.'

All four sitting at the table smiled placatingly at Bunty and she felt she had lost ground. She was annoyed that Peregrine seemed to have joined the kitchen ranks and was drinking with them. She turned to put the kettle on and began a noisy search for coffee. No one got up to help her.

The next morning Maeve went busily backwards and forwards getting Lady Pamela's breakfast and then helping her to decide what to wear. As far as Bunty knew, the old lady thought she was simply having a day out and Maeve got her up rather splendidly in a pink mohair jacket and orange and pink tweed skirt. Her own colours, in fact. She tied Sam's scarf at her neck and helped her choose some earrings and a brooch. She spent quite a time helping her with her *maquillage* and when Lady Pamela finally came downstairs at ten to ten she looked magnificent. Mrs Day stopped Hoovering the drawing room to come and admire her. Maeve had found a purple velvet beret in the hat boxes in the dressing room and had arranged it rakishly on the sleek little white head and the overall effect was certainly striking. She looked like a brightly coloured little bird.

'Lady Pamela, you look wonderful. Like a film star,' said Mrs Day.

'My dear, I hope nothing so vulgar,' said Lady Pamela.

Bunty came out of the kitchen where she had been checking for signs of extravagant consumption and counting the empty bottles in the back pantry.

'There was no need to go over the top and get all dressed up like that,' she said to Maeve. 'We're only going into Sherborne for coffee, you know.'

'Wow!' said Sophie, going through the hall with some of her stuff which she was loading into her car. 'You look great! Lady Pamela, I'll say goodbye. We're off in a moment or two, but as you know we're only going to Manor Farm. I think we'll see you tomorrow at Jane's. Isn't Matt collecting you to go over to the stables to see Dancer?'

'He is indeed,' said Lady Pamela.

'Well, it's only goodbye for now, then,' said Sophie. 'We've loved being here,' she added with typical politeness, and contrary to the truth. 'I hope it hasn't been too awful for you.'

'It's you I must thank,' said Lady Pamela, kissing her cheek, 'and let me say goodbye to these two little horrors.' Flora and Freddy had a kiss dropped on their heads. Sophie turned to say goodbye to Bunty but she had made herself scarce, disliking all this attention centred on Lady Pamela, and not wanting to appear too grateful herself. She also wished to avoid any question of reimbursement or payment. Henry could deal with that. The girl would obviously have to be paid, but there were living expenses to consider.

Maeve helped Sophie get the twins into the car. For once it was a bright sunny morning and the recent rain had given the landscape a clean, glittering look. As Sophie turned on the engine she said, 'Keep me posted, won't you? I'll be on tenterhooks all the morning.'

'Yet bet,' said Maeve, giving her a sly wink. As Sophie turned to drive through the gate she saw Peregrine taking photographs in the garden to her left with Bunty hard on his heels. She tooted and waved. Peregrine waved back while Bunty stared at her blankly and then raised a hand in an unenthusiastic gesture of farewell.

It seemed an endless morning to Maeve. First there was the business of getting Lady Pamela prepared and the anxiety of worrying whether her plan would work. After Bunty had set off with her brightly coloured little mother-in-law beside her, Maeve felt a real pang of concern. Lady P looked so small and frail in the front passenger seat, it was like seeing a technicolour lamb go to the slaughter.

The minute they had gone, Mrs Day put the kettle on and they called Peregrine in from the garden and had several cups of coffee and Maeve made toast and Marmite. Mrs Day sat nursing her mug and told them about Frank, how he had been to the doctor who said he was suffering from depression.

'Depression!' she said. 'It's not depression he's got. It's being on the scrapheap. That's his trouble. You can't get pills to cure that.'

Peregrine listened sympathetically and said that when work started at Charlton there would be the possibility of a job. 'I can't promise anything and we'll contract out the heavy stuff, but there'll be all the planting to do.'

Mrs Day sniffed. 'Odd job work,' she said. 'That's what he'll say. I can hear him now. When's all this going to start anyway?'

'Next month,' said Peregrine. 'I want to get the structural stuff out of the way so that we can be ready for planting in the spring.'

Maeve stared at him without saying anything. Don't you be too sure, she thought. She glanced at the kitchen clock. It was eleven forty-five. It might all be over by now. They could be on the way home. She did not dare think about the outcome of the morning's expedition. She got up and rinsed her mug and glanced anxiously down the drive. No sign yet. She ought to think about getting lunch ready. She was going to make soup. All the time she was chopping vegetables she was listening for the sound of the car wheels on the gravel, for Bunty's angry voice in the hall. At least, she hoped it would be angry.

Sophie was putting the children to bed when Maeve finally telephoned. Commander Digby called her down to take the call in the cold hall and the twins came bumping down the stairs after her, wrapped in their duvets. They naturally did not want to stay alone upstairs in yet another strange house.

'Maeve? Quick! Tell me!' she said at once.

'Worked a dream, matey,' said Maeve. 'Worked a dream! Bunty left about three o'clock to go back to London. She's furious.'

'What happened? Did she tell you?'

'You bet she did! I heard every outrageous detail. Apparently they were shown round this place Bunty's got her signed up for by the manager person and all was sweetness and light. Lady Pamela said quite firmly that although she was willing to see round she had no intention of moving until she had to. She was shown all the low-level light switches and door handles you can turn with your elbows and that sort of thing. She must have been furious! Anyway she said that she would like to see the communal drawing room which Bunty said was charming – all chintz and sofas and big flower arrangements. I can just picture it, can't you?

'There were several old dears nodding away in there, and one or two old men, I think, watching some television programme about a talking frog. Lady Pamela told Bunty she'd like to sit down for a moment, have a little chat, and Bunty took this as a very good sign and said she'd leave her for half an hour or so, and the manager went and organised coffee. The moment the coast was clear, Lady P got out the spliffs I brought back with me and handed them round. She's so bloody imperious that everyone took one, I think. There was one old thing who said it was a no smoking room and Lady P just said, "Oh pooh, these aren't proper cigarettes anyway – just herbal." She got them all lit up and puffing away. By the time the manager sussed there was something up, the smell of dope was wafting everywhere and they were all away with it – totally spaced out. Bunty said she'd never seen anything like it. High as kites. One old man wanted to take his trousers off. There was a bit of singing. A lot of giggling. Hand-holding. Everyone happy. Aches and pains forgotten. Sticks thrown aside, walking frames abandoned. God, I'd love to have seen it. The manager went completely wild and Lady P had to be bundled out and into the car with all the old dears calling after her and asking when she was coming again. Now it's all got to be hushed up. Nobody wants the police involved. Of course Bunty demands to know where the spliffs came from and I've had to play the total innocent and Lady P keeps saying what's wrong, they're only the cigarettes Bumper always smoked. Anyway, dearie, there's no question of Lady P going to the Old Malthouse now – not with her history of substance abuse. They wouldn't touch her with a barge pole. Bunty's livid. She knows she's been set up. She was foul to me and told Lady P she'll end up in a local authority home and that she deserves to go to prison.

'I got on to Henry's seccy the minute Bunty had gone. Diana Tripp is great. She thought it was all brill. She's one hundred per cent behind us. She says Bunty won't dare do anything for a bit. She'll be too scared of a fuss and the news somehow breaking. You know, "Dope-Smoking Dowager. Lady Pamela Peddles Pot", that sort of thing. She'll want the dust to settle and to keep things quiet. If necessary Diana is going to tell Henry that the *Western Gazette* telephoned for an interview. That'll make them shit scared. So it's round one to Lady P, I think.'

'Maeve, you are totally, totally brilliant!' said Sophie.

'Yeah, well, when I've got things sorted here I thought I might wander down and see you guys. I know three's a crowd, but I can always talk to Matt's dad.'

'You'll make his day.'

Much later when Maeve had left to cycle to the village and Charlton was quiet again, Lady Pamela sat by the fire and listened to the house settle in the dark and cold of the January night. The ashes shifted in the grate as the logs burned and fell, and outside a little owl called across the fields. For the first time she felt desperately alone. She missed Esau's snores and the scuttling of his claws on the floor, and the funny little whimpers he made when he dreamed of chasing rabbits. With him gone she was aware of being the only living soul in the old house. She watched her chest rise and fall as she breathed. Were her heart to stop now, to stall and come to a halt like a worn-out piece of machinery, her bony bird's breast would flutter and her life would drift gently to its close. It would be peaceful if death should visit her now as she sat beside her hearth. She was tired of all the fuss and commotion, of battling against Bunty, of all the toings and froings of the last few days.

If only death would come, she thought, she would wel-come it. Sam was the only thing. Leaving Sam. She didn't care to think about Sam grieving for her, missing her. In a moment she would reach for the telephone and dial his number and tell him the absurd happenings of the day. She would tell him that in the pocket of her pink mohair jacket she had two of Maeve's funny little cigarettes. She had hidden them there quite deliberately. She was keeping them for when he next came to visit. Like the old people that morning, she thought Sam would find a spliff quite delightful.

Chapter Twelve

Jane Hedderwick was too busy to care much one way or the other how the Matt, Sophie, Maeve triangle had sorted itself out. On Saturday morning when Dancer's fan club arrived in her yard she had already done a day's work by normal standards. In her usual outfit of jeans, leather half-chaps and various layers of sweaters and padded waistcoat, her thick fair hair in a knot under her woollen hat, she was dressed for survival. Her pink and white English skin was heightened by exposure to wind and cold, giving her a glowing, healthy look. By contrast, Maeve and Sophie looked like hothouse creatures with their pallid, indoor skins.

Jane was slightly surprised to see two cars drawing up. Maeve, Jack Dick and Lady Pamela were driven by Matt while Sophie, the twins and Commander Digby arrived in Sophie's car. Seeing them all together made Jane vaguely wonder which of the two girls had finally won Matt. She supposed it was Sophie because it was to her side that he gravitated as if pulled by some hidden string. One of the children in the back of the car was screaming blue murder and Jane noticed Sophie looked tired and harassed. Maeve, on the other hand, appeared cheerful and bright. God! Who'd have children? thought Jane. Putting down the tack she was carrying, she went across the yard to greet them all.

Sophie, indeed, felt exhausted. She had had a terrible night with the twins. She and Matt had made up beds for them in the room next to hers, but it was freezing in the draughty old house and although she piled on the blankets, they managed to kick them off and kept waking up, cold and crying. The move to yet another strange bedroom had thoroughly upset them and Sophie felt guilty. Really, it wasn't fair, dragging them about like this. Neither Charlton nor Manor Farm were child-orientated. There were no swings, or sandpits or climbing frames, no toys in cupboards, no other children to amuse them. The fact that they were now staying on a farm was no use at all. The cattle yards were dirty and dangerous. They couldn't be allowed to be out of her sight for one moment, so many were the potential hazards. The farm dogs were unreliable with children and they were told not to touch. Maisy, Commander Digby's warty old yellow labrador, was kept in a kennel outside and so provided little diversion. Sophie was also on edge because she was conscious of being in Matt's father's house and was anxious that the twins should make a good impression and behave well and not disturb his routine.

In fact, they could not have behaved worse. Breakfast was a disaster. Freddy wept inconsolably because she turned his egg out as he usually liked it, when this time he wanted soldiers of toast to dip into the shell. Flora shouted and threw food on the floor and upset milk over the *Daily Telegraph*. Eventually Commander Digby took his sodden paper away to read in peace in the sitting room. Sophie felt near to tears herself. Lack of sleep and stress played havoc with her looks and she felt plain and washed out. Matt seemed to have abandoned her, going out to the yard before breakfast and then after a snatched cup of coffee disappearing again to inject some cows.

Fortunately there was a television in the kitchen and with the children plonked in front of it, she slowly cleared the table and found there was no hot water when she tried to wash the breakfast dishes. She felt lonely and miserable and wished she was back in her flat following her familiar Saturday morning routine of shops and park and a Häagen-Dazs ice cream as a treat on the way home. If things didn't improve she would explain to Matt and go back to London after lunch. She wasn't sure she could stand another night like the last one.

She sensed that Matt's father had been surprised by her arrival. She wasn't sure that he had been properly warned or knew exactly how it was between her and his son. She had the impression that he deliberately made himself scarce, going out of a room shortly after she had entered, keeping conversation to a minimum. He was probably horrified by the twins, she thought, and appalled that his son was getting involved with a woman with children from a previous marriage in tow and who behaved so badly.

216

Because of this, she found conversation with David Digby awkward as she drove him to the stables. He seemed to prefer to gaze out of the window rather than talk. Now they had arrived in the yard, she was stuck again. She would have to get the children out of the car and take them off somewhere out of the way. She couldn't have them running about among the horses.

Jane, however, saved the situation. 'Do you want to take your children into the house and have a cup of coffee while we look at the horse?' she suggested. 'The puppies are still there in the washroom.' Sophie smiled at her gratefully. Matt hovered about until she said, 'Matt, go and see Dancer. I'll be fine. Come and get me when you go up to the gallops. I don't want to miss that.'

In Dancer's box, Sally was busy stripping off his rugs. He kept turning his head and trying to nip and she smacked his nose gently. 'He's got cheekier as he's got fitter,' she said. He did indeed look fit. His bay coat gleamed and he was densely muscled across his back and shoulders. He fairly exuded pent-up energy as he wove about the box. He knew he was being watched and admired.

'I should have tied him up,' said Sally, putting on a head collar and attaching the rope to a ring in the wall. 'He takes such liberties, otherwise.'

Matt squatted beside him and ran his hand down his legs. 'No trouble?' he asked Sally.

'None. Touch wood,' she replied, tapping the stable door. 'No swelling. No heat. He had a bit of an overreach here, look.' She indicated where the horse had struck into the fleshy heel of a foreleg with the shoe of his hind. 'But it's healed up fine.'

'My goodness,' said Commander Digby to Lady Pamela as they looked over the door, 'what a good sort. A real old-fashioned chaser.' In his youth he had ridden in point-to-points and still retained an interest in racehorses.

'We had high hopes of him,' said Lady Pamela. 'Bumper thought he was very talented.'

'He looks wonderful,' cried Maeve. 'Doesn't he, Jack?'

'He's a strong bugger,' said Jack, who had been mightily amused at the horse's antics and Sally's efforts to control him. 'Too much for that slip of a maid.'

Sally laughed. 'Don't you believe it,' she said. 'He knows who's boss.' She was busy putting on the saddle and then

217

slipped the bridle over Dancer's big, intelligent head.

She led him out into the yard where, as usual, Jane had assembled other horses to work alongside him. Sally was given a leg up and Dancer arched his back and side-stepped, his tail lifted like a plume in the air.

'Do you want to take a car up to the gallops?' said Jane. 'I can take four of you in the Land Rover with me.'

'I know Sophie won't want to miss this,' said Matt, loyally. 'I'll follow on with her and the children.'

'We'll see you there, then,' said Jane. 'Here, Lady Pamela, let me help you.'

Ten minutes later they were crowded round the field gate watching the four horses working up the hill towards them. It was obvious to Maeve that Dancer was pulling hard. His head was down somewhere between his knees and Sally was wrenching at the reins.

'That's one problem with him,' said Jane, 'he does pull like a train. But he settles. He just wants to get on with the job. He's so enthusiastic on the gallops. He has a sort of natural aggression. He wants to beat the hell out of the others.'

'Wouldn't he be better with a man on board?' asked Commander Digby, reasonably enough.

Jane turned to answer. 'Holding a horse has nothing to do with brute strength,' she said in a crushing tone.

Better not to pursue this line of argument, thought the Commander. Goodness, these powerful, competent women were awe-inspiring.

Sophie had the twins up on the gate. She held Freddy and Matt hung on to Flora, who kept throwing herself off backwards into his arms and shrieking with laughter.

'Be quiet, Flora, and watch the horses,' she said. 'Which one do you think will win?'

'Dancer! Dancer!' chorused the children.

The four horses were now about to start the long gallop up the hill where lack of fitness had told the last time Lady Pamela had watched her horse work. The intervening weeks had made all the difference. This time he went straight up, his strong quarters powering him along, his long stride eating the ground. The other horses kept with him. They were all racing fit, but Lady Pamela, watching intently through her field glasses, felt there was something in his rhythmic, unfaltering gallop which especially impressed. A moment later they reached the brow and were temporarily lost from sight; only to re-emerge a moment later on the other side.

Going downhill, Maeve thought that Dancer had edged in front. She could see that Sally had settled him now into a steady galloping stride and that he wasn't fighting her any more. Of course, the long stretch uphill may have taken the stuffing out of him a bit. Maeve watched as the horses, still tightly bunched, met the curve towards the five brush fences. God, Sally's brave, she thought, gnawing a fingernail. She looked so small with her short stirrups, bum in the air, head down but looking intently forward, and galloping into a line of jumps. Sitting up there, on all that freewheeling muscle and bone, she was so vulnerable. How can she do it? How can she have that confidence in an animal? She has to rely on Dancer, she thought, trust him to do what she says. If he makes a mistake, she'll be thrown off at forty miles an hour. He, maybe, could fall on top of her. Maeve could hardly bear to watch. They all stood, silent and tense, as the dull drum of hooves and rhythmic, snorting breath drifted across the bleak stubble field towards them.

It seemed to Maeve that Dancer was galloping too fast to meet the fences coming up. Although they were smaller, Jane said, than those he would meet on a racecourse, they were stiff and thick with brush. Each one stood out in a dark line along the side of the field. He's going too fast, Maeve thought. He'll never take off. She thought she saw Sally shift her weight for a moment and at the same time she seemed to collect the big horse under her. To her surprise, Maeve saw her hit Dancer a sharp smack down the ribs. His ears pricked and he took off in an effortless leap. He was over the top with miles to spare. She need not have worried. He landed in front of the others and Maeve saw that as he hit the ground he was back in his galloping stride at once.

'It's over his fences that his quality shows,' said Jane. 'You'll see he outjumps the others every time. Sally has to sit tight or she'd be jumped off, but he's listening to her now and taking off when she tells him. He's much less erratic than he was.'

Maeve understood what she meant, but as they came into the second fence something appeared to go wrong. She saw Sally give the same command to take off but Dancer seemed to scuttle in another stride, which took him almost into the bottom of the fence, and then when he jumped, he had to climb over in a corkscrew action. Sally lost a stirrup and

Dancer lost ground. The other horses galloped away from him.

'Spoke too soon,' sighed Jane, and anxiously they watched him coming into the third.

Maeve closed her eyes. She slipped a hand through Commander Digby's arm and he patted it reassuringly. This time Dancer stood right back from the fence and when Maeve looked again she saw that when Sally told him to take off, he listened and obeyed. He soared into the air and landed safely.

'That was better,' said Jane, 'but there's still room for error, as you can see!'

The riders were pulling up now and then walking their blowing horses over to the cars.

'Sorry about that!' said Sally, as they got close enough to hear. She leant forward to pat Dancer's neck. 'My fault. I didn't see the stride and let him put in a short one. I got him completely wrong at it. He was great over the others, though.'

'He's much fitter,' said Lady Pamela. 'Look at him now. He wouldn't blow out a candle. I think that mistake was more the fault of being a bit too keen. Rushing his fences. He's athletic enough to get himself out of trouble. He looks, to me, ready to run. What do you think, Jane?'

Jane smiled. 'Funny you should ask! Actually, we all think he's ready for an outing. I've listened to what the girls say, and Matt, and the farrier and the chiropractor and they all reckon he's ready to go. There's only one meeting in February at Newton Abbot and I hoped you'd agree to his having his first outing there. I've taken the liberty of entering him in the open hunter chase. He runs on Wednesday, the fifteenth of February, one thirty, all being well.'

'I'm delighted,' said Lady Pamela. 'You've done wonders with him.'

Sally beamed and patted Dancer's neck. Jack Dick stroked his nose.

'You take care of him, my girl,' he said to Sally. 'You take care of the bugger. He's the best horse you'll ever sit on.'

At Maeve's suggestion they stopped at the pub on the way home and again the party divided, with Sophie saying it was warm enough in the sun to sit outside with the twins. Matt brought her out a shandy and some crisps and orange juice for the children. He went back to get his pint and carried it to sit next to her on the grey wooden bench.

'Hey,' he said. 'Are you OK? You're very quiet.'

Sophie smiled back. 'I'm so tired,' she said. 'I told you I had very little sleep.' She closed her eyes and let the sun warm her face. Without looking at him, she went on, 'Actually, Matt, I think I'd better get on back to London. I can't face another awful night and, really, I feel a bit of an interloper. I don't think your father approves and you're so busy . . .'

'Darling,' he said. She felt him take her hand. 'Don't say that. Dad doesn't mean to be ungracious or unwelcoming. It's just how he is. He's always a bit silent.'

Not with Maeve, he's not, thought Sophie. And then, Why do I think these thoughts?

'Look, let's get the twins some sandwiches here and you can put them to have a rest when we get back and have a sleep yourself. You're in no fit state to drive if you're so tired. If you insist on going, I'll drive you and come back on the train.'

Sophie opened her eyes and looked at his concerned face and then down at his hand holding hers. 'You're so kind,' she said. 'I do feel exhausted. I could go to sleep sitting here.'

'What would you two like in your sandwiches?' Matt stood up and called to the children. 'Ham? Cheese?'

'Rule number one, never ask children what they want,' said Sophie. 'One round of each, please.' The twins had found a tiny play area behind the pub tables and were happy for the moment on the miniature slide. It wouldn't last for long, Sophie knew, and then she would have to get wearily to her feet and push them on the swings.

Inside the pub, Lady Pamela was on her second sherry and enjoying the warmth of the fire. It was years since she had been inside a public house. Commander Digby sat opposite her with half of bitter, while Jack Dick and Maeve were playing pool in the saloon. Her horse's performance, she found, had gladdened her heart. The excitement of watching the display of energy and physical strength seemed to have made her feel more vigorous and lively herself. The events of the previous day had left her feeling very weary and she was grateful that she now not only felt revitalised but also had something else to think about.

Sam had been speechless when she had described her visit to the Old Malthouse.

'It was the Irish,' she had said, 'all the Irish's doing.'

'You could have been arrested!' said Sam, horrified.

'Oh, I don't think so. Anyway I wouldn't have minded too much if I had.'

She looked across at Commander Digby who was giving her some account of church commissioners and the parish funds and wondered what he would think if she told him that yesterday she had smoked her first joint. Apart from Sophie and Diana Tripp, nobody else had been allowed into the secret. Even Maeve could see the wisdom of discretion.

'That's knocked the Old Malthouse on the head, anyway,' she had said, pleased with herself.

Only for the time being, thought Lady Pamela. Bunty won't give up that easily. She'll find somewhere else. It's a temporary reprieve, that's all. A stay of execution.

She saw plates of sandwiches going out to Sophie and the twins and felt suddenly hungry herself. 'Why don't we all have lunch?' she suggested to Commander Digby when he paused in his explanation. 'A sort of celebration.' She saw him hesitate. He had already read the menu which was chalked on a blackboard and had flinched at the prices. He had not had a meal out for twenty years. 'My treat,' she added. 'After all, this is my outing.'

Sophie did as Matt had suggested and took the twins back to Manor Farm to sleep in the afternoon. She filled herself a hot-water bottle and crept upstairs after them. Matt was busy outside strawing down the cattle yards, and Commander Digby, flushed from drink at lunchtime and the pleasure of the pub steak and kidney pie, had nodded off in the kitchen armchair, the newspaper crumpled round his feet. With a feeling of acute relief she took off her jeans, slipped into bed and cuddled down beneath the blankets and closed her eyes.

It was pitch dark when she awoke. Matt was putting a mug of tea down on the bedside table.

'Shh,' he said. 'They're still asleep. Father's outside doing the calves. Can I get in beside you for a bit?'

Sophie raised her warm arms and put them round his neck and pulled him down to her. She still felt drowsy and heavy, and as Matt's cold body slipped in beside her warm one and she wrapped her legs round him, she knew she wanted him and needed him and now was the time to show him.

Later, when the twins had woken, red-faced and cross, and she had splashed the sleep out of their eyes with water in the chilly bathroom, Sophie still insisted that she was going to drive back to London.

'The Effs will be fine now that they've had a good rest,' she said, 'and it means that a late night won't bother them. We'll be back by ten o'clock and then on Sunday I can sort everything out and get them ready for nursery on Monday. Fergus is expecting to have them tomorrow and I don't want to mess up his plans again.'

Matt put his arms round her and held her to him. The afternoon of love had left him feeling tender and protective.

'I'll miss you,' he said. 'It's been so wonderful having you at Charlton this week. It's made such a difference to me, just knowing you were nearby.'

Sophie kissed him. 'Thank you,' she said. 'Lovely for me too. But it wasn't real life, was it? Not for me, anyway. I must get back and pick up the threads again. What I am going to do, though, is to get Fergus to fix up with his sister for the twins to go there on the fifteenth of February when Dancer runs at Newton Abbot. May I come and stay the night before?'

'Darling,' said Matt, 'you don't have to ask. I hate to admit it, but it will be wonderful to have you on your own.'

That was the trouble, thought Sophie, as she drove back to London. The twins, around whom her whole world had centred, had had their position subtly shifted by her relationship with Matt. Not that for one moment did she love them any the less, but there were times now when she positively wished them out of the way. This change in attitude took some getting used to and there was a huge amount of guilt attached. To be in love was essentially to be preoccupied, and Sophie worried that she was giving the children less attention. She spent just as much time with them but it was no longer just them, the three of them bound tightly together in a mother-child relationship, exclusive and excluding. Now there was someone else, and Sophie feared that Matt had somehow elbowed the twins aside, like a cuckoo in a little bird's nest. Not deliberately, of course, but just by being important to her, by occupying her thoughts and demanding her love. She worried that there was less of her to devote to her children.

She remembered that it wasn't so long ago that she had been miserable, thinking that life was passing her by, and that she was obsessive about her children. Now she was worried that she was neglecting them. She wished she could find some balance. Why did everything have to be so weighted one way or the other? Perhaps when she and Matt had settled together, become used to one another, when the early longing and lusting had dimmed, she would feel less pulled apart. Even now, speeding up the motorway, she was absorbed in her own thoughts and reliving the lovemaking of the afternoon, ignoring Freddy, who was saying over and over again that he didn't want to go home, he wanted to stay with Maeve.

Commander Digby was glad that Sophie had gone. It was not, he told himself, that he disliked the girl, but he found her visit upsetting and uncomfortable. He was used to pottering about on his own and enjoyed the peace and stillness of his empty home. The twins, like an occupying army, had put paid to that, until there seemed to be nowhere he could find to hide. They made so much noise, hollering and roaring, and had so much clobber and kit, that it seemed they took over the entire house. Then he had seen Sophie smelling the cloth in the kitchen sink, which was a bit grey, he had to admit, and later found her boiling it up in a saucepan, and she was for ever wiping and clearing around him, as if he himself was a source of germs. He felt more at home with Maeve, who left things alone and just came for a chat and cheered him up with her outrageous conversation and sat at the kitchen table amongst all the muddle. This girl, Sophie, gave the impression that she'd take over, given half a chance. She was like a girl with a mission. He felt he should warn Matt, but did not know how. He felt deeply suspicious of single mothers. In his view children needed two parents and these girls bringing children up on their own were only after benefit and the chance to be moved up the housing list. Not that he suspected Sophie of that, but where was their father? he asked himself. Matt had told him that he had walked out on her when they were babies, but there was more to that than met the eye, he was sure. That was only half the story.

Unable to express these thoughts to his son because it would have required language and sentiments he could not articulate, he lapsed into his usual gloomy silence and mono-syllabic answers, which made Matt miss Sophie even more than he might have done. A heavy and hostile atmosphere hung over father and son, each locked in his own thoughts and yet acutely aware of each other.

He wants me to say something pleasant about Sophie, thought Commander Digby, but I shall say nothing.

I want to marry her, thought Matt. I feel I know her already, and I know I want to marry her. I don't care what he thinks.

Over the next weeks, Maeve, a migratory bird at the best of times, fought off the urge to flit. Left alone at Charlton with Lady Pamela, a grey blanket of boredom threatened to close over her head, shutting out the light, muffling her spirits. The old lady was cantankerous and difficult to please. Her arthritis was made worse by the cold and in the last week of January the east winds seemed to pierce every corner of the house. Maeve kept the fire stoked but it was impossible to eliminate the draughts. The Aga went out twice and without its warm heart, the house grew icy.

'Bunty's right, you know,' said Maeve. 'You should move out, go and live somewhere civilised. Look at you, your hands are blue.'

'Be quiet!' snapped Lady Pamela. 'I will not have you telling me what is good for me. If you had arranged to have the Aga serviced it would not have gone out.'

'Why didn't you do it? You sit around all day with nothing to do.'

Trapped together, they grated and clashed, arguing over television programmes, meals, politics, clothes. Maeve made no effort to flatter or placate, and Lady Pamela used her sharp tongue as she always had, to criticise and intimidate.

Most afternoons Maeve would bicycle or walk to Manor Farm to see Commander Digby. She would let herself in the back door and put the kettle on. When the tea was made, she would call him from where he was working in the yards and he would come willingly, wash his hands in the washroom sink and sit in his boilersuit at the kitchen table with her.

'She's an old witch, you know,' she complained. 'Yesterday it was my fault the butcher sent pig's liver instead of lamb's. She wouldn't touch it. Then she sat so close to the electric fire that she scorched her skirt and nearly set herself alight.' She pushed a slice of treacle tart across the table. 'Here, this is for you. She said it was too sweet. How can treacle tart be anything but sweet, I ask you? Not long ago it was her favourite. Well, I'm buggered if I'm going to bother making puddings. She can have shop mousse like the Cook woman gave her from now on.'

David Digby did not really listen to the details. Somehow it seemed disloyal to Lady Pamela whom he had known and

225

respected for years, but he enjoyed Maeve's lively accounts of their clashes and he enjoyed the sense of being a confidant. No one had ever shared things with him as Maeve did. Her open-heartedness was slowly freeing a seized-up mechanism within him, easing rusted joints, forcing a response from a part of him which had long fallen into disuse. She often talked openly about Matt, or described other entanglements from her harum scarum past and, creakily at first, he began to express his own concerns, his worries over the farm, his loneliness since his wife died.

Lady Pamela was irritated by the time Maeve spent at Manor Farm. If she woke from her nap after lunch and found that Maeve had gone out, she would sit and seethe with resentment.

'It's my time off. I can do what I want,' argued Maeve. 'What's the matter? Are you jealous? It's no wonder I prefer his company to yours.'

'You are employed to look after me, not gad about flirting with men old enough to be your grandfather.'

'You've a nasty mind, Lady Pamela. Do you know that?'

'No nastier than yours, my girl.'

On Mrs Day's three mornings a week, Maeve cycled to Jane Hedderwick's yard to see Dancer. She usually timed it so that she arrived at coffee break, when the girls gathered in the kitchen and the low room was full of laughter and talk and the biscuit tin did the rounds and toast was made on the Aga. Most of them had been at work since six o'clock and had already done the early feeds, cleaned the boxes and exercised the first string. Maeve enjoyed their talk, the banter about boyfriends and hangovers, and gradually she realised how the yard worked as a team. Jane sat at the top of the table and absorbed information about her horses, which one had spooked this morning and nearly come down on the lane, which had sore shins and needed time off, which was lazy and needed to work alongside something keener.

Maeve discovered that the weather conditions were vitally important, not because working outdoors in the winter could be utterly miserable but because a freeze now would spell disaster for training and fitness. Then, as far as the ground was concerned, each horse in the yard had its own particular preference. Some went better on hard ground, others preferred it soft, when the faster horses were held up and strength and staying power would tell. Dancer was a strong horse, a stayer, and Jane would not run him if it was hard because of the increased stress on his injured leg. She did not want it too deep for him either. It had to be just right.

Maeve's interest in Dancer led to a closer involvement in the yard. She began to understand the rhythm of the day, the routines and work schedules, and to lend a hand when needed. She certainly did not want to ride or handle the horses much, but she enjoyed mucking out and tidying the boxes, measuring out the feeds, each made up with the particular horse's requirements in mind, and filling the hay nets with a delicious-smelling feed called haylage. 'Christ, you could smoke this,' she said, sniffing a handful, 'or make a liqueur out of it.'

Sometimes she would perch on a saddle horse in the tack room and help clean muddy bridles after hunting. It was a laborious task, and to be repeated every other day, but there was no resentment or grumbling. Local radio poured out endless pop music in the background and the chatter was cheerful. The job had to be done and done properly. After the slack, shapeless days at Charlton, Maeve liked the tension and the focus. Sometimes it seemed nothing else existed or mattered outside the world of the stables. A cough was a disaster, a knock could put training back a couple of weeks and muck up a running schedule. The horses and their condition were watched intently. Their mechanical working parts, their legs and their joints, were, quite literally, wrapped in cotton wool and endlessly examined.

'Legs have got to be cold and tight and hard,' Jane explained to Maeve.

'God,' said Maeve, 'that sounds sexy! Like a bloke's bottom.'

She liked the sense of comradeship which Jane fostered amongst her young staff, the humour and banter of the yard, the easy democracy where all jobs were shared and everyone could express a view on a horse and its training and yet where Jane's unstated authority reigned supreme and where she took the final decisions because she was responsible to her owners. Maeve's respect for her grew. She saw her quiet professionalism as she worked in the yard, how she checked and double-checked bandages and tack, how nothing was slapdash or left to chance.

Over the kitchen table, she and Sally endlessly discussed tactics and worked out Dancer's fitness programme up to the race.

'We know he's come back from the injury OK,' said Jane, 'but what we can't know is how he'll feel being back on the course. Will he have the guts to run again? Three miles and eighteen fences is a lot to ask and, of course, the horses he's up against have been in work up to three months longer than him.'

'Attitude's no problem,' said Sally, who now identified with Dancer so strongly that she stoutly defended him. 'You've only got to look at him swaggering about in front of the other horses to know he's got bags of attitude. It's all, "Look at me, you bastards. Watch me go!" He still wants to win, to be in front.'

'All the same, first time out, I want you to hunt him round, get him enjoying it. Don't push him. Let him make his own way home. This first outing is so important.'

Maeve listened, intrigued, remembering the jargon to relay each evening to Lady Pamela.

For them both the horse provided a diversionary interest. Dancer was the one subject over which they did not scrap. Dancer and Sam, that is. For Sam's visits, Lady Pamela cheered up and painted on her face, and Maeve willingly prepared a delicious lunch when he came down from London. Sam was wintering reasonably well although his wrist had not set satisfactorily and still gave him pain and there was some loss of mobility. Mohammed had proved a great success and although it caused comment amongst his friends, Sam had started to take him to concerts and exhibitions and to treat him more like a fond nephew than an employee. Sam found himself waiting for the sound of his key in the lock and thinking of Wednesday, the one day he did not come, as a featureless grey space in the middle of the colourful days of the rest of the week.

He had laughed at Lady Pamela's description of her pot-smoking session and they had giggled together over the joints they smoked after lunch, but he felt there was something melancholy in the air at Charlton. He missed Esau and realised that the little dog's cheerful spirit had contributed significantly to the liveliness and animation of the household. Maeve, he noticed, was quieter than usual. Pammy had told him about Matt and Sophie's betrayal but he thought there was something more to it than that. At Christmas he had not noticed that Matt and Maeve were particularly close or well-suited and had witnessed the tail end of the Boxing Day row. No, he thought, there is something else troubling her. She is alone, moving through some sad and solitary landscape. It reminded him of when Pammy was unreachable, thinking of Elizabeth and revisiting a grief that was still as keen as a knife.

There was poor Mrs Day as well. She had unburdened herself to him when he had enquired after Frank. She had stopped polishing the dining-room table and told him that her husband had only two more weeks at work and then would be on the dole.

'Every day of his working life he's been up at four thirty to milk those cows,' she said. 'You'd think he'd be sick and tired of it. But no, he dreads them going. He's only got half a dozen left now – the old stock. They'll be off to the slaughterhouse next week. He's got names for them all. Betty, Daisy, Madonna. I don't know how he'll cope with it.'

Sam sighed. There was nothing he could do. Nothing he could say except offer sympathy. Everything seemed to be coming to an end, running down, drawing to a close. Bunty, he knew, would not be put off for long. He and Pammy had talked about it and agreed that although she would battle on, Charlton was all but lost. Peregrine was starting work on the garden the following week and Henry had intimated to his mother that if she was so stubborn as to insist on staying put, then building work would have to start around her and at her inconvenience.

Henry had, naturally enough, been infuriated by his mother's behaviour at the Old Malthouse. Of course he had sought an explanation but got nowhere. She affected an irritating vagueness and said that she had found the 'cigarettes' amongst Bumper's things and thought that the old people would enjoy sharing them with her. It had seemed a shame to throw them out when she knew Bumper was very particular about what he smoked. She then started to ramble on about cigars and so forth, and for a moment he wondered whether she could be telling the truth. Bunty, of course, blamed the stream of undesirables which she said now infested Charlton.

'That kitchen is always full of them,' she had exaggerated. 'God knows what they get up to.'

When pressed, it turned out that she was referring only to the friend of Maeve's who had been staying with two young children and who, as far as Henry knew, was a highly respectable young woman, whose father was ex-Blues and Royals and had been a director of Lazards, and Matthew Digby, whom he had known since he was a little boy. In Henry's view, if anyone was likely to be smoking pot and sharing it with Lady Pamela, it was Bunty's friend, Peregrine. This was not a point of view he aired to Bunty. Fortunately, in a way, his wife was temporarily deflected from the goings on at Charlton by their son, Charlie, and his behaviour at school, which was still causing considerable concern. Bunty had already suggested, darkly, that she now knew where he got his predilection for delinquency. 'Your mother, Henry, that's who.'

'You can hardly term an eighty-two-year-old a delinquent,' said Henry. 'A nuisance, maybe, but not a delinquent.'

'It's there in the blood, Henry. In the genes.'

'Listen, Lady P,' said Maeve, as the first week of February drew to a close. 'Jane says that two days before Dancer's race he's going to have a mile and a half canter. Shall we get George to take us over? We don't want to miss that, do we? Now as for the race itself, Khaled is bringing Mohammed and Sam down the day before. God, it's so exciting! Sophie's coming, but of course she's not staying here. She's defected to Manor Farm now she's bonking Matt. Mrs Day and Frank are coming. Mrs Day is going to come in here on race day and tidy up, and Frank will collect her and Jack Dick at midday. What a party! I'm going to make a fabulous picnic and we'll take buckets of drink.'

Lady Pamela smiled. It was like Christmas all over again.

'What should we wear?' asked Maeve. 'I've never been to the races. Hats and stuff?'

'It's not Ascot, my dear. One wants to be warm above all else. Certainly, I shall wear a hat, and let's think,' she shuffled off into her dressing room, 'probably this tweed suit, and this coat.' She pulled out a classic navy cashmere overcoat.

'Then I'll wear my lucky Chanel suit,' said Maeve, 'and how about this wonderful velvet beret with these pink feathers? And this lovely pink tweed coat?' She was working her way down Lady Pamela's wardrobe, pulling things out, completely unabashed, as if helping herself to her employer's clothing was perfectly normal and acceptable.

'It doesn't matter what you young things wear,' said Lady Pamela, amused, 'as long as you don't frighten the horses. But it's the country, remember. Deepest Devon. You don't want to get done up like a dog's dinner.'

'Will we be allowed into the ring please, where the horses walk round?' Maeve longed to be the centre of attention, swanking about as if she was a racehorse owner.

'The paddock, you mean? Yes, of course. I am the owner, so I will be able to go into the paddock and take one or two of you with me.'

'Not Matt and Soph,' said Maeve, narrowing her eyes. 'They're still being punished. Take Mohammed and Khaled. That'll cause a stir. It'll look as if the Arabs have come to Newton Abbot.'

It was going to be fun, thought Lady Pamela, especially lit, as it was, by Maeve's enthusiasm. She had never expected to have another chance at life like this. After her hip and the ghastly Cook woman she had almost resigned herself to being housebound and going quietly ga-ga. Bunty and Henry, inevitably, would put a stop to it all shortly, so she and this wild Irish might as well make the most of it while it lasted. If Dancer did not run well, Henry would be sure to intervene and suggest he should be put down at the end of the season. She knew that he had been over Bumper's will with a fine-tooth comb and that the conditions under which any of the horses could be destroyed were carefully detailed, but Henry could find a veterinary surgeon to testify that the horse was not fit to race and that the humane and responsible decision would be to shoot him. Which may, in fact, be the right decision, thought Lady Pamela, sadly. She could not return him to a muddy field for the rest of his life and he would have little chance of finding a secure home as a hack. He was too strong and wilful. No, she and Maeve, by starting this whole episode, were putting Dancer's future on the line. But at least they were giving him a chance.

The day before the race, it poured with rain. It had started when Maeve and Lady Pamela were at their customary gate, watching Dancer canter the day before. It had begun as a fine drizzle which continued all the grey afternoon and into the murky evening. The next morning they woke to the steady drum of persistent rain on the window and it was not until four o'clock when it was nearly dark that the sky cleared and the downpour stopped. Lady Pamela telephoned Jane.

'The course is prone to flooding at the best of times,' said Jane, gloomily. 'There will be an inspection at five this evening and another at seven tomorrow morning. Get Maeve to get Teletext for you on Channel Four. You'll find the results of the course inspections. At the moment I'm working on the assumption that we're going. We have to be there two hours before the race, so we'll be leaving about nine o'clock. If you don't hear from me, you can presume we're on. OK? If not, I'll ring you early.'

Maeve, who was pacing about with anxiety and chewing her nails, received a thumbs-up sign and capered round the room in excitement.

'I just couldn't bear it if it was cancelled after all this. I couldn't bear it, Lady P.'

'Maeve, you have to get used to disappointments with racing. There are so many things to go wrong with horses. The weather is only part of it.'

'I know, I know. I've heard Jane say that so often. But I feel so screwed up about it.'

'Screw your courage to the sticking place and we'll not fail,' said Lady Pamela.

'That's it. That's it exactly. I feel as if, with enough will-power, I can make it OK.'

The evening before the race was spent waiting for Khaled to arrive with Mohammed and Sam. Khaled had a number of bookings to honour before he could collect Sam and leave London and it was not until after ten o'clock that his taxi arrived at Charlton. Sophie and Matt had called round earlier in the evening, Sophie bringing with her a lasagne for supper, which was now bubbling gently in the bottom oven. Maeve was in a state of high excitement. She had drunk a lot of red wine and was flushed and pretty as she embraced the three arrivals. Lady Pamela waited for the commotion to die down before she reached for Sam and squeezed his hand. As usual they had planned to dine in the drawing room, while the others ate in the kitchen, but they were both past eating and preferred to go and sit by the fire and share a companionable whisky while the young people laughed and teased each other, and tucked into hearty platefuls, regardless of the time or their digestions. It was Sophie and Mohammed who remembered them and made a fuss about helping them to bed and seeing that they were both comfortable for the night. Maeve was very pissed and sitting on the men's knees and eating off their plates and was no help at all.

As they met on the landing upstairs, Mohammed caught Sophie's hand and said, 'Sophie, I am so happy for yous. I like this Matthews very much. He is good man.'

'Yes, he *is*,' said Sophie, fervently. 'Thank you, Mohammed. I'm really, truly happy. It is only Maeve I'm a bit worried about. We didn't behave very well, you know.'

Mohammed's beautiful features took on a concerned cast. 'Maeve is, what you say, a free spirits? She is always very difficult to be happy for long. She has big sadness inside.'

'Oh, don't say that!' said Sophie. 'That makes me feel much worse. What is it, Mohammed? She'll be all right, won't she?'

'She is always searching,' said Mohammed. 'Who can say? She needs someones for whom she is special person. To us all she is friend, but she needs more. Lady Pamela, she is this persons, I think.'

'But Lady Pamela won't do! She must have love,' cried Sophie, 'like me and Matt. That's what she needs. She must find that one day.'

She had all the egoism of the newly in love, thought Mohammed. 'There are many sorts of loves which you here in the West have forgotten,' he said. 'For you, all is romances and sex. These, for us, are not most valuable things. Also is love of Allah, of family, of childrens, of old peoples. This Maeve has found with Lady Pamela.'

But that is not enough, thought Sophie. Aloud, she said, 'I have my parents, my brothers, my children, but I still need Matt.'

'Of course,' said Mohammed. 'For you, Sophia, this is true, but Maeve, she is different, she has different lifes. She does not feel as you do. Always she feels unwanted, since small childs. She tells Mohammed this. Lady Pamela needs her, and this is good.'

Sophie considered. She could see that, to an extent, he could be right. His words made her feel slightly guilty, as if she had been remiss as a friend. Mohammed had seen and understood something about Maeve which she had not. He smiled at her kindly and said, 'You, Sophia, are much happier this times without your babies. It is better now, yes?'

'How right you are!' said Sophie. 'Can you remember how unhinged I was without them before Christmas? This time, I feel quite guilty because I have been really looking forward to having a break from them. I know they love it at Fergus's sister and that they'll be well looked after and so I handed them over without a qualm. Well, almost!'

Sophie did, in fact, think about the Effs a great deal. Her

time away from them seemed to resemble a pattern of peaks and troughs like a hospital chart. She thought about them almost all the time and sometimes her longing for them was so acute and physical that it almost hurt. She longed to touch their smooth warm skin, to feel their little hands in hers, to have their solid, struggling weight on her lap, their arms round her. Like an agony, this longing was too intense to last and she would lapse back into a state where she was not so conscious of being without them, only to be reminded of them again and want them once more. She couldn't explain this to Matt who saw the couple of days as a welcome respite for her and a wonderful chance to have her to himself.

Some of the time she was happy and it was easy to be his girlfriend and his guest but she also felt purposeless and adrift without her children. It was lovely on the first night to sit late in the kitchen at Charlton without a care in the world but when she and Matt crept back into Manor Farm, she felt at a loss with no babies to check and kiss goodnight, and Matt seemed too pleased to be without them. He kept saying, 'Isn't it fantastic it's just us?' and although she had to agree, in a way, that it was wonderful to be together and able to concentrate on each other, she had a hollow and sad feeling that she recognised as emptiness. As they lay in bed after they had made love, she felt a great distance separating them. Matt had fallen asleep almost at once, his arm still round her, their legs still entwined. Sophie lay on her back staring at the ceiling, listening to his shallow breathing. I am in bed with my lover, she said to herself, and all I can think about is whether Freddy has got his squirrel and whether he and Flora are sleeping peacefully, and the awful thing is that how I feel about them opens a gulf between Matt and me, because he has none of these feelings.

It was a long time before she fell asleep.

The following morning Maeve was up early, nursing a hangover but cheerful all the same, getting breakfast for Sam and Lady Pamela and chatting in the kitchen to Khaled and Mohammed. Their idea of what to wear to the races was a little unusual and Maeve smiled as she thought of what a bizarre spectacle they would make in what Lady P called deepest Devon in their black leather jackets and baseball caps. She had a look through the coats which hung in the kitchen passage and found a tweed overcoat which must have belonged to Bumper and a wax jacket. Mohammed looked devastating in the tweed coat, especially when Maeve tied a camel wool scarf round his neck. Khaled was jammed into the wax jacket and he then found a flat cap and stuck that on his head so that he looked like an exotic sort of farmer.

As Maeve prepared Lady Pamela's breakfast tray, she got Mohammed to scour Teletext and he came back to say that the meeting at Newton Abbot was on. The going, he said, was good to soft. At the same moment the telephone rang and was answered upstairs by Lady Pamela. When Maeve took up her tray, she was already getting dressed, and her eyes sparkled as she reported that the call had been from Jane to say that they were about to load Dancer and start for the course. The sun was shining weakly through her bedroom window, and the garden below and the hills beyond were swathed in a pale, wet, misty light.

Once again, the exciting prospect of an outing encouraged the imperious in Lady Pamela and she started being difficult. Sam needed a breakfast egg, she decided. Maeve must go at once and boil one. She clattered down the back stairs to do as she was told. Then there was all the performance of what to wear. This blouse would not do; that colour was wrong, not those stockings. When she was finally clothed to her satisfaction and Maeve had helped her downstairs, she started to interfere in the kitchen and poke around in the picnic which Maeve had spread out on the table.

'We need sandwiches,' she said. 'Not all this French bread nonsense. Ordinary sandwiches. And soup in the Thermos. Sam likes consommé with plenty of pepper and sherry.'

'OK! OK!' said Maeve, dashing about and making faces at Mrs Day behind Lady Pamela's back.

'Have you made a fruitcake?' demanded Lady Pamela. 'One always takes fruitcake.'

'No, I fucking haven't,' said Maeve under her breath, coming back with a battered Thermos flask she had found in the pantry. 'Did this go to war with Bumper? It looks ancient.'

'There was a fruitcake,' persisted Lady Pamela, going through tins in the larder. 'I know I haven't eaten it all.' Maeve knew exactly where this was heading. The old lady had guessed correctly that she had taken half the cake to Commander Digby. She was making a point. Maeve made an effort to control her temper.

'I've made little chocolate cakes,' she said. 'Sam's favourites.' She did not know whether this was true, but it was worth a try.

'Hmm,' said Lady Pamela. The next moment, Maeve was thankful that she was diverted by Sam coming down the stairs with Mohammed. Lady P went through to the hall and took his arm.

'Come into the drawing room, darling. Mrs Day has lit the fire, and Maeve can bring us some more coffee.'

By the time Jane's smart navy lorry pulled into the horsebox park at the racecourse, Sally was feeling sick with nerves. She always did before racing. It was all right when she was mounted and out on the course. It was the bit before that got to her. Looking back at the two horses in the rear of the box, she could see Dancer was quivering with excitement. With pricked ears he was watching through the horsebox window and Sally could tell that he knew he was at the races and that old memories must be clear in his mind. He had been plaited up the night before and his mane was now in neat little knots down his neck and his tail conjured into a woven column before it fanned out, loose and silky, halfway down its length. Last night she had shampooed his one white stocking until it glowed in the dark of his box and had washed the big white blaze down his nose. His bay coat was polished until it rippled and gleamed. He looked fit and well and edgy with tension as the box came to a halt.

He feels like I do, thought Sally. We're both bags of nerves.

Jane went to the secretary's office to declare. She was also going to have a word with the course steward to ask if Sally could take Dancer down to the start early and not wait to parade with the other runners. Sally's concern was that once the horses were out on the track, Dancer would become so excited she would not be able to hold him; she would get unceremoniously carted down to the start and before the race had even begun they would both have wasted valuable energy.

While Jane was gone, Sally and Steve, who had accompanied them in the lorry, had a cup of coffee from the flask Jane had put in the picnic box. Sally forced down two sandwiches. She had to eat; breakfast had been a long time ago. She was not going to make the twelve stone weight by a long way, even allowing around an extra stone for her saddle and her racing kit, so her weight cloth was going to be pretty heavy. This was another disadvantage for Dancer because weight carried in lead sits heavy on a horse's back and costs it more effort to carry than human weight, which can shift and move and sometimes even aid a jumping horse.

When Jane reappeared, she had a racecard with the names of the runners. There looked to be fifteen horses in the one thirty. Sally glanced down the list of names and riders. There they were: Irish Dancer, Miss S. West, The form guide read, 'Very useful chaser '95, '96. Not seen since injury forced retirement. Safe jumper and stays well. Outside chance if back to his best but unlikely to be a major player. One to watch.'

'Aren't they rude?' said Sally, indignantly.

'No, it's fair enough,' said Jane. 'There's sure to be a question mark over his fitness.'

'I wonder what our starting price will be?' asked Sally.

'Sixteen to one, something like that,' said Jane. 'Last time he ran, he was favourite.'

'And he will be again,' said Sally.

'Just remember your job is to get him safely round this one. I want him back with that leg intact. No heroics, Sal. This is just an outing to see what we've got here. OK? I want you to settle him in mid-division and stay there.'

'Yes,' said Sally. 'I know.'

'I don't know how many runners there will be,' Jane went on. 'But these five have declared already.' She indicated the Biro marks she had made beside the names of horses on her racecard. 'Just watch Billy Masters. He'll yell at you all the way round. He always does that to the girls. He tries to intimidate. He'll tell you to keep straight and get the fuck out of the way, that sort of thing. Ignore him or else tell him what he can go and do to himself. He's a cocky little bastard. He'll expect to win this race on that horse. It's won the last two times out. And watch Jo Jenks. That horse jumps to the right. Don't get inside him on the bend or he'll take you out.'

Sally nodded. She looked pale, Jane thought, and tense.

'Come on,' she said. 'Let's walk the course. Steve, I want Dancer bandaged all round. You can leave Jackpot for the time being. His race is two thirty.'

'Sure, boss,' said Steve. 'OK, Sal?' he grinned. 'Just let me know if you'd like me to ride for you.'

'In your dreams,' said Sally.

It was a mild February morning, wet and misty, and the weak sun which had shone earlier had disappeared behind pearly-grey clouds when Maeve, Lady Pamela, Sam and Mohammed arrived at the racecourse in Khaled's taxi. They had had a slow start because Lady Pamela had made a huge fuss over locking up at Charlton, giving Mrs Day endless instructions about keys and insisting on putting silver in the safe before they left. Maeve felt she had been a model of restraint not to have screamed, 'Just get into the car, for God's sake!' Then Lady Pamela had said that she knew the route, which did not prove to be the case. She kept telling Khaled to turn either right or left and then changing her mind. Maeve marvelled at his patience and in the end Sam had said, 'Pammy, dearest, I think it would be best to let Mohammed read the map, don't you?'

When they arrived, the car parks were already filling and groups of racegoers were making their way onto the course. Maeve looked head-turningly pretty in her pink suit and Lady Pamela's velvet hat. She dashed about looking for the Days and Matt and Sophie and Commander Digby, and eventually she had them all gathered round the picnic which she had spread out in the boot of Khaled's car. Matt opened the wine and Maeve and Sophie passed round the food and Frank had a can of beer and chatted to the Commander who thoroughly commiserated with him over the loss of his job. Sam perched on a shooting stick, immaculately turned out in a tweed country suit and a trilby and Mohammed waited on him lovingly. Lady P sat in the back seat, commanding operations, with her little legs stuck out of the open car door, and Maeve and Sophie made sure that she had a nip of whisky and her share of smoked salmon sandwiches. Mrs Day looked positively regal in one of Lady Pamela's hats, which Maeve had made her try on, and she was well away on white wine and having to hold on to Khaled who looked very dark and mysterious and rather prosperous, with his beard, and his round tummy encased in Bumper's old wax jacket with its fluttering clutch of old 'Owner's Badges' tied to the zip. Matt and Jack Dick went off to find Jane in the lorry park to ask her if she would like to join them. Matt returned to say that all was well but that Jane would not have a drink before the race. 'She says she'll get completely pissed after her other horse has run,' he reported. 'They've brought Steve to drive the lorry home.' Jack wanted to stay while Dancer was got

238

ready. He liked to keep an eye on things.

At about one o'clock the party made its way towards the paddock, Maeve stopping on the way to put a tenner on Irish Dancer.

'Don't waste your money,' instructed Lady Pamela. 'He's not going to win.'

'Too late,' said Maeve. 'I've put it on something called one way.'

'Each way,' corrected Matt. 'That means you get money back if he's placed, first, second or third.'

'Exactly,' said Maeve, her eyes shining, 'and I think that's excellent value, don't you?'

There were eleven runners declared for the race and the favourite, as expected, was the mount of Billy Masters, an Irish horse called Ela mana.

'What does that name mean, Maeve?' asked Matt. 'Is it Gaelic?'

'God knows,' said Maeve. 'Slow Boat to China, let's hope.'

When they reached the paddock, several horses were already being led round, still wearing rugs. 'Where's Dancer?' asked Maeve. 'Oh, look, here he comes. God, he looks wonderful.'

Silently, they watched the big bay horse enter the paddock. Steve, who was leading him, wore a yard sweatshirt with Jane's name printed on it, and Dancer's rug was in the same navy and crimson colours. He walked with a swing, his long stride forcing Steve to hurry alongside, his ears pricked, his wise eyes alert.

'He's pleased to be back,' said Sam. 'You can see that, can't you?'

Lady Pamela and Sam, accompanied by Maeve and Mohammed, made their way into the centre of the paddock. Maeve narrowed her eyes as she took in the opposition. All the horses, to her, looked fast and sleek as they jogged round. When the bell went, the jockeys appeared from the weighing room carrying their saddles and there was Sally, the only girl in the race, looking glamorous in Bumper's racing colours, an orange and white jersey and an orange cap and white nylon breeches. The rug was whipped off and Dancer saddled, with number cloth and weight cloth thrown over his back first.

'Number seven,' said Maeve. 'My lucky number. God, Sally, good luck! Good luck, Dancer!'

Sally smiled absently. Her mind was concentrating now on

what lay ahead. The girth was checked and then Steve gave her a leg up and Dancer immediately swung round, eager to start, Steve still hanging on to his head. Mohammed shepherded Lady Pamela and Sam out of the way to safety.

'Don't let him make too much of himself in the early stages,' reminded Jane. 'Remember, we want to know if he can still do the trip. Steve, are you ready?'

With good luck wishes in her ears, Sally was led down to the course and she heard the commentator saying, 'Going down early to the start is number seven, Irish Dancer ridden by Sally West.'

As she swung right onto the grassy turf of the track, Sally felt Dancer distracted by the crowds, looking this way and that, throwing himself from side to side, not concentrating and not listening to her. She touched him with her heels and gave him a reminder with her whip and he sprang into a canter. He felt bunched up and taut but Sally was in control. In front of her, his mighty shoulders were reassuring. He flexed his neck and accepted the bit and white flecks of foam flew from his mouth. Finding himself alone on the track, he was prepared to canter along, snorting and swishing his tail as he went. She could hold him at this pace and as they went away from the stand and towards the starting line, he settled into an easy rhythm and she felt him relax. She patted his neck, glad that they were moving, releasing a bit of tension and ready to start work.

Up in the stands, Matt and Sophie and Mr and Mrs Day and the Commander had found a good place from which to watch and Sophie grasped Matt's hand as Dancer went past. The sight of the powerful horse and Sally's slight figure, standing up in her stirrups, and the flash of Lady Pamela's colours, the jaunty orange of the cap, made Sophie gulp. She swallowed hard and Matt glanced at her.

'He looks great, doesn't he?' he said. 'He'll be fine. Sally knows what she's about. They'll look after one another.'

Mrs Day, who was standing on the step below them, took Frank's arm. He had borrowed a pair of field glasses and was watching their progress down to the start.

'He's settled down now,' he said. 'Here, you have a look,' and he passed them to his wife.

Sophie caught sight of Maeve and the others threading through the crowd down below and waved at them to come and join them. Khaled and Mohammed each helped Sam and

Lady Pamela up the steps and people smiled and made way for them. Jane was greeted left and right by people she knew. Several asked her about the horse she had running and she had to give a brief outline and introduce Lady Pamela. Maeve squirmed through the crowd and caught hold of Mrs Day. 'I'm not sure I'm enjoying this,' she said. 'I thought it would just be a buzz, but it's more like agony.' Jack Dick had opted to stay with Steve. He didn't like crowds and although Lady Pamela had wanted to buy him a badge for the members' enclosure, he did not want to go in. He and Steve were going to watch the race on the television above the bar.

The other horses were now cantering past in a flash of colour. Maeve stood on tiptoe trying to see over heads towards the start.

'They're down at the tape now,' Matt told her. 'Sally seems to be circling at the back.'

'She'd better get on up there if she's going to make a good start,' said Jane anxiously.

'And they're off,' said the commentator 'for this the three miles, two and a half furlong Forster Moore Challenge Hunter Chase.'

Maeve could see them now, all bunched together on the rails, going quite slowly, or so it looked.

Jane watched through her field glasses. 'Quite a good start. He's well placed,' she said, 'about the middle of the field, like I told her. They're not going fast. A good steady pace. First fence coming up. God, he jumped that well. Did you see?' Maeve hadn't. She couldn't see where he was with all the horses bunched together. She managed to identify the orange cap as the horses got to the second fence. 'Coming into the second,' said Jane. Maeve saw Sally was on the rails and that Dancer seemed to sail over. 'Over that fine. It looks as if he's pulling, but Sally's tucked him in behind the front horses, like I told her.' Maeve saw that the next fence was the first of the open ditches. She could see the dark trench dug on the take-off side. It looked enormous. She watched as the leading group of horses seemed to take off together, Dancer amongst them, and then there was a kind of collision. Maeve saw a horse skew sideways and for a moment a hind hoof pointed into the air and then it crashed to the ground, landing on its neck, the jockey thrown sideways and rolling into a ball, and then another horse came over, nearly on top, and fell too.

'Oh God!' said Jane, 'someone's gone . . . and another. No,

241

not Dancer. He's OK. That first horse brought the next one down, but it looked to me as if Billy's horse didn't jump straight. Did you see, Matt?'

Dancer was all right. Maeve groaned with relief and Sophie gripped Matt's arm so hard it hurt him.

The horses were strung out now and they could see Dancer clearly as they came to the bend and set out into the country, away from the stand. Sally was still on the rails, lying about fifth. Dancer looked to be lolloping along, not making much effort yet, and just keeping his position in the field. The two loose horses were galloping alongside, stirrups and reins flying. 'Let's hope they keep out of the way,' said Jane. 'Poor Sally, it's nerve-wracking having loose horses next to you. You have to keep an eye open for what they are going to do all the time.' The next two fences could not be seen from the stands and all heads turned to watch the television sets as the runners galloped on. The television made everything seem close and brightly coloured. Sally's cap glowed against the emerald turf. Maeve saw them jump neatly over the next fence and she started to relax. He was doing well, surely. Perhaps he could even gallop past them all and win.

'He's hunting round,' said Matt, 'really enjoying it. Sally's not pushing him at all.'

The field, strung out more and more, galloped on to the next fence.

'Irish dancer badly interfered with by a loose horse at that one,' said the commentator. Maeve had lost sight of what happened but she could see Dancer scrabbling along, nearly on his knees and Sally halfway up his neck. 'She's gone!' cried Jane, but Maeve saw Dancer's head come up and Sally somehow was back in the saddle and kicking on.

'No, he's still there,' said Matt. 'It was that loose horse, it went right across him at the fence.'

'That's knocked him back a couple of places,' said Jane. 'Can you see, Lady Pamela? He's two from the rear.' She paused, looking through her field glasses. 'But he's coming back again. He's making up the ground. He's coming back.'

The group of horses was visible again on the far side of the course, small but distinct figures strung along the white rails. Maeve could see that Dancer was moving steadily up through the field to take up a distant third position again. 'How many more of these fucking things to jump?' she asked.

'Six more,' said Jane. 'But look, the loose horses have been caught.'

From then on there were no more upsets and although three horses tailed off and pulled up at the rear, the position of the rest of the field remained the same. Dancer took his fences well, standing off and jumping boldly each time, but to Maeve's disappointment he made no impression on the lead the first two horses had established. If anything, they were galloping away from him. In the last furlong, she saw to her despair that Sally seemed to be letting Dancer ease up, not asking anything of him, and that the two horses in front were being ridden hard for the finish and were widening the gap, and the horse in fourth place was catching up, its jockey wildly kicking and working his whip arm. Sally seemed to be cantering home, unaware of the challenge from behind. Please, thought Maeve, don't be beat now. Show you can do it. Show you can still race.

As the leading horses galloped towards the line and the crowd erupted in cheers and shouts, she saw Sally glance behind, see the horse coming up on the outside and touch Dancer with her whip and heels. What happened next had them all screaming encouragement. Maeve saw the big horse flatten his ears and stretch his neck and he seemed to gallop effortlessly away, making his challenger's effort look slow and laborious. 'Irish Dancer storms home in third place,' said the commentator. Khaled threw his cap in the air, Sophie hugged Matt. Sam leaned across to kiss Lady Pamela's cheek. 'Well done, my dear!'

Maeve hid her face in her hands. It had been almost more than she could bear.

Jane worked her way swiftly through the crowd to lead Dancer in and the others were caught in the surge of people down the steps of the stand, Mohammed with his arm protectively through Sam's, and Khaled and Commander Digby supporting Lady Pamela. Maeve was now gabbling away and her obvious excitement made onlookers smile. She kissed the steward at the gate, to his great delight; he thought she must have won a great deal of money or at least owned the winning horse.

There was Dancer, led into the stall for third place, looking quite fresh, hardly blowing, although his nostrils were flared and the veins stood out like tracery on his wet neck. Sally looked jubilantly happy in a filthy, mud-splattered jersey. She banged Dancer's neck with her fist.

'He was brilliant,' she said, 'absolutely brilliant. That loose horse came right across us. It was amazing how he jumped us out of trouble. I did as I was told. I put no pressure on until the very end. He did it all himself.'

'I told you he's the best horse you'll ever ride,' said Jack, his face very red from excitement and emotion. 'I knew he'd come back all right, the old bugger.'

'Christ,' said Maeve, 'and I've won a whole lot of money!'

Chapter Thirteen

Back at Charlton, the talk was all Dancer over the next few days. Maeve and Sally and Jane sat at Jane's kitchen table and analysed his performance. 'The thing is,' insisted Sally, 'if I had kept in touch with the first two horses, he would have taken them on at the finish. It was only because I didn't ride him hard, on instructions, and because of that loose horse nearly bringing us down, that he wasn't in the frame. We could have been there, we really could.'

'He certainly did the trip,' said Jane. 'Now we know he can do the distance and come in with plenty left in the tank. And he's competitive.'

'Jackpot came in second in his race, in good company,' said Sally, 'and Dancer outguns him every time at home. I tell you, Jane, if you'd let me ride a harder race, we could have won.'

For Maeve, with no knowledge of horses, the greatest relief was that Dancer had come back from his outing fit and well. She now wanted him to go on and win and couldn't see why this was not entirely possible. The horse provided the adrenaline rush that she craved, the buzz of excitement that she longed for and it seemed to her that Jane was too cautious, too pessimistic about everything. The day after his race Dancer trotted out sound and Jane reported that his legs were cold and hard.

'And he loves his food,' added Sally. 'He never left an oat last night. Some horses,' she explained to Maeve, 'won't eat after a race and lose condition. It's difficult keeping them at peak fitness.'

'If he's so well, then we should race him as often as we can,' said Maeve. 'Lady Pamela maybe hasn't much time left. She ought to have as much fun out of him as possible.' It was easier to pretend it was Lady Pamela she was thinking of.

Jane shook her head. 'Horses aren't machines, Maeve,' she said. 'He's having three days off now. I'm turning him out every morning, and then he must have at least two to three weeks before he runs again, and if the ground is hard, I won't risk him. It wouldn't be worth it in the long term.'

'But there isn't a long term!' protested Maeve. 'I don't think Lady P will have another chance. Who knows when she'll turn up her toes?' She was completely unabashed, talking like this of Lady Pamela's death. Sally looked shocked. 'At the most,' Maeve persisted, 'how often do you think you can run him?'

'What I'm trying to tell you is that we must choose his races carefully to get the best out of him. Lady Pamela understands that. He may not run so often but the races will be right for him and he will stand a better chance in them. Don't you see?'

Maeve sighed. She knew it was reasonable, but taking things steadily was not natural to her. When you were on a roll, in her view, you didn't apply the brakes, you cranked up every second of pleasure and fun. All this caution was unbearable.

'I think we'll enter him for a Hunter Chase at the next Wincanton meeting in three weeks. He needs that sort of time to recover from Newton Abbot after the long lay-off he's had. Also it's local, a really nice course, and we can see if he can repeat his performance or even go better. You get good horses with local trainers, like me, using Wincanton as a prep for the bigger races later in the season. Depending on the result, I'll think about going for a park course for the next one.'

'What do you mean, a park course?'

'The park tracks are the larger racecourses where the fences are bigger and the horses better. Cheltenham is the ultimate.'

'Wow!' said Maeve, excited again. 'You're really nobbing him up!'

Sally laughed. 'And me! My ambition is to ride at Cheltenham! It's the same with all of us jockeys. It's like the pinnacle.'

Jane went to her desk and got out the Cheltenham race programme for the season and sat down to flick through it. Maeve and Sally made encouraging faces at one another across the table.

'At the March meeting, depending, of course, on how he goes in between, we could enter him for the National Hunt

246

Steeplechase Challenge. He hasn't won anything in the two preceding seasons, so he would be eligible. It's over four miles and he would have to carry a penalty of four pounds as far as I can see.'

'I think four miles would suit him,' said Sally eagerly. 'He felt as if he could stay all day. He's so strong and tireless but he hasn't got the speed over a short distance.'

'Is that the race he was entered for when he had his breakdown?' asked Maeve.

'No, that was the Foxhunter Chase. He'd won too much to qualify for the Challenge Cup that year. He was too good then.'

'Wouldn't it be great for Lady Pamela to have a horse at Cheltenham again? After all, that was where he was heading last time and it must have been such a letdown when it all went wrong.'

'Entries close on the third of March,' said Jane, consulting the booklet, 'so we don't have to make any decisions yet. It can be our goal.'

The three young women grinned at one another across the table.

'I can't wait to tell Lady P,' said Maeve. 'Cheltenham! Even I have heard of Cheltenham. Everyone in Ireland comes over for it, don't they? You see all the Catholic priests heading for the ferries! Will that be some party!'

She cycled flat out back to Charlton and slammed in the front door shouting, 'Lady P, where are you?' There was no answer, but through the open door of the drawing room Maeve saw the old woman standing looking out of the windows to where a JCB was moving earth in what had been the rose garden. A fresh pile, like a scoop of chocolate mousse, was mounting up on the lawn.

'Jesus!' said Maeve, and then taking Lady Pamela by the hand tried to lead her away. 'Don't look, Lady P. Don't look.'

'It must be faced,' said Lady Pamela grimly. 'I can't pretend it isn't happening.'

'That fucking Bunty,' said Maeve furiously. 'Fucking, bloody, horrible woman!'

Lady Pamela sighed. 'Really, Maeve. Your language. Although I do agree, of course.'

'Listen, I've got some great news,' said Maeve, pulling at the tiny, bony hand. 'It's about Dancer!' and she proceeded to tell Lady Pamela of Jane's plans, all the time willing her to turn from the window, away from the desecration of her garden.

'Well, that's splendid!' said Lady Pamela stoutly. 'Much better to look forward than dwell on the past.' She shook her little shoulders and stood very straight. 'Anyway, I suppose I should be glad that the garden is going to be cared for. Changed, but still cared for. That's the most important thing. I planted that rose garden after Elizabeth died, you see. But that is so long ago now. It doesn't matter any more. Lizzie loved horses. She would have loved to see Dancer run. Let him be her memorial.'

Maeve leaned forward and kissed her cheek. 'Good on yer, mate,' she said. 'And sod Bunty.'

Sophie and Matt spent the rest of February learning to adapt to the sometimes tiresome business of being in love. Matt was on the telephone every evening, trying to organise and devise ways of seeing Sophie whilst meeting the demands of his job and the farm, while Sophie found it equally hard to fit in time around the twins and her arrangements for them. Two mornings a week the Effs now went to playgroup which left Sophie gloriously free for three hours, but this was not enough time in which to see Matt and he was never available in the mornings anyway. Any time he had off tended to be at the end of the afternoon when it was too late to drive to London and be back in time to do any work on the farm. His father was able to manage less and less as winter aches and pains set in. An old knee injury bothered him and he found some of the work too strenuous. Matt had to get Rob to lend a hand when they were dehorning the calves and again when he needed someone to help with a difficult cow who had wedged herself through the bars of a yard gate. It was dangerous; she thrashed about and panicked, all the time at risk of breaking her trapped leg. In the end Matt had shouted at his father to keep out of the way and there was a moment when it looked as if there was going to be a battle. Instead, the older man had stumped away on the pretext of getting some rope, but the matter had not rested there. Later that evening he had been particularly monosyllabic and Matt knew that they had both crossed some indefinable boundary, he by giving the orders, and his father by obeying them. Overwhelmingly, Matt felt that the farm could not go on like this. He was being forced to give up all his free time and put aside the idea of ever seeing Sophie or of keeping his place on the local rugby side. Loyalty demanded that he helped, but for what? What was the future for the farm anyway? Farming was not what he had chosen for himself, and certainly not in the traditional way of his father, which he knew was doomed. He felt cornered and defeated.

Commander Digby kept up his wall of silence and if Matt tried to broach the subject of the unpaid time he was now putting in, he would always reply, 'I don't ask you to help. I can manage. I always have done.'

Obstinacy and fear of the future isolated the older man in a depressing world of his own. Any discussion with his son was out of the question because he knew already what he would say and he did not wish to hear it. Instead, most mornings he sat at the dining-room table with piles of forms from the ministry and documents relating to the herd. Recently he had had a batch of calves returned from Frome market because their passports were not in order. He had tried to hide this from Matt but of course he had discovered it and had had a go at him about everything, as usual. There was so much red tape and bloody officialdom. This was not the farming he had grown up with. He was a stockman who loved his cattle, who reared pedigree beef with pride, who cared for his land, but these days he hardly had time to lift his head and see the beauty of the landscape, the blue light over the hills, the vividness of the first green of the spring where the early grass was showing through in the valley. He saw only the knee-high mud in the yards and felt the worry of running low on feed. They were going to have to buy in hay if it was a cold, wet spring and he did not know where the money was going to come from.

The newspapers were filled with scaremongering reports of BSE. He had never had the disease on the farm, and never would, but all beef was being treated the same. The bloody Germans and French would come out of it all right. They always did, thanks to the way the government had sold British farming down the river.

Unspoken, at the back of his mind, was the anxiety raised by the appearance of Sophie in Matt's life. Maeve had been different. She blew in and out and would be gone as quickly as she had arrived, but Sophie was the marrying kind, unless he was much mistaken. What would happen if she did capture Matt? Would they move away and leave him without the help on which he knew he relied? If they stayed, she would want to take over the farmhouse. He would become an unwanted third in his own home. Really, he knew he ought to make Matt a partner, allow him a proper stake in the farm. He knew it would come to that eventually, but at the moment it was too big a step to take. As a partner, Matt would have a genuine say in how the farm was run. There would be changes forced on him. Holiday cottages, bed and breakfast. He'd be turned into a bloody hotel keeper before he knew it. No, for the moment he would resist. Dig in his heels.

Maeve wondered what was the matter. When she arrived on her bicycle and shouted for him from the back door, more often than not he was indoors, surrounded by piles of paperwork all over the dining-room table and floor. It was a dismal room, dusty, cold and dark. He had taken the shade off the central electric light so that he could see better, and the naked bulb was, to Maeve, infinitely dispiriting.

'What's all this?' she asked, poking papers with her foot. 'Why aren't you out farming?'

'Ministry stuff. Bloody officialdom. Bloody red tape,' he grumbled, looking at her over his glasses, his hair all on end.

'I thought farmers had secretaries to do this stuff.'

Commander Digby scoffed. 'Couldn't afford one.'

'Get Sophie to help. She was a seccy, you know. She'd sort it out for you. Not me, don't look at me. I can't stand those horrible envelopes with little windows. I'd just make things worse. Here, cheer up. It's a lovely day out there, quite like spring.' She went off to make him a mug of tea and when she came back and plonked it down beside him, she said, 'Anyway, if you're fed up with farming, why don't you give it up? Sell up. Someone like Bunty would love a beautiful house like this. Some swanky London person. Sell up and go and live in the sun somewhere, away from all this fucking mud and misery.'

Commander Digby realised that no one had ever dared say this to him outright. To voice the unthinkable. He sat silent for a moment and had a sudden vision of New Zealand, a country he had long wanted to visit. He saw his cousin's sheep station behind which, he knew, hung the snowy peaks of the South Island. He imagined trout fishing on a wild shallow river and tried to remember how it felt to be free of this constant anxiety. He took a gulp of his tea.

'I wish it were that easy,' he said.

'Why not?' said Maeve, sensing she had touched a hidden nerve. 'Things don't go on for ever. Why should they? You can see that from history, can't you? That everything has to change, to move on? So if I was you, I'd get the hell out and make sure I enjoyed the rest of my life. Get out while the going's good, matey. That's my advice.'

Sophie, for her part, had made up her mind that she would not bring the twins to stay at Manor Farm again.

'It just doesn't work, Matt. I am sorry, but it isn't fair on them or your father. If they were his grandchildren it would be different.' Neither would she let him stay at the flat.

'Sorry again, Matt. I made my mind up that I was never going to do that to my children. I don't want them to be brought up like that, with a mother who has boyfriends to stay.'

'But this isn't "boyfriends", it's me!'

'I know. I'm sorry. It doesn't make any difference. It's just how I feel.'

'Do you have to live in London? Couldn't you move down here?' Matt asked one evening when they had argued round and round and found no solution.

Sophie was silent. 'What are you asking?' she said finally. 'That I give up this flat and come down to Somerset and move the children away from their father and the school they've just started, and for what?'

'For me. For us!' said Matt. 'Look, Sophie. We're serious, aren't we? I know I am.'

Sophie was silent again.

'It's too fast. It's moving everything on too fast,' she said finally.

'But like this we never see one another,' Matt cried. 'How can we go on like this?'

'Fergus is having the children for a week at Easter. He's taking them down to his parents. I can see you then,' she said.

'That's miles away,' said Matt bitterly. 'Oh, Sophie, I am so sick of this. I want you. I want to see you.'

On the other end of the telephone line, Sophie heard in his voice the reassurance she needed that she was truly loved.

'It's not so long,' she said calmly. 'We can wait. After all, we have the rest of our lives.'

Off the telephone, Sophie considered what Matt had said. If things had been different between them, she would have consulted Maeve. Now it seemed inappropriate, as if she was gloating about her relationship with Matt, or rubbing salt in the wounds. She would have liked the old easy way when they would have chewed over her dilemma and she would have benefited from Maeve's bluntly expressed opinions. She was sure to have a view on whether she should think about moving nearer to Matt. It was a big step to take, but her flat was now worth considerably more than when Fergus had bought it and if she sold up she could afford somewhere much bigger in the country, with a proper garden. She imagined the twins playing outside, a climbing frame, a tree house, bicycles, keeping a rabbit, maybe having a puppy. It was an attractive proposition. She would be demonstrating a commitment to Matt by moving to Somerset. Show that she was serious. It would give his father time to get used to the idea that they were in love and that they might well marry. Ultimately, she could not help but imagine herself installed at Manor Farm. She thought of how she would do the house, changes she would make. It was silly, she knew, to think so far ahead, but she couldn't help it. Perhaps, eventually, they would do a swap, herself and Matthew and the children, with Commander Digby. There would be more children by then, and he could move into her cottage. She had it all worked out in her head. All the reasons she had wanted to stay in London, all the Fergus-based reasons, did not seem valid any more.

It was easy to reach for the telephone and make the necessary calls to put herself on the list of house agents around the Charlton area and then make an appointment for an estate agent to come and value the flat. Why not? She felt she had nothing to lose. Everything Matt said seemed to suggest that he wanted their relationship to be permanent, and marriage, after all, was the only state she would consider. 'Mrs Matthew Digby,' she said to herself. 'Mr and Mrs Matthew Digby.' It sounded right. Sophie smiled to herself. Time would tell. This time there was no rush. She could go slowly. Wait and see.

The extra freedom she now had since the twins had started at the nursery was spent mostly on her own. She read the newspaper, enjoyed a coffee at a pavement café, looked in clothes shops, but very often found herself waiting to collect them at the end of the morning. She did not have enough to do, she knew that. She would have liked to be running a proper home where there would be an evening meal to prepare, a house to clean, a garden to manage. She thought tenderly of ironing Matt's shirts, of cutting him a sandwich at lunchtime, between his calls, of helping on the farm. She wanted to be part of a busy, full, productive life, not pushed out to the sidelines like this, moping around, trying to pass the time.

She wanted to be married.

That same evening, just as she was reading Freddy a very dull story about a preachy sort of rabbit, but the one that he loved and always wanted, Maeve telephoned, bursting with news about Dancer. Sophie wondered at her enthusiasm although it was typical of Maeve to go at something hammer and tongs and then, no doubt, lose interest. Sophie wanted to interrupt and tell her of her thoughts about moving, but she still felt the awkwardness of the territory. She felt as if there was a whole mass of stuff bulking up between them, too difficult to speak of but equally hurtful if left unbroached. Sophie did not know where to begin, but the moment was anyway lost by Maeve steaming straight in.

'Can you come to Wincanton on March the third? That's next Thursday,' she demanded. 'Dancer's running again – in the three o'clock race, and depending on how he goes in that, Soph, we're going to decide whether to enter him for Cheltenham on March the sixteenth. Can you believe it? Cheltenham! You know, like you see on the telly! Lady P and I are so thrilled, we can talk of nothing else. Sam is coming, but Mohammed can't. He's promised to do a full day at the restaurant, but he's going to get to Cheltenham if Dancer runs.'

With a pang, Sophie realised that Maeve had asked the others before she had asked her. There was a time when it would have been the other way round.

'Maeve, I can't do next week,' she said, 'but there's enough time between now and Cheltenham to organise the Effs. I can't miss that! I'll take them down to my mother's which is sort of on the way. God, how exciting. Cheltenham! That's the climax of jump racing, you know? That and the Grand National meeting. I suppose everything rests now on how he goes next week.'

'You bet it does. Sally's running herself every day and I join her some mornings. I know, don't say it. It's not like me, but I've got kind of enthused, and she says she's got to be really fit and strong, so I keep her company.'

'The weather's been awful though. Do you really run in the rain?'

'Yup. Rain and dark. February fill-dyke they call it down here and they're bloody right. Thing is, we don't want the ground hard for Dancer because of his old injury, but not too heavy either.'

Sophie smiled. 'You sound like an old hand,' she said.

'Yeah. Well, you pick it up,' said Maeve, 'and I'll tell you something. Peregrine's coming racing next Wednesday. He's down here at the moment but it's too wet for them to get on with the garden so he spends his whole time with Lady P and me, playing poker. Ha ha. Bunty'd be furious.'

Bunty, indeed, would have been furious had she not been away with three of what she called her 'girlfriends' (Henry thought, privately, that this was stretching the term to its very limits) skiing in Gstaad. When she got back she had determined to remove her mother-in-law to another residential home she had found, this time on the Wiltshire Downs, and have done with it. If she didn't like it, tough. She was going to make Henry accompany her this time and then they would do an inventory of the furniture and decide what to sell and what to keep. The Irish girl could clear out all the cupboards of clothes and rubbish Henry's mother had collected over the years and then Bunty could get the architects in and begin on the house. This time the gloves were off. Yes, when she got back she would get things moving.

Henry had telephoned her and told her that the horse, whatever its name was, which had done rather well, although Bunty did not consider a third place at a tinpot racecourse anything to write home about, was going to run at Wincanton. Of course, if it turned out to be any good, it would be rather fun to go racing. Perhaps she would get Henry to take over the ownership when Lady Pamela was in residential care.

Her friends, Carol, Joanne and Angie, were totally in agreement with her plan of action. She had talked through her nightmare time with her mother-in-law while they were having a Swedish massage and afterwards over a hot chocolate. Angie in particular sympathised. Her own mother suffered from dementia and the worst thing of all was that she had completely lost her dress sense. Old people could be so difficult, they agreed. They were so rarely grateful for all that was done for them.

After Wincanton it was Matt who telephoned Sophie with news of the race. He was on his mobile and the line crackled and faded but she could just hear him say, 'Soph? Soph? It's me, Matt.' Then he seemed to be turning aside to say to someone, 'No. I've got through. I'm talking to her now . . .' and then the telephone was grabbed, Sophie supposed, and it was Maeve on the line saying, 'Soph! He won! He bloody went and won,' and then Matt was back saying, 'Did you hear that? Yes, he won. He was great, fantastic! There were only five in his race but he romped home. We all blubbed. All of us. Wish you were here, darling. Wait a minute . . . sorry, got to go. Lady P is going to be presented with a cup. Ring you this evening. 'Bye!'

Sophie sat on the floor, her eyes brimming. She felt several things quite distinctly. One was elation that Dancer had won and the other was jealousy and a sense of being left out. She should have been there. On the carpet next to her was a colour brochure for a pretty cottage for sale on the edge of a village three miles from Charlton. She had read it through several times. Now she made the first fully independent decision of her life and dialled the number of the estate agent.

As promised, Matt rang her back late that evening when he knew the twins would be asleep and she would be able to talk undistracted. Sophie answered the telephone beside her bed. It was lovely to lean back in the pillows and hear Matt's voice. Since sleeping with him she had taken to going to bed naked. She liked her body again since he had made love to her with such passion. She felt lovable, a sexual being again. She glanced down now at her breasts and saw how just thinking about sex had made her nipples hard little pink cones. She wanted to tell him how much she wanted him, how desire flooded through her, how the finger she ran between her legs was wet with longing, but Matt was in a different mood. His voice sounded eager with excitement and she wondered whether he had been drinking, celebrating. It was not the time for intimacy. Sophie felt distanced again, left out and rather resentful. Her languorous sexiness seeped away.

'There were six of us, me and Father, Maeve, Sam and Lady P and Peregrine, and then later on we saw George and Jack Dick and the Days who had all made their own way to the course. It was a really raw afternoon with a south-westerly squally wind and occasional bursts of sun and then a downpour. Foul really. It's the coldest place I know, up there on the hill. Anyway, we went early and had lunch and Sam and Lady P were in great form and my father cheered up and actually had a conversation with me which he hasn't done since Christmas, practically. He suddenly came out with the idea of a long trip to New Zealand. Dark horse, isn't he?

'Anyway, after lunch I went to find Jane in the lorry park and there she was with Sally and Steve, as usual, and Sally had a ride in the one thirty as well so they were pretty busy and involved with getting ready but Jane said that Dancer was going really well and that she had high hopes for him.

'Jack Dick was there leading him round, loosening him up and letting him have a look at things before his race. He loves that horse, you know. Jane says he's like an unpaid member of her team and that he has a real way with him with horses. Sally is quite jealous, I think. She's got a rival.

'Jane had the same arrangement with the steward that Dancer could go down to the start early and off he went, being really naughty, bucking and messing about, showing off to the crowd in the stand. When the race started he was second favourite, and he tucked in behind a horse which Jane said would take off, it always front runs apparently, and Sally had a real problem keeping him back and stopping him taking up the challenge at once. She managed pretty well although Jane kept saying, "Hold him up, hold him up." About six out, the horse in front fell and Dancer took up the lead and stayed there. Sally put him under a bit of pressure over the last furlong or so and he stormed home, lengthened his lead over the other three and won by twelve lengths. He pulled up still full of running. He'll do four miles for certain as long as Sally can hang on to him for the first couple of miles and stop him running himself into the ground. It was wonderful. Totally fucking marvellous. Afterwards there was a great celebration, as you can imagine. Because it was local and because Bumper was such a racegoer and sponsored races at Wincanton, everyone was thrilled to see his colours on the course again and made a great fuss of Lady P. She loved it. So did dear old Sam, patting her hand and saying, "Well done, old girl," as if she'd run in the race herself. George took them home in the end. Frank won three hundred pounds and thought his luck must have turned. Maeve stayed around for a bit and went back in the lorry with the girls.'

Sophie tried to sound thrilled at the end of this, but the resentment lingered and when she eventually put down the telephone she realised that she had deliberately not told Matt of the decision she had taken about the flat. He was right, the physical miles between them strained their relationship. They needed to be closer. The telephone was no good. Too much was left unsaid and too much was lost in the saying. Rather sadly she got out of bed and put on her pyjamas and made a cup of tea. Loving someone again was wonderful but it was like peeling an onion. All the papery, protective outer leaves had been peeled off and underneath was the tender core. It seemed inappropriate, comparing her heart to an onion, she thought as she put the milk back in the fridge and saw a bag of little brown supermarket onions lying in the vegetable drawer. I don't know, though, she told herself; after all, peeling an onion makes you cry, and I seem to feel miserable most of the time. When I'm not deliriously happy, that is.

What Matt had not told Sophie was that he, too, had gone back to Jane's and that after a riotous party in the kitchen, eating takeaway pizzas and drinking anything they could lay their hands on, he eventually gave Maeve a lift back to Charlton and had felt compelled to kiss her in his car and they had clung to one another and he had felt moved to say, over and over again, 'Maeve, forgive me. I loved you. I loved you, too.'

Maeve had pulled back and looked at him sternly. 'Oh yeah? You couldn't have loved me and done what you did.'

'That's not fair. You drove me away. You know you did.'

'Hmm.' Maeve considered. When she was drunk she often felt clearer about situations, as if her mind was suddenly open and imprinted with a fully developed picture of how things actually were. As if she had turned on a light in a dark room.

'What did we have then, you and me? Just bloody good sex?' she had asked.

'Yes. We did have that. But you can't found a real relationship on that alone. You know that. You didn't love me and you don't want to share my sort of life, do you?'

'I asked you to share mine,' said Maeve. 'Go away travelling with me. Have a bit of fun. You didn't love me either, come to that.'

'I couldn't just take off,' said Matt. 'A holiday, maybe, but not for any longer. I have too much happening here in Charlton. This is where my life is.'

257

'Yeah,' said Maeve, 'and so old Soph was a better bet? Falling in love is like an insurance policy with you. You read all the small print to find the best deal.'

'It's not as calculated as that,' protested Matt. 'I do love her, you know. But it is true that she and I are well matched in the sense we want the same things. Not like you.'

'You let me down, both of you. I thought better of you. Especially Sophie. You know, you've changed something by doing what you did.' She narrowed her eyes and looked at him sternly. 'You've taken something really big away from me, and not just the opportunity to shag you. Something that means more to me than that. Soph was special to me. She was like a kind of lighthouse. I could always look to her. She was reliable, like a big beam of light that kept on coming round. There might be dark bits in between, but here she'd come, round again, and everything would be all right. I know it sounds sad, but she was. That's gone now. I still love her and I suppose in the end I'll feel OK about you, but it just won't be the same.'

Matt pulled her head down onto his shoulder and put his arm round her. She seemed small and vulnerable and he regretted having hurt her. She ran a fingernail up and down his thigh and went on in a small voice, 'I used to want to be Sophie, you know? I'd have liked to be absorbed into her life and just be her, with her family and her home and being so perfect and all that. There I was with this shambolic sort of background, surrounded by people but always feeling alone. I used to hate that phrase "only child" when it was used about me. For ages I thought people said "lonely child", and there was old Soph with this wonderful support system of her family. Not a great quarrelsome tribe like my lot, but a real, loving family.

'Then she made that crap decision to marry Fergus. Anyone could see he was a jerk, but she went ahead and everything crashed round her feet. When that happened the brilliant thing was, she needed me. I don't think I'd ever been needed before, and it sort of evened things up. There was she, biting the dust, and there was me picking her up. Mates, you see. We were mates. You spoilt that. You barged in between us and wrecked it.'

'Oh, Maeve,' said Matt impatiently to the top of her head, 'don't be so melodramatic. We're still your friends. Sophie especially. She really cares about you. You can't fall out over me!'

Maeve lifted her head from his shoulder so that she could look up into his face. 'It's not about you, you plonker. Don't you understand what I've been saying?' She saw that he did not. 'Oh, forget it,' and she made a wry shape with her mouth, then kissed him lightly on the cheek and got out of the car and slammed the door. She went towards the house with a backward wave over her shoulder, not looking round, a slight figure, like a child. He drove home feeling chastened, but he did not see what he could do about it. He loved Sophie now. It was Sophie he wanted and Sophie he was going back to telephone.

Diana Tripp was not one to read the racing pages of her newspaper but the following morning she turned straight to the results from Wincanton and was pleased to see that Lady Pamela's horse had won its race. Anything that annoyed Bunty was good news as far as she was concerned. Later on in the morning Henry asked her to put a call through to Gstaad and she listened to the conversation with his wife. It was easy to go in and out of his office and hear as much as she needed. Back at her desk, and with Henry safely in a meeting, she telephoned Charlton and, as she had hoped, Maeve answered the telephone. She relayed the gist of what she had heard. 'It's a shame,' she said, 'but I'm afraid Bunty will insist this time that Lady Pamela be moved. She said she would get a doctor to certify her if necessary. I thought I ought to just ring and warn you.' She thought of her own elderly mother, so combative and contentious, still living life to the full. She could no more despatch her to an old people's home than fly to the moon.

'Yeah, well, thanks,' said Maeve. 'I suppose I knew we couldn't hold out for ever. Do you think you can keep her off until after March the sixteenth? That's the big day.'

'Why? What happens then?'

'Lady P's horse is going to Cheltenham. We're all going. All of us from down here, and Soph, my friend, and Sam from London. Heh, why don't you come? Take the day off. Come down on the train with Sam. Go on, Mrs T, have a day out. You surely deserve one, working for that pompous tosser.'

Diana Tripp considered. Henry used to take a box at Cheltenham for bank entertaining and she would organise the event for him but she had never been herself. Bunty, she knew, did not care for National Hunt racing, preferring the dressier, more flamboyant Ascot, and in recent years Henry had also given up attending. It would be fun. She was touched and pleased to be asked. Twice now Maeve had spontaneously invited her to join a party.

'I'll certainly think about it,' she said, 'and I'll keep in touch over the other business. I'll let you know if I hear anything. Now I'll have to go. Henry must be out of his meeting.'

She had educated her boss into knocking before he entered her office if the door was closed, and this he duly did.

'Come in,' said Diana grandly.

'There's the most awful smell,' complained Henry. 'What is it?'

'Possibly my aromatherapy candle,' she told him evenly. 'The essential oils restore your body harmony, Henry, by activating your magnetic aura and balancing your yin and yang.'

'Well, it gives me a headache,' said Henry. 'Please refrain from burning it in the office.'

Diana said nothing but blew out the flame of the small candle on her desk. If it is possible to blow out a candle in a manner which implies deep offence has been given and taken, Diana achieved this effect most satisfactorily.

Maeve put down the telephone thoughtfully. It was clear that Bunty and Henry would stop at nothing to pursue their intention of removing Lady Pamela from Charlton and the thought made her seethe with anger. On the other hand, Maeve knew that she did not intend to stay for ever. She didn't want to be around when the old lady died, for one thing. A touching deathbed scene was not in her repertoire. She didn't like the idea of terminal illness either. Doling out pills was about her limit. When this Dancer fun was over, she promised herself she would be off. Lady Pamela wasn't her problem. Let her family sort it out. If she was carted off into a home, so what? She'd had a privileged, indulged life up until now and, after all, that was where most people ended up. Not her own granny, as it happened, who passed away on her hands and knees scrubbing out a cupboard in her kitchen, or her grandfather who had died in the lavatory. His last reported words were 'Bloody hell' as he dropped his walking stick. That was her lot for you.

But she found she was still angry.

'It's her house, her home. It belongs to her. It's her money.

What business is it of theirs whether she lives here or not? It's as if she's lost her rights and they can bully her and take no notice of her wishes just because she's old. She's inconveniencing them by living too long, that's what it boils down to.' She said all this to Peregrine as she made him coffee in the kitchen. It was still too wet to get on with much in the garden and he seemed to have taken up residence in the house. He shrugged, not wanting to get involved in family power struggles, and helped himself to a biscuit.

'Don't you think it's scandalous?' Maeve demanded. 'They can't wait to get their hands on Charlton so they get her shipped out. I think it's like stealing.'

'No doubt it will be theirs when she dies,' said Peregrine peaceably, 'so I can't see it makes much difference.' He stirred his coffee. 'Eventually she'll be better off in a home, won't she? I think most old people end up in them these days.'

'It's like sending them off to concentration camps,' said Maeve hotly. 'You know, one day all will be revealed about how criminally we treat old people and we'll be left pretending we didn't know it was happening.'

'Don't be silly. They get well looked after. Sherry before lunch and so on.'

'Oh yeah! Big deal.'

Peregrine kept quiet. He didn't understand why Maeve seemed to mind so much. He couldn't believe that it was only because she would become redundant. He had seen a large cheque made out to her, stuck under an egg cup on the kitchen dresser. She was obviously not short of a bob or two.

The money her father had given her troubled Maeve. She had never had so large a sum and it made her feel uneasy. She had no bank or savings account and the thought of opening one bothered her. She saw it as a shackle, pinning her down, making it necessary to have an address and fill in forms and answer questions. There was nothing she wanted to spend the money on either. Her day-to-day expenses came out of the money she received from Henry for housekeeping and she had her wages as well. Of course she could easily fritter it away, take off round the world, enjoy herself, but the thought held no attraction at the moment. She was used to living a hand-to-mouth existence and the sort of options and choices that a lump sum presented made her panic. She left the cheque where she had first put it and tried to pretend it wasn't there. She might feel differently in the future, she thought. She would wait and see. If Henry and Bunty had their way she would be out of a job soon anyway and might be very glad that she had something to keep her going.

The weeks between Wincanton and Cheltenham flew past. Whenever she could, Maeve went up to the yard to see Dancer and talk to Sally and Jane. If the weather was reasonable, Jane turned the horse out into a field wearing a rug and Maeve sat on the fence and watched him roll and then high jink about, bucking and kicking before getting his head down and eating the first spring grass.

'It helps him relax,' said Jane, leaning on the fence, next to her. 'Some trainers never turn out their horses when they're in training, but I'm a great believer in giving them a bit of freedom to move around naturally. It helps Dancer, who gets pretty hyper in his box. It keeps him sweet. Lets him down a bit.'

Sally and Jane by now knew the others entered for Dancer's race. There were twenty-four declared runners and with the form books spread on the kitchen table, Jane went through them one by one. 'Laundromat used to be a useful sort and he's won a couple of reasonable races but he hasn't shown much in his two runs this season. He got rid of his last jockey last time out. I don't think we need worry about him too much. Andy Bobbett was a great point-to-pointer but he hasn't been anything like as convincing over regulation fences. Ring Home's been lightly raced. He comes with two point-to-point wins this season, but I think he has a lot to do. Castle Bridge is the one to beat, Sally. He's unbeaten in six point-to-points and jumps like an old hand. Celtic Stone is strong too. He won easily at Ludlow last time out. Then there are these six Irish horses, all good quality, all with a claim, all well rated. Look, we're rated down at ninety-six. Quite low, really, but it reflects the question mark that still hangs over Dancer's fitness and the fact that he's got relatively little form. His win won't count for much as it wasn't in great company.'

Maeve listened, entranced. She had taken on the organisation of Dancer's supporters and sent off for tickets and for parking vouchers. Lady Pamela and Sam would use the owner's badges in the club enclosure while the rest of them would go for the cheaper Tattersalls. She took the money out of her Newton Abbot winnings. She wasn't going to allow the Days or Jack or Mohammed to pay. Khaled would be back in

Cairo, visiting his family, but Mohammed had promised he would be there. Sophie and Matt and Commander Digby could refund her later.

'We want to arrive early,' said Lady Pamela. 'There are usually awful traffic jams to get in because Cheltenham is such a lovely meeting and there are all sorts of shops to look round. They have what they call a tented village. I think you will enjoy it, Maeve. Just looking at the crowds is fun. It's the country come to town. There's nothing like it. You see the most wonderful old tweed suits brought out of mothballs. And the Irish – oh, yes, the Irish everywhere. You'll feel very at home!'

'Why's it such a big Irish thing?' asked Maeve. 'I mean, more than anywhere else where there's a racecourse?'

'It happened after the war. In nineteen forty-six, I think, the Irish arrived and swept the board. It's been their preserve ever since. Believe me, Irish-trained horses and their supporters make the bookmakers tremble.'

Maeve closed her eyes. 'I can't wait,' she said.

A week or so before the race, Bunty telephoned to speak to her mother-in-law. Maeve hovered close, not wanting to miss anything. It seemed that the subject of the conversation this time was not threatening to Lady Pamela but rather concerned her grandson, Charlie. He had just been caught smoking again and his school had decided to suspend him until the end of term. Bunty and Henry, to Bunty's fury, had been summoned to meet the headmaster to discuss Charlie's future within what Bunty felt was ridiculously termed 'a tripartite relationship'.

What it boiled down to was that Charlie was out of control and the school could not cope with him. Despite the fact that the offences he had committed were against rules imposed within the school, he was being sent back to his parents for discipline. Bunty felt it was she who was being punished. Having him at home under house arrest was quite impossible. He would escape to London at every opportunity, seeing friends and clubbing, and she was certainly not going to disrupt her carefully planned social life to act as his social worker or prison warder.

She had said all this to Henry and it was then that she had her brain wave. She would despatch him to Charlton and let Lady Pamela supervise him. There were no distractions down there in the country and he was fond of his grandmother. She chose, for the moment, to overlook the unfortunate dope-smoking incident. He could drive down to Charlton in the car he had been given for his seventeenth birthday, and at the same time transport a large stone sculpture which she had bought for the Mexican garden. It was this news that she had telephoned to deliver to her mother-in-law.

'That's all very well and I don't mind having him at all, but we're going to Cheltenham, to the Festival, you know,' said Lady Pamela. 'What do we do with him then?'

'You can take him with you,' said Bunty promptly.

Lady Pamela put the telephone down and explained the situation to Maeve who immediately said, 'But what about Cheltenham? What did Bunty say? Can we leave him locked up here for the day? Chain him to the wall?'

'He'll have to come with us,' said Lady Pamela. 'He's not a bad boy, just silly and easily led. I don't think he'll be a problem. I'm rather fond of him.'

'So am I,' said Maeve. 'I'm all for him if he annoys his mother.'

Charlie, when he arrived, turned out to have grown, since Lady Pamela last saw him, into a lanky pale boy of nearly eighteen, with floppy hair and a weak chin. He was not unlike Henry at the same age, thought his grandmother, but a less secretive and more cheerful person. He settled happily into a spare bedroom, slept most of the day, played Massive Attack tapes and talked on his mobile telephone most of the night. He thought Maeve was 'cool', and Lady Pamela 'wicked'. At a rough estimate, Maeve reckoned he had a thirty-a-day cigarette habit and when he sloped off into Castle Cary to stock up she went with him and bought him a drink in the pub after she had done some shopping and been to the bank.

'Are you going to get thrown out of school?' she asked as they sat in the empty bar eating crisps and drinking cider.

He shrugged his shoulders and pushed back the sleeves of his jersey to reveal an armful of beaded bracelets. 'Dunno. Don't care much. I'm going to plough my A levels anyway. I haven't done any work.'

'What will happen then?'

'I'm going to Australia for a year, although I suppose they may make me re-sit. I'd quite like to go to a crammer in London. That'd be cool.'

Maeve grinned. Bunty had a lot of trouble stored up here in the shape of her only son. He had certainly defied any attempts to smarten him up. In enormous, baggy combat trousers and a series of black and holey sweaters and with a black woollen hat on his head, he looked as classless as any teenager loafing on a street corner. Perhaps she should introduce him to Mrs Day's errant granddaughter, Tracey. What made him different, of course, was that he already owned a car. Not a new one, but nevertheless a smart little black Golf. It was parked outside the pub with heaps of tapes in the well of the front passenger seat and Chelsea football stickers on the back window. He drove carefully, though, taking the country lanes slowly, cautiously nudging round the corners, and he refused Maeve's irresponsible offer of another drink.

He's not as wild as I was at that age, she thought. I expect he'll straighten out and be a banker by the time he's twenty-five.

That evening after a supper of macaroni cheese and salad, it was Charlie who got up to answer the telephone as the three of them sat in companionable silence watching a television fly-on-the-wall documentary of a day in the life of a chiropodist.

'It's Jane someone,' he said, passing the telephone to Lady Pamela.

Maeve gathered from hearing only one end of the conversation that there was something wrong with Dancer. She sat anxiously on the edge of her chair, fiddling with a strand of hair.

'So what do you think?' Lady Pamela said. 'How long do you think it will take?'

She listened to the answer and then said, 'You will let me know then? Obviously I don't want him to run unless he is absolutely all right.' She handed the telephone back to Charlie to replace, and turned to Maeve.

'Not good,' she said. 'Dancer's got a septic foot. It seems he's trodden on something, a nail perhaps, and it has penetrated the sole of his hoof. He's very lame. Matthew has been over and has given him a shot of antibiotic and they are poulticing the foot, but it doesn't look very hopeful.'

'Oh no!' groaned Maeve. 'Jesus! I can't bear it. What does Jane say? Will he be better in time?'

'It's a question of training, you see,' said Lady Pamela.

'With any luck he won't be lame for long, but he won't be able to work meanwhile and he will lose fitness.'

Maeve threw herself back into her chair. Charlie looked on glumly.

'Come on, Maeve,' said Lady Pamela sharply. 'This is not a tragedy. The horse will get better. He'll run again, even if he doesn't make Cheltenham. This sort of thing happens with horses.'

'It's so bloody unfair,' said Maeve angrily. 'Why did it have to happen to him and not one of Jane's other horses? It isn't as if we've got a lot of time.' She turned on Charlie furiously. 'Your bloody mother. She'll put a stop to it, you know.'

Charlie looked alarmed and Lady Pamela interrupted, 'Maeve, stop it. That's enough of that. It has nothing to do with Charlie, or his mother. It is naughty of you to say so.'

'But it's true,' said Maeve. 'She'll interfere. She'll stop you having a horse. You know she will, when she takes over here.'

Lady Pamela allowed herself a small, smug smile. 'She won't be able to. I've already thought of that. At Sam's suggestion, I have decided to pass Dancer over to Jane. She's going to lease him from me. It's not an unusual arrangement in racing and should work very well. Jane will continue to train him and although no money will pass hands, he will effectively become her horse and she will make all the decisions regarding him.'

It took Maeve a moment to take this in. 'Well!' she said eventually. 'Aren't you a sly old thing. When did you think of that?'

'The last time Sam was here we talked about it. You're not the only one to have ideas, you know.'

Maeve reached for the cushion behind her and threw it at Charlie. 'There you are, you can tell that to your bloody mother.'

'Maeve! Leave the poor boy alone.'

The next morning, as Jane was holding up Dancer's foot while Matt bound the dressing with tape, they heard voices approaching across the yard and a moment later Maeve's head appeared over the stable door.

'Well?' she demanded.

'Hard to tell,' said Matt. 'A lot of gunk has come out overnight. We've just put on a fresh poultice. He's much more comfortable on it now. He could hardly put his foot to the ground yesterday. He's had two shots of antibiotic which should help clear any infection.' He finished strapping the dressing in place and Jane let go of the foot.

'I'd guess he'll need two or three days yet and then we'll get the shoe back on,' she said. Seeing Lady Pamela appear next to Maeve, and then Charlie behind her, she added, 'We just can't tell how long it will take. Keep everything you've got crossed. We may get away with it.' She patted Dancer's neck. 'He's feeling less sorry for himself this morning.'

She and Matt let themselves out of the stable and into the yard where the sun was shining weakly and Sally and Steve were getting ready to ride out on two youngsters. Sally looked dejected, although she waved at them briefly. She clearly did not feel like talking or speculating on Dancer's chances of recovery in time.

'Come on, Matt,' said Maeve, digging him in the ribs. 'Get on with it and get him better. What kind of vet do you call yourself? Surely you can do something?'

'Nothing more than I've already done, I'm afraid. As Jane said, it's fingers crossed.'

They trooped together towards the house. 'Coffee?' asked Jane. Maeve kicked at the ground with her toe. She couldn't stand the calm and philosophical attitude everyone was taking. She felt she would explode with frustration. Jane touched her arm. 'This is a heartbreaking business,' she said. 'Things like this go wrong all the time. Believe me, you have to learn to take it.'

The one thing that Maeve could not be was philosophical. She became quite impossible over the next few days, tense and irritable and scowling. She almost gave up cooking, slamming beans on toast before Lady Pamela and Charlie, challenging them to complain. She was particularly unpleasant to Charlie, talking often of his 'bloody mother', and shut herself up in her room, lying on her bed looking at the ceiling. Lady Pamela wondered if it was all to do with Dancer or if her black mood was not the result of some other sort of imbalance in her life. Despite her openness, there was a lot of Maeve that she felt she did not know. This fury can't last, she thought, but I must face the fact that she won't want to go on here when all this excitement with the horse is over. She is young and restless. She will move on, and then what am I to do, oh, what am I to do? Lady Pamela knew that it was

Maeve's transferred touch that had put new life into her. She thought back to Mrs Cook, the dismal meals, the cheerless house. Once again the quiet, insistent desire to exit life became strong. What was the point of looking forward, of plodding on? The excitement over Dancer was temporary and altered not one jot the real tenor of her life, especially without the Irish. She would lose Charlton. That must be faced. There was little else left. The horse for the moment. Then Sam. Just Sam.

Sensing her gloom over the telephone, Sam suggested that he come down to Somerset for the day.

'Darling, how lovely, but don't expect anything to eat. The Irish is on strike.'

'We'll get Charlie to take us to the pub,' said Sam, and he duly arrived with a bottle of gin and a bunch of lilies.

'Oh, a bit funereal!' said Lady Pamela.

'But they smell so lovely,' said Sam, kissing her.

Later on, after going out for a pub lunch, they persuaded Charlie to light the drawing-room fire and Lady Pamela told Sam about Maeve.

'I thought there was something wrong,' he said, 'when she wouldn't come out with us.'

'This is all going to end,' said Pammy, gesturing with her hand. 'I doubt I will be here much longer. Maeve will leave. It's all over, really. Just a few more weeks, perhaps.'

Sam patted her hand in wordless sympathy. How easy his life was by comparison. None of this wrenching and grieving over a house. All his life, as long as he had been comfortable and things were arranged conveniently, he had never needed to make places important to him. Only Pammy. She was all he had wanted.

'There's something I have got to do, darling, before I can let go, shut up shop as it were. Would you help me? I can't somehow face it on my own.'

'Of course, my dear,' said Sam, wondering wildly what it was he was being asked to do. A vague unease flickered in his heart.

'I must go upstairs and get it,' said Pammy. 'Do you think we should have a little stiffener? I know it's only the afternoon still, but a little drop of whisky might just help.'

Sam got creakily to his feet and held out his hand to help Pammy up. She was so light that he practically lifted her out of her chair.

'Make the fire up, darling. We shall need that.'

Sam frowned as he bent down for a log. What on earth? He hoped it wasn't something he would regret. He threw the log onto the hearth and it sent out a little fountain of golden sparks. Slowly he moved over to the side table for the whisky. He splashed an inch or so into two tumblers. He could hear Pammy moving about overhead and then her feet on the stairs. He took up the two glasses and went to stand with his back to the fire, ready to face her, to read her expression when she came back into the room.

To his surprise she re-entered carrying a box, a long wooden box, and then he realised that it was a drawer pulled from a chest and that it was full of papers and what looked like packets of photographs.

She laid it reverently on the sofa and then came over to where he stood and took the glass he held out to her.

'It's Lizzie,' she said simply. 'I feel I must deal with it now. Anything relating to Bumper, Henry will want. All family letters, photographs from my side of the family Bunty will want to keep because of the title. She loves anything like that. That leaves Lizzie. No one will want these things. They'll be thrown into a heap, turned upside down on the floor and then put out for the dustmen. I don't want them blowing about on some council dump. I'd rather dispose of them myself. Now. With you. None of them matter any more. Sheer sentiment. But they have been important to me and, darling, to you too, only you didn't know.'

Sam saw the drift of this and took her in his arms and kissed the top of her little sleek white head. He felt closer to her than ever, as if their thin old skin could no longer keep them apart and they could melt and meld into one.

'Of course I knew it, Pammy dearest. Of course I knew Lizzie was mine. I knew why you pretended. It was the only way.'

She drew back and looked at him. 'Sam! And you forgave me? You let me go on lying all my life?'

'It was the best way, dearest. There wasn't another way. It was right for Lizzie.'

'I should have been bolder. More like the Irish. Not given a damn. Let people say what they liked.'

'No, Pammy, you couldn't have done that. It was different then. You did what was right. You had a husband, and there was Henry. They needed you. Here, have your drink,' and

269

they both took large gulps and smiled weakly at each other over the rims of their glasses.

'But I denied you your daughter. You should have had the pleasure of having a daughter.'

'I did,' Sam smiled. 'I always knew. I could love her from afar and Bumper was a better father than I would ever have been. Perhaps one day we would have had to tell her. I did wonder about that. But as it turned out she never had to know. She was spared the truth.'

'Oh, Sam.' They stood for a moment, two old figures holding hands.

Pammy sniffed and took up a letter from the drawer. 'Do you want to see them? Do you want to read them? There are school reports and everything in here.'

'No,' said Sam. 'I don't want to. There's no need. It is all too long ago. Shall we just let them all burn? I can remember Lizzie just as she was. I don't need anything more.'

Together they took up bundles of letters and other papers and slid them into the fire. It was a wrench to see the childish writing darken as the paper blackened, and then crumble and collapse into grey ash. The photographs followed. Sam saw images of the bright young face, the swinging bell of fair hair, the child's body and then the slim shape of a young woman. They curled and shrivelled in the flames. It did not take long and then he gave the whole lot a good stir with the poker.

'That's good, said Pammy. 'All gone now.' Her voice was falsely cheerful. 'I never guessed you knew, Sam. I sometimes thought you must, but you never gave it away.'

'Better not,' said Sam. 'Much better not.'

The drawer was now empty, just a blue plastic paperclip left in the bottom. Pammy picked it out and put it on the mantelpiece. Form upstairs came the thumping of Crash Test Dummies.

'You know,' she said, 'it's rather nice having Charlie here. This house needs new life. A fresh start. I'm glad that it will be his home.'

While Lady Pamela and Sam and Charlie were out at lunch, Maeve had dragged herself out of the house and cycled slowly down to Manor Farm. As she wheeled into the yard she could see Matt's father at the sink through the kitchen window, running water into a saucepan, and without knocking she opened the back door and went in. The radio news was turned up loud and at first he did not hear her entrance, but as he moved to the larder to see if the bread was as stale as he suspected, he saw her and his face broke into a smile of welcome.

'Don't smile,' she said. 'I'm not in a good mood.'

He turned off the radio. 'Oh. Is there anything I can do? Would a drink help? Matthew has some gin somewhere.'

'It's Dancer. At least, part of it.' She sat down on a chair and then transferred to the table, next to a bowl of tinned soup which was steaming gently. Commander Digby searched in the larder for the cheese. He knew there was some, and not blue and furry as far as he could remember. He found it in the fridge, and also some rather violent-looking Danish salami which he had bought because it was strong and cheap. He tried to arrange everything attractively on a plate, not very successfully.

'Here,' he said. 'Have some lunch. Although I realise it hardly qualifies as such.' He put the plate down and pushed the bowl of soup towards Maeve.

'I don't want that,' she said. 'It's yours anyway. You were just about to eat it.' She pushed it back and, picking up his knife, hacked off a corner of cheese and wrapped it in a slice of salami. 'This'll do me. Dancer's got a septic foot,' she said.

Commander Digby sat down and took up a spoon. 'Not the end of the world, I shouldn't have thought.'

Maeve exploded. 'You're all exactly the same. I don't need to be told that. I know it's not the end of the bloody world, but every single time anything is going right for me, something happens to mess it all up. Over and over again. It doesn't matter what. It all starts OK and I think, this is good, this is going to work out, and the moment I start to be excited or to feel just a tiny bit hopeful, wham! Disaster. I know you'll say this Dancer setback isn't about me, and of course it's not, but it's typical of what happens around me. It's what I seem to attract.'

'Don't be ridiculous,' said the Commander calmly. 'You're talking like a New Age, Glastonbury sort of half-wit. You can't really believe that there is something about you which attracts calamities, or that you somehow influence Dancer? Horses are always going wrong. Horses break hearts and empty pockets. Well-known fact.'

'I've been told that, by everyone.'

'So? Do you really want me to believe that you are so

childish that you can't take disappointments? That's all it is. A disappointment.' He took another spoonful of soup.

'Look,' said Maeve. 'I know that on the scale of human disasters it's not much, hardly registers, probably, but the point is, it's always the same with me. I so want for things to be right, and the moment I believe they will be, without exception it fucks up. Or I do. I mean, is this what to expect in life? Is this what it's really like? Don't tell me about landmines in Angola and starving babies and all that. I mean, I know about being better off than most of the world and being grateful I've got both my legs. I accept that. What I need to know is, am I wrong to go on hoping for things to be great, to work out like I want them to? Is it, like, sinful? Have I got it all wrong? Am I always barking up the wrong fucking gum tree?'

Commander Digby put down his spoon. 'Are you asking me? I'm hardly the right person to give advice. I'm not known for my optimistic outlook.'

Despite herself, his long, gloomy face made Maeve want to laugh. He went on, looking into his soup, 'However, I don't think it is wrong to pursue happiness, if that's what you're asking. Whether it can ever be attained is another matter. What's the saying? "Better to travel hopefully than to arrive"? I think you should travel hopefully through life, and I believe you do. Usually. It's when you're neither hopeful nor travelling – exactly as I feel at the moment – that you have to do something drastic, remedial, whatever.'

'Do you really think that about me?' said Maeve, fascinated by this insight into herself. 'That I'm a hopeful traveller?'

'Yes, my dear,' said Commander Digby, patting her hand. 'You couldn't be anything else. And as such, I'm afraid, you have to expect to be knocked for six every so often. It's the price you pay for enjoying life more than most other people. In that respect I would say that you and Lady Pamela are similar. What you are not so good at yet is taking the inevitable knocks.'

Maeve cut herself off another corner of cheese. 'But everything I touch seems to screw up. From birth almost.'

'How can you talk such nonsense? You have a low tolerance level, that's all, and are one of the most impatient people I've ever met. If you're counting Matthew as one of your disasters, you could have hung on to him, you know, if you'd shown a little more restraint, been a little less demanding.'

Maeve glared. 'Who says I wanted to?' she fired back.

'Exactly. Your choice. Not the malicious hand of fate, or the curse of the Delaneys.'

Maeve thought and then smiled wryly. 'Soph, of course, is exactly that, isn't she? Less demanding and a model of restraint.'

Commander Digby said nothing for a moment, and then went on, 'Many people,' he cleared his throat and wiped the soup from the corners of his mouth with the tea towel, 'find you charming as you are. Volatile, vivacious, I don't know what.' Embarrassed, he got up with his bowl and moved away, shuffling his stockinged feet over to the sink.

Maeve felt moved. She recognised that this was probably the closest he had got to a tender remark in years.

'What about you?' she asked gently. 'How can you put up with trudging about in the mud and worrying about going broke?'

'Lower set of expectations,' he said. 'Not much of a success in the navy. Joined up when defence cuts started to bite and only saw the service in decline. Ended up pushing paper when I would have liked to be on a ship. Not much of a success at farming. Some good years to start with and then possibly the worst for British agriculture since the Depression. Don't seem to have the entrepreneurial skills to see other ways of making the farm pay. Lost Matthew's mother when she was fifty, when I suppose I'd hoped for a companion more or less for life. So you see, I'm the wrong person to ask about expectations. I seem to have run short on expectations.' With a degree of dismay, David Digby wondered if he sounded as if he was trawling for sympathy. He had hoped to keep his tone jaunty.

'However,' he went on, wanting to end the conversation on a brighter note, 'I have been thinking about what you said, about selling up. Strangely, it would take more courage to do that than just sit tight and wait for the receivers, which is my natural inclination. Head in the sand kind of thing. I've been thinking about it,' he struggled on, trying to introduce a cheerful tone to his voice, 'and it might be the right thing to do. The best thing in the long run. So thank you for that.'

'It surely didn't take me to point out that chucking farming was an alternative?'

Commander Digby smiled. 'Remember all those Digby graves in the churchyard? Yes, well, I think most people who feel they know me well enough to suggest such a thing shied off the subject. Thought it was too outrageous to even discuss. You see, it would mark me out as the Digby who lost the farm which had been in the family for generations. The one who sold out. That wouldn't occur to you, would it?'

'Well, it does now you mention it but no, it wouldn't have. I can't see that the past matters. You're the one who has to deal with the present. You can't live for your ancestors. I expect they had a bloody good time, squiring about, ordering the peasants around. I bet they didn't have to shovel shit themselves, like you do.'

They smiled at each other.

'What are you going to do when this is all over?' Commander Digby asked.

'Dunno,' said Maeve. 'I've been thinking about it. Take off somewhere. I need some sun. Maybe go to Thailand where I've got a friend who runs a guesthouse up in the north somewhere.'

'A rolling stone, eh?'

'Yeah, that's me.'

As she pedalled home, Maeve realised that she felt better. Matt's father had somehow brought her back in touch with reality, stopped the awful feeling of spinning, helpless, into a black hole. She smiled to herself at the thought of him selling up the farm and bumming off somewhere. That would get them all going. Old Soph shouldn't start counting on being the lady of the manor just yet.

As she rounded the last bend she saw a cattle track turning towards Manor Farm and recognised Rob at the wheel. He pulled over, blocking the lane, and wound down his window.

'Hi there, what are you up to?'

Maeve got off her bicycle and threw it into the hedge. She climbed up on the step of the lorry. 'Open this door and I'll show you,' she said.

The next morning, Jane telephoned to say that the farrier had been and replaced Dancer's shoe, that she had plugged the hole left by the infection with Stockholm tar and cotton wool and that he seemed sound. He could start work again immediately.

The whole house seemed to sigh with relief. Poor Charlie, who was used to being shouted at, assumed a less hangdog expression and stopped skulking in his room, and Lady

Pamela found she was feeling chirpy again. She felt quite ashamed that she was as bad as Maeve, letting a setback with Dancer plunge her into gloom. Talking to Sam had made her decide to take the initiative with Bunty, have something up her sleeve, not wait for decisions to be made for her. Not only that, meals improved as well. The day that Jane telephoned, Maeve went to the butchers and came back with a rib of beef for lunch.

The second telephone call was from Sophie. Maeve knew her so well that the uncertainty and nervousness in her voice was immediately apparent. What's she coming round to saying? she thought, and then out it came, that Sophie was going to look at a cottage in South Charlton and would Maeve go with her. She was driving down the next day and would collect her if she would agree, and not to say anything to Matt. It was excluding Matt that was Sophie's master stroke and Maeve again felt the pleasure of an exclusive friendship.

''Course I will, matey. I'd love to. Well, what do you know, you must be serious about lover boy. Have you got used to the idea that the last thing he fondled was a cow?'

It was the first time that Maeve and Sophie had been properly alone and as they drove between Charlton and Snook Cottage, Maeve's normal manner made Sophie suddenly feel easy again.

'Look, Maeve, I've never really had the chance to talk to you about what happened. I terribly regret that we went behind your back, but it didn't seem like that at the time. You are the last person I would want to hurt and I now have to live with myself. I really do need to know that you forgive me. Please? All this moving down here and everything, it's all spoilt if it makes you more unhappy.'

Maeve was silent for a moment. 'It's OK, mate. I know you mean it, that you're sorry. I don't want to lose you, and I will if I hold a grudge. Yeah, I forgive you. Anyway,' she added mischievously, 'I got off with Rob the other day. There's nothing like a good fuck for putting me in a forgiving mood!'

They drew up outside Snook Cottage, laughing, and Colonel Vincent Durand, who was hoping for a quick and easy sale and was watching from the window, thought they looked too young and frivolous and not nearly rich enough to buy his cottage. And quite dangerously pretty.

The cottage was ghastly. The colonel, an impeccable

Frenchman, told them he had bought it two years ago as a base in England while he was attached to the British Army. He had fancied the idea of having 'the 'unting seat' as he called it, but Sophie suspected that one look at the blackthorn hedges and ditches and mud of the Blackmore Vale and he had had second thoughts. There were rows of highly polished and elegant riding boots in the hall and many photographs of Vincent Durand mounted on various glossy horses in terrifically glamorous uniform. As soon as he discovered that Sophie's father was a colonel he revved up his talk and there was much reminiscing about 'ze 'Orseguards' and Royal name-dropping.

'Christ, the French love it all, don't they?' said Maeve as they drove away an hour or so later. 'They go into orgasms over our monarchy. I suppose they've only got Johneee 'Alliday and old Chirac.'

'It was his knocking shop, wasn't it?' said Sophie. 'That enormous bed and all the mirrors everywhere and that ghastly wallpaper and nothing in the cupboards except booze.'

'Could you fancy him?' wondered Maeve. 'I wonder what he'd be like in bed? Imagine being snuffled by that moustache. I'm always suspicious of men who love uniform and all that stuff. Dressing up to compensate for small penises, I suspect.'

'If he only knew what we're saying about him,' laughed Sophie. 'Still, I enjoyed the champagne and he gave you his card, didn't he?'

'Yeah. For if I'm in London. He's got a flat there, in Belgrave Square. Hmm. A Frenchman's mistress. Sounds OK, doesn't it? Might be fun.'

'But what about the cottage? Apart from how he's done it up, it could be lovely, don't you think? Lovely position and pretty garden.'

'Sophie, when you and I talk about lovely positions, we refer to something quite different! Offer him ten thousand less than he's asking and you can throw me in as part of the deal.'

Sophie laughed. She felt a great weight lift from her heart. It was like old times again.

Vincent Durand collected his antique champagne glasses and took them through to the kitchen. He had enjoyed those two English girls, the one so tall and ladylike, the other so dark and small and naughty. He would like to know them better. Both of them. Together. He pulled on rubber gloves to rinse the glasses. He was asking a ridiculous price for his cottage, he knew. Perhaps he could come to some arrangement.

Chapter Fourteen

As Cheltenham approached, Sophie, too, felt excited. She was looking forward to the races but most of all she was longing to see Matt again. She spent a morning mooching about London shops looking for presents for him. She bought him a book on rugby and a keyring with a green rubber boot tag, and a knitted hat and some toilet water called New Mown Hay. She bought herself a lipstick and a mohair scarf in clashing colours, which looked more like Maeve than her own, usually subdued, taste. She bought Commander Digby some tea from Fortnum and Mason and then wondered if he would think it pretentious, and decided to give it to her mother instead.

Apart from Maeve, no one knew that she had seen Snook Cottage. Matt was going to take her to an expensive country house hotel for the night before the race. There would be blazing fires and candles, and she imagined curling up on a squashy sofa after dinner, with coffee and brandy, and telling him then. It would be their first proper night together and she felt on edge and excited. On a whim, she bought herself a beautiful nightdress from a wickedly expensive boutique. As the sales assistant wrapped it in layers of tissue, she slipped in a complimentary phial of scent called Passion and gave Sophie a knowing smile. She had tried to interest her in wisps of lacy underwear, tiny satin bras and G-strings. 'You have the figure. You'd look fabulous,' she had urged. Sophie declined. There was a limit. She felt she had strayed into the world of glamorous liaisons, of seduction, of expensive romance. She could not believe how her life had changed, how being loved by Matt had transformed her from an exhausted, abandoned single mother who slept in baggy, oversized T-shirts into this love goddess.

The next day she dropped the twins in Oxford and had to

be evasive with her mother about her whereabouts for the night. 'If you need me, ring my mobile. I'll leave it switched on,' she said.

'Aren't you going to be with Maeve?'

Sophie answered casually, 'No. Charlton is full. Other people are going to be staying before the race. I'm going to stay with a friend. I'm not sure of the number.' Her mother gave her a sharp look. Anyone could see how her daughter had changed over the past weeks. It did not take much intuition to realise that she had someone new and important in her life. It was unlike Sophie to be secretive. Mrs Gladwell said nothing. I hope she's not going to get hurt, she thought.

By not probing, Sophie knew her mother had identified the territory and cautiously retreated. The questions she would have liked to ask lay unspoken between them. I'll tell you soon, thought Sophie. When I'm sure of everything, I'll tell you. For the moment she wanted to keep Matt to herself. She did not want her relationship held up for scrutiny and discussion. She did not feel robust enough for that.

She hugged her mother and gave her a kiss.

'Have a lovely time, darling. Give our love to Maeve and we'll have our fingers crossed for Dancer.'

Sophie knelt and gathered the twins to her. Flora struggled to get free. She wanted to go and inspect the toy box in the kitchen. Sophie kissed them both. Since starting at the nursery even Freddy had become sturdily independent and there was no distress at her leaving. She was better at it as well and said goodbye without the usual pangs and wrenching doubts and terrible fear that she might never see them again. Back in the car, she felt wonderfully free. She drove fast and played loud tapes and smiled at herself in the driver's mirror.

When she arrived at the farm it was dark. There were lights on in the kitchen and she could see Matt's father moving about inside. She knocked on the back door and went in. He offered her a cup of tea and seemed less distant and almost welcoming, asking her about the journey and the traffic. Matt told her later that he had sold some calves to a dealer from Cheshire at an encouraging price. She tried to be helpful, clearing the table of lunch things and tidying up, and then the lights of Matt's car swept across the yard and the door banged and he was there, in a rush of cold air, putting his arms round her and crushing her against his wax jacket which smelled of disinfectant.

Up at the yard, Sally, Jane and Steve were putting the finishing touches to Dancer. He had been gently exercised in the morning and had had half an hour on the horse walker in the afternoon to loosen him up. Now as they rugged him for the night, Jane thought he looked as well and as fit as she could have hoped. His mane and tail had been plaited ready for the early start. He had eaten his supper, seemingly unaware of the tension surrounding him, and was now pulling at his hay net. The farrier had been in the afternoon and put on his racing plates and before she closed his door for the night Jane ran her hands down his legs for one last, anxious inspection.

Steve went over the lorry. Tank full, oil and tyres checked and all Dancer's tack already stowed. He ran his eye down the list pinned in the cab. Saddle, bridle, weight cloth, surcingle, rugs, boots, bandages. All in.

In the house, Sally tipped out her bag and went through her kit for the last time. Skull cap, silk, hair net, colours, back protector, stock, breeches, boots, whip, gloves. Her mother had stocked her up with energy drinks and glucose tablets and she had some good luck cards which she was going to take with her. She touched her neck and her fingers found the gold chain and horseshoe given her by Mark, her boyfriend, for luck. She wished she did not have the night to get through and that they were already loading the horse and starting the journey. Jane had asked her to stay and she had agreed, but now felt that she'd rather be at home in their rented cottage, sharing a beer and a takeaway with Mark, their lurcher Maisie snoring on the sofa and the television on in the background. She felt strange, like a visitor, in Jane's cold, bare spare room. She reached for her mobile telephone.

She'd ring Mark and ask him to come and get her. He needed their shared car for work but he wouldn't mind dropping her over in the morning. She knew she would not sleep unless she was in her own bed with Mark's arm round her.

Over at Charlton, Lady Pamela, Maeve, Mohammed and Sam waited for the weather forecast after the television news. From upstairs came the thump of Charlie's music. 'How would you describe the going?' asked Maeve, opening the curtains and peering out at the night sky. 'It's not going to freeze, that's for sure. There are no stars to be seen. The sky is thick with clouds.'

'It should be good to firm, I'd say,' said Lady Pamela. 'Certainly not hard, which is the main thing.'

'Has he ever run four miles before?' asked Sam.

'Three and a half,' said Lady Pamela, 'but Jane is convinced he can do the distance. The race won't be won on speed, rather jumping ability and stamina. That Cheltenham hill really makes horses dig deep at the finish. It's a punishing course but wonderful for all that. The fences are beautiful – regulation height, of course, but built solid and inviting.'

'Here comes the weather,' said Sam as the television showed a young woman with a chart behind her. 'Oh good. Mild and dry. What could be better?'

'I think early bed, don't you, darling?' asked Lady Pamela. 'We've quite a day tomorrow.'

In the kitchen, Maeve put her arms round Mohammed.

'Yous are OK?' he asked her.

'Yeah,' she said. 'I'm OK, Mohammed. I've been a bit unsettled, but I'm OK. All I'm thinking about at the moment is that horse.'

'And after the race?' he asked.

'I'll go on here for a bit. See what happens.'

'Lady Pamelas? You stay with her, I think.'

'Can't say.' Maeve felt people were always trying to box her in with these questions. 'I don't know what's going to happen with her. You know, her family want her out of Charlton and I can't hold out against them for ever. They'll pack her off sooner or later.'

Mohammed nodded. 'This, I think, will happen. I cannot be understanding, but Mr Elwes, he thinks this also. Then will be the end. You know he want Lady Pamelas to be in London with him? You knows this?'

Maeve looked unsurprised. 'I thought he probably did. But Lady Pamela is such a stubborn old bird. She has this notion that being old and infirm is undignified. She doesn't want him to see her like that – maybe bedridden, bedpans, bed baths, all that. I think that's why she won't consider it.'

'This, perhaps, is so. I am looking after Mr Elwes and it is making me very happy. You could come to be in London and look after Lady Pamela, also.'

'No thanks, Mohammed. I'm not a geriatric nurse, you know. It'd kill me before I killed her. No, I'll be off again. Don't know where, but something will turn up.' She smiled chirpily to deflect him. 'Now, come on and give me a hand getting this picnic together. We're leaving at nine tomorrow morning. I told you Matt is coming to collect you to go in his car? I need to be prepared for Lady P's usual performance. She'll interfere with everything at the last moment. I'm going to have the whole lot packed in the boot of Charlie's car before she gets downstairs.'

Maeve's experience of racecourses had not prepared her for Cheltenham. The size, the scale, the glamour of the stands and the immaculate track, the setting in a scoop of blue hills all took her by surprise.

'Christ, it's enormous. It's so smart. There are so many people!' she exclaimed as Charlie finally drew into the car park. Streams of people were already pouring into the enclosures and beyond was a coach park full of coaches from all over the country. Helicopters buzzed overhead on their way to land.

'It's the home of National Hunt racing,' explained Lady Pamela. 'The best there is.'

'Very serious gambling goes on over the Festival,' said Sam. 'These men you see studying form in the racing papers probably have a fortune at stake. A huge amount of money changes hands.'

They climbed out of the car and Maeve watched the crowds. There were the same ranks of wax jackets and tweed suits she had seen at Newton Abbot and Wincanton but heavily diluted by what she recognised immediately as groups of Irishmen, dressed for a Saturday afternoon at the betting shop back home. The smell of beer and fried onions hung over the enclosure, but up in the restaurants in the stands she could see people already drinking champagne. A girl with very long legs and a very short skirt went past on the arm of an older man in a sheepskin jacket. Her stiletto heels and thin suit looked out of place and it was not only her looks which had heads turning. 'She's his ride for the day,' laughed Maeve. Most of the women, Maeve noticed, were dressed sensibly and smartly for the cold. There were a lot of velvet and fur hats, flat shoes and boots, long wool coats. 'These horsey women,' giggled Maeve, 'they'd like to be saddled up themselves, I think. They love little snaffles and curb chains on their shoes and bags, don't they? They even wear brooches made up into saddles and boots and whips and spurs. Oh, look! There's Matt and Sophie and the others. Just arriving. Come on, Charlie, get the boot open and we'll have a glass of port straight away.'

Charlie, looking as derelict as usual in a long black overcoat and curious checked trousers, with his black knitted hat on his head, ground his cigarette stub into the grass. He'd been having a shifty smoke round the back of the car. This was miles better than school, he thought. Cheerfully he poured out port and whisky macs from the bottles Maeve had packed into a wicker basket and took a hefty one himself. He wouldn't be driving again for hours. He hoped his headmaster or his mother might see him on the television.

Sam was perfect, thought Maeve, in his beautiful old tweed suit and soft, fawn covert coat with a worn velvet collar. She put her arm through his and gave it a squeeze.

'Sam,' she said, 'I adore you, you know that? He's the best looking man here, isn't he, Lady P?' Sam looked pleased and patted her hand. Lady Pamela smiled. She looked lovely, he thought. He remembered that coat and hat from years ago and she had tied his Christmas shawl over her shoulders.

'Us old things,' she said, 'might make our way up into the stand and find somewhere to sit, don't you think, Sam? Shall we meet back here for lunch at one o'clock? The first race is at two.'

They refused all offers of supporting arms and went off together, Lady Pamela with her stick in one hand and the other hooked through Sam's elbow. Maeve looked after them fondly. 'They're quite a pair, aren't they?' she said. 'Look how even here, with all this hustle and bustle, people make way for them and smile.'

Sophie and Matt and Mohammed and Commander Digby were weaving their way through the cars to join them. Maeve and Sophie hugged each other.

'You look great, Soph,' said Maeve. 'Love, love changes everything,' she sang under her breath and gave Sophie a dig in the ribs. 'Here you are, Commander, splice the mainbrace or whatever,' and she handed him a large port.

Feeling high on alcohol and excitement they later threaded through the crowds towards the stands. Maeve heard Irish voices all around, especially in the gaggles of men grouped round the Tote, studying form and turning over the pages of the sporting press. Charlie wanted a hamburger and Maeve stole a huge bite, forcing the coatings of ketchup and mustard to ooze out of the bun and dribble down her chin. Laughing, she wiped it off on the end of his scarf.

Later they walked down to the rails and looked at the thick green turf, perfectly rolled and prepared for the day. 'This is the famous Cheltenham hill,' said Commander Digby, looking away from the finishing post. 'See what a long haul it is, and right at the end of a race. It's this which really tests the guts and the courage of a horse.'

'The fences are so huge,' wailed Maeve. 'They make me feel terrified just to look at them.'

'They're regulation minimum four foot six, more like four foot eight at the start of the season, but they're beautifully shaped, with a curving shoulder. Horses enjoy jumping them,' said Matt.

'I'm starving,' complained Charlie. 'Isn't it lunchtime yet?'

'You've got worms,' Maeve told him. 'We're supposed to meet the Days in the Persian War Bar at twelve thirty. They're coming by coach from Wincanton.' She caught Matt's arm and looked at his watch. 'It's time we went.' She was just turning away when a small, bespectacled man in a dark overcoat and a felt hat, who had been standing close to them at the rails, stepped out and touched her on the arm.

'Would it be Maeve Delaney?' he asked in an Irish accent.

Maeve spun round. 'Jesus!' she said, her eyes widening and delighted. 'Father O'Brien! I don't believe it!' and she gave him a smacker of a kiss.

'Well, well,' he said, wiping his cheek but looking pleased. 'What would you be doing here?'

'Father, you won't believe it, but I've come with a horse! Not mine, of course. It belongs to the old lady I look after.'

'Maeve Delaney! Looking after an old lady. Saints preserve us!'

'It's true, Father. Unlikely but true. You must meet my friends here!' and with a sweep of her arm she indicated them all.

The little priest shook everyone by the hand and explained that he came over every year for the Cheltenham Festival on an excursion ticket with a group of his parishioners from Belfast. He had known Maeve and her family for years, was an old friend of her father's.

'So what's the horse you've come to support? Is it one I should know? Worth a pound or two, perhaps?'

Maeve explained about Irish Dancer and Father O'Brien

marked his name in his racecard. 'It's a fine name he's got, to be sure,' he twinkled.

'Come and have lunch with us. Do, please,' she urged.

'I'd love to do just that,' he said, 'but my friends will be waiting for me. I'll be seeing you again down at the paddock. You know,' he said, drawing Maeve to one side, 'I have been asked, on occasion, to bless a horse before a race, and I've always believed it a lovely thing to do. Just think about it, will you?' and he gave her a wink before bidding them all goodbye and disappearing into the crowd.

Maeve turned to Sophie and Matt. 'It's amazing to just bump into him like that. He's my all time fave priest. He's the only one I know who could turn me into a proper Catholic.'

Sophie smiled. 'I remember you talking about him at school. He persuaded you to be confirmed, didn't he?'

'Yes, you're right. He did. Did you hear what he said? He'll bless Dancer. To bring him and Sally safely home.'

They had a noisy and happy lunch, grouped round the back of Charlie's car with Lady Pamela directing proceedings from the back seat, as usual, her little legs stuck out through the open door. She and Sam had bumped into old friends in the stand. 'I haven't seen Wally Dunlop for thirty years,' she announced. 'Hasn't he got old, Sam? Quite ancient, poor thing.'

Sam smiled at her indulgently. 'Unlike us, darling,' he said. 'Maeve, these sandwiches are delicious.'

'Fruitcake, anyone?' asked Sophie, passing round the tin. 'My mother's well-guarded recipe.'

Commander Digby and Frank were well away, grumbling about farming. Frank had a can of beer in one hand and Commander Digby another large glass of port.

Sophie and Matt leaned on the side of the car and smiled at one another. Matt bent and kissed her and slipped a hand inside her coat. 'I love you,' he mouthed, running his hand over her bottom. She was light-hearted with drink and happiness. Last night had been wonderful. Flushed by champagne, Sophie had told him the news about the cottage and Matt was elated. Having her so close would make her a proper part of his life. He could see her every day and his father would grow to love her, too. It felt as if a huge obstacle had been cleared from their path.

Mohammed and Mrs Day were looking at the other runners on the racecard and frightening each other with the descriptions of their past form.

' "Has an excellent record in the point-to-point ranks, winning four times. Won at Kelso last time out",' read Mrs Day. ' "Started his career with two wins in bumpers and has also had success over hurdles and regulation fences. He come here on the back of two recent wins".'

'Stop it, you two,' said Maeve. 'I don't care about the other horses. I don't want to hear. We all know Dancer can beat them.'

Before the first race they joined the crowds at the rails of the paddock to watch the runners parade. All the horses looked magnificent to Maeve, like glossy models striding arrogantly down a catwalk, with just as much swagger and pizzazz. She watched owners being reassured by trainers in the centre of the ring and then the jockeys appeared and there was a run of colour onto the green lawn. Red, yellow spots, red sleeves, yellow cap; white, royal blue star, red sleeves, red and white hooped cap; royal blue, yellow cross belts, black cap; they were like a flock of bright parrots released from a cage as they flitted across to their horses and, after a moment, were thrown up to perch on their backs.

'Do you think Jane's arrived? She should be here by now, shouldn't she?' asked Sophie.

'Yes, they're here,' said Charlie. 'Granny got me to call Jane's mobile. They got here about half an hour ago. They're trying to keep Sally calm and Jack's walking Dancer round.'

'Shall we go and watch this race?' asked Matt. 'Let's go up in the stand. There's a fabulous view.'

'I don't think I can bear to,' said Maeve. 'I don't want to watch horses falling over and having breakdowns and jockeys being carted off in ambulances. My nerves won't stand it. I'm going to the bar by the Tote. I'd rather have a drink in my hand and watch it on the telly. Anyone coming?'

'I'll come with you,' said Sophie unexpectedly, and the two of them went off through the crowds arm in arm.

When they met up with the others again on the steps above the parade ring before the next race, Maeve was grinning. 'We've just had our photograph taken,' she said, 'by the man from *Horse and Hound*! I told him he'd better not make the horses look fabulous and us like dogs!'

Mrs Day had won twenty pounds and was explaining her betting theory. 'I back the horse which looks me in the eye in the paddock,' she said, 'and gives me a kind of wink.'

Commander Digby, who had backed the favourite and lost a fiver, thanked her for her tip.

'Mind you,' she said, 'I don't know that it will work for anyone else.'

Sophie and Maeve disappeared again to look round the shops in the tented village and amused one another trying on hats and expensive country clothes.

'You'll have to dress like this, you know, all these puffa jackets and tweed skirts, when you live at Snook Cottage,' teased Maeve.

'Do you think I will?' asked Sophie seriously. 'I mean, do you think I'll live at Snook Cottage?'

'I'm sure of it,' said Maeve, 'and did I tell you that I had a telephone call from Monsieur le Moustache?'

'Colonel Moustache,' corrected Sophie. 'No, you didn't! Really?' She grinned.

'We 'ave ze little assignation,' said Maeve in a French accent. ''E does not let les herbes grow under ses pieds, does he?'

Sally, meanwhile, was being walked round the horsebox park by Jane. 'Just come home safe,' she said. 'You know he can do that. Just look after yourself. Keep out of trouble. You're in good company. Good horses who know the job, experienced jocks. Don't let them intimidate you, though.'

'Please, Jane, don't. I've got it in my head. I know what sort of race I'm going to ride. We've been through it so many times.' Sally ran her fingers through her hair. Her lip almost trembled. Her nerves were thrumming and she had been unable to eat a thing. The sandwich Jane had forced down her had stuck in her throat in a dry, gagging lump.

'OK, girl,' said Jane. 'Get your gear and go and get changed. Take your time. We'll bring Dancer down to the paddock.'

Sally collected her bag and made her way to the ladies' changing room. It was luxury compared to the make-do facilities provided for female jockeys at many country race-courses. It was also deserted except for the motherly woman in charge. She put down her knitting and stood up.

'Have a cup of tea, dear. You've got plenty of time and it'll steady your nerves. I haven't had many young ladies this afternoon. You're the second, in fact.' She bustled about with a kettle and teapot and made Sally sit down and fed her shortbread biscuits. She talked about the weather and holidays and the traffic, and gradually the banality of her conversation made Sally unwind a little. She was glad to be away from Jane.

Then it was time to change. With her hair loose on her shoulders she looked like some man's sexual fantasy in her breeches and boots. With it twisted into a hair net under her skullcap, she looked a professional.

'Good luck, dear. See you back soon, safe and sound,' said her new friend comfortably. 'You'll feel more like one of these nice sandwiches, then.'

The runners for the four thirty were starting to appear in the parade ring and Maeve searched through the gathering crowd at the rails and on the steps for Father O'Brien.

'He's got to be here,' she told Mohammed. 'He promised.' Commander Digby and Matt had helped Lady Pamela and Sam down from the stand where they had watched the previous races and they were now waiting to join the other owners in the ring. They had lost Charlie early on in the afternoon when he had sloped off to the amusement arcade and Mr and Mrs Day had gone to look at the starting prices offered by the bookmakers.

'Here is Dancer,' said Mohammed as the big bay horse with the long white face was led in by Steve. 'This is his day, inshallah.' He turned back and found Maeve had disappeared into the throng, but he caught sight of Sophie and went to join her.

'Look, Lady P and Sam have gone into the paddock with Jane,' she pointed out to him. 'Jane looks terrific. I've never seen her in a skirt. She's got amazing legs.' Dressed up for the occasion in a short suit and long boots, her hair caught under a fur hat, Jane was transformed from her everyday appearance.

'She is beautiful womans,' sighed Mohammed. 'All yous are beautiful womans.'

'And you're a beautiful mans.' She smiled at him affectionately and gave his arm a squeeze, and then searched the rails on either side. 'Where on earth has Maeve got to? I thought she'd be here.'

'She looks for her friend. Her god-man,' said Mohammed, turning to scan the faces of the people behind him.

A bell rang and there was a murmur from the crowd as the jockeys appeared. Sophie caught her face between her hands. 'Mohammed, I feel sick with nerves for Sally. There she is. She looks absolutely terrified.'

'No. She is good. She is quiet and strong.'

'She's the only girl in the race. Some of the men look so tough. Oh, God! Please let her be all right. Where *is* Maeve? She's missing all this.'

The horses were being called to saddle up and Jane was having a few last words with Sally, who was nodding her head solemnly, and then Steve was giving her a leg up into the saddle and Dancer spun round. Matt appeared beside Sophie. 'She's going down to the start early,' he said. 'The steward is letting her out now.'

'Maeve's missed it all,' groaned Sophie.

Steve had his shoulder braced against the excited horse, who with arched neck and high lifted tail was clearly difficult to hold.

'There she is!' cried Matt. 'Look, down by the exit. She's got that priest with her. He's blessing Dancer. He really is. He's giving him his blessing.'

Father O'Brien had taken Sally by surprise. Out of nowhere he had emerged, right in front of them, and then she had recognised Maeve with him and realised, as he lifted his right hand, that he was making the sign of the cross. 'He's blessed you, Sal,' cried Maeve, and then they had gone and she was only conscious of Dancer and a sea of faces and Steve's head bobbing at her knee as he got ready to slip the lead rein and let them go. She took a tighter hold of the reins and settled her feet well into her stirrup irons. The sun had come out and the hairs on Dancer's polished neck picked up the light in little coloured spears. She took a pinch of the skin over his shoulders and tweaked it gently. In a moment they would be out on the turf and Steve would release his hold and it would be just the two of them. She realised she longed to be moving, to settle into a canter, to feel their pent-up energy explode into the work they had to do.

Steve was shouting something and she nodded and then he jumped clear and they were off, Dancer bounding forward, and a moment when she thought he had got away from her, but she caught him back, scolding, and the grass was flashing past under his polished hooves and the stands and the crowds and the noise floated away.

On the course the only sound was the scud of Dancer's feet and his rhythmic snorting breaths. For the moment Sally felt quite calm. Looking down, she could see his powerful shoulders driving them forward and his hooves pounding the turf.

His large ears were pricked and he was looking from side to side. He felt comfortable and familiar. If nothing else, she was going to enjoy this ride, away from the stands and the enclosures and out into the country to the four-mile start.

Slowly, Lady Pamela and Sam mounted the steps to the stand. It was a long climb and they missed seeing Bumper's distinctive colours cantering to the start. Lady Pamela's heart was thumping and there was a throbbing behind her eyes. She blinked hard, trying to clear her vision. Now is not the time to have a stroke, she told herself sternly. Sophie suggested she should go inside and sit down but she preferred to lean against the rail where there was plenty of air.

'I'll get you a glass of water,' Sophie said, and disappeared. Typical that Maeve was nowhere to be seen. She had vanished with that priest of hers. Lady Pamela had heard about the blessing. Mumbo jumbo, she called it, Irish nonsense. As if the Lord should take an interest in horse racing with everything else going on in the world. Sophie came back with Mohammed and Matt and carrying a plastic tumbler of water. Lady Pamela sipped it gratefully. The other horses were going down to the start now. Seventeen runners, cantering down in a loose group. Matt, looking through her field glasses, told her he could see them being shown the first fence to remind them where they were and what they had to do.

Lady Pamela felt better and smiled reassuringly at Sam. On a step below her stood a pleasant-looking middle-aged woman with an attractive man and a teenage girl. A well-groomed, prosperous couple with intelligent, good-humoured faces. The girl said something which made them turn to her and laugh. The man put his arm round her and pulled her towards him in a rough embrace. Lady Pamela thought he called her Lizzie. The girl looked upwards and caught her eye and smiled.

It was no surprise then that when Jane, who had climbed up to join them, cried, 'Under starter's orders. They're off!' Lady Pamela was lost in thought, her mind slipped gently out of gear, freewheeling back into the past.

'They've started slowly,' said Matt. 'No one wants to take up the running.' He glanced at the television screen above their heads. 'Dancer's at the back of the first bunch.' It appeared that the horses were hardly more than cantering towards the first fence.

'She's doing well to hold him,' said Jane. 'She's fine where

291

she is.' All but Lady Pamela turned to the screen to watch the horses flow over the first fence.

'He jumped that well,' said Jane. 'Stood right off. Looks as if he's moved up a bit.'

Sam glanced at his old friend and touched her arm.

'Darling?' he said. Lady Pamela shook herself slightly and there was a moment of confusion in her eyes.

'Yes,' she said. 'Yes, Dancer. The race.'

'All safely over that one,' said Sophie. 'Wait a minute. Someone's gone at the back.'

'And the faller there was Ring Home,' said the commentator as the horses started on the left-hand bend towards the four fences on the run approaching the stands.

There was a long gallop now, slightly downhill, and it was difficult to tell how the horses were placed in the front group, bunched closely on the rails. Sam, slightly deaf, could not pick up the commentary and had to turn to Jane.

'Where is he? Can you see?'

'He's all right. Look at the screen, you can pick out the orange cap, tucked well in on the inside at the back of the first group.'

Lady Pamela peered up but the screen was a smudge of colours. Looking down the course she could see nothing at all but the snake of green track, the white railings and the dark lines of fences.

'They're coming into the fourth,' said Matt. 'It's hard to see because he's right in on the rails. Christ! He jumped that big. Did you see, Soph?'

At last Lady Pamela could make out dark bobbing shapes in the distance as the field of runners drew up the course. On the television, the pace seemed steady, but the front three or four horses were pushing ahead, opening up the pack. Into the fifth plain fence the favourite, already in front position, made a bad mistake and hit the rail. The crowd groaned as he scrabbled on his knees for a moment and then was gone, his jockey catapulted over his head and rolling instinctively into a ball, preparing for fifteen galloping horses to ride over him. Before the horse could get to his feet, it had brought down one behind. It crashed onto its side, sending its jockey flying. Another roar from the crowd.

'Laundromat and Celtic Stone the fallers there,' said the commentator. Still no more than a passing mention of Dancer who was lying about eighth, according to Matt.

As the runners moved up the course, Lady Pamela could now pick out the orange cap and colours of her horse. She recognised his steady galloping stride, relaxed and unhurried, and the rhythmic flow of his jumping. By the time the horses turned left-handed again to go away into the country and towards the water jump and the open ditches, he had moved up into sixth place. Someone at the back had pulled up, his horse clearly lame.

Down at the rails, Maeve and Father O'Brien watched silently. Some of the time Maeve had her eyes closed and once she turned her back on the track and with arms folded and head bowed listened gravely to the commentary. If she did not hear Dancer's name she knew he was all right. Father O'Brien watched through his field glasses.

'Now that was a good jump,' he told her, 'but he's got a loose horse alongside, which isn't so great. There you are, they've all flown over the water like birds. He's a great galloping horse, to be sure, by the looks of him. You can open your eyes again, Maeve.'

On the next bend, as they headed out on the far elbow of the course, Sally realised the horses in front were pushing ahead just at the moment when she wondered if Dancer was tiring and easing up a bit. They had already galloped three miles and jumped eleven fences. She was blown herself but she had to hang on. If she allowed Dancer to lose touch with the leading group they would be finished, out of the race, with nothing to do but come trailing home. Into the second open ditch she was conscious that she had a loose horse on her inside. At the split second of take-off she realised with a great rush of fear that it had swerved to jump across her. Instinctively, she yanked at the reins. Dancer hesitated only for a fraction and with a clever short stride seemed to check and then jump out of trouble but he barely made it over the fence, dragging through the top foot and skewing sideways to prevent being brought down. Sally lurched up his neck, reins flapping. I'm gone, she thought. Shit, I've had it. Almost as if in slow motion she felt herself falling. Then Dancer's neck was coming up to meet her. She clasped it with both arms, found a plait of mane with one hand and hauled herself back into the saddle.

By the time she was galloping again she saw that the near miss had cost her three or four places and the next fence was coming up quickly. She had lost a stirrup and frantically sought it with one hand. The leather had hooked over the front of the saddle and the fence was rushing to meet them by the time she had it freed. This time Dancer had to make his own arrangements. He stood right off and cleared the fence by feet and Sally thought she was gone again, unseated, jumped clean off his back. She wasn't going to last if she couldn't get her stirrup back. Her toe found the swinging iron and dug home as they rounded the last bend at the far side of the course, with four more fences and a lot of galloping left.

Getting back together and starting to ride again, Sally asked Dancer for more, pushing him not only to keep in touch but to up the pace. The big horse flattened his ears, felt her weight shift, and responded. His stride lengthened and he seemed to flatten out as he began to gallop more powerfully. He crept past the two horses immediately in front, slipping by them on the inside. At the next fence he jumped himself into sixth place, a horse falling behind him. Sally wanted to keep him on the rails to take advantage of the bend but she was blocked in front. When she tried to nose past, the jockey she was challenging swore and swerved in close. She looked for an opening but there wasn't one. This lot were old hands who raced here every season. They were not going to do her any favours. There was only one way through and that was round. Sally gave Dancer the signal to swing out on the outside. He was tired, they must all be tired, and there was a long pull ahead, three more fences and the dreaded hill. She gave Dancer a reminder with her whip and he began to edge up on the outside. If she could hold him here, towards the front, he would be in a position to challenge the leaders when they put on the pressure at the finish. As they came into the third from home, Dancer took off alongside one of the Irish favourites. The jockey turned a goggled face to see who it was and Sally saw him make an obscene gesture. 'I'll fucking take you out if you come up on me!' he screamed.

'Catch me then, you bastard!' she screamed back, feeling anger explode inside her.

Now lying fifth, they still had a lot to do. The horse in front was exhausted. Although galloping, it was nevertheless almost at a standstill, going into the ground with every stride and she thought she saw the jockey pulling up as she ploughed past. The last turn on the course brought them into the home run, and then Dancer hit the hill. It stretched out mercilessly in front of them. His stride felt leaden as the rising ground ate up his speed and consumed his effort.

He was tired, exhausted, and so was she, but if they were to make anything of this race, anything at all, he had to find a reserve of strength. Coming into the second to last from home, she jumped alongside a horse and jockey she knew from the West Country.

'Go for it, girl,' shouted Kevin. 'We're finished. He's blowing up. Go on, give it some wellie. Get your fat arse into gear.'

Feeling a great surge of elation, Sally grinned back and raised a fist in salute.

Her goggles smeared with mud, she saw the finish in the distance. Now she had to help Dancer home, ride with every ounce of strength she had left. Head down, arms and legs working, she tried to force him on. He was closing the gap between himself and the two leading horses and his great, bolshy, arrogant, competitive spirit, which she always hoped she could count on, made him fight to be ahead. He was tired, so tired. She could feel the effort it was taking to keep galloping. His shoulders were shuddering, his ears back. Exhausted horses make mistakes and there was the last fence to jump, yet she must kick him on, keep him concentrating, ask him for more. They could hear the roar of the crowd now, coming in waves across the track. It was a thrilling sound and Dancer's ears pricked. 'Come on, Dancer, let's show the bastards,' Sally screamed.

At the last fence he was a length or two behind the leader but he jumped well, the tired horse in front only scrambling over, hitting the top and dropping back. As they fought past Maeve and Father O'Brien, the priest was certain he had a nose ahead. At the winning post, a few yards further on, Irish Dancer galloped slowly home to victory and Maeve Delaney swore she would become a nun.

Up in the stands, Matt had cheered himself hoarse and Sophie was in tears. Jane and Mohammed had already bounded down the steps and were running wildly towards the finish, frantic to be there to lead Sally in victorious.

Sam wiped a tear from the corner of his eye. It had almost been too much for his old heart, he thought. The excitement, the shouting, the dreadful, searing emotion of it all. Pammy clung to his arm, frozen and speechless, unable to hear the commentary and yet swept into the last thrilling minutes as she saw her horse battling home.

The couple in front had turned and were congratulating them. The girl, fair-haired and her pale winter skin flushed with pink, blurted out, 'He's your horse, isn't he? I saw you with him in the paddock. I put my money on him. All of it. I loved his big head and his long white nose.'

'She's won a huge amount of money,' laughed her mother.

'A disgusting amount,' said her father, 'but it's for her year out, her gap year. She's off to teach children English in Chile. She has to raise two thousand pounds.'

'I'm so glad, my dear,' murmured Lady Pamela faintly. Alarmed, Sophie took her arm. She thought she might fall. She signalled to Matt to help Sam start down the steps.

The girl was still talking, gabbling away about Dancer. 'Come on, Lizzie,' said her mother, 'you must let the winning owner go. She'll have a cup to collect.'

Down below, Dancer was being led in by a jubilant Jack. Sally, her face still scarlet from exertion and emotion, was struggling not to cry as the TV cameras closed in for a brief interview as she jumped down.

'How did you plan this race?' she was asked by the commentator. 'Coming back from injury, there was always going to be a question mark hanging over the horse. Did you believe he could do it?'

Sally gulped and brushed a hand over her eyes, and spoke into the microphone thrust at her.

'I always thought he could,' she said in a rush. 'I trusted him to jump round, but I didn't know whether he could find that extra in the end. I asked him and he answered. It was wonderful. He's a great horse. I just feel so lucky that I was given a chance too. That I was given the ride.'

'Grand, too, for his owner, Lady Pamela Bentham,' said the commentator, turning back to the camera. 'I know it is not polite to mention age, but Lady Pamela is in her eighties and had retired from racing, until the decision was made to bring this horse back and give him a second chance. Lady Pamela,' and the commentator moved through the crowd, 'how do you feel? This is a great day for you, isn't it?'

'A great day,' said Lady Pamela. 'A great day for the girls, for Sally and for Jane Hedderwick, his trainer. He was on the scrapheap, you know.'

'What now? What are your plans for him?'

'We must wait and see. Jane and I will have to talk about his future. The sure thing is that he has now got a future, which was by no means certain before this race.'

The television camera swept away and Lady Pamela's friends crowded back. Maeve had reappeared with Father O'Brien, who had taken Lady Pamela's hand and said that he now could afford a new presbytery roof. Maeve was scarlet-faced with swimming eyes, but she said very little. Sally, who had been embraced and jostled between them all, went off to get weighed out, and Doug Mitchell appeared beside Jane to congratulate her.

'You've done a good job,' he said. 'I should have hung on to him.'

'Come off it, Doug,' said Jane tartly. 'You'd written him off. He'd be in a can on the shelf at Safeways if you'd had your way.'

Doug laughed. He couldn't deny it. He touched Jane's arm, and moved away. He had the favourite in the next race.

Dancer was now standing in the winner's enclosure sporting a Cheltenham winner's rug over his back, his big head held high, enjoying the crowd around him, relishing the attention. His coat was black with sweat and his sides still heaved, but he looked full of energy. Jack patted his neck, his face radiant with pride and pleasure. Watching him, Maeve knew that he would never, in his life, have a better moment, and no wonder, she thought. His vegetable plot, his fowl, his bicycle and the quiet lanes of Charlton would for ever be transformed by his afternoon of triumph at the races. Dancer, his boy, had done it.

Sam caught her eye and smiled. He reached out a hand and took hers. 'This is your doing, you know,' he said. 'You made this happen.'

Lady Pamela turned and, seeing the two of them, copied Sam and took Maeve's other hand between the two of hers.

'Yes, Irish,' she said. 'Of course, Sam is right. Without you, none of us would be here. Thank you, Maeve.'

Maeve had recovered now and, looking between the two of them, she said, 'Wasn't it just the greatest? The absolute bloody best thing ever? As they say, although I didn't believe it until now, better than sex!' and she grinned naughtily at Matt and Sophie.

Chapter Fifteen

Much later and still overwhelmed by excitement, the party made its way back to the car park and divided to travel home. Maeve, who had drunk a great deal of champagne, linked arms with Lady Pamela and said she had smiled so much her face ached. The Days took Jack Dick with them to catch the coach, Jack still saying under his breath, 'I knew the bugger could do it. I knew he could!' He had downed a lot of whisky and was happily unsteady on his feet. Sophie and Matt took Mohammed and Commander Digby, Charlie took Lady Pamela, Maeve and Sam. Dusk was falling and it had begun to rain. 'I don't think there's much point in hurrying,' said Matt. 'There's going to be one hell of a hold-up getting out of here. We're not going to be back until after eight o'clock, I wouldn't think.'

Sophie had rung her parents and they had watched the race on television and were as thrilled as she was. 'Flora and Freddy have been so excited,' said her mother. 'They're still jumping up and down now. Your father put some money on for them. I am afraid it's a very bad example to set, but they've won twelve pounds each!'

As they joined the queue of vehicles leaving the car park, Charlie's little black car roared past and cut in front of them, Maeve waving out of the back window. She was mouthing something which they couldn't catch. At the exit a policeman on traffic duty allowed Charlie through but held up Matt. 'That's the last we'll see of them,' said Commander Digby and it was five or six minutes later before they started to move again.

In the warmth of the car Sophie felt increasingly sleepy and allowed herself to close her eyes and doze in the back seat. It had been such a remarkable day. One that she and Matt, all of them in fact, would remember for ever, as a sort of milestone or marker. In the future they would say, 'Was that the year that Dancer won at Cheltenham?' It was a day that would colour all the other grey days around it, making the month special, and then the year. She and Mohammed kept smiling at each other as they sat side by side in the back. Sophie felt as if her grin was pulled from the back of her head by strings. When she closed her eyes she saw Dancer's white face and heard the cheering of the crowd. She would never forget it as long as she lived.

The traffic was moving at a snail's pace, stopping and starting, and in the rain the head and tail lights pooled on the dark road in liquid colour. She was glad that Matt was driving. She felt safe with him. She liked to watch his hands, the long fingers of his left hand moving between the gear lever and the wheel, the right resting on it lightly, as he peered through the windscreen at the road ahead.

'We'll hit the motorway soon,' was the last thing she heard him say before she fell asleep, her head resting on Mohammed's shoulder.

An hour or so later she was woken by Matt's voice, this time with an edge to it.

'God! What the hell's going on here. There's been an accident,' and as she fixed her eyes on the darkness beyond, she could see the horror of twisted metal, a scatter of glass shards across the road, police lights, an ambulance flashing and a policeman in a fluorescent jacket waving them past in a state of unusual agitation. In exactly that same moment she knew, and a heavy stone of ice fell into the pit of her stomach and her legs went weak. Her heart seemed crushed against her chest.

'It's them!' she screamed. 'It's Charlie's car.'

Then Matt was shouting at the policeman who was still trying to wave them past and he was pulling over beyond the rescue vehicles and slithering to a stop and falling from the driver's seat and Sophie felt a rush of cold, wet air and he was running along the hard shoulder and screaming back at her to stay in the car. There was a terrible moment when she couldn't get out. There was Commander Digby in the front trying to hold her and she had to climb over Mohammed who was only half awake and then she, too, was running towards the chaos, towards the figures working under a spotlight and towards something too terrible to think of.

When she reached the edge of the scene she faltered.

Which way to go? Charlie's car was recognisable but one side of it was almost flattened like a stamped-on tin. The windows were a silver web of smashed glass but the telltale football sticker still clung to the rear window. Black liquid was seeping onto the tarmac. She had a horrible vision of soft, pulsating flesh, of pink skin seared and sheared by jagged knives of metal, of skulls cracked like egg shells. She was aware of someone, a lorry driver, she thought, being given first aid by the side of the road. He looked ghastly, green almost, under the sodium light, his lorry skewed like a toy across the carriageway, its cab oddly tipped and great coils of cable hanging from the angle like loops of intestines. She saw Matt talking to a policeman and ran to him.

'Where are they?' she screamed. 'Where are they?'

He grabbed her arm hard and his face was hideous and distorted with shock as he howled back, 'They say she's dead. She was killed outright. She's gone. She's gone.'

It was three months after Maeve's funeral that Sophie prepared to move from London into Snook Cottage. Methodically, she had sorted through the Effs' clothes, washing, folding and putting away in a suitcase what was outgrown. In the bottom of the case were tiny baby clothes and she took out a little stretch suit and held it to her face. Who knows, she thought, these may be needed again before too long. Matt had asked her to marry him and she had agreed, but wanted to wait a year. When they did marry, he would come and live with her at the cottage, but first she wanted time there on her own, to establish herself.

The contents of her flat were nearly all packed now, ready for the removers on the following day, and while the twins were at nursery school Sophie wanted to finish off the cupboard in her room. She had left this until last because at the back, behind her shoes, were the two black plastic bags of Maeve's belongings and she had not felt strong enough to handle them until she was forced to. As she pulled them out she thought that she could simply lug them round the corner, unopened, and chuck them in a skip on a building site and avoid the pain of seeing Maeve's writing and hearing her voice again and having the flat filled by her presence.

The fact that she had died instantly and would have known nothing was little comfort to Sophie, who was haunted by that last glimpse of her laughing face out of the back window of Charlie's car. She missed her with a physical ache and for a few weeks after the accident often thought she saw her, a little jaunty figure in the distance, a dark mass of hair bent over a glass in a pub, a laughing face in a bus queue. She also often answered the telephone, thinking, This will be Maeve, before being hit by the pain of her absence. 'She's gone, she's gone, she's gone,' she said over and over to herself.

Everything that had happened to Sophie since, her decision to move, Matt proposing, selling the flat, had happened as if in a slow-motion dream. She felt as if she was moving underwater, pushing herself along against a dragging force. What should have caused her great bounds of happiness, things which should have lit her sky like a firework display or a hundred-watt bulb, were dimmed by the pall of grief which settled on them all. It was true what people said that the bereaved keep going because of the children, and she did. The Effs were resolutely cheerful, accepting Maeve's death with the simple understanding of the very young. Why should Mummy be so sad if Maeve was in heaven with Jesus? asked Flora, who was happy to think of her with the angels looking after her. Freddy found it comforting, whenever they saw a particularly grizzly bit of carnage on the lanes round Snook Cottage, a flattened badger or a rabbit, that Maeve was already in heaven to arrange a welcome.

Matt had been wonderful and if Sophie had ever had any doubts about him they would have been utterly dispelled by how he took over during the nightmare days immediately after the accident. Sam and Lady Pamela were both in hospital in Bath, Lady Pamela with a broken leg and chest injuries and Sam with broken ribs. It was remarkable that they had escaped relatively unscathed. Charlie was in intensive care with a suspected fractured neck and two broken legs, but in a few days was off the critical list and making good progress. As soon as was possible Bunty had moved him to a private hospital in London. It made it easier for her to supervise his recovery and for family and friends to visit him.

He was subdued after the accident. The trauma of the crash had knocked the easy confidence out of him and although there was no question that it had not been his fault, he relived the fairground skid on the patch of oil, the dazzling lights of the lorry as his little car spun round into its path, the moment he took his hands off the wheel to cover his face. Bunty and Henry worried as much about his damaged mind as they did about his physical injuries. However much they reassured him that it was not his fault, and even an awkward policeman turning his cap round and round in large red hands had sat by his bedside and told him so, Charlie could not come to terms with his involvement in the accident. It was the first time that he had encountered death and the first time that he had considered his own mortality.

Matt had had to telephone Maeve's father and break the news. Sophie had said she would do it but had frozen at the sound of Mr Delaney's voice and then released great gulping sobs of pain and Matt had to take over. Mr Delaney was very quiet and dignified. At first he had wanted to take her body back to Ireland but Matt had persuaded him to allow her to be buried in the little churchyard at South Charlton. Maeve's mother was undergoing rehabilitation for alcohol addiction and was unable to express a view or even attend the service.

Matt's father had been wonderful too. He organised the service, the vicar and the organist, and offered to put up anyone who needed a bed for the night. He was all right while he had something to do. At other times he was sunk into a deep, impenetrable gloom. Watching him, Sophie thought it couldn't be grief. After all, he hadn't known Maeve for long.

Sophie remembered the funeral as if she was watching a black and white film. Maeve's father, looking small and grey and with an angle of his head, a set of his jaw, painfully like his daughter, the Days, Rob, Jane, Sally and Steve, and the girls from the yard, Jack Dick, George, some of her friends from the rugby club, Mohammed and Khaled, of course, and Commander Digby had filled the front rows of the little church. Sophie's parents had accompanied her, her mother with her arm protectively through hers, her father looking anxiously to see how she was coping. Sister Davina from St Theresa's had come and also Father O'Brien. A woman nobody recognised came in late. Afterwards she introduced herself as Diana Tripp, Henry Bentham's secretary. She said that Henry and Bunty had asked her to send flowers but she had wanted to come, that she'd only met Maeve once but knew the moment she saw her that she was someone special.

The same bearded vicar whom Sophie remembered from Christmas took the service. The coffin was so tiny, like a child's, and Sophie could only think of Maeve lying in it, cold and pale and, stupidly, how lonely she would be, she who had loved life and people and noise and laughter. Someone had put a small vase of snowdrops on the coffin and the little white flowers looked cold and delicate with their slender stems and drooping heads. They had sung a hymn and there were prayers – Commander Digby had arranged all that. Sophie couldn't make any decisions. During the service Mr Delaney had read a passage from *A Midsummer Night's Dream*:

> *O, when she's angry she is keen and shrewd*
> *She was a vixen when she went to school*
> *And though she be but little she is fierce.*

Then he went on to say these were the qualities he'd loved in Maeve, and Sophie thought, Yes, I did, too, and then he spoke about how she had lived life to the full and in her own way, and Sophie could not listen any more because of the blood banging in her head and the tears congesting behind her eyes.

When they buried her in the grave Jack Dick had dug, in the corner of the churchyard, Sophie felt it was all wrong and as if she couldn't let her be lowered into the ground. She could hear her saying, 'Don't leave me here in this fucking place. I want a bit of life around me,' but when she looked up and saw the calm beauty of the hills and the quiet air filled with early birdsong she hoped that Maeve would find the peace that had eluded her in life.

When Matt told Sophie that she and Mrs Day must clear Maeve's things out of Charlton, she managed to complete the task by divorcing herself from what she was doing and not allowing herself to think, This is that lovely bright jumper she always wore when it was very cold, or, These are the pink jeans she had on when she last came to London. Maeve's bedroom at the top of the house was incredibly untidy and she and Mrs Day had been forced to smile at the mess she had created around her. Mrs Day did up black bags for Oxfam and Sophie saw with a pang the pink Chanel suit folded on the top. There were bags of clothes too tatty to be passed on and they made a tiny pile of her bracelets and beads and earrings. It was looking at them, so frail and pretty and insubstantial, that made Sophie cry again and Mrs Day put her arms round her shaking shoulders and cried as well.

'I'll take these,' said Sophie eventually, sniffing and looking at them, cupped in her hand. 'No one else will want them. They aren't worth anything.'

At the bottom of a drawer, Sophie found the photograph of Lizzie.

'I wonder who this is?' she said, picking it up and peering at it.

Mrs Day stopped moving the bin bags onto the landing and came to look over her shoulder. 'That's Lady Pamela's daughter. I know that. She has one photograph of her by her bed. Only the one. I wonder how that came to be here.' She paused, hand on hip, remembering. 'Funny thing, though, Maeve sometimes talked about her – about Lizzie. It seemed to fascinate her, how close the two of them were. She asked me about my daughter, whether we got on, like. When I told her we were best friends, I could see it upset her. It was as if she knew she had missed something.'

Sophie considered. 'Well, she had. Her mother wasn't a mother to her at all. She ran off when Maeve was young and hardly saw her again. Much too selfish. But I never thought Maeve cared that much. She always said she hated being mothered, fussed over.' She put the photograph to one side. How well had she really known her friend? Had Maeve kept the snap as a curiosity, because this girl with her smooth fair hair and sweet smile had known a deep and nourishing maternal love which she had been denied? Sophie hoped that Maeve had not felt that she herself was in some way undeserving. Maddening though she could be, she had never been hard to love.

'And there's her money,' said Mrs Day, remembering the cheque.

'What money?' asked Sophie, and they went downstairs together and found the cheque still under the egg cup on the dresser in the kitchen. Sophie stood looking at it.

'I suppose I'd better send it back to her father,' she said. 'It's so strange that she should have had all this money and not said anything and not cashed it. She started off, you know, with nothing. That's why she took this job. That's why she came to Charlton.'

David Digby found the weeks after the funeral almost too painful to bear. Maeve's death served to confirm his view that life was arbitrary and cruel and shook his belief in God to its foundation. Why, he asked, had it not been his useless life that had been taken? He would gladly have died in her place.

Acutely, too, he felt his loss. Maeve had thawed his heart. He had loved her, he recognised that now. Unsuitable, inappropriate, whatever, it didn't matter . . . he had loved her. He had loved the warmth she brought into his chilly life, her acceptance of him as he was, the affection she was bold enough to show him. Whatever it was she had done to him, what transformation she was responsible for, it was now all gone. He felt a physical ache where he imagined his heart must be. How, he thought miserably, was he ever going to recover? Nobody offered him any comfort. Why should they when they could not guess at his grief? Instead they crowded round Sophie, whose shoulders shook as her tears flowed. What sort of friend had she been, anyway? he thought angrily. No one had loved Maeve as he did.

How easy it would be to finish himself off. He had a shotgun in the gun cupboard, a cardboard box full of cartridges. There were two things which stopped him. One was his reluctance to be a nuisance. Such an action would create a bother for everyone. Someone would have to clean up. There would be a residue of guilt and pain. He did not want to leave all that behind. And then there were his cows. Calving was about to start in earnest. His heifers trusted him, his older cows were used to him. He did not want them unsettled and upset and it would be hard for Matt to find someone to take them over. No, just for the time being he had a job to do. He would have to see it through.

He thought of the last time Maeve had cycled over to the farm. She had been full of horse talk, with Cheltenham only days away. Then she had asked him if he had thought any more about New Zealand. He told her he was still mulling it over and she came out with the words which he would never forget: 'Hey! I've got some dosh. I could come with you. How about that? We'd have some fun, wouldn't we? We'd get those Kiwis going!' and his foolish old heart had leapt.

It *was* foolish, he knew that. He was not a deluded old man and had no expectation of her returning his love. It was enough that she seemed to seek his company and was fond of him. The idea that they might travel together was absurd but the very fact that she had suggested it, and had included him in this vision of carefree freewheeling to the other side of the world, meant more to him than he could describe.

Now the travel agent brochures lay beneath a pile of *Farmers Weekly*. He could still hear Maeve urging him to pack up and get out, to believe he had a future, but with her gone, a door had slammed shut. David Digby no longer believed in anything.

Sophie had dreaded breaking the news to Lady Pamela. In the end it was Bunty who blurted it out and whose feeling was, naturally enough, one of gratitude that Charlie had survived. Maeve's death was mentioned as a tragic afterthought. 'Terrible, of course, but a miracle that Charlie came out of it alive. And you and Sam, of course. The police said . . .'

Lady Pamela turned her head away and for a long time lay with her eyes closed. Bunty imagined that she was asleep.

The old lady said very little. She knew that Sam was lying in a bed in the same hospital, but not so badly injured, and it became imperative for her to see him. When Sophie and Matt visited her she was vague and remote, hardly recognising them or acknowledging the flowers which Sophie had taken such trouble choosing. She did not mention Maeve.

'Do you think she understands what has happened?' asked Sophie, as they left. She stopped a nurse on their way out. 'Lady Pamela, she seems so far away. Does she know about the accident? Does she know that someone died?' The nurse, trained to fob off enquiries said, 'It's the trauma and the drugs she is on. It will leave her confused for a week or two. Are you a relative?'

'No, no. I'm not. But it was my best friend who died in the car with her.' Sophie felt the blood rushing to her face. 'Sorry,' she blurted, and made a run for the swing doors. The nurse, who was used to drama, shrugged and walked on.

At last Sam was brought to see Lady Pamela in a wheelchair, wearing his old striped pyjamas and a silk dressing gown, his thick white hair brushed, his face a healthy pink. A nurse, with whom he was already a favourite, pushed him to her bedside and thoughtfully drew the curtains round the bed. The two old people reached out frail arms to each other but could only grasp hands. For the first time tears slid down Lady Pamela's cheeks and Sam wept too.

'Why not us?' she whispered. 'Sam, why not me? It's too cruel. It's too cruel that it should happen again. I loved her, Sam. I loved her.'

'Darling, darling. We all loved her. In a funny way she was a blessing to us all.'

'But Sam, who did she belong to? You and I have each

other. Charlie has his family. It's as if she was the dispensable one in that car and I can't bear it that she was.'

'Pammy, don't think like that. You or I would have gladly died in her place. She was so young and so full of life, but accidents defy reason and so does violent death. You know that. Think about the war. Think who we lost.'

They sat in silence, remembering. 'Can you recollect how we felt then, Pammy? That if we escaped, we had a duty to live fully? We must do the same for Maeve. You must get better, darling. We must trudge on with life.'

Sam was released from hospital two weeks later and Mohammed arranged to be at his London flat full time to look after him. Khaled came to collect him from the hospital and when Sam got back to London and Mohammed helped him into the lift and he unlocked his front door, he found the place clean and bright, with flowers on the table and a meal from the restaurant in the kitchen under a clean tea cloth, waiting to be warmed for his supper. He was so glad to be home. Hospital had been a nightmare. After that first time it had been too difficult to get the busy nurses to take him to visit Pammy. They had to content themselves with seeing one another whenever a visitor could be persuaded to bully a nurse into arranging a wheelchair and allowing a meeting in the dismal ward sitting room where the television played constantly at full volume and the plastic chairs were scarred and stained and the magazines a year out of date and tatty.

Lady Pamela's recovery had been slow. There was fear of infection and when Sophie next went to visit, she found the old woman sadly diminished. The nurses had got her up and she was walking about on sticks but looked so tiny and somehow as if her spirit had been dimmed. She and Sam had discussed the future and the decision they had taken to live together was not taken lightly. Sam's flat was on the second floor, but there was a lift, and dear Mohammed had promised that he would take over looking after them as soon as they were fit enough to be discharged. 'We're going to live in sin, dear,' she told Sophie. 'Maeve would have approved, don't you think?'

It was only after Sam left hospital that Lady Pamela seemed to rouse herself to get better. One of the nurses, a cheerful black girl called Louella, who understood that there was more to nursing than administering drugs, started to help her with make-up and arranged for the hairdresser to come and trim

her hair. She had a manicure and began to read the newspaper which so far had been left unopened on her locker. The
better news about Charlie cheered her.

'I must see him,' she said to Henry. 'He needs to know that
we love him very much.' It was as if life had gained a hold
again. When the doctor commented on her improvement, she
answered tartly, 'I'm not ready to fall off the twig. I want to
see that horse of mine run again.'

Sally and Jane had been to see her, looking almost too
healthy with their pink cheeks and outdoor complexions.
They both had stable manure on their boots and left little
wisps of straw on the floor. They brought photographs of the
race and newspaper cuttings and a great draft of vitality.
Dancer was well, they said. He had been pottery after the race
but was fit enough again now and soon they would decide
when he would race again.

'It's your decision, Jane,' Lady Pamela reminded her. 'He's
your horse now, remember.'

'We want you there,' said Jane, squeezing her hand. 'It
won't be the same if you're not.'

'Nonsense,' said Lady Pamela. 'Sam and I will be perfectly
content watching on the television. The dear old thing is
going to get the Racing Channel for me. You know that I'm
moving to London?'

The young women nodded. For a moment there was a
silence as they each remembered how much Maeve had been
part of it all.

'I'm glad you're going to be with your friend,' said Jane
awkwardly. She disliked venturing into these complicated
areas. 'Maeve would have been pleased.'

'Yes, I think she would,' said Lady Pamela.

It was after they had gone, while she was leafing through
the photographs cut from newspapers, that she saw that Jane
had trimmed off the text beneath each one. She realised that
they had been used, not on the racing pages, but to highlight
the tragedy of the fatal accident which was so shortly to befall
the happy, smiling, victorious group, all stretching up to pat
the neck of the big horse with the white blaze. It made a good
newspaper story.

Commander Digby was another visitor. He sat, turning his
flat cap round in his large bony hands, the backs weathered
brown, the palms hard and cracked with outdoor work. He
found the hospital unsettling. It was too warm and overlit,

and he felt large and awkward on the tubular chair beside Lady Pamela's bed. Every time a nurse approached he got to his feet, alarmed that he might inadvertently witness some intimate medical procedure. He was as out of place as his beaten-up muddy old Land Rover, trailing straw in the car park outside. In the back, Jess and Gyp, his working collies, snarled and barked at passers by.

Lady Pamela noticed the dull eyes, the stiff face of her visitor and saw his grief. Why, he loved her, she thought. She held out her little hand with its tracery of veins and fragile bones.

He took it gratefully. 'David,' she said, 'we all loved her, in a way, you know. She was very naughty and wild, but she had something very special. Sam says she blessed us all and I think that's exactly right. She was a blessing, wasn't she? She made us see opportunities.'

Commander Digby gazed out of the window at a skyline of office blocks. His eyes found some pigeons squabbling in the branches of a sycamore tree in the hospital grounds. He did not want to betray his feelings.

'She suggested to me that I should sell up and go abroad,' he said gruffly, trying to imply by his tone that it was a nonsensical idea. 'Even said she'd come with me.' He could hardly bear to bring the words out in the open, to lay them out for scrutiny, for ridicule.

Lady Pamela said nothing. She wondered what she could give this gaunt, suffering man to relieve his pain.

'She was very fond of you, David,' she said finally. 'In fact, it rather annoyed me. It was petty of me, but I told her off for spending so much time at Manor Farm. Frankly, I was jealous.'

He turned to look at her with astonishment. Was it true, then? Not a figment of his imagination, an absurd fancy? Maeve had really been fond of him? 'Jealous?' he snorted. 'Hardly any need for that.'

'Perhaps not, but true all the same.'

There was another long pause and Lady Pamela felt very, very tired. Commander Digby watched the pigeons in the tree. They had settled down into huddled shapes, side by side on the bare branch. With a start he remembered where he was and stood up, coughing nervously. He felt for a handkerchief in his pocket and pulled it out with the desiccated remains of some calf nuts. He blew his nose. 'So glad to see

you are improving. Must leave you to rest . . .' he mumbled.
He glanced anxiously at the bed.

Lady Pamela knew what she must do. 'You should go,' she
said. 'Go off on your travels. New Zealand, wasn't it? Maeve
told me. She would have gone with you, you know.'

Driving home in the dark, David Digby felt his spirits lift.
He felt as if he was redeemed, as if he had been given a
benediction. When he had finished with the calving he would
make his plans.

It wasn't long before Bunty took over at Charlton and work
began on an extension to the drawing room and alterations to
the kitchen and new bathrooms. Sophie drove past often after
she had the keys to Snook Cottage and she saw that the
overgrown drive had been cleared, new wrought-iron gates
erected and that a gravel sweep was being laid at the front.
She felt that the house had given up its secrets. The façade,
stripped of the old-fashioned climbers and the vine, no longer
seemed to smile in the way that Maeve had once described. It
looked like any other handsome Queen Anne house.

Peregrine was often busy in the garden. Once or twice he
saw her car and waved but turned hurriedly away. Maeve's
death had been difficult. He did not like being associated with
tragedies. He had stayed away from her funeral which had
surprised Sophie, who thought that they had been friends.
Later she realised that Peregrine was like one of his exotic
annuals that would bloom once and then fade away. Unlike
Jack, who had already planted up Maeve's grave and kept it
weeded and tidy.

'She was a grand maid,' he said gruffly, when he met
Sophie in the lane. 'There aren't many like her.' He had been
asked to stay on at Charlton as an odd job man, but had gone
to work for Jane at the racing stable. Now there was a tussle
with Bunty about his cottage. Commander Digby, on the
parish council, had taken up his case.

Mrs Day had given in her notice and was working in the
cheese factory in Frome and Mr Day was doing contract
gardening and quite enjoying it.

Everything different, everything changed, thought Sophie
as she opened the first of Maeve's bags. She tipped the
contents onto the floor and sorted through them. Maeve had
kept everything, it seemed, lugged things around with her
despite her itinerant lifestyle. There were old concert tickets,

programmes, school reports, tapes, books, photographs all jumbled together. Sophie made a pile of things she thought she should return to Maeve's father. There was a photograph of Maeve aged about six with stick arms and legs and a big grin, standing between her father and mother, and looking with a triumphant, upturned face at her father, who was looking down at her, expressionless.

There were many more and Sophie swept them into a large envelope before starting on the bunches of letters. With a start she recognised her own juvenile handwriting. Maeve had kept every letter she'd ever written. Sophie loathed hearing the echoes of her own voice as she scanned the neatly written pages. How smug she sounded with her reports of pony club rallies and parties and family fun. Her instinct was to destroy them, to shred them, but if Maeve had kept them . . . Sadly, she put them to one side. They were evidence of how she was, the girl she'd been.

Then there were the diaries. Sophie opened one of the exercise books and glanced at a line or two and then closed it. There were some things, she thought, that should remain private, some things which are too personal for anyone else to share. She'd take them with her to Somerset and one day she would build a little fire outside in the garden and she would burn Maeve's diaries one by one. Somewhere she remembered having read that in India, she thought, fire was seen as a purifier and that burning released the human spirit to float up to its god. She thought of how troubled she had been at leaving Maeve lying in the cold wet earth. These little scuffed exercise books in which she had recorded her hopes and fears contained her life. She could imagine the bright burst of blue and yellow flame and the trail of smoke curling into the sky. That is what she would do. She would set Maeve free.

Sitting back on her heels, she wiped the back of her hand across her nose. Maeve would hate all this moping around, all these long faces. She would have thought the Effs were right. Be sad for a bit and then look on the bright side. She would have been impatient with her grief. She would have called it self-pity. Sophie smiled, remembering. It was Vincent Durand who had done the strangest thing. He had missed the funeral but had sent a case of champagne. The accompanying note in his foreign-looking handwriting had said, 'There will come a time when you can be glad – to remember Maeve as she would wish.' He was right, of course. Maybe she and Matt would have a party when she had settled in at Snook Cottage. Invite Maeve's friends and drink to her in very expensive French champagne. She'd like that.

Sophie was nearly done. She shook the last objects out of the bag. She recognised the battered cloth-covered book at once – their old school hymnal. She flicked it open. It was as defaced as she expected. Maeve had altered the words of many of the hymns to her own lewd version and covered the pages with doodles and drawings. Sophie put the book on the pile to be thrown out.

The last thing was a cheap plastic heart-shaped frame in which there was a photograph of two happy, laughing school-girls in checked school dresses, one tall and thin and fair with hair scraped back from her face by an Alice band and the other, gap-toothed and grinning with a cloud of dark curls.

SZKEL